Murder
at the Manor

Murder at the Manor

Country House Mysteries

Edited and Introduced by
Martin Edwards

Poisoned Pen Press

Introduction and notes copyright © 2016 Martin Edwards

Published by Poisoned Pen Press in association with the British Library

First Edition 2015
First US Trade Paperback Edition

10 9 8 7 6 5 4 3 2 1

Library of Congress Catalog Card Number: 2015946477
ISBN: 9781464205736   Trade Paperback

Poisoned Pen Press
6962 E. First Ave., Ste. 103
Scottsdale, AZ 85251
www.poisonedpenpress.com
info@poisonedpenpress.com

Printed in the United States of America

Contents

Introduction

Murder at the Manor is an anthology of short stories celebrating the British country house mystery. A sinister mansion set in lonely grounds offers an eerie backdrop for dark deeds, as in Arthur Conan Doyle's "The Copper Beeches" and W. W. Jacobs' "The Well". And the country house party with a richly varied assortment of guests provides an ideal "closed circle" of suspects when a crime is committed. An enjoyable example is Nicholas Blake's "The Long Shot", a story written by a former Communist who went on to become Poet Laureate.

Today, enthusiasm for the country house crime story remains as strong as ever. Murder mystery evenings and weekends in country house hotels have become hugely popular, and a thriving industry provides interactive entertainment for guests who want to try their hand at amateur detective work in a suitable setting. The appeal is driven in part by nostalgia for a vanished way of life, and partly by the pleasure of trying to solve a puzzle.

This collection gathers together stories written over a span of (very roughly) sixty-five years, during which British society, and life in country houses, was transformed out of all recognition. "Gentlemen and Players", written by Conan Doyle's brother-in-law, "Willie" Hornung, recalls a seemingly genteel and tranquil age, when members of the aristocracy hosted cricket matches at their country estates. But, as usual in crime fiction, all is not as it seems; A. J. Raffles, that charming gentleman and gifted cricketer, is also a thief with a fondness for diamonds and sapphires.

Some of the stories included in this anthology were written before or after the Golden Age of Murder between the two world wars, but the Golden Age is well represented, and for good reason—it yielded many of the finest examples of this type of fiction. Renowned detectives who made their first appearance investigating crime in a country house include Hercule Poirot (*The Mysterious Affair at Styles*), Albert Campion (*The Crime at Black Dudley*), Mrs Bradley (*Speedy Death*) and Roderick Alleyn (*A Man Lay Dead*).

A small minority of detective novelists not only wrote mysteries set in country houses but actually owned a country house themselves. Most famous of these country estates is Greenway in Devon, a house purchased by Agatha Christie and her husband in 1938, and now a much-loved visitor attraction in the care of the National Trust. Christie used Greenway as a setting more than once in her work, turning it into Nasse House in *Dead Man's Folly*, a relatively late (1956) example of the classic country house whodunit. Margery Allingham and her husband Pip Youngman Carter lived in D'Arcy House at Tolleshunt D'Arcy in Essex from 1935. The Georgian house, still in private hands, is now adorned by a blue plaque commemorating the connection with Allingham, one of whose neatly crafted country house mysteries is included here.

Anthony Berkeley Cox, who wrote as Anthony Berkeley and Francis Iles, also bought a country estate in Devon— Linton Hills. He used it as a setting for a murder mystery novel, *The Second Shot*, published in 1930. A map on endpapers of the book, in keeping with the fashion of the times, showed "Minton Deeps" estate in elaborate detail, identifying the "supposed positions" of the prime suspects. The short story by Berkeley in this book, "The Mystery of Horne's Copse", is much less familiar, but shares some ingredients with *The Second Shot*. A lively example of the traditional whodunit, it offers a cleverly crafted problem complete with vanishing corpses.

The upstairs-downstairs life of a country house provided potential suspects among the staff when murder occurred. "The butler did it" became a cliché, although in fact this particular solution is seldom found in Golden Age whodunits. Herbert Jenkins used the device in one of his stories featuring the detective Malcolm Sage, but in 1928, the American detective novelist S. S. Van Dine published "Twenty rules for writing detective stories", which today seem both amusing and absurd, not least for their insistence that "a servant must not be chosen by the author as the culprit". Servants were sometimes suspects, and sometimes victims, perhaps most poignantly in Christie's *A Pocket Full of Rye*, when one of Miss Marple's former parlour maids meets a cruel end.

The notion of finding "a body in the library" of a country house was another trope of the genre. Christie had fun with it in *The Body in the Library*, where the corpse is found in Gossington Hall, owned by Miss Marple's cronies, Colonel Arthur Bantry and his wife Dolly. But profound changes were taking place in British society as war was followed by peace-time austerity, and high taxes made it impossible for many families to cling on to old houses that were cripplingly expensive to run. Country house parties fell out of fashion, and although traditional whodunits continued to be written and enjoyed, detective novelists could not altogether ignore the reality. The scale of upheaval is apparent in another Marple story, *The Mirror Crack'd from Side to Side*, published twenty years after *The Body in the Library*.

Gossington Hall has been sold off, and been run as a guest house, divided into flats, bought by a government body, and finally snapped up for use as a rich woman's playground by a much-married film star. Her entourage provides a "closed circle" of suspects suited to the 1960s.

The tropes of classic detective fiction make the genre a prime target for humorists, and I was keen to include one of the best send-ups of the country house murder, "The Murder at the Towers". Among the other contributors are such distinguished writers as G. K. Chesterton, and the gifted James Hilton, famed as the author of *Goodbye, Mr Chips*, and as the creator of Shangri-La, whose ventures into crime fiction were sadly infrequent. *Murder at the Manor* also includes little-known stories by the likes of J. J. Bell, and Michael Gilbert. Readers may not hanker after the days of the country house party—after all, attending them often placed one at risk of sudden death or arrest and the prospect of the gallows—but they will, I am sure, relish these entertaining reminders of a bygone age.

Martin Edwards

www.martinedwardsbooks.com

The Copper Beeches

Arthur Conan Doyle

The accomplishments of Arthur Conan Doyle (1859–1930) were many and varied, but he is remembered above all as the creator of Sherlock Holmes. Holmes first appeared in two long stories, *A Study in Scarlet* and *The Sign of Four*, which enjoyed modest success. His investigations proved to be ideally suited to the short story form, and once Conan Doyle embarked on writing up a series of Holmes' cases for the recently established *Strand Magazine*, literary immortality was assured.

Country house mysteries are at the heart of several of the finest Holmes stories, including "The Speckled Band," set at sinister Stoke Moran, which concerns a classic "impossible crime". "The Copper Beeches" features the eponymous mansion, to be found "five miles on the far side of Winchester... it is the most lovely country, and the dearest old country house." But devilry is afoot, and as Holmes and Watson travel by train, the detective remarks that "the lowest and vilest alleys in London do not present a more dreadful record of sin than does the smiling and beautiful countryside". The truth of this famous line is borne out as the story unfolds.

◇◇◇

'To the man who loves art for its own sake,' remarked Sherlock Holmes, tossing aside the advertisement sheet of the *Daily Telegraph*, 'it is frequently in its least important and lowliest manifestations that the keenest pleasure is to be derived. It is pleasant to me to observe, Watson, that you have so far grasped this truth that in these little records of our cases which you have been good enough to draw up, and, I am bound to say, occasionally to embellish, you have given prominence not so much to the many *causes célèbres* and sensational trials in which I have figured, but rather to those incidents which may have been trivial in themselves, but which have given room for those faculties of deduction and of logical synthesis which I have made my special province.'

'And yet,' said I, smiling, 'I cannot quite hold myself absolved from the charge of sensationalism which has been urged against my records.'

'You have erred, perhaps,' he observed, taking up a glowing cinder with the tongs, and lighting with it the long cherrywood pipe which was wont to replace his clay when he was in a disputatious rather than a meditative mood—'you have erred, perhaps, in attempting to put colour and life into each of your statements, instead of confining yourself to the task of placing upon record that severe reasoning from cause to effect which is really the only notable feature about the thing.'

'It seems to me that I have done you full justice in the matter,' I remarked with some coldness, for I was repelled by the egotism which I had more than once observed to be a strong factor in my friend's singular character.

'No, it is not selfishness or conceit,' said he, answering, as was his wont, my thoughts rather than my words. 'If I claim full justice for my art, it is because it is an impersonal thing—a thing beyond myself. Crime is common. Logic is rare. Therefore it is upon the logic rather than upon the crime that you should dwell. You have degraded what should have been a course of lectures into a series of tales.'

It was a cold morning of the early spring, and we sat after breakfast on either side of a cheery fire in the old room in Baker Street. A thick fog rolled down between the lines of dun-coloured houses, and the opposing windows loomed like dark, shapeless blurs, through the heavy yellow wreaths. Our gas was lit, and shone on the white cloth, and glimmer of china and metal, for the table had not been cleared yet. Sherlock Holmes had been silent all the morning, dipping continuously into the advertisement columns of a succession of papers, until at last, having apparently given up his search, he had emerged in no very sweet temper to lecture me upon my literary shortcomings.

'At the same time,' he remarked, after a pause, during which he had sat puffing at his long pipe and gazing down into the fire, 'you can hardly be open to a charge of sensationalism, for out of these cases which you have been so kind as to interest yourself in, a fair proportion do not treat of crime, in its legal sense, at all. The small matter in which I endeavoured to help the King of Bohemia, the singular experience of Miss Mary Sutherland, the problem connected with the man with the twisted lip, and the incident of the noble bachelor, were all matters which are outside the pale of the law. But in avoiding the sensational, I fear that you may have bordered on the trivial.'

'The end may have been so,' I answered, 'but the methods I hold to have been novel and of interest.'

'Pshaw, my dear fellow, what do the public, the great unobservant public, who could hardly tell a weaver by his tooth or a compositor by his left thumb, care about the finer shades of analysis and deduction! But, indeed, if you are trivial, I cannot blame you, for the days of the great cases are past. Man, or at least criminal man, has lost all enterprise and originality. As to my own little practice, it seems to be degenerating into an agency for recovering lost lead pencils and giving advice to young ladies from boarding-schools. I think that I have touched bottom at last, however. This note I had this morning marks my zero point, I fancy. Read it!' He tossed a crumpled letter across to me.

It was dated from Montague Place upon the preceding evening, and ran thus:

> 'DEAR MR HOLMES—I am very anxious to consult you as to whether I should or should not accept a situation which has been offered to me as governess. I shall call at half-past ten tomorrow, if I do not inconvenience you—Yours faithfully, VIOLET HUNTER'

'Do you know the young lady?' I asked.

'Not I.'

'It is half-past ten now.'

'Yes, and I have no doubt that is her ring.'

'It may turn out to be of more interest than you think. You remember that the affair of the blue carbuncle, which appeared to be a mere whim at first, developed into a serious investigation. It may be so in this case also.'

'Well, let us hope so! But our doubts will very soon be solved, for here, unless I am much mistaken, is the person in question.'

As he spoke the door opened, and a young lady entered the room. She was plainly but neatly dressed, with a bright, quick face, freckled like a plover's egg, and with the brisk manner of a woman who has had her own way to make in the world.

'You will excuse my troubling you, I am sure,' said she, as my companion rose to greet her; 'but I have had a very strange experience, and as I have no parents or relations of any sort from whom I could ask advice, I thought that perhaps you would be kind enough to tell me what I should do.'

'Pray take a seat, Miss Hunter. I shall be happy to do anything that I can to serve you.'

I could see that Holmes was favourably impressed by the manner and speech of his new client. He looked her over in his searching fashion, and then composed himself with his lids drooping and his finger-tips together to listen to her story.

'I have been a governess for five years,' said she, 'in the family of Colonel Spence Munro, but two months ago the Colonel received an appointment at Halifax, in Nova Scotia, and took his children over to America with him, so that I found myself without a situation. I advertised and I answered advertisements, but without success. At last the little money which I had saved began to run short, and I was at my wits' end as to what I should do.

'There is a well-known agency for governesses in the West End called Westaway's, and there I used to call about once a week in order to see whether anything had turned up which might suit me. Westaway was the name of the founder of the business, but it is really managed by Miss Stoper. She sits in her own little office, and the ladies who are seeking employment wait in an ante-room, and are then shown in one by one, when she consults her ledgers, and sees whether she has anything which would suit them.

'Well, when I called last week I was shown into the little office as usual, but I found that Miss Stoper was not alone. A prodigiously stout man with a very smiling face, and a great heavy chin which rolled down in fold upon fold over his throat, sat at her elbow with a pair of glasses on his nose, looking very earnestly at the ladies who entered. As I came in he gave quite a jump in his chair, and turned quickly to Miss Stoper:

'"That will do," said he; "I could not ask for anything better. Capital! Capital!" He seemed quite enthusiastic and rubbed his hands together in the most genial fashion. He was such a comfortable-looking man that it was quite a pleasure to look at him.

'"You are looking for a situation, miss?" he asked.

'"Yes, sir."

'"As governess?"

'"Yes, sir."

'"And what salary do you ask?"

'"I had four pounds a month in my last place with Colonel Spence Munro."

'"Oh, tut, tut! sweating—rank sweating!" he cried, throwing his fat hands out into the air like a man who is in a boiling passion. "How could anyone offer so pitiful a sum to a lady with such attractions and accomplishments?"

'"My accomplishments, sir, may be less than you imagine," said I. "A little French, a little German, music and drawing—"

'"Tut, tut!" he cried. "This is all quite beside the question. The point is, have you or have you not the bearing and deportment of a lady? There it is in a nutshell. If you have not, you are not fitted for the rearing of a child who may some day play a considerable part in the history of the country. But if you have, why, then how could any gentleman ask you to condescend to accept anything under the three figures? Your salary with me, madam, would commence at a hundred pounds a year."

'You may imagine, Mr Holmes, that to me, destitute as I was, such an offer seemed almost too good to be true. The gentleman, however, seeing perhaps the look of incredulity upon my face, opened a pocket-book and took out a note.

'"It is also my custom," said he, smiling in the most pleasant fashion until his eyes were just two shining slits, amid the white creases of his face, "to advance to my young ladies half their salary beforehand, so that they may meet any little expenses of their journey and their wardrobe."

'It seemed to me that I had never met so fascinating and so thoughtful a man. As I was already in debt to my tradesmen, the advance was a great convenience, and yet there was something unnatural about the whole transaction which made me wish to know a little more before I quite committed myself.

'"May I ask where you live, sir?" said I.

'"Hampshire. Charming rural place. The Copper Beeches, five miles on the far side of Winchester. It is the most lovely country, my dear young lady, and the dearest old country house."

'"And the duties, sir? I should be glad to know what they would be."

'"One child—one dear little romper just six years old. Oh, if you could see him killing cockroaches with a slipper! Smack! smack! smack! Three gone before you could wink!" He leaned back in his chair and laughed his eyes into his head again.

'I was a little startled at the nature of the child's amusement, but the father's laughter made me think that perhaps he was joking.

'"My sole duties, then," I asked, "are to take charge of a single child?"

'"No, no, not the sole, not the sole, my dear young lady," he cried. "Your duty would be, as I am sure your good sense would suggest, to obey any little commands which my wife might give, provided always that they were such commands as a lady might with propriety obey. You see no difficulty, heh?"

"'I should be happy to make myself useful."

"'Quite so. In dress now, for example! We are faddy people, you know—faddy, but kind-hearted. If you were asked to wear any dress which we might give you, you would not object to our little whim. Heh?"

"'No,' said I, considerably astonished at his words.

"'Or to sit here, or sit there, that would not be offensive to you?"

"'Oh, no."

"'Or to cut your hair quite short before you come to us?"

'I could hardly believe my ears. As you may observe, Mr Holmes, my hair is somewhat luxuriant, and of a rather peculiar tint of chestnut. It has been considered artistic. I could not dream of sacrificing it in this off-hand fashion.

"'I am afraid that that is quite impossible,' said I. He had been watching me eagerly out of his small eyes, and I could see a shadow pass over his face as I spoke.

"'I am afraid that it is quite essential,' said he. "It is a little fancy of my wife's, and ladies' fancies, you know, madam, ladies' fancies must be consulted. And so you won't cut your hair?"

"'No, sir, I really could not,' I answered firmly.

"'Ah, very well; then that quite settles the matter. It is a pity, because in other respects you would really have done very nicely. In that case, Miss Stoper, I had best inspect a few more of your young ladies."

'The manageress had sat all this while busy with her papers without a word to either of us, but she glanced at me now with so much annoyance upon her face that I could not help suspecting that she had lost a handsome commission through my refusal.

"'Do you desire your name to be kept upon the books?" she asked.

"'If you please, Miss Stoper."

'"Well, really, it seems rather useless, since you refuse the most excellent offers in this fashion," said she sharply. "You can hardly expect us to exert ourselves to find another such opening for you. Good day to you, Miss Hunter." She struck a gong upon the table, and I was shown out by the page.

'Well, Mr Holmes, when I got back to my lodgings and found little enough in the cupboard, and two or three bills upon the table, I began to ask myself whether I had not done a very foolish thing. After all, if these people had strange fads, and expected obedience on the most extraordinary matters, they were at least ready to pay for their eccentricity. Very few governesses in England are getting a hundred a year. Besides, what use was my hair to me? Many people are improved by wearing it short, and perhaps I should be among the number. Next day I was inclined to think that I had made a mistake, and by the day after I was sure of it. I had almost overcome my pride, so far as to go back to the agency and inquire whether the place was still open, when I received this letter from the gentleman himself. I have it here, and I will read it to you:

'THE COPPER BEECHES, NEAR WINCHESTER

'DEAR MISS HUNTER—Miss Stoper has very kindly given me your address, and I write from here to ask you whether you have reconsidered your decision. My wife is very anxious that you should come, for she has been much attracted by my description of you. We are willing to give thirty pounds a quarter, or £120 a year, so as to recompense you for any little inconvenience which our fads may cause you. They are not very exacting after all. My wife is fond of a particular shade of electric blue, and would like you to wear such a dress indoors in the mornings. You need not, however, go to the expense of purchasing one, as we have one belonging to my dear daughter Alice (now in Philadelphia) which would, I should think, fit you very well. Then, as to sitting here or there, or amusing yourself in any manner indicated, that need cause you no inconvenience. As regards your hair, it is no doubt a pity, especially as I could not help remarking its beauty during our short interview, but I am afraid that I must remain firm upon this point, and I only hope that the increased salary may recompense you for the loss. Your duties, as far as the child is concerned, are very light. Now do try to come, and I shall meet you with the dog-cart at Winchester. Let me know your train.—Yours faithfully,

'JEPHRO RUCASTLE'

'That is the letter which I have just received, Mr Holmes, and my mind is made up that I will accept it. I thought, however, that before taking the final step, I should like to submit the whole matter to your consideration.'

'Well, Miss Hunter, if your mind is made up, that settles the question,' said Holmes, smiling.

'But you would not advise me to refuse?'

'I confess that it is not the situation which I should like to see a sister of mine apply for.'

'What is the meaning of it all, Mr Holmes?'

'Ah, I have no data. I cannot tell. Perhaps you have yourself formed some opinion?'

'Well, there seems to me to be only one possible solution. Mr Rucastle seemed to be a very kind, good-natured man. Is it not possible that his wife is a lunatic, that he desires to keep the matter quiet for fear she should be taken to an asylum, and that he humours her fancies in every way in order to prevent an outbreak?'

'That is a possible solution—in fact, as matters stand, it is the most probable one. But in any case it does not seem to be a nice household for a young lady.'

'But the money, Mr Holmes, the money!'

'Well, yes, of course, the pay is good—too good. That is what makes me uneasy. Why should they give you £120 a year, when they could have their pick for £40? There must be some strong reason behind.'

'I thought that if I told you the circumstances you would understand afterwards if I wanted your help. I should feel so much stronger if I felt that you were at the back of me.'

'Oh, you may carry that feeling away with you. I assure you that your little problem promises to be the most interesting which has come my way for some months. There is something distinctly novel about some of the features. If you should find yourself in doubt or in danger—'

'Danger! What danger do you foresee?'

Holmes shook his head gravely. 'It would cease to be a danger if we could define it,' said he. 'But at any time, day or night, a telegram would bring me down to your help.'

'That is enough.' She rose briskly from her chair with the anxiety all swept from her face. 'I shall go down to Hampshire quite easy in my mind now. I shall write to Mr Rucastle at once, sacrifice my poor hair tonight, and start for Winchester tomorrow.' With a few grateful words to Holmes she bade us both good night, and bustled off upon her way.

'At least,' said I, as we heard her quick, firm step descending the stairs, 'she seems to be a young lady who is very well able to take care of herself.'

'And she would need to be,' said Holmes gravely; 'I am much mistaken if we do not hear from her before many days are past.'

It was not very long before my friend's prediction was fulfilled. A fortnight went by, during which I frequently found my thoughts turning in her direction, and wondering what strange side-alley of human experience this lonely woman had strayed into. The unusual salary, the curious conditions, the light duties, all pointed to something abnormal, though whether a fad or a plot, or whether the man were a philanthropist or a villain, it was quite beyond my powers to determine. As to Holmes, I observed that he sat frequently for half an hour on end, with knitted brows and an abstracted air, but he swept the matter away with a wave of his hand when I mentioned it. 'Data! data! data!' he cried impatiently. 'I can't make bricks without clay.' And yet he would always wind up by muttering that no sister of his should ever have accepted such a situation.

The telegram which we eventually received came late one night, just as I was thinking of turning in, and Holmes was settling down to one of those all-night researches which he frequently indulged in, when I would leave him stooping over a retort and a test-tube at night, and find him in the same position when I came down to breakfast in the morning. He opened the yellow envelope, and then, glancing at the message, threw it across to me.

'Just look up the trains in Bradshaw,' said he, and turned back to his chemical studies.

The summons was a brief and urgent one.

'Please be at the Black Swan Hotel at Winchester at midday tomorrow,' it said. 'Do come! I am at my wits' end. hunter'

'Will you come with me?' asked Holmes, glancing up.
'I should wish to.'
'Just look it up, then.'
'There is a train at half-past nine,' said I, glancing over my Bradshaw. 'It is due at Winchester at 11.30.'

'That will do very nicely. Then perhaps I had better postpone my analysis of the acetones, as we may need to be at our best in the morning.'

By eleven o'clock the next day we were well upon our way to the old English capital. Holmes had been buried in the morning papers all the way down, but after we had passed the Hampshire border he threw them down, and began to admire the scenery. It was an ideal spring day, a light blue sky, flecked with little fleecy white clouds drifting across from west to east. The sun was shining very brightly, and yet there was an exhilarating nip in the air, which set an edge to a man's energy. All over the countryside, away to the rolling hills around Aldershot, the little red and grey roofs of the farm-steadings peeped out from amidst the light green of the new foliage.

'Are they not fresh and beautiful?' I cried, with all the enthusiasm of a man fresh from the fogs of Baker Street.

But Holmes shook his head gravely.

'Do you know, Watson,' said he, 'that it is one of the curses of a mind with a turn like mine that I must look at everything with reference to my own special subject. You look at these scattered houses, and you are impressed by their beauty. I look at them, and the only thought which comes to me is a feeling of their isolation, and of the impunity with which crime may be committed there.'

'Good heavens!' I cried. 'Who would associate crime with these dear old homesteads?'

'They always fill me with a certain horror. It is my belief, Watson, founded upon my experience, that the lowest and vilest alleys in London do not present a more dreadful record of sin than does the smiling and beautiful countryside.'

'You horrify me!'

'But the reason is very obvious. The pressure of public opinion can do in the town what the law cannot accomplish. There is no lane so vile that the scream of a tortured child, or the thud of a drunkard's blow, does not beget sympathy and indignation among the neighbours, and then the whole machinery of justice is ever so close that a word of complaint can set it going, and there is but a step between the crime and the dock. But look at these lonely houses, each in its own fields, filled for the most part with poor ignorant folk who know little of the law. Think of the deeds of hellish cruelty, the hidden wickedness which may go on, year in, year out, in such places, and none the wiser. Had this lady who appeals to us for help gone to live in Winchester, I should never had had a fear for her. It is the five miles of country which makes the danger. Still, it is clear that she is not personally threatened.'

'No. If she can come to Winchester to meet us she can get away.'

'Quite so. She has her freedom.'

'What *can* be the matter, then? Can you suggest no explanation?'

'I have devised seven separate explanations, each of which would cover the facts as far as we know them. But which of these is correct can only be determined by the fresh information which we shall no doubt find waiting for us. Well, there is the tower of the Cathedral, and we shall soon learn all that Miss Hunter has to tell.'

The 'Black Swan' is an inn of repute in the High Street, at no distance from the station, and there we found the young lady waiting for us. She had engaged a sitting-room, and our lunch awaited us upon the table.

'I am so delighted that you have come,' she said earnestly, 'it is so kind of you both; but indeed I do not know what I should do. Your advice will be altogether invaluable to me.'

'Pray tell us what has happened to you.'

'I will do so, and I must be quick, for I have promised Mr Rucastle to be back before three. I got his leave to come into town this morning, though he little knew for what purpose.'

'Let us have everything in its due order.' Holmes thrust his long thin legs out towards the fire, and composed himself to listen.

'In the first place, I may say that I have met, on the whole, with no actual ill-treatment from Mr and Mrs Rucastle. It is only fair to them to say that. But I cannot understand them, and I am not easy in my mind about them.'

'What can you not understand?'

'Their reasons for their conduct. But you shall have it all just as it occurred. When I came down Mr Rucastle met me here, and drove me in his dog-cart to Copper Beeches. It is, as he said, beautifully situated, but it is not beautiful in itself, for it is a large square block of a house, whitewashed, but all stained and streaked with damp and bad weather. There are grounds round it, woods on three sides, and on the fourth a field which slopes down to the Southampton high-road, which curves past about a hundred yards from the front door. This ground in front belongs to the house, but the woods all round are part of Lord Southerton's preserves. A clump of copper beeches immediately in front of the hall door has given its name to the place.

'I was driven over by my employer, who was as amiable as ever, and was introduced by him that evening to his wife and the child. There was no truth, Mr Holmes, in the conjecture which seemed to us to be probable in your rooms at Baker Street. Mrs Rucastle is not mad. I found her to be a silent, pale-faced woman, much younger than her husband, not more than thirty, I should think, while he can hardly be less than forty-five. From their conversation I have gathered that they have been married about seven years, that he was a widower, and that his only child by the first wife was the daughter who has gone to Philadelphia. Mr Rucastle told me in private that the reason why she had left them was that she had an unreasoning aversion to her step-mother. As the daughter could not have been less than twenty, I can quite imagine that her position must have been uncomfortable with her father's young wife.

'Mrs Rucastle seemed to me to be colourless in mind as well as in feature. She impressed me neither favourably nor the reverse. She was a nonentity. It was easy to see that she was passionately devoted both to her husband and to her little son. Her light grey eyes wandered continually from one to the other, noting every little want and forestalling it if possible. He was kind to her also in his bluff boisterous fashion, and on the whole they seemed to be a happy couple. And yet she had some secret sorrow, this woman. She would often be lost in deep thought, with the saddest look upon her face. More than once I have surprised her in tears. I have thought sometimes that it was the disposition of her child which weighed upon her mind, for I have never met so utterly spoilt and so ill-natured a little creature. He is small for his age, with a head which is quite disproportionately large. His whole life appears to be spent in an alternation between savage fits of passion and gloomy intervals of sulking. Giving pain to any creature weaker than himself seems to be his one idea of amusement, and he shows quite remarkable talent in planning the capture of mice, little birds, and insects. But I would rather not talk about the creature, Mr Holmes, and, indeed he has little to do with my story.'

'I am glad of all details,' remarked my friend, 'whether they seem to you to be relevant or not.'

'I shall try not to miss anything of importance. The one unpleasant thing about the house, which struck me at once, was the appearance and conduct of the servants. There are only two, a man and his wife. Toller, for that's his name, is a rough, uncouth man, with grizzled hair and whiskers, and a perpetual smell of drink. Twice since I have been with them he has been quite drunk, and yet Mr Rucastle seemed to take no notice of it. His wife is a very tall and strong woman with a sour face, as silent as Mrs Rucastle, and much less amiable. They are a most unpleasant couple, but fortunately I spend most of my time in the nursery and my own room, which are next to each other in one corner of the building.

'For two days after my arrival at the Copper Beeches my life was very quiet; on the third, Mrs Rucastle came down just after breakfast and whispered something to her husband.

'"Oh yes," said he, turning to me, "we are very much obliged to you, Miss Hunter, for falling in with our whims so far as to cut your hair. I assure you that it has not detracted in the tiniest iota from your appearance. We shall now see how the electric blue dress will become you. You will find it laid out upon the bed in your room, and if you would be so good as to put it on we should both be extremely obliged."

'The dress which I found waiting for me was of a peculiar shade of blue. It was of excellent material, a sort of beige, but it bore unmistakable signs of having been worn before. It could not have been a better fit if I had been measured for it. Both Mr and Mrs Rucastle expressed a delight at the look of it which seemed quite exaggerated in its vehemence. They were waiting for me in the drawing-room, which is a very large room, stretching along the entire front of the house, with three long windows reaching down to the floor. A chair had been placed close to the central window, with its back turned towards it. In this I was asked to sit, and then Mr Rucastle, walking up and down on the other side of the room, began to tell me a series of the funniest stories that I have ever listened to. You cannot imagine how comical he was, and I laughed until I was quite weary. Mrs Rucastle, however, who has evidently no sense of humour, never so much as smiled, but sat with her hands in her lap, and a sad, anxious look upon her face. After an hour or so, Mr Rucastle suddenly remarked that it was time to commence the duties of the day, and that I might change my dress, and go to little Edward in the nursery.

'Two days later this same performance was gone through under exactly similar circumstances. Again I changed my dress, again I sat in the window, and again I laughed very heartily at the funny stories of which my employer had an immense repertoire, and which he told inimitably. Then he handed me a yellow-backed novel, and, moving my chair a little sideways, that my own shadow might not fall upon the page, he begged me to read aloud to him. I read for about ten minutes, beginning in the heart of a chapter, and then suddenly, in the middle of a sentence, he ordered me to cease and change my dress.

'You can easily imagine, Mr Holmes, how curious I became as to what the meaning of this extraordinary performance could possibly be. They were always very careful, I observed, to turn my face away from the window, so that I became consumed with the desire to see what was going on behind my back. At first it seemed to be impossible, but I soon devised a means. My hand mirror had been broken, so a happy thought seized me, and I concealed a little of the glass in my handkerchief. On the next occasion, in the midst of my laughter, I put my handkerchief up to my eyes, and was able with a little management to see all that there was behind me. I confess that I was disappointed. There was nothing.

'At least, that was my first impression. At the second glance, however, I perceived that there was a man standing in the Southampton road, a small bearded man in a grey suit, who seemed to be looking in my direction. The road is an important highway, and there are usually people there. This man, however, was leaning against the railings which bordered our field, and was looking earnestly. I lowered my handkerchief, and glanced at Mrs Rucastle to find her eyes fixed upon me with a most searching gaze. She said nothing, but I am convinced that she had divined that I had a mirror in my hand, and had seen what was behind me. She rose at once.

'"Jephro," said she, "there is an impertinent fellow upon the road there who stares up at Miss Hunter."

'"No friend of yours, Miss Hunter?" he asked.

'"No; I know no one in these parts."

'"Dear me! How very impertinent! Kindly turn round, and motion him to go away."

'"Surely it would be better to take no notice?"

'"No, no, we should have him loitering here always. Kindly turn round, and wave him away like that."

'I did as I was told, and at the same instant Mrs Rucastle drew down the blind. That was a week ago, and from that time I have not sat again in the window, nor have I worn the blue dress, nor seen the man in the road.'

'Pray continue,' said Holmes. 'Your narrative promises to be a most interesting one.'

'You will find it rather disconnected, I fear, and there may prove to be little relation between the different incidents of which I speak. On the very first day that I was at Copper Beeches, Mr Rucastle took me to a small outhouse which stands near the kitchen door. As we approached it I heard the sharp rattling of a chain, and the sound as of a large animal moving about.

'"Look in here!" said Mr Rucastle, showing me a slit between two planks. "Is he not a beauty?"

'I looked through, and was conscious of two glowing eyes, and of a vague figure huddled up in the darkness.

'"Don't be frightened," said my employer, laughing at the start which I had given. "It's only Carlo, my mastiff. I call him mine, but really old Toller, my groom, is the only man who can do anything with him. We feed him once a day, and not too much then, so that he is always as keen as mustard. Toller lets him loose every night, and God help the trespasser whom he lays his fangs upon. For goodness' sake don't you ever on any pretext set your foot over the threshold at night, for it is as much as your life is worth."

'The warning was no idle one, for two nights later I happened to look out of my bedroom window about two o'clock in the morning. It was a beautiful moonlight night, and the lawn in front of the house was silvered over and almost as bright as day. I was standing wrapt in the peaceful beauty of the scene, when I was aware that something was moving under the shadow of the copper beeches. As it emerged into the moonshine I saw what it was. It was a giant dog, as large as a calf, tawny-tinted, with hanging jowl, black muzzle, and huge projecting bones. It walked slowly across the lawn and vanished into the shadow upon the other side. That dreadful silent sentinel sent a chill to my heart, which I do not think that any burglar could have done.

'And now I have a very strange experience to tell you. I had, as you know, cut off my hair in London, and I had placed it in a great coil at the bottom of my trunk. One evening, after the child was in bed, I began to amuse myself by examining the furniture of my room, and by rearranging my own little things. There was an old chest of drawers in the room, the two upper ones empty and open, the lower one locked. I had filled the two first with my linen, and as I had still much to pack away, I was naturally annoyed at not having the use of the third drawer. It struck me that it might have been fastened by a mere oversight, so I took out my bunch of keys and tried to open it. The very first key fitted to perfection, and I drew the drawer open. There was only one thing in it, but I am sure that you would never guess what it was. It was my coil of hair.

'I took it up and examined it. It was of the same peculiar tint, and the same thickness. But then the impossibility of the thing obtruded itself upon me. How *could* my hair have been locked in the drawer? With trembling hands I undid my trunk, turned out the contents, and drew from the bottom my own hair. I laid the two tresses together, and I assure you they were identical. Was it not extraordinary? Puzzle as I would, I could make nothing at all of what it meant. I returned the strange hair to the drawer, and I said nothing of the matter to the Rucastles, as I felt that I had put myself in the wrong by opening a drawer which they had locked.

'I am naturally observant as you may have remarked, Mr Holmes, and I soon had a pretty good plan of the whole house in my head. There was one wing, however, which appeared not to be inhabited at all. A door which faced that which led into the quarters of the Tollers opened into this suite, but it was invariably locked. One day, however, as I ascended the stair, I met Mr Rucastle coming out through this door, his keys in his hand, and a look on his face which made him a very different person to the round jovial man to whom I was accustomed. His cheeks were red, his brow was all crinkled with anger, and the veins stood out at his temples with passion. He locked the door, and hurried past me without a word or a look.

'This aroused my curiosity; so when I went out for a walk in the grounds with my charge, I strolled round to the side from which I could see the windows of this part of the house. There were four of them in a row, three of which were simply dirty, while the fourth was shuttered up. They were evidently all deserted. As I strolled up and down, glancing at them occasionally, Mr Rucastle came out to me, looking as merry and jovial as ever.

'"Ah!" said he, "you must not think me rude if I passed you without a word, my dear young lady. I was preoccupied with business matters."

'I assured him that I was not offended. "By the way," said I, "you seem to have quite a suite of spare rooms up there, and one of them has the shutters up."

'"Photography is one of my hobbies," said he. "I have made my dark-room up there. But, dear me! what an observant young lady we have come upon. Who would have believed it? Who would have ever believed it?" He spoke in a jesting tone, but there was no jest in his eyes as he looked at me. I read suspicion there, and annoyance, but no jest.

'Well, Mr Holmes, from the moment that I understood that there was something about that suite of rooms which I was not to know, I was all on fire to go over them. It was not mere curiosity, though I have my share of that. It was more a feeling of duty—a feeling that some good might come from my penetrating to this place. They talk of woman's instinct; perhaps it was woman's instinct which gave me that feeling. At any rate, it was there; and I was keenly on the look-out for any chance to pass the forbidden door.

'It was only yesterday that the chance came. I may tell you that, besides Mr Rucastle, both Toller and his wife find something to do in these deserted rooms, and I once saw him carrying a large black linen bag with him through the door. Recently he has been drinking hard, and yesterday evening he was very drunk; and, when I came upstairs, there was the key in the door. I have no doubt at all that he had left it there. Mr and Mrs Rucastle were both downstairs, and the child was with them, so that I had an admirable opportunity. I turned the key gently in the lock, opened the door, and slipped through.

'There was a little passage in front of me, unpapered and uncarpeted, which turned at a right angle at the farther end. Round this corner were three doors in a line, the first and third of which were open. They each led into an empty room, dusty and cheerless, with two windows in the one, and one in the other, so thick with dirt that the evening light glimmered dimly through them. The centre door was closed, and across the outside of it had been fastened one of the broad bars of an iron bed, padlocked at one end to a ring in the wall, and fastened at the other with stout cord. The door itself was locked as well, and the key was not there. This barricaded door corresponded clearly with the shuttered window outside, and yet I could see by the glimmer from beneath it that the room was not in darkness. Evidently there was a skylight which let in light from above. As I stood in the passage gazing at this sinister door, and wondering what secret it might veil, I suddenly heard the sound of steps within the room, and saw a shadow pass backwards and forwards against the little slit of dim light which shone out from under the door. A mad, unreasoning terror rose up in me at the sight, Mr Holmes. My overstrung nerves failed me suddenly, and I turned and ran—ran as though some dreadful hand were behind me, clutching at the skirt of my dress. I rushed down the passage, through the door, and straight into the arms of Mr Rucastle, who was waiting outside.

'"So," said he, smiling, "it was you, then. I thought it must be when I saw the door open."

'"Oh, I am so frightened!" I panted.

'"My dear young lady! my dear young lady!"—you cannot think how caressing and soothing his manner was—"and what has frightened you, my dear young lady?"

'But his voice was just a little too coaxing. He overdid it. I was keenly on my guard against him.

"'I was foolish enough to go into the empty wing," I answered. "But it is so lonely and eerie in this dim light that I was frightened and ran out again. Oh, it is so dreadfully still in there!"

"'Only that?' said he, looking at me keenly.

"'Why, what do you think?' I asked.

"'Why do you think that I lock this door?'

"'I am sure that I do not know.'

"'It is to keep people out who have no business there. Do you see?' He was still smiling in the most amiable manner.

"'I am sure if I had known—'

"'Well, then, you know now. And if you ever put your foot over that threshold again—' here in an instant the smile hardened into a grin of rage, and he glared down at me with the face of a demon, "I'll throw you to the mastiff."

'I was so terrified that I do not know what I did. I suppose that I must have rushed past him into my room. I remember nothing until I found myself lying on my bed trembling all over. Then I thought of you, Mr Holmes. I could not live there longer without some advice. I was frightened of the house, of the man, of the woman, of the servants, even of the child. They were all horrible to me. If I could only bring you down all would be well. Of course I might have fled from the house, but my curiosity was almost as strong as my fears. My mind was soon made up. I would send you a wire. I put on my hat and cloak, went down to the office, which is about half a mile from the house, and then returned, feeling very much easier. A horrible doubt came into my mind as I approached the door lest the dog might be loose, but I remembered that Toller had drunk himself into a state of insensibility that evening, and I knew that he was the only one in the household who had any influence with the savage creature, or who would venture to set him free. I slipped in in safety, and lay awake half the night in my joy at the thought of seeing you. I had no difficulty in getting leave to come into Winchester this morning, but I must be back before three o'clock, for Mr and Mrs Rucastle are going on a visit, and will be away all the evening, so that I must look after the child. Now I have told you all my adventures, Mr Holmes, and I should be very glad if you could tell me what it all means, and, above all, what I should do.'

Holmes and I had listened spellbound to this extraordinary story. My friend rose now, and paced up and down the room, his hands in his pockets, and an expression of the most profound gravity upon his face.

'Is Toller still drunk?' he asked.

'Yes. I heard his wife tell Mrs Rucastle that she could do nothing with him.'

'That is well. And the Rucastles go out tonight?'

'Yes.'

'Is there a cellar with a good strong lock?'

'Yes, the wine cellar.'

'You seem to me to have acted all through this matter like a brave and sensible girl, Miss Hunter. Do you think that you could perform one more feat? I should not ask it of you if I did not think you a quite exceptional woman.'

'I will try. What is it?'

'We shall be at the Copper Beeches by seven o'clock, my friend and I. The Rucastles will be gone by that time, and Toller will, we hope, be incapable. There only remains Mrs Toller, who might give the alarm. If you could send her into the cellar, on some errand, and then turn the key upon her, you would facilitate matters immensely.'

'I will do it.'

'Excellent! We shall then look thoroughly into the affair. Of course there is only one feasible explanation. You have been brought there to personate someone, and the real person is imprisoned in this chamber. That is obvious.

As to who this prisoner is, I have no doubt that it is the daughter, Miss Alice Rucastle, if I remember right, who was said to have gone to America. You were chosen, doubtless, as resembling her in height, figure, and the colour of your hair. Hers had been cut off, very possibly in some illness through which she has passed, and so, of course, yours had to be sacrificed also. By a curious chance you came upon her tresses. The man in the road was, undoubtedly, some friend of hers—possibly her fiancé—and no doubt as you wore the girl's dress, and were so like her, he was convinced from your laughter, whenever he saw you, and afterwards from your gesture, that Miss Rucastle was perfectly happy, and that she no longer desired his attentions. The dog is let loose at night to prevent him from endeavouring to communicate with her. So much is fairly clear. The most serious point in the case is the disposition of the child.'

'What on earth has that to do with it?' I ejaculated.

'My dear Watson, you as a medical man are continually gaining light as to the tendencies of a child by the study of the parents. Don't you see that the converse is equally valid? I have frequently gained my first real insight into the character of parents by studying their children. This child's disposition is abnormally cruel, merely for cruelty's sake, and whether he derives this from his smiling father, as I should suspect, or from his mother, it bodes evil for the poor girl who is in their power.'

'I am sure that you are right, Mr Holmes,' cried our client. 'A thousand things come back to me which make me certain that you have hit it. Oh, let us lose not an instant in bringing help to this poor creature.'

'We must be circumspect, for we are dealing with a very cunning man. We can do nothing until seven o'clock. At that hour we shall be with you, and it will not be long before we solve the mystery.'

We were as good as our word, for it was just seven when we reached the Copper Beeches, having put up our trap at a wayside public-house. The group of trees, with their dark leaves shining like burnished metal in the light of the setting sun, were sufficient to mark the house even had Miss Hunter not been standing smiling on the doorstep.

'Have you managed it?' asked Holmes.

A loud thudding noise came from somewhere downstairs. 'That is Mrs Toller in the cellar,' said she. 'Her husband lies snoring on the kitchen rug. Here are his keys, which are the duplicates of Mr Rucastle's.'

'You have done well indeed!' cried Holmes, with enthusiasm. 'Now lead the way, and we shall soon see the end of this black business.'

We passed up the stair, unlocked the door, followed on down a passage, and found ourselves in front of the barricade which Miss Hunter had described. Holmes cut the cord and removed the transverse bar. Then he tried the various keys in the lock, but without success. No sound came from within, and at the silence Holmes' face clouded over.

'I trust that we are not too late,' said he. 'I think, Miss Hunter, that we had better go in without you. Now, Watson, put your shoulder to it, and we shall see whether we cannot make our way in.'

It was an old rickety door and gave at once before our united strength. Together we rushed into the room. It was empty. There was no furniture save a little pallet bed, a small table, and a basketful of linen. The skylight above was open, and the prisoner gone.

'There has been some villainy here,' said Holmes; 'this beauty has guessed Miss Hunter's intentions, and has carried his victim off.'

'But how?'

'Through the skylight. We shall soon see how he managed it.' He swung himself up on to the roof. 'Ah, yes,' he cried, 'here's the end of a long light ladder against the eaves. That is how he did it.'

'But it is impossible,' said Miss Hunter, 'the ladder was not there when the Rucastles went away.'

'He has come back and done it. I tell you that he is a clever and dangerous man. I should not be very much surprised if this were he whose step I hear now upon the stair. I think, Watson, that it would be as well for you to have your pistol ready.'

The words were hardly out of his mouth before a man appeared at the door of the room, a very fat and burly man, with a heavy stick in his hand. Miss Hunter screamed and shrunk against the wall at the sight of him, but Sherlock Holmes sprang forward and confronted him.

'You villain,' said he, 'where's your daughter?'

The fat man cast his eyes round, and then up at the open skylight.

'It is for me to ask you that,' he shrieked, 'you thieves! Spies and thieves! I have caught you, have I? You are in my power. I'll serve you!' He turned and clattered down the stairs as hard as he could go.

'He's gone for the dog!' cried Miss Hunter.

'I have my revolver,' said I.

'Better close the front door,' cried Holmes, and we all rushed down the stairs together. We had hardly reached the hall when we heard the baying of a hound, and then a scream of agony, with a horrible worrying sound which it was dreadful to listen to. An elderly man with a red face and shaking limbs came staggering out at a side-door.

'My God!' he cried. 'Someone has loosed the dog. It's not been fed for two days. Quick, quick, or it'll be too late!'

Holmes and I rushed out, and round the angle of the house, with Toller hurrying behind us. There was the huge famished brute, its black muzzle buried in Rucastle's throat, while he writhed and screamed upon the ground. Running up, I blew its brains out, and it fell over with its keen white teeth still meeting in the great creases of his neck. With much labour we separated them, and carried him, living but horribly mangled, into the house. We laid him upon the drawing-room sofa, and having dispatched the sobered Toller to bear the news to his wife, I did what I could to relieve his pain. We were all assembled round him when the door opened, and a tall, gaunt woman entered the room.

'Mrs Toller!' cried Miss Hunter.

'Yes, miss. Mr Rucastle let me out when he came back before he went up to you. Ah, miss, it is a pity you didn't let me know what you were planning, for I would have told you that your pains were wasted.'

'Ha!' said Holmes, looking keenly at her. 'It is clear that Mrs Toller knows more about this matter than anyone else.'

'Yes, sir, I do, and I am ready enough to tell what I know.'

'Then pray sit down, and let us hear it, for there are several points on which I must confess that I am still in the dark.'

'I will soon make it clear to you,' said she; 'and I'd have done so before now if I could ha' got out from the cellar. If there's police-court business over this, you'll remember that I was the one that stood your friend, and that I was Miss Alice's friend too.

'She was never happy at home, Miss Alice wasn't, from the time that her father married again. She was slighted like, and had no say in anything; but it never really became bad for her until after she met Mr Fowler at a friend's house. As well as I could learn, Miss Alice had rights of her own by will, but she was so quiet and patient, she was, that she never said a word about them, but just left everything in Mr Rucastle's hands. He knew he was safe with her; but when there was a chance of a husband coming forward, who would ask for all that the law could give him, then her father thought it time to put a stop on it. He wanted her to sign a paper so that whether she married or not, he could use her money. When she wouldn't do it, he kept on worrying her until she got brain fever, and for six weeks was at death's door. Then she got better at last, all worn to a shadow, and with her beautiful hair cut off; but that didn't make no change in her young man, and he stuck to her as true as man could be.'

'Ah,' said Holmes, 'I think that what you have been good enough to tell us makes the matter fairly clear, and that I can deduce all that remains. Mr Rucastle, then, I presume, took to this system of imprisonment?'

'Yes, sir.'

'And brought Miss Hunter down from London in order to get rid of the disagreeable persistence of Mr Fowler.'

'That was it, sir.'

'But Mr Fowler, being a persevering man, as a good seaman should be, blockaded the house, and, having met you, succeeded by certain arguments, metallic or otherwise, in convincing you that your interests were the same as his.'

'Mr Fowler was a very kind-spoken, free-handed gentleman,' said Mrs Toller serenely.

'And in this way he managed that your good man should have no want of drink, and that a ladder should be ready at the moment when your master had gone out.'

'You have it, sir, just as it happened.'

'I am sure we owe you an apology, Mrs Toller,' said Holmes, 'for you have certainly cleared up everything which puzzled us. And here comes the country surgeon and Mrs Rucastle, so I think, Watson, that we had best escort Miss Hunter back to Winchester, as it seems to me that our *locus standi* now is rather a questionable one.'

And thus was solved the mystery of the sinister house with the copper beeches in front of the door. Mr Rucastle survived, but was always a broken man, kept alive solely through the care of his devoted wife. They still live with their old servants, who probably know so much of Rucastle's past life that he finds it difficult to part from them. Mr Fowler and Miss Rucastle were married, by special licence, in Southampton the day after their flight, and he is now the holder of a Government appointment in the Island of Mauritius. As to Miss Violet Hunter, my friend Holmes, rather to my disappointment, manifested no further interest in her when once she had ceased to be the centre of one of his problems, and she is now the head of a private school at Walsall, where I believe that she has met with considerable success.

The Problem of
Dead Wood Hall

Dick Donovan

Dick Donovan was a pen-name of James Edward Preston Muddock (1843–1934), a journalist and prolific author of crime and horror fiction who also called himself Joyce Emmerson Preston Muddock. Two of Muddock's daughters later achieved celebrity. Dorothy, an Olympic medal-winning figure skater, married Herbert Greenough-Smith, a legendary editor of the *Strand Magazine* who gave Conan Doyle much encouragement. Evangeline, who borrowed her father's idea of improving her name, called herself Eva Mudocci. A beautiful violinist, she became Edvard Munch's muse; his lithograph of her in its turn inspired a print by Andy Warhol.

Dick Donovan began life as a fictional sleuth, and as his popularity grew, Muddock started writing under the character's name; a similar ploy was later used for the long line of "Nick Charles" stories, and by the two American cousins who wrote as Ellery Queen about a gifted detective of that name. "The Problem of Dead Wood Hall" is one of Donovan's best-remembered stories, and although he was no match for Conan Doyle as a literary stylist, the story's zest helps to explain why this formidably hard-working writer was for a brief period almost as popular as Holmes' creator.

◇◇◇

'Mysterious Case In Cheshire'. So ran the heading to a paragraph in all the morning papers some years ago, and prominence was given to the following particulars:

A gentleman, bearing the somewhat curious name of Tuscan Trankler, resided in a picturesque old mansion, known as Dead Wood Hall, situated in one of the most beautiful and lonely parts of Cheshire, not very far from the quaint and old-time village of Knutsford. Mr Trankler had given a dinner-party at his house, and amongst the guests was a very well-known county magistrate and landowner, Mr Manville Charnworth. It appeared that, soon after the ladies had retired from the table, Mr Charnworth rose and went into the grounds, saying he wanted a little air. He was smoking a cigar, and in the enjoyment of perfect health. He had drunk wine, however, rather freely, as was his wont, but though on exceedingly good terms with himself and every one else, he was perfectly sober. An hour passed, but Mr Charnworth had not returned to the table. Though this did not arouse any alarm, as it was thought that he had probably joined the ladies, for he was what is called 'a ladies' man,' and preferred the company of females to that of men. A tremendous sensation, however, was caused when, a little later, it was announced that Charnworth had been found insensible, lying on his back in a shrubbery. Medical assistance was at once summoned, and when it arrived the opinion expressed was that the unfortunate gentleman had been stricken with apoplexy. For some reason or other, however, the doctors were led to modify that view, for symptoms were observed which pointed to what was thought to be a peculiar form of poisoning, although the poison could not be determined. After a time, Charnworth recovered consciousness, but was quite unable to give any information. He seemed to be dazed and confused, and was evidently suffering great pain. At last his limbs began to swell, and swelled to an enormous size; his eyes sunk, his cheeks fell in, his lips turned black, and mortification appeared in the extremities. Everything that could be done for the unfortunate man was done, but without avail. After six hours' suffering, he died in a paroxysm of raving madness, during which he had to be held down in the bed by several strong men.

The post-mortem examination, which was necessarily held, revealed the curious fact that the blood in the body had become thin and purplish, with a faint strange odour that could not be identified. All the organs were extremely congested, and the flesh presented every appearance of rapid decomposition. In fact, twelve hours after death putrefaction had taken place. The medical gentlemen who had the case in hand were greatly puzzled, and were at a loss to determine the precise cause of death. The deceased had been a very healthy man, and there was no actual organic disease of any kind. In short, everything pointed to poisoning. It was noted that on the left side of the neck was a tiny scratch, with a slightly livid appearance, such as might have been made by a small sharply pointed instrument. The viscera having been secured for purposes of analysis, the body was hurriedly buried within thirty hours of death.

The result of the analysis was to make clear that the unfortunate gentleman had died through some very powerful and irritant poison being introduced into the blood. That it was a case of blood-poisoning there was hardly room for the shadow of a doubt, but the science of that day was quite unable to say what the poison was, or how it had got into the body. There was no reason—so far as could be ascertained—to suspect foul play, and even less reason to suspect suicide. Altogether, therefore, the case was one of profound mystery, and the coroner's jury were compelled to return an open verdict. Such were the details that were made public at the time of Mr Charnworth's death; and from the social position of all the parties, the affair was something more than a nine days' wonder; while in Cheshire itself, it created a profound sensation. But, as no further information was forthcoming, the matter ceased to interest the outside world, and so, as far as the public were concerned, it was relegated to the limbo of forgotten things.

Two years later, Mr Ferdinand Trankler, eldest son of Tuscan Trankler, accompanied a large party of friends for a day's shooting in Mere Forest. He was a young man, about five and twenty years of age; was in the most perfect health, and had scarcely ever had a day's illness in his life. Deservedly popular and beloved, he had a large circle of warm friends, and was about to be married to a charming young lady, a member of an old Cheshire family who were extensive landed proprietors and property owners. His prospects therefore seemed to be unclouded, and his happiness complete.

The shooting-party was divided into three sections, each agreeing to shoot over a different part of the forest, and to meet in the afternoon for refreshments at an appointed rendezvous.

Young Trankler and his companions kept pretty well together for some little time, but ultimately began to spread about a good deal. At the appointed hour the friends all met, with the exception of Trankler. He was not there. His absence did not cause any alarm, as it was thought he would soon turn up. He was known to be well acquainted with the forest, and the supposition was he had strayed further afield than the rest. By the time the repast was finished, however, he had not put in an appearance. Then, for the first time, the company began to feel some uneasiness, and vague hints that possibly an accident had happened were thrown out. Hints at last took the form of definite expressions of alarm, and search parties were at once organized to go in search of the absent young man, for only on the hypothesis of some untoward event could his prolonged absence be accounted for, inasmuch as it was not deemed in the least likely that he would show such a lack of courtesy as to go off and leave his friends without a word of explanation. For two hours the search was kept up without any result. Darkness was then closing in, and the now painfully anxious searchers began to feel that they would have to desist until daylight returned. But at last some of the more energetic and active members of the party came upon Trankler lying on his side, and nearly entirely hidden by masses of half withered bracken. He was lying near a little stream that meandered through the forest, and near a keeper's shelter that was constructed with logs and thatched with pine boughs. He was stone dead, and his appearance caused his friends to shrink back with horror, for he was not only black in the face, but his body was bloated, and his limbs seemed swollen to twice their natural size.

Amongst the party were two medical men, who, being hastily summoned, proceeded at once to make an examination. They expressed an opinion that the young man had been dead for some time, but they could not account for his death, as there was no wound to be observed. As a matter of fact, his gun was lying near him with both barrels loaded. Moreover, his appearance was not compatible at all with death from a gun-shot wound. How then had he died? The consternation amongst those who had known him can well be imagined, and with a sense of suppressed horror, it was whispered that the strange condition of the dead man coincided with that of Mr Manville Charnworth, the county magistrate who had died so mysteriously two years previously.

As soon as it was possible to do so, Ferdinand Trankler's body was removed to Dead Wood Hall, and his people were stricken with profound grief when they realized that the hope and joy of their house was dead. Of course an autopsy had to be performed, owing to the ignorance of the medical men as to the cause of death. And this post-mortem examination disclosed the fact that all the extraordinary appearances which had been noticed in Mr Charnworth's case were present in this one. There was the same purplish coloured blood; the same gangrenous condition of the limbs; but as with Charnworth, so with Trankler, all the organs were healthy. There was no organic disease to account for death. As it was pretty certain, therefore, that death was not due to natural causes, a coroner's inquest was held, and while the medical evidence made it unmistakably clear that young Trankler had been cut down in the flower of his youth and while he was in radiant health by some powerful and potent means which had suddenly destroyed his life, no one had the boldness to suggest what those means were, beyond saying that blood-poisoning of a most violent character had been set up. Now, it was very obvious that blood-poisoning could not have originated without some specific cause, and the most patient investigation was directed to trying to find out the cause, while exhaustive inquiries were made, but at the end of them, the solution of the mystery was as far off as ever, for these investigations had been in the wrong channel, not one scrap of evidence was brought forward which would have justified a definite statement that this or that had been responsible for the young man's death.

It was remembered that when the post-mortem examination of Mr Charnworth took place, a tiny bluish scratch was observed on the left side of the neck. But it was so small, and apparently so unimportant that it was not taken into consideration when attempts were made to solve the problem of 'How did the man die?' When the doctors examined Mr Trankler's body, they looked to see if there was a similar puncture or scratch, and, to their astonishment, they did find rather a curious mark on the left side of the neck, just under the ear. It was a slight abrasion of the skin, about an inch long as if he had been scratched with a pin, and this abrasion was a faint blue, approximating in colour to the tattoo marks on a sailor's arm. The similarity in this scratch to that which had been observed on Mr Charnworth's body, necessarily gave rise to a good deal of comment amongst the doctors, though they could not arrive at any definite conclusion respecting it. One man went so far as to express an opinion that it was due to an insect or the bite of a snake. But this theory found no supporters, for it was argued that the similar wound on Mr Charnworth could hardly have resulted from an insect or snake bite, for he had died in his friend's garden. Besides, there was no insect or snake in England capable of killing a man as these two men had been killed. That theory, therefore, fell to the ground; and medical science as represented by the local gentlemen had to confess itself baffled; while the coroner's jury were forced to again return an open verdict.

'There was no evidence to prove how the deceased had come by his death.'

This verdict was considered highly unsatisfactory, but what other could have been returned. There was nothing to support the theory of foul play; on the other hand, no evidence was forthcoming to explain away the mystery which surrounded the deaths of Charnworth and Trankler. The two men had apparently died from precisely the same cause, and under circumstances which were as mysterious as they were startling, but what the cause was, no one seemed able to determine.

Universal sympathy was felt with the friends and relatives of young Trankler, who had perished so unaccountably while in pursuit of pleasure. Had he been taken suddenly ill at home and had died in his bed, even though the same symptoms and morbid appearances had manifested themselves, the mystery would not have been so great. But as Charnworth's end came in his host's garden after a dinner-party, so young Trankler died in a forest while he and his friends were engaged in shooting. There was certainly something truly remarkable that two men, exhibiting all the same post-mortem effects, should have died in such a way; their deaths, in point of time, being separated by a period of two years. On the face of it, it seemed impossible that it could be merely a coincidence. It will be gathered from the foregoing, that in this double tragedy were all the elements of a romance well calculated to stimulate public curiosity to the highest pitch; while the friends and relatives of the two deceased gentlemen were of opinion that the matter ought not to be allowed to drop with the return of the verdict of the coroner's jury. An investigation seemed to be urgently called for. Of course, an investigation of a kind had taken place by the local police, but something more than that was required, so thought the friends. And an application was made to me to go down to Dead Wood Hall; and bring such skill as I possessed to bear on the case, in the hope that the veil of mystery might be drawn aside, and light let in where all was then dark.

Dead Wood Hall was a curious place, with a certain gloominess of aspect which seemed to suggest that it was a fitting scene for a tragedy. It was a large, massive house, heavily timbered in front in a way peculiar to many of the old Cheshire mansions. It stood in extensive grounds, and being situated on a rise commanded a very fine panoramic view which embraced the Derbyshire Hills. How it got its name of Dead Wood Hall no one seemed to know exactly. There was a tradition that it had originally been known as Dark Wood Hall; but the word 'Dark' had been corrupted into 'Dead'. The Tranklers came into possession of the property by purchase, and the family had been the owners of it for something like thirty years.

With great circumstantiality I was told the story of the death of each man, together with the results of the post-mortem examination, and the steps that had been taken by the police. On further inquiry I found that the police, in spite of the mystery surrounding the case, were firmly of opinion that the deaths of the two men were, after all, due to natural causes, and that the similarity in the appearance of the bodies after death *was* a mere coincidence. The superintendent of the county constabulary, who had had charge of the matter, waxed rather warm; for he said that all sorts of ridiculous stories had been set afloat, and absurd theories had been suggested, not one of which would have done credit to the intelligence of an average schoolboy.

'People lose their heads so, and make such fools of themselves in matters of this kind,' he said warmly; 'and of course the police are accused of being stupid, ignorant, and all the rest of it. They seem, in fact, to have a notion that we are endowed with super-human faculties, and that nothing should baffle us. But, as a matter of fact, it is the doctors who are at fault in this instance. They are confronted with a new disease, about which they are ignorant; and, in order to conceal their want of knowledge, they at once raise the cry of "foul play".'

'Then you are clearly of opinion that Mr Charnworth and Mr Trankler died of a disease,' I remarked.

'Undoubtedly I am.'

'Then how do you explain the rapidity of the death in each case, and the similarity in the appearance of the dead bodies?'

'It isn't for me to explain that at all. That is doctors' work not police work. If the doctors can't explain it, how can I be expected to do so? I only know this, I've put some of my best men on to the job, and they've failed to find anything that would suggest foul play.'

'And that convinces you absolutely that there has been no foul play?'

'Absolutely.'

'I suppose you were personally acquainted with both gentlemen? What sort of man was Mr Charnworth?'

'Oh, well, he was right enough, as such men go. He made a good many blunders as a magistrate; but all magistrates do that. You see, fellows get put on the bench who are no more fit to be magistrates than you are, sir. It's a matter of influence more often as not. Mr Charnworth was no worse and no better than a lot of others I could name.'

'What opinion did you form of his private character?'

'Ah, now, there, there's another matter,' answered the superintendent, in a confidential tone, and with a smile playing about his lips. 'You see, Mr Charnworth was a bachelor.'

'So are thousands of other men,' I answered. 'But bachelorhood is not considered dishonourable in this country.'

'No, perhaps not. But they say as how the reason was that Mr Charnworth didn't get married was because he didn't care for having only one wife.'

'You mean he was fond of ladies generally. A sort of general lover.'

'I should think he was,' said the superintendent, with a twinkle in his eye, which was meant to convey a good deal of meaning. 'I've heard some queer stories about him.'

'What is the nature of the stories?' I asked, thinking that I might get something to guide me.

'Oh, well, I don't attach much importance to them myself,' he said, half-apologetically; 'but the fact is, there was some social scandal talked about Mr Charnworth.'

'What was the nature of the scandal?'

'Mind you,' urged the superintendent, evidently anxious to be freed from any responsibility for the scandal whatever it was, 'I only tell you the story as I heard it. Mr Charnworth liked his little flirtations, no doubt, as we all do; but he was a gentleman and a magistrate, and I have no right to say anything against him that I know nothing about myself.'

'While a gentleman may be a magistrate, a magistrate is not always a gentleman,' I remarked.

'True, true; but Mr Charnworth was. He was a fine specimen of a gentleman, and was very liberal. He did me many kindnesses.'

'Therefore, in your sight, at least, sir, he was without blemish.'

'I don't go as far as that,' replied the superintendent, a little warmly; 'I only want to be just.'

'I give you full credit for that,' I answered; 'but please do tell me about the scandal you spoke of. It is just possible it may afford me a clue.'

'I don't think that it will. However, here is the story. A young lady lived in Knutsford by the name of Downie. She is the daughter of the late George Downie, who for many years carried on the business of a miller. Hester Downie was said to be one of the prettiest girls in Cheshire, or, at any rate, in this part of Cheshire, and rumour has it that she flirted with both Charnworth and Trankler.'

'Is that all that rumour says?' I asked.

'No, there was a good deal more said. But, as I have told you, I know nothing for certain, and so must decline to commit myself to any statement for which there could be no better foundation than common gossip.'

'Does Miss Downie still live in Knutsford?'

'No; she disappeared mysteriously soon after Charnworth's death.'

'And you don't know where she is?'

'No; I have no idea.'

As I did not see that there was much more to be gained from the superintendent I left him, and at once sought an interview with the leading medical man who had made the autopsy of the two bodies. He was a man who was somewhat puffed up with the belief in his own cleverness, but he gave me the impression that, if anything, he was a little below the average country practitioner. He hadn't a single theory to advance to account for the deaths of Charnworth and Trankler. He confessed that he was mystified; that all the appearances were entirely new to him, for neither in his reading nor his practice had he ever heard of a similar case.

'Are you disposed to think, sir, that these two men came to their end by foul play?' I asked.

'No, I am not,' he answered definitely, 'and I said so at the inquest. Foul play means murder, cool and deliberate, and planned and carried out with fiendish cunning. Besides, if it was murder how was the murder committed?'

'*If it was murder?*' I asked significantly. 'I shall hope to answer that question later on.'

'But I am convinced it wasn't murder,' returned the doctor, with a self-confident air. 'If a man is shot, or bludgeoned, or poisoned, there is something to go upon. I scarcely know of a poison that cannot be detected. And not a trace of poison was found in the organs of either man. Science has made tremendous strides of late years, and I doubt if she has much more to teach us in that respect. Anyway,

I assert without fear of contradiction that Charnworth and Trankler did not die of poison.'

'What killed them, then?' I asked, bluntly and sharply.

The doctor did not like the question, and there was a roughness in his tone as he answered—

'I'm not prepared to say. If I could have assigned a precise cause of death the coroner's verdict would have been different.'

'Then you admit that the whole affair is a problem which you are incapable of solving?'

'Frankly, I do,' he answered, after a pause. 'There are certain peculiarities in the case that I should like to see cleared up. In fact, in the interests of my profession, I think it is most desirable that the mystery surrounding the death of the unfortunate men should be solved. And I have been trying experiments recently with a view to attaining that end, though without success.'

My interview with this gentleman had not advanced matters, for it only served to show me that the doctors were quite baffled, and I confess that that did not altogether encourage me. Where they had failed, how could I hope to succeed? They had the advantage of seeing the bodies and examining them, and though they found themselves confronted with signs which were in themselves significant, they could not read them. All that I had to go upon was hearsay, and I was asked to solve a mystery which seemed unsolvable. But, as I have so often stated in the course of my chronicles, the seemingly impossible is frequently the most easy to accomplish, where a mind specially trained to deal with complex problems is brought to bear upon it.

In interviewing Mr Tuscan Trankler, I found that he entertained a very decided opinion that there had been foul play, though he admitted that it was difficult in the extreme to suggest even a vague notion of how the deed had been accomplished. If the two men had died together or within a short period of each other, the idea of murder would have seemed more logical. But two years had elapsed, and yet each man had evidently died from precisely the same cause. Therefore, if it *was* murder, the same hand that had slain Mr Charnworth slew Mr Trankler. There was no getting away from that; and then of course arose the question of *motive*. Granted that the same hand did the deed, did the same motive prompt in each case? Another aspect of the affair that presented itself to me was that the crime, if crime it was, was not the work of any ordinary person. There was an originality of conception in it which pointed to the criminal being, in certain respects, a genius. And, moreover, the motive underlying it must have been a very powerful one; possibly, nay probably, due to a sense of some terrible wrong inflicted, and which could only be wiped out with the death of the wronger. But this presupposed that each man, though unrelated, had perpetrated the same wrong. Now, it was within the grasp of intelligent reasoning that Charnworth, in his capacity of a county justice, might have given mortal offence to some one, who, cherishing the memory of it, until a mania had been set up, resolved that the magistrate should die. That theory was reasonable when taken singly, but it seemed to lose its reasonableness when connected with young Trankler, unless it was that he had been instrumental in getting somebody convicted. To determine this I made very pointed inquiries, but received the most positive assurances that never in the whole course of his life had he directly or indirectly been instrumental in prosecuting any one. Therefore, so far as he was concerned, the theory fell to the ground; and if the same person killed both men, the motive prompting in each case was a different one, assuming that Charnworth's death resulted from revenge for a fancied wrong inflicted in the course of his administration of justice.

Although I fully recognized all the difficulties that lay in the way of a rational deduction that would square in with the theory of murder, and of murder committed by one and the same hand, I saw how necessary it was to keep in view the points I have advanced as factors in the problem that had to be worked out, and I adhered to my first impression, and felt tolerably certain that, granted the men had been murdered, they were murdered by the same hand. It may be said that this deduction required no great mental effort. I admit that that is so; but it is strange that nearly all the people in the district were opposed to the theory. Mr Tuscan Trankler spoke very highly of Charnworth. He believed him to be an upright, conscientious man, liberal to a fault with his means, and in his position of magistrate erring on the side of mercy. In his private character he was a *bon vivant*; fond of a good dinner, good wine, and good company. He was much in request at dinner-parties and other social gatherings, for he was accounted a brilliant *raconteur*, possessed of an endless fund of racy jokes and anecdotes. I have already stated that with ladies he was an especial favourite, for he had a singularly suave, winning way, which with most women was irresistible. In age he was more than double that of young Trankler, who was only five and twenty at the time of his death, whereas Charnworth had turned sixty, though I was given to understand that he was a well-preserved, good-looking man, and apparently younger than he really was.

Coming to young Trankler, there was a consensus of opinion that he was an exemplary young man. He had been partly educated at home and partly at the Manchester Grammar School; and, though he had shown a decided talent for engineering, he had not gone in for it seriously, but had dabbled in it as an amateur, for he had ample means and good prospects, and it was his father's desire that he should lead the life of a country gentleman, devote himself to country pursuits, and to improving and keeping together the family estates. To the lady who was to have become his bride, he had been engaged but six months, and had only known her a year. His premature and mysterious death had caused intense grief in both families; and his intended wife had been so seriously affected that her friends had been compelled to take her abroad.

With these facts and particulars before me, I had to set to work and try to solve the problem which was considered unsolvable by most of the people who knew anything about it. But may I be pardoned for saying very positively that, even at this point, I did not consider it so. Its complexity could not be gainsaid; nevertheless, I felt that there were ways and means of arriving at a solution, and I set to work in my own fashion. Firstly, I started on the assumption that both men had been deliberately murdered by the same person. If that was not so, then they had died of some remarkable and unknown disease which had stricken them down under a set of conditions that were closely allied, and the coincidence in that case would be one of the most astounding the world had ever known. Now, if that was correct, a pathological conundrum was propounded which it was for the medical world to answer, and practically I was placed out of the running, to use a sporting phrase. I found that, with few exceptions—the exceptions being Mr Trankler and his friends—there was an undisguised opinion that what the united local wisdom and skill had failed to accomplish, could not be accomplished by a stranger. As my experience, however, had inured me against that sort of thing, it did not affect me. Local prejudices and jealousies have always to be reckoned with, and it does not do to be thin-skinned. I worked upon my own lines, thought with my own thoughts, and, as an expert in the art of reading human nature, I reasoned from a different set of premises to that employed by the irresponsible chatterers, who cry out 'Impossible', as soon as the first difficulty presents itself. Marshalling all the facts of the case so far as I had been able to gather them, I arrived at the conclusion that the problem could be solved, and, as a preliminary step to that end, I started off to London, much to the astonishment of those who had secured my services. But my reply to the many queries addressed to me was, 'I hope to find the key-note to the solution in the metropolis.' This reply only increased the astonishment, but later on I will explain why I took the step, which may seem to the reader rather an extraordinary one.

After an absence of five days I returned to Cheshire, and I was then in a position to say, 'Unless a miracle has happened, Charnworth and Trankler were murdered beyond all doubt, and murdered by the same person in such a cunning, novel, and devilish manner, that even the most astute inquirer might have been pardoned for being baffled.' Of course there was a strong desire to know my reasons for the positive statement, but I felt that it was in the interests of justice itself that I should not allow them to be known at that stage of the proceedings.

The next important step was to try and find out what had become of Miss Downie, the Knutsford beauty, with whom Charnworth was said to have carried on a flirtation. Here, again, I considered secrecy of great importance.

Hester Downie was about seven and twenty years of age. She was an orphan, and was believed to have been born in Macclesfield, as her parents came from there. Her father's calling was that of a miller. He had settled in Knutsford about fifteen years previous to the period I am dealing with, and had been dead about five years. Not very much was known about the family, but it was thought there were other children living. No very kindly feeling was shown for Hester Downie, though it was only too obvious that jealousy was at the bottom of it. Half the young men, it seemed, had lost their heads about her, and all the girls in the village were consumed with envy and jealousy. It was said she was 'stuck up', 'above her position', 'a heartless flirt', and so forth. From those competent to speak, however, she was regarded as a nice young woman, and admittedly good-looking. For years she had lived with an old aunt, who bore the reputation of being rather a sullen sort of woman, and somewhat eccentric. The girl had a little over fifty pounds a year to live upon, derived from a small property left to her by her father; and she and her aunt occupied a cottage just on the outskirts of Knutsford. Hester was considered to be very exclusive, and did not associate much with the people in Knutsford. This was sufficient to account for the local bias, and as she often went away from her home for three and four weeks at a time, it was not considered extraordinary when it was known that she had left soon after Trankler's death. Nobody, however, knew where she had gone to; it is right, perhaps, that I should here state that not a soul breathed a syllable of suspicion against her, that either directly or indirectly she could be connected with the deaths of Charnworth or Trankler. The aunt, a widow by the name of Hislop, could not be described as a pleasant or genial woman, either in appearance or manner. I was anxious to ascertain for certain whether there was any truth in the rumour or not that Miss Downie had flirted with Mr Charnworth. If it was true that she did, a clue might be afforded which would lead to the ultimate unravelling of the mystery. I had to approach Mrs Hislop with a good deal of circumspection, for she showed an inclination to resent any inquiries being made into her family matters. She gave me the impression that she was an honest woman, and it was very apparent that she was strongly attached to her niece Hester. Trading on this fact, I managed to draw her out. I said that people in the district were beginning to say unkind things about Hester, and that it would be better for the girl's sake that there should be no mystery associated with her or her movements.

The old lady fired up at this, and declared that she didn't care a jot about what the 'common people' said. Her niece was superior to all of them, and she would 'have the law on any one who spoke ill of Hester.'

'But there is one thing, Mrs Hislop,' I replied, 'that ought to be set at rest. It is rumoured—in fact, something more than rumoured—that your niece and the late Mr Charn-worth were on terms of intimacy, which, to say the least, if it is true, was imprudent for a girl in her position.'

'Them what told you that,' exclaimed the old woman, 'is like the adders the woodmen get in Delamere forest: they're full of poison. Mr Charnworth courted the girl fair and square, and led her to believe he would marry her. But, of course, he had to do the thing in secret. Some folk will talk so, and if it had been known that a gentleman like Mr Charnworth was coming after a girl in Hester's position, all sorts of things would have been said.'

'Did she believe that he was serious in his intentions towards her?'

'Of course she did.'

'Why was the match broken off?'

'Because he died.'

'Then do you mean to tell me seriously, Mrs Hislop, that Mr Charnworth, had he lived, would have married your niece?'

'Yes, I believe he would.'

'Was he the only lover the girl had?'

'Oh dear no. She used to carry on with a man named Job Panton. But, though they were engaged to be married, she didn't like him much, and threw him up for Mr Charnworth.'

'Did she ever flirt with young Mr Trankler?'

'I don't know about flirting; but he called here now and again, and made her some presents. You see, Hester is a superior sort of girl, and I don't wonder at gentlefolk liking her.'

'Just so,' I replied; 'beauty attracts peasant and lord alike. But you will understand that it is to Hester's interest that there should be no concealment—no mystery; and I advise that she return here, for her very presence would tend to silence the tongue of scandal. By the way, where is she?'

'She's staying in Manchester with a relative, a cousin of hers, named Jessie Turner.'

'Is Jessie Turner a married woman?'

'Oh yes: well, that is, she has been married; but she's a widow now, and has two little children. She is very fond of Hester, who often goes to her.'

Having obtained Jessie Turner's address in Manchester, I left Mrs Hislop, feeling somehow as if I had got the key of the problem, and a day or two later I called on Mrs Jessie Turner, who resided in a small house, situated in Tamworth Street, Hulme, Manchester.

She was a young woman, not more than thirty years of age, somewhat coarse, and vulgar-looking in appearance, and with an unpleasant, self-assertive manner. There was a great contrast between her and her cousin, Hester Downie, who was a remarkably attractive and pretty girl, with quite a classical figure, and a childish, winning way, but a painful want of education which made itself very manifest when she spoke; and a harsh, unmusical voice detracted a good deal from her winsomeness, while in everything she did, and almost everything she said, she revealed that vanity was her besetting sin.

I formed my estimate at once of this young woman—indeed, of both of them. Hester seemed to me to be shallow, vain, thoughtless, giddy; and her companion, artful, cunning, and heartless.

'I want you, Miss Downie,' I began, 'to tell me truthfully the story of your connection, firstly, with Job Panton; secondly, with Mr Charnworth; thirdly, with Mr Trankler.'

This request caused the girl to fall into a condition of amazement and confusion, for I had not stated what the nature of my business was, and, of course, she was unprepared for the question.

'What should I tell you my business for?' she cried snappishly, and growing very red in the face.

'You are aware,' I remarked, 'that both Mr Charnworth and Mr Trankler are dead?'

'Of course I am.'

'Have you any idea how they came by their death?'

'Not the slightest.'

'Will you be surprised to hear that some very hard things are being said about you?'

'About me!' she exclaimed, in amazement.

'Yes.'

'Why about me?'

'Well, your disappearance from your home, for one thing.'

She threw up her hands and uttered a cry of distress and horror, while sudden paleness took the place of the red flush that had dyed her cheeks. Then she burst into almost hysterical weeping, and sobbed out:

'I declare it's awful. To think that I cannot do anything or go away when I like without all the old cats in the place trying to blacken my character! It's a pity that people won't mind their own business, and not go out of the way to talk about that which doesn't concern them.'

'But, you see, Miss Downie, it's the way of the world,' I answered, with a desire to soothe her; 'one mustn't be too thin-skinned. Human nature is essentially spiteful. However, to return to the subject, you will see, perhaps, the importance of answering my questions. The circumstances of Charn-worth's and Trankler's deaths are being closely inquired into, and I am sure you wouldn't like it to be thought that you were withholding information which, in the interest of law and justice, might be valuable.'

'Certainly not,' she replied, suppressing a sob. 'But I have nothing to tell you.'

'But you knew the three men I have mentioned.'

'Of course I did, but Job Panton is an ass. I never could bear him.'

'He was your sweetheart, though, was he not?'

'He used to come fooling about, and declared that he couldn't live without me.'

'Did you never give him encouragement?'

'I suppose every girl makes a fool of herself sometimes.'

'Then you did allow him to sweetheart you?'

'If you like to call it sweethearting you can,' she answered, with a toss of her pretty head. 'I did walk out with him sometimes. But I didn't care much for him. You see, he wasn't my sort at all.'

'In what way?'

'Well, surely I couldn't be expected to marry a game-keeper, could I?'

'He is a gamekeeper, then?'

'Yes.'

'In whose employ is he?'

'Lord Belmere's.'

'Was he much disappointed when he found that you would have nothing to do with him?'

'I really don't know. I didn't trouble myself about him,' she answered, with a coquettish heartlessness.

'Did you do any sweethearting with Mr Trankler?'

'No, of course not. He used to be very civil to me, and talk to me when he met me.'

'Did you ever walk out with him?'

The question brought the colour back to her face, and her manner grew confused again.

'Once or twice I met him by accident, and he strolled along the road with me—that's all.'

This answer was not a truthful one. Of that I was convinced by her very manner. But I did not betray my mistrust or doubts. I did not think there was any purpose to be served in so doing. So far the object of my visit was accomplished, and as Miss Downie seemed disposed to resent any further questioning, I thought it was advisable to bring the interview to a close; but before doing so, I said:

'I have one more question to ask you, Miss Downie. Permit me to preface it, however, by saying I am afraid that, up to this point, you have failed to appreciate the situation, or grasp the seriousness of the position in which you are placed. Let me, therefore, put it before you in a somewhat more graphic way. Two men—gentlemen of good social position—with whom you seem to have been well acquainted, and whose attentions you encouraged—pray do not look at me so angrily as that; I mean what I say. I repeat that you encouraged their attentions, otherwise they would not have gone after you.' Here Miss Downie's nerves gave way again, and she broke into a fit of weeping, and, holding her handkerchief to her eyes, she exclaimed with almost passionate bitterness:

'Well, whatever I did, I was egged on to do it by my cousin, Jessie Turner. She always said I was a fool not to aim at high game.'

'And so you followed her promptings, and really thought that you might have made a match with Mr Charnworth; but, he having died, you turned your thoughts to young Trankler.' She did not reply, but sobbed behind her handkerchief. So I proceeded. 'Now the final question I want to ask you is this: Have you ever had anyone who has made serious love to you but Job Panton?'

'Mr Charnworth made love to me,' she sobbed out.

'He flirted with you,' I suggested.

'No; he made love to me,' she persisted. 'He promised to marry me.'

'And you believed him?'

'Of course I did.'

'Did Trankler promise to marry you?'

'No.'

'Then I must repeat the question, but will add Mr Charnworth's name. Besides him and Panton, is there any one else in existence who has courted you in the hope that you would become his wife?'

'No—no one,' she mumbled in a broken voice.

As I took my departure I felt that I had gathered up a good many threads, though they wanted arranging, and, so to speak, classifying; that done, they would probably give me the clue I was seeking. One thing was clear, Miss Downie was a weak-headed, giddy, flighty girl, incapable, as it seemed to me, of seriously reflecting on anything. Her cousin was crafty and shallow, and a dangerous companion for Downie, who was sure to be influenced and led by a creature like Jessie Turner. But, let it not be inferred from these remarks that I had any suspicion that either of the two women had in any way been accessory to the crime, for crime I was convinced it was. Trankler and Charnworth had been murdered, but by whom I was not prepared to even hint at at that stage of the proceedings. The two unfortunate gentlemen had, beyond all possibility of doubt, both been attracted by the girl's exceptionally good looks, and they had amused themselves with her. This fact suggested at once the question, was Charnworth in the habit of seeing her before Trankler made her acquaintance? Now, if my theory of the crime was correct, it could be asserted with positive certainty that Charnworth was the girl's lover before Trankler. Of course it was almost a foregone conclusion that Trankler must have been aware of her existence for a long time. The place, be it remembered, was small; she, in her way, was a sort of local celebrity, and it was hardly likely that young Trankler was ignorant of some of the village gossip in which she figured. But, assuming that he was, he was well acquainted with Charnworth, who was looked upon in the neighbourhood as 'a gay dog'. The female conquests of such men are often matters of notoriety; though, even if that was not the case, it was likely enough that Charnworth may have discussed Miss Downie in Trankler's presence. Some men—especially those of Charnworth's characteristics—are much given to boasting of their flirtations, and Charnworth may have been rather proud of his ascendency over the simple village beauty. Of course, all this, it will be said, was mere theorizing. So it was; but it will presently be seen how it squared in with the general theory of the whole affair, which I had worked out after much pondering, and a careful weighing and nice adjustment of all the evidence, such as it was, I had been able to gather together, and the various parts which were necessary before the puzzle could be put together.

It was immaterial, however, whether Trankler did or did not know Hester Downie before or at the same time as Charnworth. A point that was not difficult to determine was this—he did not make himself conspicuous as her admirer until after his friend's death, probably not until some time afterwards. Otherwise, how came it about that the slayer of Charnworth waited two years before he took the life of young Trankler? The reader will gather from this remark how my thoughts ran at that time. Firstly, I was clearly of opinion that both men had been murdered. Secondly, the murder in each case was the outcome of jealousy. Thirdly, the murderer must, as a logical sequence, have been a rejected suitor. This would point necessarily to Job Panton as the criminal, assuming my information was right that the girl had not had any other lover. But against that theory this very strong argument could be used: By what extraordinary and secret means—means that had baffled all the science of the district—had Job Panton, who occupied the position of a gamekeeper, been able to do away with his victims, and bring about death so horrible and so sudden as to make one shudder to think of it? Herein was displayed a devilishness of cunning, and a knowledge which it was difficult to conceive that an ignorant and untravelled man was likely to be in possession of. Logic, deduction, and all the circumstances of the case were opposed to the idea of Panton being the murderer at the first blush; and yet, so far as I had gone, I had been irresistibly drawn towards the conclusion that Panton was either directly or indirectly responsible for the death of the two gentlemen. But, in order to know something more of the man whom I suspected, I disguised myself as a travelling showman on the look-out for a good pitch for my show, and I took up my quarters for a day or two at a rustic inn just on the skirts of Knutsford, and known as the Woodman. I had previously ascertained that this inn was a favourite resort of the gamekeepers for miles round about, and Job Panton was to be found there almost nightly.

In a short time I had made his acquaintance. He was a young, big-limbed, powerful man, of a pronounced rustic type. He had the face of a gipsy—swarthy and dark, with keen, small black eyes, and a mass of black curly hair, and

in his ears he wore tiny, plain gold rings. Singularly enough
his expression was most intelligent; but allied with—as it
seemed to me—a certain suggestiveness of latent ferocity.
That is to say, I imagined him liable to outbursts of temper
and passion, during which he might be capable of anything.
As it was, then, he seemed to me subdued, somewhat sullen,
and averse to conversation. He smoked heavily, and I soon
found that he guzzled beer at a terrible rate. He had received,
for a man in his position, a tolerably good education. By
that I mean he could write a fair hand, he read well, and
had something more than a smattering of arithmetic. I was
told also that he was exceedingly skilful with carpenter's
tools, although he had had no training that way; he also
understood something about plants, while he was considered
an authority on the habits, and everything appertaining to
game. The same informant thought to still further enlighten
me by adding:

'Poor Job bëan't the chap he wur a year or more ago. His
gal cut un, and that kind a took a hold on un. He doän't say
much; but it wur a terrible blow, it wur.'

'How was it his girl cut him?' I asked.

'Well, you see, maäster, it wur this way; she thought
hersel' a bit too high for un. Mind you, I bäan't a saying as
she wur; but when a gel thinks hersel' above a chap, it's no
use talking to her.'

'What was the girl's name?'

'They call her Downie. Her father was a miller here in
Knutsford, but his gal had too big notions of hersel'; and
she chucked poor Job Panton overboard, and they do say
as how she took on wi' Meäster Charnworth and also wi'
Meäster Trankler. I doän't know nowt for certain myself, but
there wur some rum kind o' talk going about. Leastwise,
I know that Job took it badly, and he ain't been the same
kind o' chap since. But there, what's the use of a braking

one's 'art about a gal? Gals is a queer lot, I tell you. My old grandfaither used to say, "Women folk be curious folk. They be necessary evils, they be, and pleasant enough in their way, but a chap mustn't let 'em get the upper hand. They're like harses, they be, and if you want to manage 'em, you must show 'em you're their meäster".'

The garrulous gentleman who entertained me thus with his views on women, was a tough, sinewy, weather-tanned old codger, who had lived the allotted span according to the psalmist, but who seemed destined to tread the earth for a long time still; for his seventy years had neither bowed nor shrunk him. His chatter was interesting to me because it served to prove what I already suspected, which was that Job Panton had taken his jilting very seriously indeed. Job was by no means a communicative fellow. As a matter of fact, it was difficult to draw him out on any subject; and though I should have liked to have heard *his* views about Hester Downie, I did not feel warranted in tapping him straight off. I very speedily discovered, however, that his weakness was beer. His capacity for it seemed immeasurable. He soaked himself with it; but when he reached the muddled stage, there was a tendency on his part to be more loquacious, and, taking advantage at last of one of these opportunities, I asked him one night if he had travelled. The question was an exceedingly pertinent one to my theory, and I felt that to a large extent the theory I had worked out depended upon the answers he gave. He turned his beady eyes upon me, and said, with a sort of sardonic grin—

'Yes, I've travelled a bit in my time, meäster. I've been to Manchester often, and I once tramped all the way to Edinburgh. I had to rough it, I tell thee.'

'Yes, I dare say,' I answered. 'But what I mean is, have you ever been abroad? Have you ever been to sea?'

'No, meäster, not me.'

'You've been in foreign countries?'

'No. I've never been out of this one. England was good enough for me. But I would like to go away now to Australia, or some of those places.'

'Why?'

'Well, meäster, I have my own reasons.'

'Doubtless,' I said, 'and no doubt very sound reasons.'

'Never thee mind whether they are, or whether they beän't,' he retorted warmly. 'All I've got to say is, I wouldn't care where I went to if I could only get far enough away from this place. I'm tired of it.'

In the manner of giving his answer, he betrayed the latent fire which I had surmised, and showed that there was a volcanic force of passion underlying his sullen silence, for he spoke with a suppressed force which clearly indicated the intensity of his feelings, and his bright eyes grew brighter with the emotion he felt. I now ventured upon another remark. I intended it to be a test one.

'I heard one of your mates say that you had been jilted. I suppose that's why you hate the place?'

He turned upon me suddenly. His tanned, ruddy face took on a deeper flush of red; his upper teeth closed almost savagely on his nether lip; his chest heaved, and his great, brawny hands clenched with the working of his passion. Then, with one great bang of his ponderous fist, he struck the table until the pots and glasses on it jumped as if they were sentient and frightened; and in a voice thick with smothered passion, he growled, 'Yes, damn her! She's been my ruin.'

'Nonsense!' I said. 'You are a young man and a young man should not talk about being ruined because a girl has jilted him.'

Once more he turned that angry look upon me, and said fiercely—

'Thou knows nowt about it, governor. Thou're a stranger to me; and I doän't allow no strangers to preach to me. So shut up! I'll have nowt more to say to thee.'

There was a peremptoriness, a force of character, and a display of firmness and self-assurance in his tone and manner, which stamped him with a distinct individualism, and made it evident that in his own particular way he was distinct from the class in which his lot was cast. He, further than that, gave me the idea that he was designing and secretive; and given that he had been educated and well trained, he might have made his mark in the world. My interview with him had been instructive, and my opinion that he might prove a very important factor in working out the problem was strengthened; but at that stage of the inquiry I would not have taken upon myself to say, with anything like definiteness, that he was directly responsible for the death of the two gentlemen, whose mysterious ending had caused such a profound sensation. But the reader of this narrative will now see for himself that of all men, so far as one could determine then, who might have been interested in the death of Mr Charnworth and Mr Trankler, Job Panton stood out most conspicuously. His motive for destroying them was one of the most powerful of human passions—namely, jealousy, which in his case was likely to assume a very violent form, inasmuch as there was no evenly balanced judgment, no capability of philosophical reasoning, calculated to restrain the fierce, crude passion of the determined and self-willed man.

A wounded tiger is fiercer and more dangerous than an unwounded one, and an ignorant and unreasoning man is far more likely to be led to excess by a sense of wrong, than one who is capable of reflecting and moralizing. Of course, if I had been the impossible detective of fiction, endowed with the absurd attributes of being able to tell the story of a man's life from the way the tip of his nose was formed, or the number of hairs on his head, or by the shape and size of his teeth, or by the way he held his pipe when smoking, or from the kind of liquor he consumed, or the hundred and one utterly ridiculous and burlesque signs which are so easily read by the detective prig of modern creation, I might have come to a different conclusion with reference to Job Panton. But my work had to be carried out on very different lines, and I had to be guided by certain deductive inferences, aided by an intimate knowledge of human nature, and of the laws which, more or less in every case of crime, govern the criminal.

I have already set forth my unalterable opinion that Charnworth and Trankler had been murdered; and so far as I had proceeded up to this point, I had heard and seen enough to warrant me, in my own humble judgment, in at least suspecting Job Panton of being guilty of the murder. But there was one thing that puzzled me greatly. When I first commenced my inquiries, and was made acquainted with all the extraordinary medical aspects of the case, I argued with myself that if it *was* murder, it was murder carried out upon very original lines. Some potent, swift and powerful poison must have been suddenly and secretly introduced into the blood of the victim. The bite of a cobra, or of the still more fearful and deadly Fer de lance of the West Indies, might have produced symptoms similar to those observed in the two men; but happily our beautiful and quiet woods and gardens of England are not infested with these deadly reptiles, and one had to search for the causes elsewhere. Now every one knows that the notorious Lucrezia Borgia, and the Marchioness of Brinvilliers, made use of means for accomplishing the death of those whom they were anxious to get out of the way, which were at once effective and secret. These means consisted, amongst others, of introducing into the blood of the intended victim some subtle poison, by the medium of a scratch or puncture. This little and fatal wound could be given by the scratch of a pin, or the sharpened stone of a ring, and in such a way that the victim would be all unconscious of it until the deadly poison so insidiously introduced began to course through his veins, and to sap the props of his life. With these facts in my mind, I asked myself if in the Dead Wood Hall tragedies some similar means had been used; and in order to have competent and authoritative opinion to guide me, I journeyed back to London to consult the eminent chemist and scientist, Professor Lucraft. This gentleman had made a lifelong study of the toxic effect of ptomaines on the human system, and of the various poisons used by savage tribes for tipping their arrows and spears. Enlightened as he was on the subject, he confessed that there were hundreds of these deadly poisons, of which the modern chemist knew absolutely nothing; but he expressed a decided opinion that there were many that would produce all the effects and symptoms observable in the cases of Charnworth and Trankler. And he particularly instanced some of the herbal extracts used by various tribes of Indians, who wander in the interior of the little known country of Ecuador, and he cited as an authority Mr Hart Thompson, the botanist, who travelled from Quito right through Ecuador to the Amazon. This gentleman reported that he found a vegetable poison in use by the natives for poisoning the tips of their arrows and spears of so deadly and virulent a nature, that a scratch even on a panther would bring about the death of the animal within an hour.

Armed with these facts, I returned to Cheshire, and continued my investigations on the assumption that some such deadly destroyer of life had been used to put Charnworth and Trankler out of the way. But necessarily I was led to question whether or not it was likely that an untravelled and ignorant man like Job Panton could have known anything about such poisons and their uses. This was a stumbling-block; and while I was convinced that Panton had a strong motive for the crime, I was doubtful if he could have been in possession of the means for committing it. At last, in order to try and get evidence on this point, I resolved to search the place in which he lived. He had for a long time occupied lodgings in the house of a widow woman in Knutsford, and I subjected his rooms to a thorough and critical search, but without finding a sign of anything calculated to justify my suspicion.

I freely confess that at this stage I began to feel that the problem was a hopeless one, and that I should fail to work it out. My depression, however, did not last long. It was not my habit to acknowledge defeat so long as there were probabilities to guide me, so I began to make inquiries about Panton's relatives, and these inquiries elicited the fact that he had been in the habit of making frequent journeys to Manchester to see an uncle. I soon found that this uncle had been a sailor, and had been one of a small expedition which had travelled through Peru and Ecuador in search of gold. Now, this was a discovery indeed, and the full value of it will be understood when it is taken in connection with the information given to me by Professor Lucraft. Let us see how it works out logically.

Panton's uncle was a sailor and a traveller. He had travelled through Peru, and had been into the interior of Ecuador.

Panton was in the habit of visiting his uncle.

Could the uncle have wandered through Ecuador without hearing something of the marvellous poisons used by the natives?

Having been connected with an exploring expedition, it was reasonable to assume that he was a man of good intelligence, and of an inquiring turn of mind.

Equally probable was it that he had brought home some of the deadly poisons or poisoned implements used by the Indians. Granted that, and what more likely than that he talked of his knowledge and possessions to his nephew? The nephew, brooding on his wrongs, and seeing the means within his grasp of secretly avenging himself on those whom he counted his rivals, obtained the means from his uncle's collection of putting his rivals to death, in a way which to him would seem to be impossible to detect. I had seen enough of Panton to feel sure that he had all the intelligence and cunning necessary for planning and carrying out the deed.

A powerful link in the chain of evidence had now been forged, and I proceeded a step further. After a consultation with the chief inspector of police, who, however, by no means shared my views, I applied for a warrant for Panton's arrest, although I saw that to establish legal proof of his guilt would be extraordinarily difficult, for his uncle at that time was at sea, somewhere in the southern hemisphere. Moreover, the whole case rested upon such a hypothetical basis, that it seemed doubtful whether, even supposing a magistrate would commit, a jury would convict. But I was not daunted; and, having succeeded so far in giving a practical shape to my theory, I did not intend to draw back. So I set to work to endeavour to discover the weapon which had been used for wounding Charnworth and Trankler, so that the poison might take effect. This, of course, was the *crux* of the whole affair. The discovery of the medium by which the death-scratch was given would forge almost the last link necessary to ensure a conviction.

Now, in each case there was pretty conclusive evidence that there had been no struggle. This fact justified the belief that the victim was struck silently, and probably unknown to himself. What were the probabilities of that being the case? Assuming that Panton was guilty of the crime, how was it that he, being an inferior, was allowed to come within striking distance of his victims? The most curious thing was that both men had been scratched on the left side of the neck. Charnworth had been killed in his friend's garden on a summer night. Trankler had fallen in mid-day in the depths of a forest. There was an interval of two years between the death of the one man and the death of the other, yet each had a scratch on the left side of the neck. That could not have been a mere coincidence. It was design.

The next point for consideration was, how did Panton— always assuming that he was the criminal—get access to Mr Trankler's grounds? Firstly, the grounds were extensive, and in connection with a plantation of young fir trees. When Charnworth was found, he was lying behind a clump of rhododendron bushes, and near where the grounds were merged into the plantation, a somewhat dilapidated oak fence separating the two. These details before us make it clear that Panton could have had no difficulty in gaining access to the plantation, and thence to the grounds. But how came it that he was there just at the time that Charnworth was strolling about? It seemed stretching a point very much to suppose that he could have been loafing about on the mere chance of seeing Charnworth. And the only hypothesis that squared in with intelligent reasoning, was that the victim had been lured into the grounds. But this necessarily presupposed a confederate. Close inquiry elicited the fact that Panton was in the habit of going to the house. He knew most of the servants, and frequently accompanied young Trankler on his shooting excursions, and periodically he spent half a day or so in the gun room at the house, in order that he might clean up all the guns, for which he was paid a small sum every month. These circumstances cleared the way of difficulties to a very considerable extent. I was unable, however, to go beyond that, for I could not ascertain the means that had been used to lure Mr Charnworth into the garden—if he had been lured; and I felt sure that he had been. But so much had to remain for the time being a mystery.

Having obtained the warrant to arrest Panton, I proceeded to execute it. He seemed thunderstruck when told that he was arrested on a charge of having been instrumental in bringing about the death of Charnworth and Trankler. For a brief space of time he seemed to collapse, and lose his presence of mind. But suddenly, with an apparent effort, he recovered himself, and said, with a strange smile on his face—

'You've got to prove it, and that you can never do.'

His manner and this remark were hardly compatible with innocence, but I clearly recognized the difficulties of proof.

From that moment the fellow assumed a self-assured air, and to those with whom he was brought in contact he would remark:

'I'm as innocent as a lamb, and them as says I done the deed have got to prove it.'

In my endeavour to get further evidence to strengthen my case, I managed to obtain from Job Panton's uncle's brother, who followed the occupation of an engine-minder in a large cotton factory in Oldham, an old chest containing a quantity of lumber. The uncle, on going to sea again, had left this chest in charge of his brother. A careful examination of the contents proved that they consisted of a very miscellaneous collection of odds and ends, including two or three small, carved wooden idols from some savage country; some stone weapons, such as are used by the North American Indians; strings of cowrie shells, a pair of moccasins, feathers of various kinds; a few dried specimens of strange birds; and last, though not least, a small bamboo case containing a dozen tiny sharply pointed darts, feathered at the thick end; while in a stone box, about three inches square, was a viscid thick gummy looking substance of a very dark brown colour, and giving off a sickening and most disagreeable, though faint odour. These things I at once submitted to Professor Lucraft, who expressed an opinion that the gummy substance in the stone box was a vegetable poison, used probably to poison the darts with. He lost no time in experimentalizing with this substance, as well as with the darts. With these darts he scratched guinea-pigs, rabbits, a dog, a cat, a hen, and a young pig, and in each case death ensued in periods of time ranging from a quarter of an hour to two hours. By means of a subcutaneous injection into a rabbit of a minute portion of the gummy substance, about the size of a pea, which had been thinned with alcohol, he produced death in exactly seven minutes. A small monkey was next procured, and slightly scratched on the neck with one of the poisoned darts. In a very short time the poor animal exhibited the most distressing symptoms, and in half an hour it was dead, and a post-mortem examination revealed many of the peculiar effects which had been observed in Charnworth's and Trankler's bodies. Various other exhaustive experiments were carried out, all of which confirmed the deadly nature of these minute poison-darts, which could be puffed through a hollow tube to a great distance, and after some practice, with unerring aim. Analysis of the gummy substance in the box proved it to be a violent vegetable poison; innocuous when swallowed, but singularly active and deadly when introduced direct into the blood.

On the strength of these facts, the magistrate duly committed Job Panton to take his trial at the next assizes, on a charge of murder, although there was not a scrap of evidence forthcoming to prove that he had ever been in possession of any of the darts or the poison; and unless such evidence was forthcoming, it was felt that the case for the prosecution must break down, however clear the mere guilt of the man might seem.

In due course, Panton was put on his trial at Chester, and the principal witness against him was Hester Downie, who was subjected to a very severe cross-examination, which left not a shadow of a doubt that she and Panton had at one time been close sweethearts. But her cousin Jessie Turner proved a tempter of great subtlety. It was made clear that she poisoned the girl's mind against her humble lover. Although it could not be proved, it is highly probable that Jessie Turner was a creature of and in the pay of Mr Charnworth, who seemed to have been very much attracted by him. Hester's connection with Charnworth half maddened Panton, who made frantic appeals to her to be true to him, appeals to which she turned a deaf ear. That Trankler knew her in Charnworth's time was also brought out, and after Charnworth's death she smiled favourably on the young man. On the morning that Trankler's shooting-party went out to Mere Forest, Panton was one of the beaters employed by the party.

So much was proved; so much was made as clear as daylight, and it opened the way for any number of inferences. But the last and most important link was never forthcoming. Panton was defended by an able and unscrupulous counsel, who urged with tremendous force on the notice of the jury, that firstly, not one of the medical witnesses would undertake to swear that the two men had died from the effects of poison similar to that found in the old chest which had belonged to the prisoner's uncle; and secondly, there was not one scrap of evidence tending to prove that Panton had ever been in possession of poisoned darts, or had ever had access to the chest in which they were kept. These two points were also made much of by the learned judge in his summing up. He was at pains to make clear that there was a doubt involved, and that mere inference ought not to be allowed to outweigh the doubt when a human being was on trial for his life. Although circumstantially the evidence very strongly pointed to the probability of the prisoner having killed both men, nevertheless, in the absence of the strong proof which the law demanded, the way was opened for the escape of a suspected man, and it was far better to let the law be cheated of its due, than that an innocent man should suffer. At the same time, the judge went on, two gentlemen had met their deaths in a manner which had baffled medical science, and no one was forthcoming who would undertake to say that they had been killed in the manner suggested by the prosecution, and yet it had been shown that the terrible and powerful poison found in the old chest, and which there was reason to believe had been brought from some part of the little known country near the sources of the mighty Amazon, would produce all the effects which were observed in the bodies of Charnworth and Trankler. The chest, furthermore, in which the poison was discovered, was in the possession of Panton's uncle. Panton had a powerful motive in the shape of consuming jealousy for getting rid of his more favoured rivals; and though he was one of the shooting-party in Mere Forest on the day that Trankler lost his life, no evidence had been produced to prove that he was on the premises of Dead Wood Hall, on the night that Charnworth died. If, in weighing all these points of evidence, the jury were of opinion the circumstantial evidence was inadequate, then it was their duty to give the prisoner—whose life was in their hands—the benefit of the doubt.

The jury retired, and were absent three long hours, and it became known that they could not agree. Ultimately, they returned into court, and pronounced a verdict of 'Not guilty'. In Scotland the verdict must and would have been *non proven*.

And so Job Panton went free, but an evil odour seemed to cling about him; he was shunned by his former companions, and many a suspicious glance was directed to him, and many a bated murmur was uttered as he passed by, until in a while he went forth beyond the seas, to the far wild west, as some said, and his haunts knew him no more.

The mystery is still a mystery; but how near I came to solving the problem of Dead Wood Hall it is for the reader to judge.

Gentlemen and Players

E. W. Hornung

Ernest William Hornung (1866–1921) was a talented but unlucky man. He suffered poor health in his teens, and spent time recuperating in Australia; following his return to England, and the death of his father, he turned to journalism. He also started to publish fiction, often drawing on his knowledge of Australian life. His early stories about A. J. Raffles, the amateur cracksman, earned widespread acclaim, but after his son was killed at Ypres, grief as well as continuing health problems brought an end to his literary career, and he died relatively young.

The background of "Gentlemen and Players" reflects Hornung's love of cricket; he was a member of the same cricket club as Arthur Conan Doyle, and married Conan Doyle's sister, Connie. He dedicated the first book of Raffles stories to his brother-in-law, although Conan Doyle had reservations about the daring concept of making a criminal the hero. Yet the best Raffles stories are highly entertaining. Ironically, it was only in later years, when Hornung tried to present Raffles in a more conventionally heroic light, that the quality of his work slipped.

◇◇◇

Old Raffles may or may not have been an exceptional criminal, but as a cricketer I dare swear he was unique. Himself a dangerous bat, a brilliant field, and perhaps the very finest slow bowler of his decade, he took incredibly little interest in the game at large. He never went up to Lord's without his cricket-bag, or showed the slightest interest in the result of a match in which he was not himself engaged. Nor was this mere hateful egotism on his part. He professed to have lost all enthusiasm for the game, and to keep it up only from the very lowest motives.

"Cricket," said Raffles, "like everything else, is good enough sport until you discover a better. As a source of excitement it isn't in it with other things you wot of, Bunny, and the involuntary comparison becomes a bore. What's the satisfaction of taking a man's wicket when you want his spoons? Still, if you can bowl a bit your low cunning won't get rusty, and always looking for the weak spot's just the kind of mental exercise one wants. Yes, perhaps there's some affinity between the two things after all. But I'd chuck up cricket to-morrow, Bunny, if it wasn't for the glorious protection it affords a person of my proclivities."

"How so?" said I. "It brings you before the public, I should have thought, far more than is either safe or wise."

"My dear Bunny, that's exactly where you make a mistake. To follow Crime with reasonable impunity you simply *must* have a parallel, ostensible career—the more public the better. The principle is obvious. Mr Peace, of pious memory, disarmed suspicion by acquiring a local reputation for playing the fiddle and taming animals, and it's my profound conviction that Jack the Ripper was a really eminent public man, whose speeches were very likely reported alongside his atrocities. Fill the bill in some prominent part, and you'll never be suspected of doubling it with another of equal prominence. That's why I want you to cultivate journalism, my boy, and sign all you can. And it's the one and only reason why I don't burn my bats for firewood."

Nevertheless, when he did play there was no keener performer on the field, nor one more anxious to do well for his side. I remember how he went to the nets, before the first match of the season, with his pocket full of sovereigns, which he put on the stumps instead of bails. It was a sight to see the professionals bowling like demons for the hard cash, for whenever a stump was hit a pound was tossed to the bowler and another balanced in its stead, while one man took £3 with a ball that spread-eagled the wicket. Raffles's practice cost him either eight or nine sovereigns; but he had absolutely first-class bowling all the time; and he made fifty-seven runs next day.

It became my pleasure to accompany him to all his matches, to watch every ball he bowled, or played, or fielded, and to sit chatting with him in the pavilion when he was doing none of these three things. You might have seen us there, side by side, during the greater part of the Gentlemen's first innings against the Players (who had lost the toss) on the second Monday in July. We were to be seen, but not heard, for Raffles had failed to score, and was uncommonly cross for a player who cared so little for the game. Merely taciturn with me, he was positively rude to more than one member who wanted to know how it had happened, or who ventured to commiserate him on his luck; there he sat, with a straw hat tilted over his nose and a cigarette stuck between lips that curled disagreeably at every advance. I was therefore much surprised when a young fellow of the exquisite type came and squeezed himself in between us, and met with a perfectly civil reception despite the liberty. I did not know the boy by sight, nor did Raffles introduce us; but their conversation proclaimed at once a slightness of acquaintanceship and a licence on the lad's part which combined to puzzle me. Mystification reached its height when Raffles was informed that the other's father was anxious to meet him, and he instantly consented to gratify that whim.

"He's in the Ladies' Enclosure. Will you come round now?"

"With pleasure," says Raffles. "Keep a place for me, Bunny."

And they were gone.

"Young Crowley," said some voice further back. "Last year's Harrow Eleven."

"I remember him. Worst man in the team."

"Keen cricketer, however. Stopped till he was twenty to get his colours. Governor made him. Keen breed. Oh, pretty, sir! Very pretty!"

The game was boring me. I only came to see old Raffles perform. Soon I was looking wistfully for his return, and at length I saw him beckoning me from the palings to the right.

"Want to introduce you to old Amersteth," he whispered, when I joined him. "They've a cricket week next month, when this boy Crowley comes of age, and we've both got to go down and play."

"Both!" I echoed. "But I'm no cricketer!"

"Shut up," says Raffles. "Leave that to me. I've been lying for all I'm worth," he added sepulchrally as we reached the bottom of the steps. "I trust to you not to give the show away."

There was the gleam in his eye that I knew well enough elsewhere, but was unprepared for in those healthy, sane surroundings; and it was with very definite misgivings and surmises that I followed the Zingari blazer through the vast flower-bed of hats and bonnets that bloomed beneath the ladies' awning.

Lord Amersteth was a fine-looking man with a short moustache and a double chin. He received me with much dry courtesy, through which, however, it was not difficult to read a less flattering tale. I was accepted as the inevitable appendage of the invaluable Raffles, with whom I felt deeply incensed as I made my bow.

"I have been bold enough," said Lord Amersteth, "to ask one of the Gentlemen of England to come down and play some rustic cricket for us next month. He is kind enough to say that he would have liked nothing better, but for this little fishing expedition of yours, Mr.—, Mr.—," and Lord Amersteth succeeded in remembering my name.

It was, of course, the first I had ever heard of that fishing expedition, but I made haste to say that it could easily, and should certainly, be put off. Raffles gleamed approval through his eyelashes. Lord Amersteth bowed and shrugged.

"You're very good, I'm sure," said he. "But I understand you're a cricketer yourself?"

"He was one at school," said Raffles, with infamous readiness.

"Not a real cricketer," I was stammering meanwhile.

"In the eleven?" said Lord Amersteth.

"I'm afraid not," said I.

"But only just out of it," declared Raffles, to my horror.

"Well, well, we can't all play for the Gentlemen," said Lord Amersteth slyly. "My son Crowley only just scraped into the eleven at Harrow, and *he's* going to play. I may even come in myself at a pinch; so you won't be the only duffer, if you are one, and I shall be very glad if you will come down and help us too. You shall flog a stream before breakfast and after dinner, if you like."

"I should be very proud," I was beginning, as the mere prelude to resolute excuses; but the eye of Raffles opened wide upon me; and I hesitated weakly, to be duly lost.

"Then that's settled," said Lord Amersteth, with the slightest suspicion of grimness. "It's to be a little week, you know, when my son comes of age. We play the Free Foresters, the Dorsetshire Gentlemen, and probably some local lot as well. But Mr. Raffles will tell you all about it, and Crowley shall write. Another wicket! By Jove, they're all out! Then I rely on you both." And, with a little nod, Lord Amersteth rose and sidled to the gangway.

Raffles rose also, but I caught the sleeve of his blazer.

"What are you thinking of?" I whispered savagely. "I was nowhere near the eleven. I'm no sort of cricketer. I shall have to get out of this!"

"Not you," he whispered back. "You needn't play, but come you must. If you wait for me after half-past six I'll tell you why."

But I could guess the reason; and I am ashamed to say that it revolted me much less than did the notion of making a public fool of myself on a cricket-field. My gorge rose at this as it no longer rose at crime, and it was in no tranquil humour that I strolled about the ground while Raffles disappeared in the pavilion. Nor was my annoyance lessened by a little meeting I witnessed between young Crowley and his father, who shrugged as he stopped and stooped to convey some information which made the young man look a little blank. It may have been pure self-consciousness on my part, but I could have sworn that the trouble was their inability to secure the great Raffles without his insignificant friend.

Then the bell rang, and I climbed to the top of the pavilion to watch Raffles bowl. No subtleties are lost up there; and if ever a bowler was full of them, it was A. J. Raffles on his day, as, indeed, all the cricket world remembers. One had not to be a cricketer oneself to appreciate his perfect command of pitch and break, his beautifully easy action, which never varied with the varying pace, his great ball on the leg-stump—his dropping head-ball—in a word, the infinite ingenuity of that versatile attack. It was no mere exhibition of athletic prowess, it was an intellectual treat, and one with a special significance in my eyes. I saw the "affinity between the two things," saw it in that afternoon's tireless warfare against the flower of professional cricket. It was not that Raffles took many wickets for few runs; he was too fine a bowler to mind being hit; and time was short, and the wicket good. What I admired, and what I remember, was the combination of resource and cunning, of patience and precision, of head-work and handiwork, which made every over an artistic whole. It was all so characteristic of that other Raffles whom I alone knew!

"I felt like bowling this afternoon," he told me later in the hansom. "With a pitch to help me, I'd have done something big; as it is, three for forty-one, out of the four that fell, isn't so bad for a slow bowler on a plumb wicket against those fellows. But I felt venomous! Nothing riles me more than being asked about for my cricket as though I were a pro. myself."

"Then why on earth go?"

"To punish them, and—because we shall be jolly hard up, Bunny, before the season's over!"

"Ah!" said I. "I thought it was that."

"Of course, it was! It seems they're going to have the very devil of a week of it—balls—dinner-parties—swagger house-party—general junketings—and obviously a houseful of diamonds as well. Diamonds galore! As a general rule nothing would induce me to abuse my position as a guest. I've never done it, Bunny. But in this case we're engaged like the waiters and the band, and by heaven we'll take our toll! Let's have a quiet dinner somewhere and talk it over."

"It seems rather a vulgar sort of theft," I could not help saying; and to this, my single protest, Raffles instantly assented.

"It *is* a vulgar sort," said he; "but I can't help that. We're getting vulgarly hard up again, and there's an end on 't. Besides, these people deserve it, and can afford it. And don't you run away with the idea that all will be plain sailing; nothing will be easier than getting some stuff, and nothing harder than avoiding all suspicion, as, of course, we must. We may come away with no more than a good working plan of the premises. Who knows? In any case there's weeks of thinking in it for you and me."

But with those weeks I will not weary you further than by remarking that the "thinking," was done entirely by Raffles, who did not always trouble to communicate his thoughts to me. His reticence, however, was no longer an irritant. I began to accept it as a necessary convention of these little enterprises. And, after our last adventure of the kind, more especially after its *dénouement*, my trust in Raffles was much too solid to be shaken by a want of trust in me, which I still believe to have been more the instinct of the criminal than the judgment of the man.

It was on Monday, the tenth of August, that we were due at Milchester Abbey, Dorset; and the beginning of the month found us cruising about that very county, with fly-rods actually in our hands. The idea was that we should acquire at once a local reputation as decent fishermen, and some knowledge of the countryside, with a view to further and more deliberate operations in the event of an unprofitable week. There was another idea which Raffles kept to himself until he had got me down there. Then one day he produced a cricket-ball in a meadow we were crossing, and threw me catches for an hour together. More hours he spent in bowling to me on the nearest green; and, if I was never a cricketer, at least I came nearer to being one, by the end of that week, than ever before or since.

Incident began early on the Monday. We had sallied forth from a desolate little junction within quite a few miles of Milchester, had been caught in a shower, had run for shelter to a wayside inn. A florid, overdressed man was drinking in the parlour, and I could have sworn it was at the sight of him that Raffles recoiled on the threshold, and afterwards insisted on returning to the station through the rain. He assured me, however, that the odour of stale ale had almost knocked him down. And I had to make what I could of his speculative, downcast eyes and knitted brows.

Milchester Abbey is a grey, quadrangular pile, deep-set in rich woody country, and twinkling with triple rows of quaint windows, every one of which seemed alight as we drove up just in time to dress for dinner. The carriage had whirled us under I know not how many triumphal arches in process of construction, and past the tents and flag-poles of a juicy-looking cricket-field, on which Raffles undertook to bowl up to his reputation. But the chief signs of festival were within, where we found an enormous house-party assembled, including more persons of pomp, majesty, and dominion than I had ever encountered in one room before. I confess I felt overpowered. Our errand and my own pretences combined to rob me of an address upon which I have sometimes plumed myself; and I have a grim recollection of my nervous relief when dinner was at last announced. I little knew what an ordeal it was to prove.

I had taken in a much less formidable young lady than might have fallen to my lot. Indeed I began by blessing my good fortune in this respect. Miss Melhuish was merely the rector's daughter, and she had only been asked to make an even number. She informed me of both facts before the soup reached us, and her subsequent conversation was characterised by the same engaging candour. It exposed what was little short of a mania for imparting information.

I had simply to listen, to nod, and to be thankful. When I confessed to knowing very few of those present, even by sight, my entertaining companion proceeded to tell me who everybody was, beginning on my left and working conscientiously round to her right. This lasted quite a long time, and really interested me; but a great deal that followed did not; and, obviously to recapture my unworthy attention, Miss Melhuish suddenly asked me, in a sensational whisper, whether I could keep a secret.

I said I thought I might, whereupon another question followed, in still lower and more thrilling accents:

"Are you afraid of burglars?"

Burglars! I was roused at last. The word stabbed me. I repeated it in horrified query.

"So I've found something to interest you at last!" said Miss Melhuish, in naïve triumph. "Yes—burglars! But don't speak so loud. It's supposed to be kept a great secret. I really oughtn't to tell you at all!"

"But what is there to tell?" I whispered with satisfactory impatience.

"You promise not to speak of it?"

"Of course!"

"Well, then, there are burglars in the neighbourhood."

"Have they committed any robberies?"

"Not yet."

"Then how do you know?"

"They've been seen. In the district. Two well-known London thieves!"

Two! I looked at Raffles. I had done so often during the evening, envying him his high spirits, his iron nerve, his buoyant wit, his perfect ease and self-possession. But now I pitied him; through all my own terror and consternation, I pitied him as he sat eating and drinking, and laughing and talking, without a cloud of fear or of embarrassment on his handsome, taking, daredevil face. I caught up my champagne and emptied the glass.

"Who has seen them?" I then asked calmly.

"A detective. They were traced down from town a few days ago. They are believed to have designs on the Abbey!"

"But why aren't they run in?"

"Exactly what I asked papa on the way here this evening; he says there is no warrant out against the men at present, and all that can be done is to watch their movements."

"Oh! so they are being watched?"

"Yes, by a detective who is down here on purpose. And I heard Lord Amersteth tell papa that they had been seen this afternoon at Warbeck Junction!"

The very place where Raffles and I had been caught in the rain! Our stampede from the inn was now explained; on the other hand, I was no longer to be taken by surprise by anything that my companion might have to tell me; and I succeeded in looking her in the face with a smile.

"This is really quite exciting, Miss Melhuish," said I. "May I ask how you come to know so much about it?"

"It's papa," was the confidential reply. "Lord Amersteth consulted him, and he consulted me. But for goodness' sake don't let it get about! I can't think *what* tempted me to tell you!"

"You may trust me, Miss Melhuish. But—aren't you frightened?"

Miss Melhuish giggled.

"Not a bit! They won't come to the rectory. There's nothing for them there. But look round the table: look at the diamonds: look at old Lady Melrose's necklace alone!"

The Dowager Marchioness of Melrose was one of the few persons whom it had been unnecessary to point out to me. She sat on Lord Amersteth's right, flourishing her ear-trumpet, and drinking champagne with her usual notorious freedom, as dissipated and kindly a dame as the world has ever seen. It was a necklace of diamonds and sapphires that rose and fell about her ample neck.

"They say it's worth five thousand pounds at least," continued my companion. "Lady Margaret told me so this morning (that's Lady Margaret next your Mr. Raffles, you know); and the old dear *will* wear them every night. Think what a haul they would be! No; we don't feel in immediate danger at the rectory."

When the ladies rose, Miss Melhuish bound me to fresh vows of secrecy; and left me, I should think, with some remorse for her indiscretion, but more satisfaction at the importance which it had undoubtedly given her in my eyes. The opinion may smack of vanity, though, in reality, the very springs of conversation reside in that same human, universal itch to thrill the auditor. The peculiarity of Miss Melhuish was that she must be thrilling at all costs. And thrilling she had surely been.

I spare you my feelings of the next two hours. I tried hard to get a word with Raffles, but again and again I failed. In the dining-room he and Crowley lit their cigarettes with the same match, and had their heads together all the time. In the drawing-room I had the mortification of hearing him talk interminable nonsense into the ear-trumpet of Lady Melrose, whom he knew in town. Lastly, in the billiard-room, they had a great and lengthy pool, while I sat aloof and chafed more than ever in the company of a very serious Scotch-man, who had arrived since dinner, and who would talk of nothing but the recent improvements in instantaneous photography. He had not come to play in the matches (he told me), but to obtain for Lord Amersteth such a series of cricket photographs as had never been taken before; whether as an amateur or a professional photographer I was unable to determine. I remember, however, seeking distraction in little bursts of resolute attention to the conversation of this bore. And so at last the long ordeal ended; glasses were emptied, men said good-night, and I followed Raffles to his room.

"It's all up!" I gasped, as he turned up the gas and I shut the door. "We're being watched. We've been followed down from town. There's a detective here on the spot!"

"How do *you* know?" asked Raffles, turning upon me quite sharply, but without the least dismay. And I told him how I knew.

"Of course," I added, "it was the fellow we saw in the inn this afternoon."

"The detective?" said Raffles. "Do you mean to say you don't know a detective when you see one, Bunny?"

"If that wasn't the fellow, which is?"

Raffles shook his head.

"To think that you've been talking to him for the last hour in the billiard-room, and couldn't spot what he was!"

"The Scotch photographer—"

I paused aghast.

"Scotch he is," said Raffles, "and photographer he may be. He is also Inspector Mackenzie of Scotland Yard—the very man I sent the message to that night last April. And you couldn't spot who he was in a whole hour! O Bunny, Bunny, you were never built for crime!"

"But," said I, "if that was Mackenzie, who was the fellow you bolted from at Warbeck?"

"The man he's watching."

"But he's watching us!"

Raffles looked at me with a pitying eye, and shook his head again before handing me his open cigarette-case.

"I don't know whether smoking's forbidden in one's bedroom, but you'd better take one of these and stand tight, Bunny, because I'm going to say something offensive."

I helped myself with a laugh.

"Say what you like, my dear fellow, if it really isn't you and I that Mackenzie's after."

"Well, then, it isn't, and it couldn't be, and nobody but a born Bunny would suppose for a moment that it was! Do you seriously think he would sit there and knowingly watch his man playing pool under his nose? Well, he might; he's a cool hand, Mackenzie; but I'm not cool enough to win a pool under such conditions. At least I don't think I am; it would be interesting to see. The situation wasn't free from strain as it was, though I knew he wasn't thinking of us. Crowley told me all about it after dinner, you see, and then I'd seen one of the men for myself this afternoon. You thought it was a detective who made me turn tail at that inn. I really don't know why I didn't tell you at the time, but it was just the opposite. That loud, red-faced brute is one of the cleverest thieves in London, and I once had a drink with him and our mutual fence. I was an Eastender from tongue to toe at the moment, but you will understand that I don't run unnecessary risks of recognition by a brute like that."

"He's not alone, I hear."

"By no means; there's at least one other man with him; and it's suggested that there may be an accomplice here in the house."

"Did Lord Crowley tell you so?"

"Crowley and the champagne between them. In confidence, of course, just as your girl told you; but even in confidence he never let on about Mackenzie. He told me there was a detective in the background, but that was all. Putting him up as a guest is evidently their big secret, to be kept from the other guests because it might offend them, but more particularly from the servants whom he's here to watch. That's my reading of the situation, Bunny, and you will agree with me that it's infinitely more interesting than we could have imagined it would prove."

"But infinitely more difficult for us," said I, with a sigh of pusillanimous relief. "Our hands are tied for this week, at all events."

"Not necessarily, my dear Bunny, though I admit that the chances are against us. Yet I'm not so sure of that either. There are all sorts of possibilities in these three-cornered combinations. Set A to watch B, and he won't have an eye left for C. That's the obvious theory, but then Mackenzie's a very big A. I should be sorry to have any boodle about me with that man in the house. Yet it would be great to nip in between A and B and score off them both at once! It would be worth a risk, Bunny, to do that; it would be worth risking something merely to take on old hands like B and his men at their own old game! Eh, Bunny? That would be something like a match. Gentlemen and Players at single wicket, by Jove!"

His eyes were brighter than I had known them for many a day. They shone with the perverted enthusiasm which was roused in him only by the contemplation of some new audacity. He kicked off his shoes and began pacing his room with noiseless rapidity; not since the night of the Old Bohemian dinner to Reuben Rosenthall had Raffles exhibited such excitement in my presence; and I was not sorry at the moment to be reminded of the fiasco to which that banquet had been the prelude.

"My dear A. J.," said I in his very own tone, "you're far too fond of the uphill game; you will eventually fall a victim to the sporting spirit and nothing else. Take a lesson from our last escape, and fly lower as you value our skins. Study the house as much as you like, but do—not—go and shove your head into Mackenzie's mouth!"

My wealth of metaphor brought him to a standstill, with his cigarette between his fingers and a grin beneath his shining eyes.

"You're quite right, Bunny. I won't. I really won't. Yet—
you saw old Lady Melrose's necklace? I've been wanting it
for years! But I'm not going to play the fool; honour bright,
I'm not; yet—by Jove!—to get to windward of the professors and Mackenzie too! It would be a great game, Bunny,
it would be a great game!"

"Well, you mustn't play it this week."

"No, no, I won't. But I wonder how the professors think
of going to work? That's what one wants to know. I wonder
if they've really got an accomplice in the house? How I wish
I knew their game! But it's all right, Bunny; don't you be
jealous; it shall be as you wish."

And with that assurance I went off to my own room, and
so to bed with an incredibly light heart. I had still enough
of the honest man in me to welcome the postponement of
our actual felonies, to dread their performance, to deplore
their necessity: which is merely another way of stating the
too patent fact that I was an incomparably weaker man than
Raffles, while every whit as wicked. I had, however, one rather
strong point. I possessed the gift of dismissing unpleasant
considerations, not intimately connected with the passing
moment, entirely from my mind. Through the exercise of this
faculty I had lately been living my frivolous life in town with
as much ignoble enjoyment as I had derived from it the year
before; and similarly, here at Milchester, in the long-dreaded
cricket week, I had after all a quite excellent time.

It is true that there were other factors in this pleasing
disappointment. In the first place, *mirabile dictu*, there were
one or two even greater duffers than I on the Abbey cricket
field. Indeed, quite early in the week, when it was of most
value to me, I gained considerable kudos for a lucky catch;
a ball, of which I had merely heard the hum, stuck fast in
my hand, which Lord Amersteth himself grasped in public
congratulation. This happy accident was not to be undone

even by me, and, as nothing succeeds like success, and the constant encouragement of the one great cricketer on the field was in itself an immense stimulus, I actually made a run or two in my very next innings. Miss Melhuish said pretty things to me that night at the great ball in honour of Viscount Crowley's majority; she also told me that was the night on which the robbers would assuredly make their raid, and was full of arch tremors when we sat out in the garden, though the entire premises were illuminated all night long. Meanwhile, the quiet Scotchman took countless photographs by day, which he developed by night in a dark room admirably situated in the servants' part of the house; and it is my firm belief that only two of his fellow-guests knew Mr. Clephane of Dundee for Inspector Mackenzie of Scotland Yard.

The week was to end with a trumpery match on the Saturday, which two or three of us intended abandoning early in order to return to town that night. The match, however, was never played. In the small hours of the Saturday morning a tragedy took place at Milchester Abbey.

Let me tell of the thing as I saw and heard it. My room opened upon the central gallery, and was not even on the same floor as that on which Raffles—and I think all the other men—were quartered. I had been put, in fact, into the dressing-room of one of the grand suites, and my two near neighbours were old Lady Melrose and my host and hostess. Now, by the Friday evening the actual festivities were at an end, and, for the first time that week, I must have been sound asleep since midnight, when all at once I found myself sitting up breathless. A heavy thud had come against my door, and now I heard hard breathing and the dull stamp of muffled feet.

"I've got ye," muttered a voice. "It's no use struggling."

It was the Scotch detective, and a new fear turned me cold. There was no reply, but the hard breathing grew harder still, and the muffled feet beat the floor to a quicker measure. In sudden panic I sprang out of bed and flung open my door. A light burnt low on the landing, and by it I could see Mackenzie swaying and staggering in a silent tussle with some powerful adversary.

"Hold this man!" he cried, as I appeared. "Hold the rascal!"

But I stood like a fool until the pair of them backed into me, when, with a deep breath I flung myself on the fellow, whose face I had seen at last. He was one of the footmen who waited at table; and no sooner had I pinned him than the detective loosed his hold.

"Hang on to him," he cried. "There's more of 'em below."

And he went leaping down the stairs, as other doors opened and Lord Amersteth and his son appeared simultaneously in their pyjamas. At that my man ceased struggling; but I was still holding him when Crowley turned up the gas.

"What the devil's all this?" asked Lord Amersteth, blinking. "Who was that ran downstairs?"

"Mac—Clephane!" said I hastily.

"Aha!" said he, turning to the footman. "So you're the scoundrel, are you? Well done! Well done! Where was he caught?"

I had no idea.

"Here's Lady Melrose's door open," said Crowley. "Lady Melrose! Lady Melrose!"

"You forget she's deaf," said Lord Amersteth. "Ah! that'll be her maid."

An inner door had opened; next instant there was a little shriek, and a white figure gesticulated on the threshold.

"Où donc est l'écrin de Madame la Marquise? La fenêtre est ouverte. Il a disparu!"

"Window open and jewel-case gone, by Jove!" exclaimed Lord Amersteth. "Mais comment est Madame la Marquise? Est-elle bien?"

"Oui, milor. Elle dort."

"Sleeps through it all," said my lord. "She's the only one, then!"

"What made Mackenzie—Clephane—bolt?" young Crowley asked me.

"Said there were more of them below."

"Why the devil couldn't you tell us so before?" he cried, and went leaping downstairs in his turn.

He was followed by nearly all the cricketers, who now burst upon the scene in a body, only to desert it for the chase. Raffles was one of them, and I would gladly have been another, had not the footman chosen this moment to hurl me from him, and to make a dash in the direction from which they had come. Lord Amersteth had him in an instant; but the fellow fought desperately, and it took the two of us to drag him downstairs, amid a terrified chorus from half-open doors. Eventually we handed him over to two other footmen who appeared with their nightshirts tucked into their trousers, and my host was good enough to compliment me as he led the way outside.

"I thought I heard a shot," he added. "Didn't you?"

"I thought I heard three."

And out we dashed into the darkness.

I remember how the gravel pricked my feet, how the wet grass numbed them as we made for the sound of voices on an outlying lawn. So dark was the night that we were in the cricketers' midst before we saw the shimmer of their pyjamas; and then Lord Amersteth almost trod on Mackenzie as he lay prostrate in the dew.

"Who's this?" he cried. "What on earth's happened?"

"It's Clephane," said a man who knelt over him. "He's got a bullet in him somewhere."

"Is he alive?"

"Barely."

"Good God! Where's Crowley?"

"Here I am," called a breathless voice. "It's no good, you fellows. There's nothing to show which way they've gone. Here's Raffles; he's chucked it, too." And they ran up panting.

"Well, we've got one of them, at all events," muttered Lord Amersteth. "The next thing is to get this poor fellow indoors. Take his shoulders, somebody. Now his middle. Join hands under him. Altogether, now; that's the way. Poor fellow! Poor fellow! His name isn't Clephane at all. He's a Scotland Yard detective, down here for these very villains!"

Raffles was the first to express surprise; but he had also been the first to raise the wounded man. Nor had any of them a stronger or more tender hand in the slow procession to the house. In a little we had the senseless man stretched on a sofa in the library. And there, with ice on his wound and brandy in his throat, his eyes opened and his lips moved.

Lord Amersteth bent down to catch the words.

"Yes, yes," said he; "we've got one of them safe and sound. The brute you collared upstairs." Lord Amersteth bent lower. "By Jove! Lowered the jewel-case out of the window, did he? And they've got clean away with it! Well, well! I only hope we'll be able to pull this good fellow through. He's off again."

An hour passed: the sun was rising.

It found a dozen young fellows on the settees in the billiard-room, drinking whisky and soda-water in their overcoats and pyjamas, and still talking excitedly in one breath. A time-table was being passed from hand to hand: the doctor was still in the library. At last the door opened, and Lord Amersteth put in his head.

"It isn't hopeless," said he, "but it's bad enough. There'll be no cricket to-day."

Another hour, and most of us were on our way to catch the early train; between us we filled a compartment almost to suffocation. And still we talked all together of the night's event; and still I was a little hero in my way, for having kept my hold of the one ruffian who had been taken; and my gratification was subtle and intense. Raffles watched me under lowered lids. Not a word had we had together; not a word did we have until we had left the others at Paddington, and were skimming through the streets in a hansom with noiseless tyres and a tinkling bell.

"Well, Bunny," said Raffles, "so the professors have it, eh?"

"Yes," said I. "And I'm jolly glad!"

"That poor Mackenzie has a ball in his chest?"

"That you and I have been on the decent side for once."

He shrugged his shoulders.

"You're hopeless, Bunny, quite hopeless! I take it you wouldn't have refused your share if the boodle had fallen to us? Yet you positively enjoy coming off second best—for the second time running! I confess, however, that the professors' methods were full of interest to me. I, for one, have probably gained as much in experience as I have lost in other things. That lowering the jewel-case out of the window was a very simple and effective expedient; two of them had been waiting below for it for hours."

"How do you know?" I asked.

"I saw them from my own window, which was just above the dear old lady's. I was fretting for that necklace in particular, when I went up to turn in for our last night—and I happened to look out of my window. In point of fact, I wanted to see whether the one below was open, and whether there was the slightest chance of working the oracle with my sheet for a rope. Of course I took the precaution of turning my light off first, and it was a lucky thing I did. I saw the pros. right down below, and they never saw me. I saw a little tiny luminous disc just for an instant, and then again for an instant a few minutes later. Of course I knew what it was, for I have my own watch-dial daubed with luminous paint; it makes a lantern of sorts when you can get no better. But these fellows were not using theirs as a lantern. They were under the old lady's window. They were watching the time. The whole thing was arranged with their accomplice inside. Set a thief to catch a thief: in a minute I had guessed what the whole thing proved to be."

"And you did nothing!" I exclaimed.

"On the contrary, I went downstairs and straight into Lady Melrose's room—"

"You did?"

"Without a moment's hesitation. To save her jewels. And I was prepared to yell as much into her ear-trumpet for all the house to hear. But the dear lady is too deaf and too fond of her dinner to wake easily."

"Well?"

"She didn't stir."

"And yet you allowed the professors, as you call them, to take her jewels, case and all!"

"All but this," said Raffles, thrusting his fist into my lap. "I would have shown it you before, but really, old fellow, your face all day has been worth a fortune to the firm!"

And he opened his fist, to shut it next instant on the bunch of diamonds and of sapphires that I had last seen encircling the neck of Lady Melrose.

The Well

W. W. Jacobs

William Wymark Jacobs (1863–1945) was a Londoner who took a clerical job with the Post Office Savings Bank while trying to establish himself as a writer. By the time he married a suffragette, and moved with her to Loughton in Essex, he had become a well-regarded author of macabre short stories. The most famous is "The Monkey's Paw", which has been adapted for stage, radio, film, television, and even operatic performance.

The success of "The Monkey's Paw" has meant that Jacobs' other work has tended to suffer from undeserved neglect. Many of his stories benefit from flashes of humour, and his literary style has occasionally been compared to Dickens'. It is, however, his gift for building suspense that is most impressive. He did not write conventional detective stories, but this tale is a study of the consequences of crime.

⟩⟩⟩

Two men stood in the billiard-room of an old country house, talking. Play, which had been of a half-hearted nature, was over, and they sat at the open window, looking out over the park stretching away beneath them, conversing idly.

"Your time's nearly up, Jem," said one at length; "this time six weeks you'll be yawning out the honeymoon and cursing the man—woman I mean—who invented them."

Jem Benson stretched his long limbs in the chair and grunted in dissent.

"I've never understood it," continued Wilfred Carr, yawning. "It's not in my line at all; I never had enough money for my own wants, let alone for two. Perhaps if I were as rich as you or Crœsus I might regard it differently."

There was just sufficient meaning in the latter part of the remark for his cousin to forbear to reply to it. He continued to gaze out of the window and to smoke slowly.

"Not being as rich as Crœsus—or you," resumed Carr, regarding him from beneath lowered lids, "I paddle my own canoe down the stream of Time, and, tying it to my friends' door-posts, go in to eat their dinners."

"Quite Venetian," said Jem Benson, still looking out of the window. "It's not a bad thing for you, Wilfred, that you have the door-posts and dinners—and friends."

Carr grunted in his turn. "Seriously though, Jem," he said slowly, "you're a lucky fellow, a very lucky fellow. If there is a better girl above ground than Olive, I should like to see her."

"Yes," said the other quietly.

"She's such an exceptional girl," continued Carr, staring out of the window. "She's so good and gentle. She thinks you are a bundle of all the virtues."

He laughed frankly and joyously, but the other man did not join him.

"Strong sense of right and wrong, though," continued Carr musingly. "Do you know, I believe that if she found out that you were not—"

"Not what?" demanded Benson, turning upon him fiercely, "not what?"

"Everything that you are," returned his cousin, with a grin that belied his words, "I believe she'd drop you."

"Talk about something else," said Benson slowly; "your pleasantries are not always in the best taste."

Wilfred Carr rose, and taking a cue from the rack, bent over the board and practised one or two favourite shots. "The only other subject I can talk about just at present is my own financial affairs," he said slowly, as he walked round the table.

"Talk about something else," said Benson again bluntly.

"And the two things are connected," said Carr, and dropping his cue he half sat on the table and eyed his cousin.

There was a long silence. Benson pitched the end of his cigar out of the window, and leaning back closed his eyes.

"Do you follow me?" inquired Carr at length.

Benson opened his eyes and nodded at the window.

"Do you want to follow my cigar?" he demanded.

"I should prefer to depart by the usual way for your sake," returned the other, unabashed. "If I left by the window all sorts of questions would be asked, and you know what a talkative chap I am."

"So long as you don't talk about my affairs," returned the other, restraining himself by an obvious effort, "you can talk yourself hoarse."

"I'm in a mess," said Carr slowly, "a devil of a mess. If I don't raise fifteen hundred by this day fortnight, I may be getting my board and lodging free."

"Would that be any change?" questioned Benson.

"The quality would," retorted the other. "The address also would not be good. Seriously, Jem, will you let me have the fifteen hundred?"

"No," said the other simply.

Carr went white. "It's to save me from ruin," he said thickly.

"I've helped you till I'm tired," said Benson, turning and regarding him, "and it is all to no good. If you've got into a mess, get out of it. You should not be so fond of giving autographs away."

"It's foolish, I admit," said Carr deliberately. "I won't do so any more. By the way, I've got some to sell. You needn't sneer. They're not my own."

"Whose are they?" inquired the other.

"Yours."

Benson got up from his chair and crossed over to him. "What is this?" he asked quietly. "Blackmail?"

"Call it what you like," said Carr. "I've got some letters for sale, price fifteen hundred. And I know a man who would buy them at that price for the mere chance of getting Olive from you. I'll give you first offer."

"If you have got any letters bearing my signature, you will be good enough to give them to me," said Benson very slowly.

"They're mine," said Carr lightly; "given to me by the lady you wrote them to. I must say that they are not all in the best possible taste."

His cousin reached forward suddenly, and catching him by the collar of his coat pinned him down on the table.

"Give me those letters," he breathed, sticking his face close to Carr's.

"They're not here," said Carr, struggling. "I'm not a fool. Let me go, or I'll raise the price."

The other man raised him from the table in his powerful hands, apparently with the intention of dashing his head against it. Then suddenly his hold relaxed as an astonished-looking maid-servant entered the room with letters. Carr sat up hastily.

"That's how it was done," said Benson, for the girl's benefit as he took the letters.

"I don't wonder at the other man making him pay for it, then," said Carr blandly.

"You will give me those letters?" said Benson suggestively, as the girl left the room.

"At the price I mentioned, yes," said Carr; "but so sure as I am a living man, if you lay your clumsy hands on me again, I'll double it. Now, I'll leave you for a time while you think it over."

He took a cigar from the box and lighting it carefully quitted the room. His cousin waited until the door had closed behind him, and then turning to the window sat there in a fit of fury as silent as it was terrible.

The air was fresh and sweet from the park, heavy with the scent of new-mown grass. The fragrance of a cigar was now added to it, and glancing out he saw his cousin pacing slowly by. He rose and went to the door, and then, apparently altering his mind, he returned to the window and watched the figure of his cousin as it moved slowly away into the moonlight. Then he rose again, and, for a long time, the room was empty.

◇◇◇

It was empty when Mrs. Benson came in some time later to say good-night to her son on her way to bed. She walked slowly round the table, and pausing at the window gazed from it in idle thought, until she saw the figure of her son advancing with rapid strides toward the house. He looked up at the window.

"Good-night," said she.

"Good-night," said Benson, in a deep voice.

"Where is Wilfred?"

"Oh, he has gone," said Benson.

"Gone?"

"We had a few words; he was wanting money again, and I gave him a piece of my mind. I don't think we shall see him again."

"Poor Wilfred!" sighed Mrs. Benson. "He is always in trouble of some sort. I hope that you were not too hard upon him."

"No more than he deserved," said her son sternly. "Good-night."

II

The well, which had long ago fallen into disuse, was almost hidden by the thick tangle of undergrowth which ran riot at that corner of the old park. It was partly covered by the shrunken half of a lid, above which a rusty windlass creaked in company with the music of the pines when the wind blew strongly. The full light of the sun never reached it, and the ground surrounding it was moist and green when other parts of the park were gaping with the heat.

Two people walking slowly round the park in the fragrant stillness of a summer evening strayed in the direction of the well.

"No use going through this wilderness, Olive," said Benson, pausing on the outskirts of the pines and eyeing with some disfavour the gloom beyond.

"Best part of the park," said the girl briskly; "you know it's my favourite spot."

"I know you're very fond of sitting on the coping," said the man slowly, "and I wish you wouldn't. One day you will lean back too far and fall in."

"And make the acquaintance of Truth," said Olive lightly. "Come along."

She ran from him and was lost in the shadow of the pines, the bracken crackling beneath her feet as she ran. Her companion followed slowly, and emerging from the gloom saw her poised daintily on the edge of the well with her feet hidden in the rank grass and nettles which surrounded it. She motioned her companion to take a seat by her side, and smiled softly as she felt a strong arm passed about her waist.

"I like this place," said she, breaking a long silence, "it is so dismal—so uncanny. Do you know I wouldn't dare to sit here alone, Jem. I should imagine that all sorts of dreadful things were hidden behind the bushes and trees, waiting to spring out on me. Ugh!"

"You'd better let me take you in," said her companion tenderly; "the well isn't always wholesome, especially in the hot weather. Let's make a move."

The girl gave an obstinate little shake, and settled herself more securely on her seat.

"Smoke your cigar in peace," she said quietly. "I am settled here for a quiet talk. Has anything been heard of Wilfred yet?"

"Nothing."

"Quite a dramatic disappearance, isn't it?" she continued. "Another scrape, I suppose, and another letter for you in the same old strain: 'Dear Jem, help me out.'"

Jem Benson blew a cloud of fragrant smoke into the air, and holding his cigar between his teeth brushed away the ash from his coat sleeves.

"I wonder what he would have done without you," said the girl, pressing his arm affectionately. "Gone under long ago, I suppose. When we are married, Jem, I shall presume upon the relationship to lecture him. He is very wild, but he has his good points, poor fellow."

"I never saw them," said Benson, with startling bitterness. "God knows I never saw them."

"He is nobody's enemy but his own," said the girl, startled by this outburst.

"You don't know much about him," said the other sharply. "He was not above blackmail; not above ruining the life of a friend to do himself a benefit. A loafer, a cur, and a liar!"

The girl looked up at him soberly but timidly and took his arm without a word, and they both sat silent while evening deepened into night and the beams of the moon, filtering through the branches, surrounded them with a silver network. Her head sank upon his shoulder, till suddenly with a sharp cry she sprang to her feet.

"What was that?" she cried breathlessly.

"What was what?" demanded Benson, springing up and clutching her fast by the arm.

She caught her breath and tried to laugh. "You're hurting me, Jem."

His hold relaxed.

"What is the matter?" he asked gently. "What was it startled you?"

"I was startled," she said slowly, putting her hands on his shoulder. "I suppose the words I used just now are ringing in my ears, but I fancied that somebody behind us whispered '*Jem, help me out.*'"

"Fancy," repeated Benson, and his voice shook; "but these fancies are not good for you. You—are frightened—at the dark and the gloom of these trees. Let me take you back to the house."

"No, I'm not frightened," said the girl, reseating herself. "I should never be really frightened of anything when you were with me, Jem. I'm surprised at myself for being so silly."

The man made no reply but stood, a strong, dark figure, a yard or two from the well, as though waiting for her to join him.

"Come and sit down, sir," cried Olive, patting the brick-work with her small, white hand; "one would think that you did not like your company."

He obeyed slowly and took a seat by her side, drawing so hard at his cigar that the light of it shone upon his face at every breath. He passed his arm, firm and rigid as steel, behind her, with his hand resting on the brickwork beyond.

"Are you warm enough?" he asked tenderly, as she made a little movement.

"Pretty fair," she shivered; "one oughtn't to be cold at this time of the year, but there's a cold, damp air comes up from the well."

As she spoke a faint splash sounded from the depths below, and for the second time that evening, she sprang from the well with a little cry of dismay.

"What is it now?" he asked in a fearful voice. He stood by her side and gazed at the well, as though half expecting to see the cause of her alarm emerge from it.

"Oh, my bracelet," she cried in distress, "my poor mother's bracelet. I've dropped it down the well."

"Your bracelet!" repeated Benson dully. "Your bracelet? The diamond one?"

"The one that was my mother's," said Olive. "Oh, we can get it back surely. We must have the water drained off."

"Your bracelet!" repeated Benson stupidly.

"Jem," said the girl in terrified tones, "dear Jem, what is the matter?"

For the man she loved was standing regarding her with horror. The moon which touched it was not responsible for all the whiteness of the distorted face, and she shrank back in fear to the edge of the well. He saw her fear and by a mighty effort regained his composure and took her hand.

"Poor little girl," he murmured, "you frightened me. I was not looking when you cried, and I thought that you were slipping from my arms, down—down—"

His voice broke, and the girl throwing herself into his arms clung to him convulsively.

"There, there," said Benson fondly, "don't cry, don't cry."

"To-morrow," said Olive, half-laughing, half-crying, "we will all come round the well with hook and line and fish for it. It will be quite a new sport."

"No, we must try some other way," said Benson. "You shall have it back."

"How?" asked the girl.

"You shall see," said Benson. "To-morrow morning at latest you shall have it back. Till then promise me that you will not mention your loss to any one. Promise."

"I promise," said Olive wonderingly. "But why not?"

"It is of great value, for one thing, and—But there—there are many reasons. For one thing it is my duty to get it for you."

"Wouldn't you like to jump down for it?" she asked mischievously. "Listen."

She stooped for a stone and dropped it down.

"Fancy being where that is now," she said, peering into the blackness; "fancy going round and round like a mouse in a pail, clutching at the slimy sides, with the water filling your mouth, and looking up to the little patch of sky above."

"You had better come in," said Benson, very quietly. "You are developing a taste for the morbid and horrible."

The girl turned, and taking his arm walked slowly in the direction of the house; Mrs. Benson, who was sitting in the porch, rose to receive them.

"You shouldn't have kept her out so long," she said chidingly. "Where have you been?"

"Sitting on the well," said Olive, smiling, "discussing our future."

"I don't believe that place is healthy," said Mrs. Benson emphatically. "I really think it might be filled in, Jem."

"All right," said her son slowly. "Pity it wasn't filled in long ago."

He took the chair vacated by his mother as she entered the house with Olive, and with his hands hanging limply over the sides sat in deep thought. After a time he rose, and going upstairs to a room which was set apart for sporting requisites selected a sea fishing line and some hooks and stole softly downstairs again. He walked swiftly across the park in the direction of the well, turning before he entered the shadow of the trees to look back at the lighted windows of the house. Then having arranged his line he sat on the edge of the well and cautiously lowered it.

He sat with his lips compressed, occasionally looking about him in a startled fashion, as though he half expected to see something peering at him from the belt of trees. Time after time he lowered his line until at length in pulling it up he heard a little metallic tinkle against the side of the well.

He held his breath then, and forgetting his fears drew the line in inch by inch, so as not to lose its precious burden. His pulse beat rapidly, and his eyes were bright. As the line came slowly in he saw the catch hanging to the hook, and with a steady hand drew the last few feet in. Then he saw that instead of the bracelet he had hooked a bunch of keys.

With a faint cry he shook them from the hook into the water below, and stood breathing heavily. Not a sound broke the stillness of the night. He walked up and down a bit and stretched his great muscles; then he came back to the well and resumed his task.

For an hour or more the line was lowered without result. In his eagerness he forgot his fears, and with eyes bent down the well fished slowly and carefully. Twice the hook became entangled in something, and was with difficulty released. It caught a third time, and all his efforts failed to free it. Then he dropped the line down the well, and with head bent walked toward the house.

He went first to the stables at the rear, and then retiring to his room for some time paced restlessly up and down. Then without removing his clothes he flung himself upon the bed and fell into a troubled sleep.

III

Long before anybody else was astir he arose and stole softly downstairs. The sunlight was stealing in at every crevice, and flashing in long streaks across the darkened rooms. The dining-room into which he looked struck chill and cheerless in the dark yellow light which came through the lowered blinds. He remembered that it had the same appearance when his father lay dead in the house; now, as then, everything seemed ghastly and unreal; the very chairs standing as their occupants had left them the night before, seemed to be indulging in some dark communication of ideas.

Slowly and noiselessly he opened the hall door and passed into the fragrant air beyond. The sun was shining on the drenched grass and trees, and a slowly vanishing white mist rolled like smoke about the grounds. For a moment he stood, breathing deeply the sweet air of the morning, and then walked slowly in the direction of the stables.

The rusty creaking of a pump-handle and a spatter of water upon the red-tiled courtyard showed that somebody else was astir, and a few steps farther he beheld a brawny, sandy-haired man gasping wildly under severe self-infliction at the pump.

"Everything ready, George?" he asked quietly.

"Yes, sir," said the man, straightening up suddenly and touching his forehead. "Bob's just finishing the arrangements inside. It's a lovely morning for a dip. The water in that well must be just icy."

"Be as quick as you can," said Benson impatiently.

"Very good, sir," said George, burnishing his face harshly with a very small towel which had been hanging over the top of the pump. "Hurry up, Bob."

In answer to his summons a man appeared at the door of the stable with a coil of stout rope over his arm and a large metal candlestick in his hand.

"Just to try the air, sir," said George, following his master's glance; "a well gets rather foul sometimes, but if a candle can live down it, a man can."

His master nodded, and the man, hastily pulling up the neck of his shirt and thrusting his arms into his coat, followed him as he led the way slowly to the well.

"Beg pardon, sir," said George, drawing up to his side, "but you are not looking over and above well this morning. If you'll let me go down I'd enjoy the bath."

"No, no," said Benson peremptorily.

"You ain't fit to go down, sir," persisted his follower. "I've never seen you look so before. Now if—"

"Mind your business," said his master curtly.

George became silent, and the three walked with swinging strides through the long wet grass to the well. Bob flung the rope on the ground, and at a sign from his master handed him the candlestick.

"Here's the line for it, sir," said Bob, fumbling in his pockets.

Benson took it from him and slowly tied it to the candlestick. Then he placed it on the edge of the well, and striking a match, lit the candle and began slowly to lower it.

"Hold hard, sir," said George quickly, laying his hand on his arm, "you must tilt it or the string'll burn through."

Even as he spoke the string parted and the candlestick fell into the water below.

Benson swore quietly.

"I'll soon get another," said George, starting up.

"Never mind, the well's all right," said Benson.

"It won't take a moment, sir," said the other over his shoulder.

"Are you master here, or am I?" said Benson hoarsely.

George came back slowly, a glance at his master's face stopping the protest upon his tongue, and he stood by watching him sulkily as he sat on the well and removed his outer garments. Both men watched him curiously, as having completed his preparations he stood grim and silent with his hands by his sides.

"I wish you'd let me go, sir," said George, plucking up courage to address him. "You ain't fit to go, you've got a chill or something. I shouldn't wonder it's the typhoid. They've got it in the village bad."

For a moment Benson looked at him angrily, then his gaze softened. "Not this time, George," he said quietly. He took the looped end of the rope and placed it under his arms, and sitting down threw one leg over the side of the well.

"How are you going about it, sir?" queried George, laying hold of the rope and signing to Bob to do the same.

"I'll call out when I reach the water," said Benson; "then pay out three yards more quickly so that I can get to the bottom."

"Very good, sir," answered both.

Their master threw the other leg over the coping and sat motionless. His back was turned toward the men as he sat with head bent, looking down the shaft. He sat for so long that George became uneasy.

"All right, sir?" he inquired.

"Yes," said Benson slowly. "If I tug at the rope, George, pull up at once. Lower away."

The rope passed steadily through their hands until a hollow cry from the darkness below and a faint splashing warned them that he had reached the water. They gave him three yards more and stood with relaxed grasp and strained ears, waiting.

"He's gone under," said Bob in a low voice.

The other nodded, and moistening his huge palms took a firmer grip of the rope.

Fully a minute passed, and the men began to exchange uneasy glances. Then a sudden tremendous jerk followed by a series of feebler ones nearly tore the rope from their grasp.

"Pull!" shouted George, placing one foot on the side and hauling desperately. "Pull! pull! He's stuck fast; he's not coming; P—U—LL!"

In response to their terrific exertions the rope came slowly in, inch by inch, until at length a violent splashing was heard, and at the same moment a scream of unutterable horror came echoing up the shaft.

"What a weight he is!" panted Bob. "He's stuck fast or something. Keep still, sir; for heaven's sake, keep still."

For the taut rope was being jerked violently by the struggles of the weight at the end of it. Both men with grunts and sighs hauled it in foot by foot.

"All right, sir," cried George cheerfully.

He had one foot against the well, and was pulling manfully; the burden was nearing the top. A long pull and a strong pull, and the face of a dead man with mud in the eyes and nostrils came peering over the edge. Behind it was the ghastly face of his master; but this he saw too late, for with a great cry he let go his hold of the rope and stepped back.

The suddenness overthrew his assistant, and the rope tore through his hands. There was a frightful splash.

"You fool!" stammered Bob, and ran to the well helplessly.

"Run!" cried George. "Run for another line."

He bent over the coping and called eagerly down as his assistant sped back to the stables shouting wildly. His voice re-echoed down the shaft, but all else was silence.

The White Pillars Murder

G. K. Chesterton

Gilbert Keith Chesterton (1874–1936) was a brilliant poly-
math who would no doubt be surprised to learn that, eighty
years after his death, his continuing fame rests mainly on his
creation of the sleuthing priest, Father Brown. A theologian,
journalist, broadcaster and campaigner, he used his newspaper, *G. K.'s Weekly*, as a soap box, and frequently debated
issues of the day with the likes of George Bernard Shaw.

Chesterton manifested a keen interest in detective fiction
long before he became a skilled exponent of the genre; his
article "A Defence of Detective Stories" appeared in 1901,
and *The Man Who Was Thursday*, often described as a meta-
physical thriller, appeared seven years later. Father Brown
quickly became his best-loved character, and this resulted
in a tendency to overlook Chesterton's other detectives,
including that unorthodox criminologist, Dr Adrian Hyde.

◇◇◇

Those who have discussed the secret of the success of the
great detective, Dr. Adrian Hyde, could find no finer example
of his remarkable methods than the affair which came to be

called "The White Pillars Mystery." But that extraordinary man left no personal notes and we owe our record of it to his two young assistants, John Brandon and Walter Weir. Indeed, as will be seen, it was they who could best describe the first investigations in detail, from the outside; and that for a rather remarkable reason.

They were both men of exceptional ability; they had fought bravely and even brilliantly in the Great War; they were cultivated, they were capable, they were trustworthy, and they were starving. For such was the reward which England in the hour of victory accorded to the deliverers of the world. It was a long time before they consented in desperation to consider anything so remote from their instincts as employment in a private detective agency. Jack Brandon, who was a dark, compact, resolute, restless youth, with a boyish appetite for detective tales and talk, regarded the notion with a half-fascinated apprehension, but his friend Weir, who was long and fair and languid, a lover of music and metaphysics, with a candid disgust.

"I believe it might be frightfully interesting," said Brandon. "Haven't you ever had the detective fever when you couldn't help overhearing somebody say something—'If only he knew what she did to the Archdeacon,' or 'And then the whole business about Susan and the dog will come out.'?"

"Yes," replied Weir, "but you only heard snatches because you didn't mean to listen and almost immediately left off listening. If you were a detective, you'd have to crawl under the bed or hide in the dust-bin to hear the whole secret, till your dignity was as dirty as your clothes."

"Isn't it better than stealing," asked Brandon, gloomily, "which seems to be the next step?"

"Why, no; I'm not sure that it is!" answered his friend.

Then, after a pause, he added, reflectively, "Besides, it isn't as if we'd get the sort of work that's relatively decent. We can't claim to know the wretched trade. Clumsy eavesdropping must be worse than the blind spying on the blind. You've not only got to know what is said, but what is meant. There's a lot of difference between listening and hearing. I don't say I'm exactly in a position to fling away a handsome salary offered me by a great criminologist like Dr. Adrian Hyde, but, unfortunately, he isn't likely to offer it."

But Dr. Adrian Hyde was an unusual person in more ways than one, and a better judge of applicants than most modern employers. He was a very tall man with a chin so sunk on his chest as to give him, in spite of his height, almost a look of being hunchbacked; but though the face seemed thus fixed as in a frame, the eyes were as active as a bird's, shifting and darting everywhere and observing everything; his long limbs ended in large hands and feet, the former being almost always thrust into his trouser-pockets, and the latter being loaded with more than appropriately large boots. With all his awkward figure he was not without gaiety and a taste for good things, especially good wine and tobacco; his manner was grimly genial and his insight and personal judgment marvellously rapid. Which was how it came about that John Brandon and Walter Weir were established at comfortable desks in the detective's private office, when Mr. Alfred Morse was shown in, bringing with him the problem of White Pillars.

Mr. Alfred Morse was a very stolid and serious person with stiffly-brushed brown hair, a heavy brown face and a heavy black suit of mourning of a cut somewhat provincial, or perhaps colonial. His first words were accompanied with an inoffensive but dubious cough and a glance at the two assistants.

"This is rather confidential business," he said.

"Mr. Morse," said Dr. Hyde, with quiet good humour, "if you were knocked down by a cab and carried to a hospital, your life might be saved by the first surgeon in the land: but you couldn't complain if he let students learn from the operation. These are my two cleverest pupils, and if you want good detectives, you must let them be trained."

"Oh, very well," said the visitor, "perhaps it is not quite so easy to talk of the personal tragedy as if we were alone; but I think I can lay the main facts before you.

"I am the brother of Melchior Morse, whose dreadful death is so generally deplored. I need not tell you about him; he was a public man of more than average public spirit; and I suppose his benefactions and social work are known throughout the world. I had not seen so much of him as I could wish till the last few years; for I have been much abroad; I suppose some would call me the rolling stone of the family, compared with my brother, but I was deeply attached to him, and all the resources of the family estate will be open to anyone ready to avenge his death. You will understand I shall not lightly abandon that duty.

"The crime occurred, as you probably know, at his country place called 'White Pillars,' after its rather unique classical architecture; a colonnade in the shape of a crescent, like that at St. Peter's, runs half-way round an artificial lake, to which the descent is by a flight of curved stone steps. It is in the lake that my brother's body was found floating in the moonlight; but as his neck was broken, apparently with a blow, he had clearly been killed elsewhere. When the butler found the body, the moon was on the other side of the house and threw the inner crescent of the colonnade and steps into profound shadow. But the butler swears he saw the figure of the fleeing man in dark outline against the moonlight as it turned the corner of the house. He says it was a striking outline, and he would know it again."

"Those outlines are very vivid sometimes," said the detective, thoughtfully, "but of course very difficult to prove. Were there any other traces? Any footprints or fingerprints?"

"There were no fingerprints," said Morse, gravely, "and the murderer must have meant to take equal care to leave no footprints. That is why the crime was probably committed on the great flight of stone steps. But they say the cleverest murderer forgets something; and when he threw the body in the lake there must have been a splash, which was not quite dry when it was discovered; and it showed the edge of a pretty clear footprint. I have a copy of the thing here, the original is at home." He passed a brown slip across to Hyde, who looked at it and nodded. "The only other thing on the stone steps that might be a clue was a cigar-stump. My brother did not smoke."

"Well, we will look into those clues more closely in due course," said Dr. Hyde. "Now tell me something about the house and the people in it."

Mr. Morse shrugged his shoulders, as if the family in question did not impress him.

"There were not many people in it," he replied, "putting aside a fairly large staff of servants, headed by the butler, Barton, who has been devoted to my brother for years. The servants all bear a good character; but of course you will consider all that. The other occupants of the house at the time were my brother's wife, a rather silent elderly woman, devoted almost entirely to religion and good works; a niece, of whose prolonged visits the old lady did not perhaps altogether approve, for Miss Barbara Butler is half Irish and rather flighty and excitable; my brother's secretary, Mr. Graves, a very silent young man (I confess I could never make out whether he was shy or sly), and my brother's solicitor, Mr. Caxton, who is an ordinary snuffy lawyer, and happened to be down there on legal business. They might all be guilty in theory, I suppose, but I'm a practical man, and I don't imagine such things in practice."

"Yes, I realized you were a practical man when you first came in," said Dr. Hyde, rather dryly. "I realized a few other details as well. Is that all you have to tell me?"

"Yes," replied Morse, "I hope I have made myself clear."

"It is well not to forget anything," went on Adrian Hyde, gazing at him calmly. "It is still better not to suppress anything, when confiding in a professional man. You may have heard, perhaps, of a knack I have of noticing things about people. I knew some of the things you told me before you opened your mouth; as that you long lived abroad and had just come up from the country. And it was easy to infer from your own words that you are the heir of your brother's considerable fortune."

"Well, yes, I am," replied Alfred Morse, stolidly.

"When you said you were a rolling stone," went on Adrian Hyde, with the same placid politeness, "I fear some might say you were a stone which the builders were justified in rejecting. Your adventures abroad have not all been happy. I perceive that you deserted from some foreign navy, and that you were once in prison for robbing a bank. If it comes to an inquiry into your brother's death and your present inheritance—"

"Are you trying to suggest," cried the other fiercely, "that appearances are against me?"

"My dear sir," said Dr. Adrian Hyde blandly, "appearances are most damnably against you. But I don't always go by appearances. It all depends. Good day."

When the visitor had withdrawn, looking rather black, the impetuous Brandon broke out into admiration of the Master's methods and besieged him with questions.

"Look here," said the great man, good-humouredly, "you've no business to be asking how I guessed right. You ought to be guessing at the guesses yourselves. Think it out."

"The desertion from a foreign navy," said Weir, slowly, "might be something to do with those bluish marks on his wrist. Perhaps they were some special tattooing and he'd tried to rub them out."

"That's better," said Dr. Hyde, "you're getting on."

"I know!" cried Brandon, more excitedly, "I know about the prison! They always say, if you once shave your moustache it never grows the same; perhaps there's something like that about hair that's been cropped in gaol. Yes, I thought so. The only thing I can't imagine, is why you should guess he had robbed a bank."

"Well, you think that out too," said Adrian Hyde. "I think you'll find it's the key to the whole of this riddle. And now I'm going to leave this case to you. I'm going to have a half-holiday." As a signal that his own working hours were over, he lit a large and sumptuous cigar, and began pishing and poohing over the newspapers.

"Lord, what rubbish!" he cried. "My God, what headlines! Look at this about White Pillars: 'Whose Was the Hand?' They've murdered even murder with clichés like clubs of wood. Look here, you two fellows had better go down to White Pillars and try to put some sense into them. I'll come down later and clear up the mess."

The two young detectives had originally intended to hire a car, but by the end of their journey they were very glad they had decided to travel by train with the common herd. Even as they were in the act of leaving the train, they had a stroke of luck in the matter of that collecting of stray words and whispers which Weir found the least congenial, but Brandon desperately clung to as the most practicable, of all forms of detective inquiry. The steady scream of a steam-whistle, which was covering all the shouted conversation, stopped suddenly in the fashion that makes a shout shrivel into a whisper. But there was one whisper caught in the silence and sounding clear as a bell; a voice that said, "There were excellent reasons for killing him. I know them, if nobody else does."

Brandon managed to trace the voice to its origin; a sallow face with a long shaven chin and a rather scornful lower lip. He saw the same face more than once on the remainder of his journey, passing the ticket collector, appearing in a car behind them on the road, haunting him so significantly, that he was not surprised to meet the man eventually in the garden of White Pillars, and to have him presented as Mr. Caxton, the solicitor.

"That man evidently knows more than he's told the authorities," said Brandon to his friend, "but I can't get anything more out of him."

"My dear fellow," cried Weir, "that's just what they're all like. Don't you feel by this time that it's the atmosphere of the whole place? It's not a bit like those delightful detective stories. In a detective story all the people in the house are gaping imbeciles, who can't understand anything, and in the midst stands the brilliant sleuth who understands everything. Here am I standing in the midst, a brilliant sleuth, and I believe, on my soul, I'm the only person in the house who doesn't know all about the crime."

"There's one other anyhow," said Brandon, with gloom, "two brilliant sleuths."

"Everybody else knows except the detective," went on Weir; "everybody knows something, anyhow, if it isn't everything. There's something odd even about old Mrs. Morse; she's devoted to charity, yet she doesn't seem to have agreed with her husband's philanthropy. It's as if they'd quarrelled about it. Then there's the secretary, the quiet, good-looking young man, with a square face like Napoleon. He looks as if he would get what he wants, and I've very little doubt that what he wants is that red-haired Irish girl they call Barbara.

I think she wants the same thing; but if so there's really no reason for them to hide it. And they are hiding it, or hiding something. Even the butler is secretive. They can't all have been in a conspiracy to kill the old man."

"Anyhow, it all comes back to what I said first," observed Brandon. "If they're in a conspiracy, we can only hope to overhear their talk. It's the only way."

"It's an excessively beastly way," said Weir, calmly, "and we will proceed to follow it."

They were walking slowly round the great semicircle of colonnade that looked inwards upon the lake, that shone like a silver mirror to the moon. It was of the same stretch of clear moonlit nights as that recent one, on which old Morse had died mysteriously in the same spot. They could imagine him as he was in many portraits, a little figure in a skull cap with a white beard thrust forward, standing on those steps, till a dreadful figure that had no face in their dreams descended the stairway and struck him down. They were standing at one end of the colonnade, full of these visions, when Brandon said suddenly:

"Did you speak?"

"I? No," replied his friend staring.

"Somebody spoke," said Brandon, in a low voice, "yet we seem to be quite alone."

Then their blood ran cold for an instant. For the wall behind them spoke; and it seemed to say quite plainly, in a rather harsh voice:

"Do you remember exactly what you said?"

Weir stared at the wall for an instant; then he slapped it with his hand with a shaky laugh.

"My God," he cried, "what a miracle! And what a satire! We've sold ourselves to the devil as a couple of damned eavesdroppers; and he's put us in the very chamber of eaves-dropping—into the ear of Dionysius, the Tyrant. Don't you see this is a whispering gallery, and people at the other end of it are whispering?"

"No, they're talking too loud to hear us, I think," whispered Brandon, "but we'd better lower our voices. It's Caxton the lawyer, and the young secretary."

The secretary's unmistakable and vigorous voice sounded along the wall saying:

"I told him I was sick of the whole business; and if I'd known he was such a tyrant, I'd never have had to do with him. I think I told him he ought to be shot. I was sorry enough for it afterwards."

Then they heard the lawyer's more croaking tones saying, "Oh, you said that, did you? Well, there seems no more to be said now. We had better go in," which was followed by echoing feet and then silence.

The next day Weir attached himself to the lawyer with a peculiar pertinacity and made a new effort to get something more out of that oyster. He was pondering deeply on the very little that he had got, when Brandon rushed up to him with hardly-restrained excitement.

"I've been at that place again," he cried. "I suppose you'll say I've sunk lower in the pit of slime, and perhaps I have, but it's got to be done. I've been listening to the young people this time, and I believe I begin to see something; though heaven knows, it's not what I want to see. The secretary and the girl are in love all right, or have been; and when love is loose pretty dreadful things can happen. They were talking about getting married, of course, at least she was, and what do you think she said? 'He made an excuse of my being under age.' So it's pretty clear the old man opposed the match. No doubt that was what the secretary meant by talking about his tyranny."

"And what did the secretary say when the girl said that?"

"That's the queer thing," answered Brandon, "rather an ugly thing, I begin to fancy. The young man only answered, rather sulkily, I thought: 'Well, he was within his rights there; and perhaps it was for the best.' She broke out in protest: 'How can you say such a thing'; and certainly it was a strange thing for a lover to say."

"What are you driving at?" asked his friend.

"Do you know anything about women?" asked Brandon. "Suppose the old man was not only trying to break off the engagement but *succeeding* in breaking it off. Suppose the young man was weakening and beginning to wonder whether she was worth losing his job for. The woman might have waited any time or eloped any time. But if she thought she was in danger of losing him altogether, don't you think she might have turned on the tempter with the fury of despair? I fear we have got a glimpse of a very heart-rending tragedy. Don't you believe it, too?"

Walter Weir unfolded his long limbs and got slowly to his feet, filling a pipe and looking at his friend with a sort of quizzical melancholy.

"No, I don't believe it," he said, "but that's because I'm such an unbeliever. You see, I don't believe in all this eavesdropping business; I don't think we shine at it. Or, rather, I think you shine too much at it and dazzle yourself blind. I don't believe in all this detective romance about deducing everything from a trifle. I don't believe in your little glimpse of a great tragedy. It would be a great tragedy no doubt, and does you credit as literature or a symbol of life; you can build imaginative things of that sort on a trifle. You can build everything on the trifle except the truth. But in the present practical issue, I don't believe there's a word of truth in it. I don't believe the old man was opposed to the engagement; I don't believe the young man was backing out of it; I believe the young people are perfectly happy and ready to be married tomorrow. I don't believe anybody in this house had any motive to kill Morse or has any notion of how he was killed. In spite of what I said, the poor shabby old sleuth enjoys his own again. I believe I am the only person who knows the truth; and it only came to me in a flash a few minutes ago."

"Why, how do you mean?" asked the other.

"It came to me in a final flash," said Weir, "when you repeated those words of the girl: 'He made the excuse that I was under age'."

After a few puffs of his pipe, he resumed reflectively: "One queer thing is, that the error of the eavesdropper often comes from a thing being too clear. We're so sure that people mean what we mean, that we can't believe they mean what they say. Didn't I once tell you that it's one thing to listen and another to hear? And sometimes the voice talks too plain. For instance, when young Graves, the secretary, said that he was sick of the business, he meant it literally, and not metaphorically. He meant he was sick of Morse's trade, because it was tyrannical."

"Morse's trade? What trade?" asked Brandon, staring.

"Our saintly old philanthropist was a money-lender," replied Weir, "and as great a rascal as his rascally brother. That is the great central fact that explains everything. That is what the girl meant by talking about being under age. She wasn't talking about her love-affair at all, but about some small loan she'd tried to get from the old man and which he refused because she was a minor. Her fiancé made the very sensible comment that perhaps it was all for the best; meaning that she had escaped the net of a usurer. And her momentary protest was only a spirited young lady's lawful privilege of insisting on her lover agreeing with all the silly things she says. That is an example of the error of the eavesdropper, or the fallacy of detection by trifles. But, as I say, it's the moneylending business that's the clue to everything in this house. That's what all of them, even the secretary and solicitor, out of a sort of family pride, are trying to hush up and hide from detectives and newspapers. But the old man's murder was much more likely to get it into the newspapers. They had no motive to murder him, and they didn't murder him."

"Then who did?" demanded Brandon.

"Ah," replied his friend, but with less than his usual languor in the ejaculation and something a little like a hissing intake of the breath. He had seated himself once more, with his elbows on his knees, but the other was surprised to realize something rigid about his new attitude; almost like a creature crouching for a spring. He still spoke quite dryly, however, and merely said:

"In order to answer that, I fancy we must go back to the first talk that we overheard, before we came to the house; the very first of all."

"Oh, I see," said Brandon, a light dawning on his face. "You mean what we heard the solicitor say in the train."

"No," replied Weir, in the same motionless manner, "that was only another illustration touching the secret trade. Of course his solicitor knew he was a money-lender; and knew that any such money-lender has a crowd of victims, who might kill him. It's quite true he was killed by one of those victims. But it wasn't the lawyer's remark in the train that I was talking about, for a very simple reason."

"And why not?" inquired his companion.

"Because that was not the first conversation we overheard."

Walter Weir clutched his knees with his long bony hands, and seemed to stiffen still more as if in a trance, but he went on talking steadily.

"I have told you the moral and the burden of all these things; that it is one thing to hear what men say and another to hear what they mean. And it was at the very first talk that we heard all the words and missed all the meaning. We did not overhear that first talk slinking about in moonlit gardens and whispering galleries. We overheard that first talk sitting openly at our regular desks in broad daylight, in a bright and businesslike office. But we no more made sense of that talk than if it had been half a whisper, heard in a black forest or a cave."

He sprang to his feet as if a stiff spring were released and began striding up and down, with what was for him an unnatural animation.

"That was the talk we really misunderstood," he cried. "That was the conversation that we heard word for word, and yet missed entirely! Fools that we were! Deaf and dumb and imbecile, sitting there like dummies and being stuffed with a stage play! We were actually allowed to be eavesdroppers, tolerated, ticketed, given special permits to be eavesdroppers; and still we could not eavesdrop! I never even guessed till ten minutes ago the meaning of that conversation in the office. That terrible conversation! That terrible meaning! Hate and hateful fear and shameless wickedness and mortal peril—death and hell wrestled naked before our eyes in that office, and we never saw them. A man accused another man of murder across a table, and we never heard it."

"Oh," gasped Brandon at last, "you mean that the Master accused the brother of murder?"

"No!" retorted Weir, in a voice like a volley, "I mean that the brother accused the Master of murder."

"The Master!"

"Yes," answered Weir, and his high voice fell suddenly, "and the accusation was true. The man who murdered old Morse was our employer, Dr. Adrian Hyde."

"What can it all mean?" asked Brandon, and thrust his hand through his thick brown hair.

"That was our mistake at the beginning," went on the other calmly, "that we did not think what it could all mean. Why was the brother so careful to say the reproduction of the footprint was a proof and not the original? Why did Dr. Hyde say the outline of the fugitive would be difficult to prove? Why did he tell us, with that sardonic grin, that the brother having robbed a bank was the key of the riddle? Because the whole of that consultation of the client and the specialist was a fiction for our benefit. The whole course of events was determined by that first thing that happened; that the young and innocent detectives were allowed to remain in the room. Didn't you think yourself the interview was a little too like that at the beginning of every damned detective story? Go over it speech by speech, and you will see that every speech was a thrust or parry under a cloak. That blackmailing blackguard Alfred hunted out Doctor Hyde simply to accuse and squeeze him. Seeing us there, he said, 'This is confidential,' meaning, 'You don't want to be accused before them.' Dr. Hyde answered, 'They're my favourite pupils,' meaning, 'I'm less likely to be blackmailed before them; they shall stay.' Alfred answered, 'Well, I can state my business, if not quite so personally,' meaning, 'I can accuse you so that you understand, if they don't.' And he did. He presented his proofs like pistols across the table; things that sounded rather thin, but, in Hyde's case, happened to be pretty thick. His boots, for instance, happened to be very thick. His huge footprint would be unique enough to be a clue. So would the cigar-end; for very few people can afford to smoke his cigars. Of course, that's what got him tangled up with the moneylender—extravagance. You see how much money you get through if you smoke those cigars all day and never drink anything but the best vintage champagne. And though a black silhouette against the moon sounds as vague as moonshine, Hyde's huge figure and hunched shoulders would be rather marked. Well, you know how the black-mailed man hit back: 'I perceive by your left eyebrow that you are a deserter; I deduce from the pimple on your nose that you were once in gaol,' meaning, 'I know you, and you're as much a crook as I am; expose me and I'll expose you.' Then he said he had deduced in the Sherlock Holmes manner that Alfred had robbed a bank, and that was where he went too far. He presumed on the incredible credulity, which is the mark of the modern mind when anyone has uttered the magic word 'science.' He presumed on the priestcraft of our time; but he presumed the least little bit too much, so far as I was concerned. It was then I first began to doubt. A man might possibly deduce by scientific detection that another man had been in a certain navy or prison, but by no possibility could he deduce from a man's appearance that what he had once robbed was a bank. It was simply impossible. Dr. Hyde knew it was his biggest bluff; that was why he told you in mockery, that it was the key to the riddle. It was; and I managed to get hold of the key."

He chuckled in a hollow fashion as he laid down his pipe. "That jibe at his own bluff was like him; he really is a remarkable man or a remarkable devil. He has a sort of horrible sense of humour. Do you know, I've got a notion that sounds rather a nightmare, about what happened on that great slope of steps that night. I believe Hyde jeered at the journalistic catchword, 'Whose Was the Hand?' partly because he, himself, had managed it without hands. I believe he managed to commit a murder entirely with his feet. I believe he tripped up the poor old usurer and stamped on him on the stone steps with those monstrous boots. An idyllic moonlight scene, isn't it? But there's something that seems to make it worse. I think he had the habit anyhow, partly to avoid leaving his fingerprints, which may be known to the police. Anyhow, I believe he did the whole murder with his hands in his trouser-pockets."

Brandon shuddered suddenly; then collected himself and said, rather weakly:

"Then you don't think the science of observation—"

"Science of observation be damned!" cried Weir. "Do you still think private detectives get to know about criminals by smelling their hair-oil, or counting their buttons? They do it, a whole gang of them do it just as Hyde did. They get to know about criminals by being half criminals themselves, by being of the same rotten world, by belonging to it and by betraying it, by setting a thief to catch a thief, and proving there is no honour among thieves. I don't say there are no honest private detectives, but if there are, you don't get into their service as easily as you and I got into the office of the distinguished Dr. Adrian Hyde. You ask what all this means, and I tell you one thing it means. It means that you and I are going to sweep crossings or scrub out drains. I feel as if I should like a clean job."

The Secret of Dunstan's Tower

Ernest Bramah

Ernest Brammah Smith (1868–1942) wrote under the pseudonym Ernest Bramah. At the start of the twentieth century, he created Kai Lung, a Chinese story-teller, who became highly popular with readers. It is his blind detective Max Carrados, however, whose appeal has proved more enduring. The first of three successful collections of stories about Carrados appeared in 1914. Like A. J. Raffles, Carrados made his final appearance in an unsatisfactory novel; Bramah, like Conan Doyle and Hornung, was a writer whose skills were better suited to the short form.

Carrados is assisted in this story by his butler, Parkinson, but his customary "Watson" is Louis Carlyle, formerly a lawyer and now a private enquiry agent. In his preface to *The Eyes of Max Carrados*, in which this story first appeared in book form, Bramah explained the concept of the character: "so far from [blindness] crippling his interests in life or his energies, it has merely impelled him to develop those senses which in most us lie half dormant…while he may be at a disadvantage when you are at an advantage, he is at an advantage when you are at a disadvantage."

◇◇◇

It was a peculiarity of Mr Carrados that he could drop the most absorbing occupation of his daily life at a moment's notice if need be, apply himself exclusively to the solution of some criminological problem, possibly a matter of several days, and at the end of the time return and take up the thread of his private business exactly where he had left it.

On the morning of the 3rd of September he was dictating to his secretary a monograph to which he had given the attractive title, "The Portrait of Alexander the Great, as Jupiter Ammon, on an unedited octadrachm of Macedonia," when a telegram was brought in. Greatorex, the secretary, dealt with such communications as a matter of course, and, taking the envelope from Parkinson's salver, he cut it open in the pause between a couple of sentences.

"This is a private matter of yours, sir," he remarked, after glancing at the message. "Handed in at Netherhempsfield, 10.48 a.m. Repeated. One step higher. Quite baffled. Tulloch."

"Oh yes; that's all right," said Carrados. "No reply, Parkinson. Have you got down 'the Roman supremacy'?"

"'…the type of workmanship that still enshrined the memory of Spartan influence down to the era of Roman supremacy,'" read the secretary.

"That will do. How are the trains for Netherhempsfield?"

Greatorex put down the notebook and took up an "ABC."

"Waterloo departure 11—" He cocked an eye towards the desk clock. "Oh, that's no good. 12.17, 2.11, 5.9, 7.25."

"The 5.9 should do," interposed Carrados. "Arrival?"

"6.48."

"Now what has the gazetteer to say about the place?"

The yellow railway guide gave place to a weightier volume, and the secretary read out the following details:

"Netherhempsfield, parish and village, pop. 732, South Downshire. 2728 acres land and 27 water; soil rich loam, occupied as arable, pasture, orchard and woodland; subsoil various. The church of St Dunstan (restored 1740) is Saxon and Early English. It possesses an oak roof with curious grotesque bosses, and contains brasses and other memorials (earliest 13th century) of the Aynosforde family. In the 'Swinefield,' 1 1/2 miles south-west of the village, are 15 large stones, known locally as the Judge and Jury, which constitute the remains of a Druidical circle and temple. Dunstan's Tower, a moated residence built in the baronial style, and probably dating from the 14th century, is the seat of the Aynosfordes."

"I can give three days easily," mused Carrados. "Yes, I'll go down by the 5.9."

"Do I accompany you, sir?" inquired Greatorex.

"Not this time, I think. Have three days off yourself. Just pick up the correspondence and take things easy. Send on anything to me, care of Dr Tulloch. If I don't write, expect me back on Friday."

"Very well, Mr Carrados. What books shall I put out for Parkinson to pack?"

"Say…Gessner's *Thesaurus* and—yes, you may as well add Hilarion's *Celtic Mythology*."

Six hours later Carrados was on his way to Netherhempsfield. In his pocket was the following letter, which may be taken as offering the only explanation why he should suddenly decide to visit a place of which he had never even heard until that morning:—

"Dear Mr Carrados ('old Wynn,' it used to be),—
Do you remember a fellow at St Michael's who used
to own insects and the name of Tulloch—'Earwigs,'
they called him? Well, you will find it at the end of
this epistle, if you have the patience to get there. I
ran across Jarvis about six months ago on Euston
platform—you'll recall him by his red hair and great
feet—and we had a rapid and comprehensive pow-
wow. He told me who you were, having heard of you
from Lessing, who seems to be editing a high-class
review. He always was a trifle eccentric, Lessing.

"As for yours t., well, at the moment I'm local
demon in a G-f-s little place that you'd hardly find
on anything less than a 4-inch ordnance. But I won't
altogether say it mightn't be worse, for there's trout in
the stream, and after half-a-decade of Cinder Moor,
in the Black Country, a great and holy peace broods
on the smiling land.

"But you will guess that I wouldn't be taking up
the time of a busy man of importance unless I had
something to say, and you'd be right. It may interest
you, or it may not, but here it is.

"Living about two miles out of the village, at a sort
of mediæval stronghold known as Dunstan's Tower,
there is an ancient county family called Aynosforde.
And, for the matter of that, they are about all there
is here, for the whole place seems to belong to them,
and their authority runs from the power to charge you
two-pence if you sell a pig between Friday night and
Monday morning to the right to demand an exchange
of scabbards with the reigning sovereign whenever
he comes within seven bowshot flights of the highest
battlement of Dunstan's Tower. (I don't gather that
any reigning sovereign ever has come, but that isn't

the Aynosfordes' fault.) But, levity apart, these Aynosfordes, without being particularly rich, or having any title, are accorded an extraordinary position. I am told that scarcely a living duchess could hold out against the moral influence old dame Aynosforde could bring to bear on social matters, and yet she scarcely ever goes beyond Netherhempsfield now.

"My connection with these high-and-mighties ought to be purely professional, and so, in a manner, it is, but on the top of it I find myself drawn into a full-blooded, old haunted house mystery that takes me clean out of my depth.

"Darrish, the man whose place I'm taking for three months, had a sort of arrangement that once a week he should go up to the Tower and amuse old Mrs Aynosforde for a couple of hours under the pretence of feeling her pulse. I found that I was let in for continuing this. Fortunately the old dame was quite amiable at close quarters. I have no social qualifications whatever, and we got on very well together on those terms. I have heard that she considers me 'thoroughly responsible.'

"For five or six weeks everything went on swimmingly. I had just enough to do to keep me from doing nothing; people have a delightful habit of not being taken ill in the night, and there is a comfortable cob to trot round on.

"Tuesday is my Dunstan's Tower day. Last Tuesday I went as usual. I recall now that the servants about the place seemed rather wild and the old lady did not keep me quite as long as usual, but these things were not sufficiently noticeable to make any impression on me at the time. On Friday a groom rode over with a note from Swarbrick, the butler. Would I go up that afternoon and see Mrs Aynosforde? He had taken the liberty of asking me on his own responsibility as he thought that she ought to be seen. Deuced queer it struck me, but of course I went.

"Swarbrick was evidently on the look-out. He is a regular family retainer, taciturn and morose rather than bland. I saw at once that the old fellow had something on his mind, and I told him that I should like a word with him. We went into the morning-room.

"'Now, Swarbrick,' I said, 'you sent for me. What is the matter with your mistress since Tuesday?'

"He looked at me dourly, as though he was still in two minds about opening his mouth. Then he said slowly:

"'It isn't since Tuesday, sir. It was on that morning.'

"'What was?' I asked.

"'The beginning of it, Dr Tulloch. Mrs Aynosforde slipped at the foot of the stairs on coming down to breakfast.'

"'She did?' I said. 'Well, it couldn't have been very serious at the time. She never mentioned it to me.'

"'No, sir,' the old monument assented, with an appalling surface of sublime pride, 'she would not.'

"'Why wouldn't she if she was hurt?' I demanded. 'People do mention these things to their medical men, in strict confidence.'

"'The circumstances are unusual, sir,' he replied, without a ruffle of his imperturbable respect. 'Mrs Aynosforde was not hurt, sir. She did not actually fall, but she slipped—on a pool of blood.'

"'That's unpleasant,' I admitted, looking at him sharply, for an owl could have seen that there was something behind all this. 'How did it come there? Whose was it?'

"'Sir Philip Bellmont's, sir.'

"I did not know the name. 'Is he a visitor here?' I asked.

"'Not at present, sir. He stayed with us in 1662. He died here, sir, under rather unpleasant circumstances.'

"There you have it, Wynn. That is the keystone of the whole business. But if I keep to my conversation with the still reluctant Swarbrick I shall run out of foolscap and into midnight. Briefly, then, the 'unpleasant circumstances' were as follows:—Just about two and a half centuries ago, when Charles II. was back, and things in England were rather gay, a certain Sir Philip Bellmont was a guest at Dunstan's Tower. There were dice, and there was a lady—probably a dozen, but the particular one was the Aynosforde's young wife. One night there was a flare-up. Bellmont was run through with a rapier, and an ugly doubt turned on whether the point came out under the shoulder-blade, or went in there. Dripping on to every stair, the unfortunate man was carried up to his room. He died within a few hours, convinced, from the circumstances, of treachery all round, and with his last breath he left an anathema on every male and female Aynosforde as the day of their death approached. There are fourteen steps in the flight that Bellmont was carried up, and when the pool appears in the hall some Aynosforde has just two weeks to live. Each succeeding morning the stain may be found one stair higher. When it reaches the top there is a death in the family.

"This was the gist of the story. As far as you and I are concerned, it is, of course, merely a matter as to what form our scepticism takes, but my attitude is complicated by the fact that my nominal patient has become a real one. She is seventy-two and built to be a nonagenarian, but she has gone to bed with the intention of dying on Tuesday week. And I firmly believe she will.

"'How does she know that she is the one?' I asked. There aren't many Aynosfordes, but I knew that there were some others.

"To this Swarbrick maintained a discreet ambiguity. It was not for him to say, he replied, but I can see that he, like most of the natives round here, is obsessed with Aynosfordism.

"'And for that matter,' I objected, 'your mistress is scarcely entitled to the distinction. She will not really be an Aynosforde at all—only one by marriage.'

"'No, sir,' he replied readily, 'Mrs Aynosforde was also a Miss Aynosforde, sir—one of the Dorset Aynosfordes. Mr Aynosforde married his cousin.'

"'Oh,' I said, 'do the Aynosfordes often marry cousins?'

"'Very frequently, sir. You see, it is difficult otherwise for them to find eligible partners.'

"Well, I saw the lady, explaining that I had not been altogether satisfied with her condition on the Tuesday. It passed, but I was not able to allude to the real business. Swarbrick, in his respectful, cast-iron way, had impressed on me that Sir Philip Bellmont must not be mentioned, assuring me that even Darrish would not venture to do so. Mrs Aynosforde was certainly a little feverish, but there was nothing the matter with her. I left, arranging to call again on the Sunday.

"When I came to think it over, the first form it took was: Now who is playing a silly practical joke, or working a deliberate piece of mischief? But I could not get any further on those lines, because I do not know enough of the circumstances. Darrish might know, but Darrish is cruising off Spitzbergen, suffering from a nervous breakdown. The people here are amiable enough superficially, but they plainly regard me as an outsider.

"It was then that I thought of you. From what Jarvis had told me I gathered that you were keen on a mystery for its own sake. Furthermore, though I understand that you are now something of a dook, you might not be averse to a quiet week in the country, jogging along the lanes, smoking a peaceful pipe of an evening and yarning over old times. But I was not going to lure you down and then have the thing turn out to be a ridiculous and transparent hoax, no matter how serious its consequences. I owed it to you to make some reasonable investigation myself. This I have now done.

"On Sunday when I went there Swarbrick, with a very long face, reported that on each morning he had found the stain one step higher. The patient, needless to say, was appreciably worse. When I came down I had made up my mind.

"'Look here, Swarbrick,' I said, 'there is only one thing for it. I must sit up here to-night and see what happens.'

"He was very dubious at first, but I believe the fellow is genuine in his attachment to the house. His final scruple melted when he learned that I should not require him to sit up with me. I enjoined absolute secrecy, and this, in a large rambling place like the Tower, is not difficult to maintain. All the maidservants had fled. The only people sleeping within the walls now, beyond those I have mentioned, are two of Mrs Aynosforde's grandchildren (a girl and a young man whom I merely know by sight), the housekeeper

and a footman. All these had retired long before the
butler admitted me by an obscure little door, about
half-an-hour after midnight.

"The staircase with which we are concerned goes
up from the dining hall. A much finer, more modern
way ascends from the entrance hall. This earlier one,
however, only gives access now to three rooms, a lovely
oak-panelled chamber occupied by my patient and
two small rooms, turned nowadays into a boudoir
and a bathroom. When Swarbrick had left me in an
easy-chair, wrapped in a couple of rugs, in a corner
of the dark dining hall, I waited for half-an-hour
and then proceeded to make my own preparations.
Moving very quietly, I crept up the stairs, and at the
top drove one drawing-pin into the lintel about a
foot up, another at the same height into the baluster
opposite, and across the stairs fastened a black thread,
with a small bell hanging over the edge. A touch and
the bell would ring, whether the thread broke or not.
At the foot of the stairs I made another attachment
and hung another bell.

"'I think, my unknown friend,' I said, as I went back
to the chair, 'you are cut off above and below now.'

"I won't say that I didn't close my eyes for a minute
through the whole night, but if I did sleep it was
only as a watchdog sleeps. A whisper or a creak of a
board would have found me alert. As it was, however,
nothing happened. At six o'clock Swarbrick appeared,
respectfully solicitous about my vigil.

"'We've done it this time, Swarbrick,' I said in
modest elation. 'Not the ghost of a ghost has appeared.
The spell is broken.'

"He had crossed the hall and was looking rather
strangely at the stairs. With a very queer foreboding

I joined him and followed his glance. By heavens, Wynn, there, on the sixth step up, was a bright red patch! I am not squeamish; I cleared four steps at a stride, and stooping down I dipped my finger into the stuff and felt its slippery viscidity against my thumb. There could be no doubt about it; it was the genuine thing. In my baffled amazement I looked in every direction for a possible clue to human agency. Above, more than twenty feet above, were the massive rafters and boarding of the roof itself. By my side reared a solid stone wall, and beneath was simply the room we stood in, for the space below the stairway was not enclosed.

"I pointed to my arrangement of bells.

"'Nobody has gone up or down, I'll swear,' I said a little warmly. Between ourselves, I felt a bit of an ass for my pains, before the monumental Swarbrick.

"'No, sir,' he agreed. 'I had a similar experience myself on Saturday night.'

"'The deuce you did,' I exclaimed. 'Did you sit up then?'

"'Not exactly, sir,' he replied, 'but after making all secure at night I hung a pair of irreplaceable Dresden china cups in a similar way. They were both still intact in the morning, sir.'

"Well, there you are. I have nothing more to say on the subject. 'Hope not,' you'll be muttering. If the thing doesn't tempt you, say no more about it. If it does, just wire a time and I'll be at the station. Welcome isn't the word.—Yours as of yore.

"Jim Tulloch.

"*P.S.*—Can put your man up all right.

"J. T."

Carrados had "wired a time," and he was seized on the platform by the awaiting and exuberant Tulloch and guided with elaborate carefulness to the doctor's cart, which was, as its temporary owner explained, "knocking about somewhere in the lane outside."

"Splendid little horse," he declared. "Give him a hedge to nibble at and you can leave him to look after himself for hours. Motors? He laughs at them, Wynn, merely laughs."

Parkinson and the luggage found room behind, and the splendid little horse shook his shaggy head and launched out for home. For a mile the conversation was a string of, "Do you ever come across Brown now?" "You know Sugden was killed flying?" "Heard of Marling only last week; he's gone on the stage." "By the way, that appalling ass Sanders married a girl with a pot of money and runs horses now," and doubtless it would have continued in a similar strain to the end of the journey if an encounter with a farmer's country trap had not interrupted its tenor.

The lane was very narrow at that point and the driver of the trap drew into the hedge and stopped to allow the doctor to pass. There was a mutual greeting, and Tulloch pulled up also when their hubs were clear.

"No more sheep killed, I hope?" he called back.

"No, sir; I can't complain that we have," said the driver cheerfully. "But I do hear that Mr Stone, over at Daneswood, lost one last night."

"In the same way, do you mean?"

"So I heard. It's a queer business, doctor."

"It's a blackguardly business. It's a marvel what the fellow thinks he's doing."

"He'll get nabbed, never fear, sir. He'll do it once too often."

"Hope so," said the doctor. "Good-day." He shook the reins and turned to his visitor. "One of our local 'Farmer Jarges.' It's part of the business to pass the time o' day with them all and ask after the cow or the pig, if no other member of the family happens to be on the sick list."

"What is the blackguardly business?" asked Carrados.

"Well, that is a bit out of the common, I'll admit. About a week ago this man, Bailey, found one of his sheep dead in the field. It had been deliberately killed—head cut half off. It hadn't been done for meat, because none was taken. But, curiously enough, something else had been taken. The animal had been opened and the heart and intestines were gone. What do you think of that, Wynn?"

"Revenge, possibly."

"Bailey declares that he hasn't got the shadow of an enemy in the world. His three or four labourers are quite content. Of course a thing like that makes a tremendous sensation in a place like this. You may see as many as five men talking together almost any day now. And here, on the top of it, comes another case at Stone's. It looks like one of those outbreaks that crop up from time to time for no obvious reason and then die out again."

"No reason, Jim?"

"Well, if it isn't revenge, and if it isn't food, what is there to be got by it?"

"What is there to be got when an animal is killed?"

Tulloch stared without enlightenment.

"What is there that I am here to trace?"

"Godfrey Dan'l, Wynn! You don't mean to say that there is any connection between—?"

"I don't say it," declared Carrados promptly. "But there is very strong reason why we should consider it. It solves a very obvious question that faces us. A pricked thumb does not produce a pool. Did you microscope it?"

"Yes, I did. I can only say that it's mammalian. My limited experience doesn't carry me beyond that. Then what about the entrails, Wynn? Why take those?"

"That raises a variety of interesting speculations certainly."

"It may to you. The only thing that occurs to me is that it might be a blind."

"A very unfortunate one, if so. A blind is intended to allay curiosity—to suggest an obvious but fictitious motive. This, on the contrary, arouses curiosity. The abstraction of a haunch of mutton would be an excellent blind. Whereas now, as you say, what about the entrails?"

Tulloch shook his head.

"I've had my shot," he answered. "Can you suggest anything?"

"Frankly, I can't," admitted Carrados.

"On the face of it, I don't suppose anyone short of an oracle could. Pity our local shrine has got rusty in the joints." He levelled his whip and pointed to a distant silhouette that showed against the last few red streaks in the western sky a mile away. "You see that solitary old outpost of paganism—"

The splendid little horse leapt forward in indignant surprise as the extended whip fell sharply across his shoulders. Tulloch's ingenuous face seemed to have caught the rubicundity of the distant sunset.

"I'm beastly sorry, Wynn, old man," he muttered. "I ought to have remembered."

"My blindness?" contributed Carrados. "My dear chap, everyone makes a point of forgetting that. It's quite a recognised form of compliment among friends. If it were baldness I probably should be touchy on the subject; as it's only blindness I'm not."

"I'm very glad you take it so well," said Tulloch. "I was referring to a stone circle that we have here. Perhaps you have heard of it?"

"The Druids' altar!" exclaimed Carrados with an inspiration. "Jim, to my everlasting shame, I had forgotten it."

"Oh, well, it isn't much to look at," confessed the practical doctor. "Now in the church there are a few decent monuments—all Aynosfordes, of course."

"Aynosfordes—naturally. Do you know how far that remarkable race goes back?"

"A bit beyond Adam I should fancy," laughed Tulloch. "Well, Darrish told me that they really can trace to somewhere before the Conquest. Some antiquarian Johnny has claimed that the foundations of Dunstan's Tower cover a Celtic stronghold. Are you interested in that sort of thing?"

"Intensely," replied Carrados; "but we must not neglect other things. This gentleman who owned the unfortunate sheep, the second victim, now? How far is Daneswood away?"

"About a mile—mile and a half at the most."

Carrados turned towards the back seat.

"Do you think that in seven minutes' time you would be able to distinguish the details of a red mark on the grass, Parkinson?"

Parkinson took the effect of three objects, the sky above, the herbage by the roadside, and the back of his hand, and then spoke regretfully.

"I'm afraid not, sir; not with any certainty," he replied.

"Then we need not trouble Mr Stone to-night," said Carrados philosophically.

After dinner there was the peaceful pipe that Tulloch had forecast, and mutual reminiscences until the long clock in the corner, striking the smallest hour of the morning, prompted Tulloch to suggest retirement.

"I hope you have everything," he remarked tentatively, when he had escorted the guest to his bedroom. "Mrs Jones does for me very well, but you are an unknown quantity to her as yet."

"I shall be quite all right, you may be sure," replied Carrados, with his engagingly grateful smile. "Parkinson will already have seen to everything. We have a complete system, and I know exactly where to find anything I require."

Tulloch gave a final glance round.

"Perhaps you would prefer the window closed?" he suggested.

"Indeed I should not. It is south-west, isn't it?"

"Yes."

"And a south-westerly breeze to bring the news. I shall sit here for a little time." He put his hand on the top rail of a chair with unhesitating precision and drew it to the open casement. "There are a thousand sounds that you in your arrogance of sight ignore, a thousand individual scents of hedge and orchard that come to me up here. I suppose it is quite dark to you now, Jim? What a lot you seeing people must miss!"

Tulloch guffawed, with his hand on the door-knob.

"Well, don't let your passion for nocturnal nature study lead you to miss breakfast at eight. My eyes won't, I promise you. Ta-ta."

He jigged off to his own room and in ten minutes was soundly asleep. But the oak clock in the room beneath marked the quarters one by one until the next hour struck, and then round the face again until the little finger stood at three, and still the blind man sat by the open window that looked out over the south-west, interpreting the multitudinous signs of the quiet life that still went on under the dark cover of the warm summer night.

"The word lies with you, Wynn," remarked Tulloch at breakfast the next morning—he was twelve minutes late, by the way, and found his guest interested in the titles of Dr Darrish's excellent working library. "I am supposed to be on view here from nine to ten, and after that I am due at Abbot's Farm somewhere about noon. With those reservations, I am at your disposal for the day."

"Do you happen to go anywhere near the 'Swinefield' on your way to Abbot's Farm?" asked Carrados.

"The 'Swinefield'? Oh, the Druids' circle. Yes, one way—and it's as good as any other—passes the wheel-track that leads up to it."

"Then I should certainly like to inspect the site."

"There's really nothing to see, you know," apologised the doctor. "Only a few big rocks on end. They aren't even chiselled smooth."

"I am curious," volunteered Carrados, "to discover why fifteen stones should be called 'The Judge and Jury.'"

"Oh, I can explain that for you," declared Tulloch. "Two of them are near together with a third block across the tops. That's the Judge. The twelve jurymen are scattered here and there. But we'll go, by all means."

"There is a public right-of-way, I suppose?" asked Carrados, when, in due course, the trap turned from the highway into a field track.

"I don't know about a right," said Tulloch, "but I imagine that anyone goes across who wants to. Of course it's not a Stonehenge, and we have very few visitors, or the Aynosfordes might put some restrictions. As for the natives, there isn't a man who wouldn't sooner walk ten miles to see a five-legged calf than cross the road to look at a Phidias. And for that matter," he added thoughtfully, "this is the first time I've been really up to the place myself."

"It's on Aynosforde property, then?"

"Oh yes. Most of the parish is, I believe. But this 'Swinefield' is part of the park. There is an oak plantation across there or Dunstan's Tower would be in sight."

They had reached the gate of the enclosure. The doctor got down to open it, as he had done the former ones.

"This is locked," he said, coming back to the step, "but we can climb over easy enough. You can get down all right?"

"Thanks," replied Carrados. He descended and followed Tulloch, stopping to pat the little horse's neck.

"He'll be all right," remarked the doctor with a backward nod. "I fancy Tommy's impressionable years must have been spent between the shafts of a butcher's cart. Now, Wynn, how do we proceed?"

"I should like to have your arm over this rough ground. Then if you will take me from stone to stone—"

They paced the broken circle leisurely, Carrados judging the appearance of the remains by touch and by the answers to the innumerable questions that he put. They were approaching the most important monument, the Judge—when Tulloch gave a shout of delight.

"Oh, the beauty!" he cried with enthusiasm. "I must see you closer. Wynn, do you mind—a minute—"

"Lady, Jim?" murmured Carrados. "Certainly not. I'll stand like Tommy."

Tulloch shot off with a laugh and Carrados heard him racing across the grass in the direction of the trilithon. He was still amused when he returned, after a very short interval.

"No, Wynn, not a lady, but it occurred to me that you might have been farther off. A beautiful airy creature very brightly clad. A Purple Emperor, in fact. I haven't netted a butterfly for years, but the sight gave me all the old excitement of the chase."

"Tolerably rare, too, aren't they?"

"Generally speaking, they are. I remember waiting in an oak grove with a twenty-foot net for a whole day once, and not a solitary Emperor crossed my path."

"An oak grove; yes, you said there was an oak plantation here."

"I didn't know the trick then. You needn't go to that trouble. His Majesty has rather peculiar tastes for so elegant

a being. You just hang a piece of decidedly ripe meat anywhere near."

"Yes, Jim?"

"Do you notice anything?" demanded the doctor, with
his face up to the wind.

"Several things," replied Carrados.

"Apropos of high meat? Do you know, Wynn, I lost that
Purple Emperor here, round the blocks. I thought it must
have soared, as I couldn't quite fathom its disappearance.
This used to be the Druids' altar, they say. I don't know if
you follow me, but it would be a devilish rum go if—eh?"

Carrados accepted the suggestion of following Jim's idea
with impenetrable gravity.

"I haven't the least doubt that you are right," he assented.
"Can you get up?"

"It's about ten feet high," reported Tulloch, "and not an
inch of crevice to get a foothold on. If only we could bring
the trap in here—"

"I'll give you a back," said Carrados, taking a position
against one of the pillars. "You can manage with that?"

"Sure you can stand it?"

"Only be as quick as you can."

"Wait a minute," said Tulloch with indecision. "I think
someone is coming."

"I know there is," admitted Carrados, "but it is only a
matter of seconds. Make a dash for it."

"No," decided Tulloch. "One looks ridiculous. I believe
it is Miss Aynosforde. We'd better wait."

A young girl with a long thin face, light hair and the palest
blue eyes that it would be possible to imagine had come from
the wood and was approaching them hurriedly. She might
have been eighteen, but she was "dressed young," and when
she spoke she expressed the ideas of a child.

"You ought not to come in here," was her greeting. "It belongs to us."

"I am sorry if we are trespassing," apologised Tulloch, colouring with chagrin and surprise. "I was under the impression that Mrs Aynosforde allowed visitors to inspect these ruins. I am Dr Tulloch."

"I don't know anything about that," said the girl vaguely. "But Dunstan will be very cross if he sees you here. He is always cross if he finds that anyone has been here. He will scold me afterwards. And he makes faces in the night."

"We will go," said Tulloch quietly. "I am sorry that we should have unconsciously intruded."

He raised his hat and turned to walk away, but Miss Aynosforde detained him.

"You must not let Dunstan know that I spoke to you about it," she implored him. "That would be as bad. Indeed," she added plaintively, "whatever I do always makes him cruel to me."

"We will not mention it, you may be sure," replied the doctor. "Good-morning."

"Oh, it is no good!" suddenly screamed the girl. "He has seen us; he is coming!"

Tulloch looked round in the direction that Miss Aynosforde's frightened gaze indicated. A young man whom he knew by sight as her brother had left the cover of the wood and was strolling leisurely towards them. Without waiting to encounter him the girl turned and fled, to hide herself behind the farthest pillar, running with ungainly movements of her long, wispish arms and uttering a low cry as she went.

As young Aynosforde approached he courteously raised his hat to the two elder men. He appeared to be a few years older than his sister, and in him her colourless ovine features were moulded to a firmer cast.

"I am afraid that we are trespassing," said the doctor, awkward between his promise to the girl and the necessity of glossing over the situation. "My friend is interested in antiquities—"

"My unfortunate sister!" broke in Aynosforde quietly, with a sad smile. "I can guess what she has been saying. You are Dr Tulloch, are you not?"

"Yes."

"Our grandmother has a foolish but amiable weakness that she can keep poor Edith's infirmity dark. I cannot pretend to maintain that appearance before a doctor...and I am sure that we can rely on the discretion of your friend?"

"Oh, certainly," volunteered Tulloch. "He is—"

"Merely an amateur," put in Carrados suavely, but with the incisiveness of a scalpel.

"You must, of course, have seen that Edith is a little unusual in her conversation," continued the young man. "Fortunately, it is nothing worse than that. She is not helpless, and she is never violent. I have some hope, indeed, that she will outgrow her delusions. I suppose"—he laughed a little as he suggested it—"I suppose she warned you of my displeasure if I saw you here?"

"There was something of the sort," admitted Tulloch, judging that the circumstances nullified his promise.

Aynosforde shook his head slowly.

"I am sorry that you have had the experience," he remarked. "Let me assure you that you are welcome to stay as long as you like under the shadows of these obsolete fossils, and to come as often as you please. It is a very small courtesy; the place has always been accessible to visitors."

"I am relieved to find that I was not mistaken," said the doctor.

"When I have read up the subject I should like to come again," interposed Carrados. "For the present we have gone all over the ground." He took Tulloch's arm, and under the insistent pressure the doctor turned towards the gate. "Good-morning, Mr Aynosforde."

"What a thing to come across!" murmured Tulloch when they were out of earshot. "I remember Darrish making the remark that the girl was simple for her years or something of that sort, but I only took it that she was backward. I wonder if the old ass knew more than he told me!"

They were walking without concern across the turf and had almost reached the gate when Carrados gave a sharp, involuntary cry of pain and wrenched his arm free. As he did so a stone of dangerous edge and size fell to the ground between them.

"Damnation!" cried Tulloch, his face darkening with resentment. "Are you hurt, old man?"

"Come on," curtly replied Carrados between his set teeth.

"Not until I've given that young cub something to remember," cried the outraged doctor truculently. "It was Aynosforde, Wynn. I wouldn't have believed it, but I just caught sight of him in time. He laughed and ran behind a pillar when you were hit."

"Come on," reiterated Carrados, seizing his friend's arm and compelling him towards the gate. "It was only the funny bone, fortunately. Would you stop to box the village idiot's ears because he puts out his tongue at you?"

"Village idiot!" exclaimed Tulloch. "I may only be a thick-skulled, third-rate general practitioner of no social pretension whatever, but I'm blistered if I'll have my guest insulted by a long-eared pedigree blighter without putting up a few plain words about it. An Aynosforde or not, he must take the consequences; he's no village idiot."

"No," was Carrados's grim retort; "he is something much more dangerous—the castle maniac."

Tulloch would have stopped in sheer amazement, but the recovered arm dragged him relentlessly on.

"Aynosforde! Mad!"

"The girl is on the borderline of imbecility; the man has passed beyond the limit of a more serious phase. The ground has been preparing for generations; doubtless in him the seed has quietly germinated for years. Now his time has come."

"I heard that he was a nice, quiet young fellow, studious and interested in science. He has a workshop and a laboratory."

"Yes, anything to occupy his mind. Well, in future he will have a padded room and a keeper."

"But the sheep killed by night and the parts exposed on the Druids' altar? What does it mean, Wynn?"

"It means madness, nothing more and nothing less. He is the receptacle for the last dregs of a rotten and decrepit stock that has dwindled down to mental atrophy. I don't believe that there is any method in his midnight orgies. The Aynosfordes are certainly a venerable line, and it is faintly possible that its remote ancestors were Druid priests who sacrificed and practised haruspicy on the very spot that we have left. I have no doubt that on that questionable foundation you would find advocates of a more romantic theory."

"Moral atavism?" suggested the doctor shrewdly.

"Yes—reincarnation. I prefer the simpler alternative. Aynosforde has been so fed up with pride of family and traditions of his ancient race that his mania takes this natural trend. You know what became of his father and mother?"

"No, I have never heard them mentioned."

"The father is in a private madhouse. The mother—another cousin, by the way—died at twenty-five."

"And the blood-stains on the stairs? Is that his work?"

"Short of actual proof, I should say yes. It is the realisation of another family legend, you see. Aynosforde may have an insane grudge against his grandmother, or it may be simply apeish malignity, put into his mind by the sight of blood."

"What do you propose doing, then? We can't leave the man at large."

"We have nothing yet to commit him on. You would not sign for a reception order on the strength of seeing him throw a stone? We must contrive to catch him in the act to-night, if possible."

Tulloch woke up the little horse with a sympathetic touch—they were ambling along the highroad again by this time—and permitted himself to smile.

"And how do you propose to do that, Excellency?" he asked.

"By sprinkling the ninth step with iodide of nitrogen. A warm night…it will dry in half-an-hour."

"Well, do you know, I never thought of that," admitted the doctor. "Certainly that would give us the alarm if a feather brushed it. But we don't possess a chemist's shop, and I very much doubt if I can put my hand on any iodine."

"I brought a couple of ounces," said Carrados with diffidence. "Also a bottle of .880 ammonia to be on the safe side."

"You really are a bit of a *sine qua non*, Wynn," declared Tulloch expressively.

"It was such an obvious thing," apologised the blind man. "I suppose Brook Ashfield is too far for one of us to get over to this afternoon?"

"In Dorset?"

"Yes. Colonel Eustace Aynosforde is the responsible head of the family now, and he should be on the spot if possible. Then we ought to get a couple of men from the county lunatic asylum. We don't know what may be before us."

"If it can't be done by train we must wire, or perhaps Colonel Aynosforde is on the telephone. We can go into that as soon as we get back. We are almost at Abbot's Farm now. I will cut it down to fifteen minutes at the outside. You don't mind waiting here?"

"Don't hurry," replied Carrados. "Few cases are matters of minutes. Besides, I told Parkinson to come on here from Daneswood on the chance of our picking him up."

"Oh, it's Parkinson, to be sure," said the doctor. "Thought I knew the figure crossing the field. Well, I'll leave you to him."

He hastened along the rutty approach to the farmhouse, and Tommy, under the pretext of being driven there by certain pertinacious flies, imperceptibly edged his way towards the long grass by the roadside. In a few minutes Parkinson announced his presence at the step of the vehicle.

"I found what you described, sir," he reported. "These are the shapes."

Tulloch kept to his time. In less than a quarter of an hour he was back again and gathering up the reins.

"That little job is soon worked off," he remarked with mild satisfaction. "Home now, I suppose, Wynn?"

"Yes," assented Carrados. "And I think that the other little job is morally worked off." He held up a small piece of note-paper, cut to a neat octagon, with two long sides and six short ones. "What familiar object would just about cover that plan, Jim?"

"If it isn't implicating myself in any devilment, I should say that one of our four-ounce bottles would be about the ticket," replied Tulloch.

"It very likely does implicate you to the extent of being one of your four-ounce bottles, then," said Carrados. "The man who killed Stone's sheep had occasion to use what we will infer to be a four-ounce bottle. It does not tax the imagination to suggest the use he put it to, nor need we wonder that he found it desirable to wash it afterwards—this small, flat bottle that goes conveniently into a waistcoat pocket. On one side of the field—the side remote from the road, Jim, but in the direct line for Dunstan's Tower—there is a stream. There he first washed his hands, carefully placing the little bottle on the grass while he did so. That indiscretion has put us in possession of a ground plan, so to speak, of the vessel."

"Pity it wasn't of the man instead."

"Of the man also. In the field the earth is baked and unimpressionable, but down by the water-side the conditions are quite favourable, and Parkinson got perfect reproductions of the footprints. Soon, perhaps, we may have an opportunity of making a comparison."

The doctor glanced at the neat lines to which the papers Carrados held out had been cut.

"It's a moral," he admitted. "There's nothing of the hobnailed about those boots, Wynn."

◇◇◇

Swarbrick had been duly warned, and obedience to his instructions had been ensured by the note that conveyed them bearing the signature of Colonel Aynosforde. Between eleven and twelve o'clock a light in a certain position gave the intelligence that Dunstan Aynosforde was in his bedroom and the coast quite clear. A little group of silent men approached the Tower, and four, crossing one of the two bridges that spanned the moat, melted spectrally away in a dark angle of the walls.

Every detail had been arranged. There was no occasion for whispered colloquies about the passages, and with the exception of the butler's sad and respectful greeting of an Aynosforde, scarcely a word was spoken. Carrados, the Colonel and Parkinson took up their positions in the great dining hall, where Dr Tulloch had waited on the occasion of his vigil. A screen concealed them from the stairs and the chairs on which they sat did not creak—all the blind man asked for. The doctor, who had carried a small quantity of some damp powder wrapped in a saturated sheet of blotting-paper, occupied himself for five minutes distributing it minutely over the surface of the ninth stair. When this was accomplished he disappeared and the silence of a sleeping house settled upon the ancient Tower.

A party, however, is only as quiet as its most restless member, and the Colonel soon discovered a growing inability to do nothing at all and to do it in absolute silence. After an exemplary hour he began to breathe whispered comments on the situation into his neighbour's ear, and it required all Carrados's tact and good humour to repress his impatience. Two o'clock passed and still nothing had happened.

"I begin to feel uncommonly dubious, you know," whispered the Colonel, after listening to the third clock strike the hour. "We stand to get devilishly chaffed if this gets about. Suppose nothing happens?"

"Then your aunt will probably get up again," replied Carrados.

"True, true. We shall have broken the continuity. But, you know, Mr Carrados, there are some things about this portent, visitation—call it what you will—that even I don't fully understand down to this day. There is no doubt that my grandfather, Oscar Aynosforde, who died in 1817, did receive a similar omen, or summons, or whatever it may be. We have it on the authority—"

Carrados clicked an almost inaudible sound of warning and laid an admonishing hand on the Colonel's arm.

"Something going on," he breathed.

The soldier came to the alert like a terrier at a word, but his straining ears could not distinguish a sound beyond the laboured ticking of the hall clock beyond.

"I hear nothing," he muttered to himself.

He had not long to wait. Half-way up the stairs something snapped off like the miniature report of a toy pistol. Before the sound could translate itself to the human brain another louder discharge had swallowed it up and out of its echo a crackling fusillade again marked the dying effects of the scattered explosive.

At the first crack Carrados had swept aside the screen. "Light, Parkinson!" he cried.

An electric lantern flashed out and centred its circle of brilliance on the stairs opposite. Its radiance pierced the nebulous balloon of violet smoke that was rising to the roof and brought out every detail of the wall beyond.

"Good heavens!" exclaimed Colonel Aynosforde, "there is a stone out. I knew nothing of this."

As he spoke the solid block of masonry slid back into its place and the wall became as blankly impenetrable as before.

"Colonel Aynosforde," said Carrados, after a hurried word with Parkinson, "you know the house. Will you take my man and get round to Dunstan's work-room at once? A good deal depends upon securing him immediately."

"Am I to leave you here without any protection, sir?" inquired Parkinson in mild rebellion.

"Not without any protection, thank you, Parkinson. I shall be in the dark, remember."

They had scarcely gone when Dr Tulloch came stumbling in from the hall and the main stairs beyond, calling on Carrados as he bumped his way past a succession of inopportune pieces of furniture.

"Are you there, Wynn?" he demanded, in high-strung irritation. "What the devil's happening? Aynosforde hasn't left his room, we'll swear, but hasn't the iodide gone off?"

"The iodide has gone off and Aynosforde has left his room, though not by the door. Possibly he is back in it by now."

"The deuce!" exclaimed Tulloch blankly. "What am I to do?"

"Return—" began Carrados, but before he could say more there was a confused noise and a shout outside the window.

"We are saved further uncertainty," said the blind man. "He has thrown himself down into the moat."

"He will be drowned!"

"Not if Swarbrick put the drag-rake where he was instructed, and if those keepers are even passably expert," replied Carrados imperturbably. "After all, drowning…But perhaps you had better go and see, Jim."

In a few minutes men began to return to the dining hall as though where the blind man was constituted their headquarters. Colonel Aynosforde and Parkinson were the first, and immediately afterwards Swarbrick entered from the opposite side, bringing a light.

"They've got him out," exclaimed the Colonel. "Upon my word, I don't know whether it's for the best or the worst, Mr Carrados." He turned to the butler, who was lighting one after another of the candles of the great hanging centre-pieces. "Did you know anything of a secret passage giving access to these stairs, Swarbrick?" he inquired.

"Not personally, sir," replied Swarbrick, "but we always understood that formerly there was a passage and hiding chamber somewhere, though the positions had been lost. We last had occasion to use it when we were defeated at Naseby, sir."

Carrados had walked to the stairs and was examining the wall.

"This would be the principal stairway then?" he asked.

"Yes, sir, until we removed the Elizabethan gallery when we restored in 1712."

"It is on the same plan as the 'Priest's Chamber' at Lapwood. If you investigate in the daylight, Colonel Aynosforde, you will find that you command a view of both bridges when the stone is open. Very convenient sometimes, I dare say."

"Very, very," assented the Colonel absently. "Every moment," he explained, "I am dreading that Aunt Eleanor will make her appearance. She must have been disturbed."

"Oh, I took that into account," said Tulloch, catching the remark as he put his head in at the door and looked round. "I recommended a sleeping draught when I was here this— no, last evening. We have got our man in all right now," he continued, "and if we can have a dry suit—"

"I will accompany you, sir," said Swarbrick.

"Is he—violent?" asked the Colonel, dropping his voice.

"Violent? Well," admitted Tulloch, holding out two dripping objects that he had been carrying, "we thought it just as well to cut his boots off." He threw them down in a corner and followed the butler out of the room.

Carrados took two pieces of shaped white paper from his pocket and ran his fingers round the outlines. Then he picked up Dunstan Aynosforde's boots and submitted them to a similar scrutiny.

"Very exact, Parkinson," he remarked approvingly.

"Thank you, sir," replied Parkinson with modest pride.

The Manor House Mystery

J. S. Fletcher

Joseph Smith Fletcher (1863–1935) was born in Yorkshire, and worked there as a newspaperman before relocating to London, where he established himself as a hard-working novelist. His reputation received a powerful boost when President Woodrow Wilson expressed his enthusiasm for *The Middle Temple Murder,* and Fletcher continued to write crime novels until his death, although by then his fame had been superseded by that of younger authors, notably Agatha Christie and Dorothy L. Sayers.

Fletcher never lost his love of north England; he set a good deal of his fiction there, and his recurrent characters included the Yorkshireman Archer Dawe ("the famous amateur detective, expert criminologist, a human ferret.") Fletcher was as prolific a writer of short stories as he was of novels, and although sometimes quantity came at the expense of quality, at his best he was one of the most entertaining authors of popular fiction of his day.

◇◇◇

1
Misadventure—Or Murder?

In a private sitting-room of an old-fashioned country town hotel, a man sat at a writing-desk absent-mindedly drawing unmeaning scrawls on a blotting-pad. On the table in the centre of the room lay the remains of the last course of a simple dinner; he himself had almost forgotten that he had eaten any dinner. In fact, he had left untouched most of what he had last taken on his plate—in the middle of a spoonful of apple-tart he had got up from his chair to walk up and down the room, thinking, speculating, racking his brain; just as abstractedly he had sat down at the desk, to lay hand on a pen, and begin to scribble lines and curves. He went on scribbling lines and curves and circles and various hieroglyphics, until an old waiter came in and laid the evening newspaper at his side. He started then and looked up, and the waiter glanced at the table.

"You can clear away," said the absent-minded man. "I've finished."

He remained where he was until the table had been cleared and he was once more alone; then he turned his chair to the fire, put his slippered feet on the fender, and picked up the paper. It was a small, four-page sheet, printed at the county town twenty miles away, and it contained little news which had not already appeared in the morning journals. The man turned it over with listless indifference, until his eye lighted on a paragraph, headed "The Flamstock Mystery." The indifference went out of his face then; he lifted the folded sheet nearer and read with eagerness.

"The mystery attending the death of Mr. Septimus Walshawe, J.P., of Flamstock, remains still unsolved. That this much-respected townsman and magistrate died of poisoning there is no doubt. It is inconceivable that Mr. Walshawe took his own life; no one who was familiar with him could believe for a moment that a man of his cheery temperament, his optimistic character, and his interest in life could ever terminate a useful and fully occupied existence by suicide. Nor is there any evidence that Mr. Walshawe took poison by misadventure. There is a growing feeling in Flamstock that the deceased gentleman was—to put it in plain language—murdered, but, although the services of a noted expert in criminal detection have been employed in this case, nothing, we understand, has so far transpired which is likely to lead to the detection of the cowardly—and clever—murderer."

The reader threw the newspaper aside with a smile. He was the noted expert in criminal detection to whom the paragraph referred, and, after several days' investigation of the Walshawe case, he was not quite so certain about the facts which appertained to it as the writer of the paragraph appeared to be. All that he was actually certain about was that he was very much puzzled. He had done a good deal of thinking during the last few days; he knew that a lot of thinking was still to be done. And, realising that there was no likelihood of his thinking of anything else that evening, he lighted a cigar, and settling himself comfortably before the dancing flames, fell to representing the case to his own judgment for perhaps the hundredth time.

This was how the case stood. Mr. Septimus Walshawe, a gentleman of about sixty years of age at the time of his sudden death, had lived in Flamstock, a small country town, for twenty-five years. He rented the Manor House, a quaint old mansion at the top of the High Street. He was a man of considerable means, and a bachelor. His tastes were literary and antiquarian. He was the possessor of a notable library; he collected old china, old silver; he had a small but valuable museum of antiquities. He was never so happy as when he was busied about his books and his curiosities, but he was by no means a recluse. From the time of his coming to Flamstock he took a good deal of interest in the life of the town.

He had served on its town council; he had been mayor; he had founded a literary and philosophical institute, and once a year he lectured to its members on some subject of importance. Also, he was a magistrate, and he never failed in his attendance at petty sessions or quarter sessions. In short, he was a feature of the town; everybody knew him; his face and figure was as familiar in High Street as the tower of the old church, or the queer figures which ornamented the town-hall clock.

So much for Mr. Walshawe's public life. His private life appeared to have been a very quiet one. His household consisted of a housekeeper, a cook, three female servants, and a boy in buttons; he also employed two gardeners and a groom-coachman, who drove his one equipage, an old-fashioned landau.

He seemed to have no near relations—in fact, the only relation who ever came to see him was a niece, married far away in the North of England, who visited Flamstock for a week or two every year, and for the last few years had brought her two small children with her. It was understood by those Flamstockians who were admitted to Mr. Walshawe's confidence that this lady would inherit all he had. And she had inherited it now that he was dead, and it was by her express desire and on her instructions that the New Scotland Yard man who toasted his feet at the fire of his private parlour in the Bull and Bucket had come down to Flamstock to find out the truth about the mystery which surrounded her uncle's death.

That Mr. Walshawe's death had taken place under mysterious circumstances there was no doubt. He was found dead in bed at noon on the tenth day of November on a Thursday. The detective had no need to refer to his memoranda for these precise facts as regards Mr. Walshawe's doings for some days previous to the day of his death.

Nothing had occurred which could be taken as presaging his decease; he had shown no sign of illness, had made no complaint of any feeling of illness. In fact, he had been rather more than usually active that week.

On the Monday evening he had delivered his annual lecture at the institute; on the Tuesday he had sat on the bench at the town hall from eleven in the morning till five in the afternoon; on the Wednesday he had lunched at Sir Anthony Cleeke's house, just outside the town; that evening he had entertained a few friends to dinner; one or two of whom had stayed rather late.

The fact that they had stayed rather late had relieved Mrs. Whiteside, the housekeeper, of any fear when Mr. Walshawe did not come down to breakfast at his usual hour next morning. She knew that he had not gone to bed until quite two o'clock.

When breakfast-time had been passed by two hours, however, she went to call him, and, getting no answer, walked into his room to find him asleep, but looking so strange and breathing so uneasily that she had become alarmed and sent at once for medical help.

There was delay in getting that. Dr. Thorney, Mr. Walshawe's medical attendant, was away from home, and his assistant had gone into the country on a round of visits. Consequently an hour elapsed before medical help was brought to his bedside. And when it arrived Mr. Walshawe was dead.

In the opinion of the coroner this was decidedly a case for a post-mortem examination, and it was immediately carried out. Its results went to prove that Mr. Walshawe had died from veronal poisoning. Thereupon the mystery began.

It was not known to any member of his household that he ever took such things. There was no trace of such things in the house. His private apartments were searched from top to bottom; his desks, his drawers, every receptacle, every nook and cranny where drugs could have been concealed, were scrupulously examined. Nothing was found.

Nor could anybody be found who had ever sold veronal or any similar drug to Mr. Walshawe. There were three chemists in Flamstock; none of them had ever known him as a customer for any drug of that sort. Advertisements asking for information on this point were inserted first in the local papers of the neighbouring towns, then in the London newspapers. Had any chemist ever sent veronal to Mr. Walshawe by post?

There was no reply to these advertisements. Of course, as plenty of people were quick to point out, Mr. Walshawe could have purchased veronal when he was away from the town.

But, as a matter of fact, he had not been away from Flamstock for well over a year. And, in addition to that, those who knew him best and most intimately agreed that he was given to boasting of his general robust health, his good appetite, and, above everything, his power of sleeping. He was the last man in the world, said they, to have need of sleeping draughts; he had been heard to say, a thousand times, that he slept like a top from eleven o'clock until seven. He had said so, Sir Anthony Cleeke remembered, only the day before he was found dead.

It was inconceivable that he should have taken veronal in a sufficient quantity to kill him. Yet the fact remained that he had died from veronal poisoning, and must have taken a considerable dose.

When the man from New Scotland Yard came on the scene, brought there by Mr. Walshawe's niece, he had at first come to an immediate conclusion that the dead man had taken the veronal himself. He had had his own reasons, he said, for taking the drug, and being—possibly or probably—unaccustomed to it, he had taken too much.

But he was faced with the fact that no trace of Mr. Walshawe ever having bought or possessed such a drug could be found. He was also faced with the general habits and tone of the dead man. He was further having it impressed upon him, day by day, that Mr. Walshawe's niece was sure, certain, convinced that somebody had administered the veronal to her uncle in order to do him to death.

She pointed out that there was nothing to show that he was likely to take a sleeping draught; certainly nothing to indicate that he was tired of life. Tired of life, indeed! Why, he was just then full of spirits, full of interests. He was looking forward to attending, on the very day on which he died, a sale by auction at a neighbouring country house, where there were certain antiquities and objects of art which he ardently desired to possess.

He had been talking of them when he lunched at Sir Anthony Cleeke's; he talked of them at his own dinner-party in the evening. No—no; nothing would persuade her that her uncle had done anything to bring about his own death. Nothing!

"Misadventure?" suggested the detective.

"No misadventure!" retorted Mr. Walshawe's niece. "My uncle was murdered. It is your place to find out who murdered him."

This was the problem which vexed the mind of the detective as he sat musing and reflecting in his quiet room at the

Bull and Bucket. It seemed to him that he was doing little good. He had been in Flamstock nearly a fortnight, pursuing all sorts of inquiries, following up all manner of suggestions, and he was no nearer any solution of the mystery. Nevertheless, he knew what he wanted. And he muttered a word unconsciously.

"Motive!" he said. "Motive! Motive!"

A tap came at the door, and the old waiter put his head into the room.

"Mr. Peasegood to see you, sir," he said.

The detective, with the alacrity of a man who is relieved at the prospect of exchanging ideas with a fellow-creature, rose.

"Show Mr. Peasegood in, William," he answered.

2
The Legal Visitor

The man who came into the room, contenting himself with a nod of greeting until the waiter had gone away, was known to the detective as Mr. Septimus Walshawe's solicitor. He had already had several interviews with him, and they had discussed the details of the case until it seemed as if they had covered every inch of the debatable ground. Yet it now appeared to him that Mr. Peasegood had something new to communicate; there was the suggestion of news in his face, and the detective wheeled an easy-chair to the hearth with an eagerness which really meant that he was anxious to know what his visitor had to say.

"Good evening, Mr. Peasegood," he said. "Glad to see you. Can I offer you anything now—a drink, a cigar?"

Mr. Peasegood was slowly drawing off his gloves, which he deposited carefully within his hat. He also divested himself of his overcoat, and, having run his fingers over his smooth hair, he dropped into the seat and smiled.

"Not just now, Mr. Marshford," he answered. "Perhaps a little later. Business first—eh?"

"There is business, then!" exclaimed the detective. "Ah! Something to do with the case, of course?"

"Something to do with the case, of course," repeated Mr. Peasegood, blandly. "Very much to do with the case."

Marshford threw his cigar into the fire and, leaning forward in his chair, looked fixedly at his visitor.

"Yes?" he said.

"You are aware," continued Peasegood, "of the tenor of Mr. Walshawe's will, which was executed by myself some years ago?"

"Yes—yes," replied Marshford; "of course. That is, I know what you told me—that, with the exception of a few trifling legacies, everything was left to the niece, Mrs. Carstone?"

"Just so," assented Peasegood. "It is ten years since I drew up that will. I have been under the impression that it was Walshawe's last word as to the disposition of his property."

The detective started.

"And—wasn't it?" he asked eagerly.

Peasegood smiled in an odd fashion.

"Another will—a later will—has come to light," he replied. He looked narrowly at the detective, and he smiled again. "It is a perfectly good will," he added; "and, of course, it upsets the other."

"Bless me!" said Marshford. "I'm sorry to hear it—for Mrs. Carstone's sake."

Peasegood laughed.

"Oh, it doesn't make any great amount of difference to Mrs. Carstone!" he remarked. "Oh, no! But it may make a considerable difference to somebody else in a way which that somebody else won't quite appreciate; a very considerable difference."

Marshford looked an inquiry. He was eager with inquisitiveness, but he recognised that Peasegood was one of those men who will tell a story in their own way, and he waited.

"This is how it is," continued Peasegood after a pause; "and you're the first person I've spoken to about it. This afternoon, just as I was about to leave my office for the day, Mrs. Whiteside called on me."

"Walshawe's housekeeper!" exclaimed Marshford.

"Walshawe's housekeeper—exactly. She requested an interview. Her manner was mysterious. She was some time in coming to a point—I had to ask her, at last, what she really wanted. Eventually she told me that not many months before his death Mr. Walshawe made a new will, and entrusted it to her keeping."

The detective whistled.

"Just so," continued Peasegood. "I, too, felt inclined to whistle. Instead, I asked to see the will she spoke of. She produced it. I read it hastily. It is a perfectly good will; nothing can upset it. Or, rather, there's only one thing that might upset it—we'll talk of what that is later. But—to give you particulars of it—it was made on the twenty-fourth of last May; it was written out by Walshawe himself on a sheet of foolscap; it is duly and properly signed and witnessed. Quite a good will."

"And its provisions?" asked Marshford.

"Simple—very!" replied Peasegood. "It appoints the same executors—myself and Mr. John Entwhistle. Mrs. Carstone is left the residue of everything—real and personal estate—as before. The trifling legacies are as before. But a sum of ten thousand pounds is left to Jane Whiteside, and a like sum to her son Richard."

Peasegood paused and laughed a little.

"That's the difference," he said—"a little difference of twenty thousand pounds. I said it would make no difference to Mrs. Carstone. It doesn't. Walshawe, first and last, died worth a quarter of a million. Mrs. Carstone can easily afford to drop twenty thousand. Twenty thousand is nothing to her. But ten thousand is a lot to Mrs. Whiteside—and to her son."

"To anybody but wealthy people!" exclaimed the detective. "Um! Well, that's news, Mr. Peasegood. But—do you think it has any bearing on the mystery of Walshawe's death?"

Peasegood's eyes and mouth became inscrutable for a minute. Then he smiled.

"You asked me if I'd take anything," he said. "I'll take a little whisky, and I'll smoke a cigar. Then—I'll tell you something."

His face became inscrutable again, and remained so until Marshford had summoned the waiter and his demands for refreshment had been supplied, and he kept silence until he had smoked a good inch of his cigar. When he turned to the detective again it was with a smile that seemed to suggest much.

"I dare say you're as well aware as I am that—especially in professions like yours and mine—men who are practised in deducing one thing from another are apt to think pretty sharply at times," he said. "I thought with unusual sharpness when Mrs. Whiteside revealed the existence of this will and I'd convinced myself that it would stand. Or, rather, I didn't so much think as remember. I remembered—that's the word—remembered."

"Remembered—what?" asked Marshford.

Peasegood bent forward with a sidelong glance at the door, and he tapped the detective's knee.

"I remembered two very striking facts—striking in connection with what we know," he replied, in a whisper. "First that Jane Whiteside's son, her co-beneficiary, is a chemist in London; second, that he was in Flamstock during the evening and night immediately preceding Walshawe's death. That's what I remembered."

Marshford opened his eyes to their widest extent. Once more he whistled.

"Whew!" he exclaimed, supplementing the whistle. "That's—gad, I don't know what that isn't, or—is! Anyway, it's news of rare significance."

"Some people," observed Peasegood, calmly—"some people would call it news of sinister significance. It's news that's worth thinking about, anyway. I," he continued, smiling grimly—"I have been thinking about it ever since I remembered it."

"What have you thought?" asked Marshford.

"Nothing that's very clear yet," replied the solicitor. "But you may be sure that Mrs. Whiteside had long since told her son of the will which she kept locked-up in her private repository for such things. He'd no doubt seen it. And a man will dare much for ten thousand pounds."

"You think he—or he and his mother between them—administered the stuff to Walshawe?" suggested the detective.

"I think," answered Peasegood deliberately; "I think that when a man dies as suddenly as Walshawe did, when it's found that he was poisoned, when it's discovered that two people benefit by his death to the extent of twenty thousand pounds, to be paid to them in cash and unconditionally soon after his decease, and when one of these persons is a man acquainted with drugs and their properties—why, then, it's high time that some inquiry should be made."

"Did you say as much to Mrs. Whiteside?" asked Marshford.

"No, I didn't," replied the solicitor. "All that I said to Mrs. Whiteside was—to ask her why she didn't bring forward this will at once. She replied that she didn't know that there was any occasion for hurry, and that she'd thought she'd wait until things had got settled down a bit."

The detective reflected in silence for a while.

"What about her manner?" he suddenly asked. "You'd have thought—good heavens!—why, if they're guilty, you'd have thought they'd be afraid to bring that will forward. They can't be—fools?"

"Apart from her mysterious way of introducing the subject, the woman's manner was calm enough," answered Peasegood. "And, as to their being fools, you've got to remember this—the *onus probandi* rests on us if we accuse them. We've got to prove—prove, mind you!—that they, or one of them, poisoned Walshawe, I repeat—prove!"

"The man may be the guilty party, his mother may be perfectly innocent," remarked Marshford.

"And the mother may be the guilty party, and the son as innocent as you are," said Peasegood.

Marshford nodded.

"Anyway, there's a motive," he said. "But I can see certain things that are in their favour. And the first is—since the son's a chemist, his knowledge would surely show him a cleverer way of getting rid of Walshawe than that. Considering that he's a chemist, and, of course, supposing that he's guilty, it was clumsy—clumsy."

"I'm not so sure," replied Peasegood. "You've got to remember this—good sleeper as Walshawe boasted himself to be, there's nobody can prove that he didn't take drugs at times. For instance, that particular night he'd been giving a dinner-party, he sat up, to my knowledge—I was one of his guests—until quite two o'clock. He may have said to himself, as on many similar occasions, "I'm a bit excited. I'll take something to make me sleep," and he may have taken this stuff. You can't prove that he hadn't it by him, any more than you can prove that these people—or one of them—contrived to administer it to him. All you can say is this: Walshawe undoubtedly died of veronal poisoning. There is nothing to show that he ever took veronal. Jane Whiteside and Richard Whiteside benefit by his death to the extent of twenty thousand pounds. They had the opportunity of administering—"

"For that matter," said Marshford suddenly, "Jane Whiteside had abundant opportunities—daily opportunities. Why choose that particular night?"

Peasegood got up and began to put on his coat.

"I said, to begin with, that Richard may be the sole guilty party," he answered. "He was in Flamstock that night. He came by the six train that Wednesday evening; he left at eight next morning, having spent the night at the Manor House. And it seems to me that the first thing to do is to find out if Richard Whiteside is in particular need of—his legacy—eh?"

"Just so—just so," agreed Marshford. "Leave that to me. I shall want his address."

Peasegood laid a slip of paper on the table.

"That's his address," he said. "Be cautious, Marshford. Well, I'm going."

The detective accompanied his visitor downstairs. In the hall, a little, middle-aged, blue-spectacled man, who carried a bag and a travelling-rug, was booking a room at the office window. And when the detective came back from the door, after saying "good night" to Peasegood, the landlady called to him, glancing at the new arrival.

"Here's a gentleman asking for you, Mr. Marshford," she said.

The little, blue-spectacled man made a bow, and presented the detective with a card.

"My name and address, sir," he said politely, in a sharp, businesslike fashion. "Can I have a few words with you?"

Marshford looked at the card, and read:

"William W. Williams, M.P.S., Dispensing and Family Chemist, The Pharmacy, Llandinas."

"Come this way, Mr. Williams," responded Marshford.

And as he led his second caller up the stairs, he said to himself that the evening was certainly yielding fruit. For he had no doubt whatever that Mr. William W. Williams had come to tell him something about the Walshawe case.

3
The Scientific Visitor

Once within the private sitting-room the caller unwound the shawl and comforter in which he was swathed, and took off a heavy travelling overcoat that lay beneath them. He then presented himself as a little, spare man of active frame and movements. What Marshford could see of his eyes beneath his spectacles, and his mouth beneath his beard and moustache, seemed to show that his mind was as active as his body.

He bustled into the chair which Peasegood had just vacated, accepted the detective's offer of a drink with ready cordiality, and, having expressed his thanks in a set phrase, clapped his hands on his knees and looked searchingly at his host.

"I have come a long way to see you, Mr. Marshford," he said. "Yes, indeed, a long way I have come, sir?"

"That shows that you want to see me on important business, Mr. Williams," observed Marshford. "I gather that, of course."

"Important business, sir; oh, yes, indeed! Of the first importance, in my opinion, Mr. Marshford," replied the visitor. He cleared his throat, as if he meant to indulge in a lengthy speech. "I have read what has been in the papers, sir, about Mr. Septimus Walshawe," he began. "I gathered from the papers that you are in charge of that case?"

"I am," said Marshford. "And if you can throw any light on it, I shall be much obliged to you."

Williams again cleared his throat.

"I can, sir," he answered. "Yes, indeed I can. I knew the late Mr. Septimus Walshawe, sir, though I have not set eyes on him for twenty-five years. Mr. Walshawe, sir, used to live in Llandinas, and though I have not seen Mr. Walshawe since he left—five-and-twenty years ago—I know something about him which, as I gather from the papers, nobody here in Flamstock knows, and you do not know, either. Yes, indeed!"

"Yes?" said Marshford. "What?"

Williams drew his chair close to the detective's. He wagged his head with a knowing air.

"This, sir," he said. "The late Septimus Walshawe was a victim of drugs—or, rather, of one drug. Of one drug, Mr. Marshford."

"What drug?" asked Marshford quietly.

Williams slapped his knees, put his face close to the detective's and rapped out one word.

"Opium!" he said. "Opium!"

Marshford stared silently at his visitor for a minute or two. Here, indeed, was a revelation which he had not expected—a revelation which might mean a great deal.

"You're quite sure of what you allege?" he asked at last.

"Allege!" exclaimed the chemist, with a laugh. "I know! Oh, yes, indeed, Mr. Marshford! As if I should come all this way, whatever, to talk about something that I wasn't sure of! Oh, yes; I know, sir!"

"What do you know?" said Marshford.

"I know this," replied Williams. "Mr. Walshawe lived in Llandinas—at a house called Plas Newydd, Mr. Marshford—for five years before he came to live here. Soon after he came into Llandinas, he came to my shop for opium. He told me that he had become accustomed to taking it at times for a certain internal disorder which he had contracted while abroad. I made it up for him in five-grain pills. He had so many a month, and as time went on he began to increase his doses. But when he left our neighbourhood he was not taking so much—not nearly so much—as he did later on."

"How," asked Marshford, "how do you know what he took later on?"

The chemist smiled slyly.

"How do I know indeed?" he said. "Because I have sent him his opium pills to his house here in Flamstock ever since he came here. Yes, indeed; five-and-twenty years I have sent them, once a month. And he needed more and more a month every year. That man, sir, was a victim to the opium habit."

"You sent him a supply of opium pills regularly?" asked Marshford.

"Once a month I sent them—yes," replied Williams. "In a neat box, sir, sealed. Oh, yes; for five-and-twenty years, Mr. Marshford!"

"I thought," remarked Marshford, reflectively, "that a confirmed opium-taker showed marked signs of the vice?"

"Not always, sir—not always! He wouldn't," said Williams. "He was a fresh-coloured, lively-looking man when I knew him, and was to the end, judging from the accounts I've read in the papers. No, sir; I don't think he would show the usual signs much."

"You don't think that anybody else would detect it?" suggested Marshford.

Williams looked round him, and sank his voice to a whisper.

"I think that somebody here did detect it—was well aware of it," he answered. "Yes, indeed, I do, Mr. Marshford—oh, yes!"

"Who?" asked Marshford bluntly.

"Whoever poisoned him," replied the chemist with another sly smile. "Yes, sir—whoever poisoned him."

Marshford considered this suggestion awhile. It was some time before he spoke; meanwhile his visitor sat tapping his knees and watching him.

"Look here, Mr. Williams," said the detective at last. "You've got a theory, and you've come here to tell me what it is. I'm much obliged to you. And now—what is it?"

Williams cleared his throat with one of his sharp, dry coughs.

"This, sir," he said. "It seems certain that somebody wanted to get Walshawe out of the way. That somebody knew that he took opium in the shape of pills—probably knew how many he took, and the chemical value of the pills, and made the veronal up to resemble the pills—so closely, indeed, that Walshawe didn't know they weren't opium pills. Yes, indeed!"

"That argues a certain amount of chemical knowledge, Mr. Williams," said Marshford—"I mean on the part of the poisoner."

"Oh, it does!" agreed Williams. "Or it argues that the poisoner knew where to get veronal made up in the form and of the strength he wanted. Oh, yes!"

"That's your theory?" said Marshford.

"That's my theory, sir," answered the chemist. "I formed that theory as soon as I read the case in the papers. And having business in London to-morrow I took this place on my way so that I could tell you what I thought. And I venture to predict, sir, that if you ever do get to the bottom of this mystery, you'll find that theory to be correct. Yes, indeed! You don't know of anything that fits in with it, I suppose?"

"I may tell you something about that later, Mr. Williams," replied Marshford. "I suppose you are going to stay the night here?"

The chemist rose and began to gather together his belongings.

"I am, sir," he said. "I am now about to take some much-needed refreshment, and then I am going to bed—I have had a long journey, whatever. I shall have the pleasure of seeing you in the morning, Mr. Marshford?"

"Yes, that's it—see me in the morning," replied Marshford. "I'm going to think over what you've told me."

He sat for some time after the chemist had gone away, thinking steadily on the news just given to him. He was beginning to see a clear line now as regards the administration of the veronal, and it certainly seemed to lead to a strong suggestion of the guilt of the Whitesides, mother and son—or, at any rate, one or other of them. It might be that both were concerned; it might be that only the son was concerned. And it might be that the son was innocent and the mother guilty.

"Anyhow," he murmured, as he drew up a chair to the writing-desk, "the first thing to do is to find out all about the son, and I'll set Chivvins on to that at once."

But he had scarcely written a line of his letter when the old waiter put his grey head inside the door again and announced the third visitor of the evening.

4

The Imaginative Visitor

"Mr. Pitt-Carnaby, sir," said the waiter, mouthing the double-barrelled name with a reverence which showed Marshford that this latest caller was a person of importance. He bowed the visitor in and moved across the room on pretence of mending the fire. "Followed me straight in, sir—wouldn't wait," he whispered to the detective as he passed him.

Marshford looked up from his writing and recognised an elderly gentleman whom he had once or twice seen in the streets of Flamstock and who was chiefly remarkable for the fact that he always wore a knickerbocker suit and a Scotch cap with ribbons depending from its hinder end. He was a bearded and spectacled gentleman. Marshford, on the rare occasions on which he had seen him, had set him down as being a little eccentric. All the same Mr. Pitt-Carnaby looked business-like enough as he took the chair which had already been twice occupied that evening.

"Allow me to introduce myself," said the third visitor. "I am Mr. Pitt-Carnaby, of the Hollies. I have come to speak to you about Mr. Walshawe's mysterious death. Mr. Walshawe was one of my colleagues on the magisterial bench; he was also a personal friend of mine. We had many tastes in common—we were, for instance, both collectors of antiquities. Naturally, I have thought and reflected a great deal on the circumstances of his sudden decease."

"I should be very glad of any information, sir," replied Marshford, almost mechanically. He was not greatly disposed to listen to any further theorisings that night, and he wanted to write his letter to Chivvins. "Is there something you can tell?" he asked.

Mr. Pitt-Carnaby smiled.

"That is a very definite question," he answered. "Perhaps I can't reply to it quite so definitely. However, I will say what I came to say. Has it ever struck you, in the exercise of your calling, that imagination is a very valuable asset?"

Marshford was not quite clear as to his visitor's meaning, and he said so.

"Some people," continued Mr. Pitt-Carnaby, "bring science—in some shape or other—to bear on these things; I believe that imagination is a surer thing—eh?"

Marshford began to fear that he was in for a very long dissertation from an obvious crank. Nevertheless, it was impossible to get rid of Mr. Pitt-Carnaby in summary fashion.

"I suppose you have some theory, sir?" he said, thinking it best to put a direct question.

But the visitor was evidently not the sort of man to be forced into answering direct questions.

"I have allowed my imagination to play round the closing hours of my unfortunate friend's life," he said. "Perhaps the result is a theory, though I won't call it so. Instead, I will invite your attention to a few facts. And please to understand that I am not going to mention any names. If I make suggestions, I shall leave you to follow them up."

Marshford's face lightened; suggestions and facts—especially facts—were things with which he could deal. He left the mantelpiece, against which he had been leaning, and took a chair close to his visitor. Mr. Pitt-Carnaby noticed the sudden revival of interest and smiled.

"Very well!" he said. "The late Mr. Walshawe was, like myself, a collector of books, curiosities, and antiquities. On the evening before his death he entertained some friends—myself amongst them—at dinner. Our conversation during the evening turned very largely on a sale by auction which was to be held next day at a certain country house in this neighbourhood. Many interesting articles were to be offered; the late tenant of the house in question had been a great collector. Amongst those articles was a jar, fashioned of malachite, which, as you may or may not know, Mr. Marshford, is a mineral scientifically known as basic cupric carbonate. This jar was of the finer quality of malachite—the malachite found in a certain district in Siberia, which is used in the manufacture of mosaics and ornaments. Also, it has a well-authenticated history—it had once belonged to Peter the Great of Russia, and it was given by him, during his stay in England in 1698, to an ancestor of the gentleman whose effects were being disposed of. Mr. Walshawe was very anxious to acquire this malachite jar. He had a collection of articles which had belonged to

Tsars and Tsarinas of Russia during the past two centuries, and he wished to add this to it. Concentrate your attention, then, Mr. Marshford, on the fact that on the evening before his death Mr. Walshawe's mind was fixed on buying a certain malachite jar which was to be offered for sale nearly twenty miles away at about one o'clock next day."

Marshford nodded silently. He was beginning to think that something might come out of this. And Mr. Pitt-Carnaby saw his increasing interest, and went on with his story.

"I repeat," he said, "for it is a highly important point, that Mr. Walshawe was absolutely determined to buy this antique. At dinner that night he talked of it a great deal; he said what figure he would go to—a heavy one. He anticipated a certain amount of opposition, for the jar was famous, and there were likely to be competitors from London, and even from Paris. However, Mr. Walshawe was, as you know, a man of very large means, and he meant to outbid anybody and everybody. When I left him, a good deal after midnight, he was still gloating over his determination to carry home the malachite jar in triumph from the sale."

"And he never went to the sale," remarked Marshford reflectively.

"He never went to the sale—true!" replied Mr. Pitt-Carnaby. "We know, of course, that when that sale began, my unfortunate friend was dead. But I went to the sale, as also did several of my fellow-guests of the previous evening. We expected to meet Mr. Walshawe there, but he never arrived. One o'clock came—he was still absent. At a quarter-past one the famous malachite jar was put up—Mr. Walshawe was not there to bid for it. There were many competitors—there were competitors from London and from Paris, as we had thought likely. The bidding began at five hundred guineas and advanced to two thousand guineas, at which sum the malachite jar was knocked down."

"To whom?" asked Marshford, eagerly.

Mr. Pitt-Carnaby rose, and picked up his Scotch cap, his stout stick, and his hand-knitted gloves.

"I said I should mention no names," he said with a smile, "but one name I must mention. The malachite jar was sold for two thousand guineas to John Pethington, the house and estate agent in our High Street. Of course, Pethington bought for somebody else. Well, I must now say good-night, Mr. Marshford."

"But," exclaimed Marshford, surprised at this sudden termination of the visit, "but—what do you expect me to do? What—"

Mr. Pitt-Carnaby wandered towards the door.

"Oh, what you please!" he answered. "Of course, if I were in your case, I should find out from Pethington the name of the person for whom he bought the malachite jar."

"And then?" asked Marshford.

Mr. Pitt-Carnaby laid his hand on the door and turned with a sharp look.

"Then?" he said. "Then you will have the name of the man who poisoned Septimus Walshawe!"

5
The Plain Truth

Marshford looked at his watch when Mr. Pitt-Carnaby had departed. It was close upon ten o'clock. He believed that most people in Flamstock went to bed at ten o'clock; nevertheless, there was a possibility that some did not. Anyway, it would do him no harm to take a stroll up the High Street. And he threw the scarcely begun letter to Chivvins into the fire, and, putting on his ulster and a travelling cap, went out into the night.

There were lights in the windows of Mr. Pethington's house, and when Marshford rang the bell, Mr. Pethington, a fat-faced, stolid-looking man, answered the summons in person. As the light of his hall-lamp fell on Marshford's face Pethington silently moved aside, motioning the detective to enter. When Marshford stepped within, Pethington just as silently showed him into a small room near the door. He turned up a solitary gas-jet, and looked at his visitor with the calm interrogation of a man who expects to be asked questions.

"You know me, Mr. Pethington, and what my business is?" said Marshford, in a low voice. "I can take that for granted, of course?"

Pethington leaned back against his desk, and put his hands in his pockets.

"I don't know what it is at present," he answered, "I know what you're after in the town, of course."

"I want to ask a very simple question," said Marshford. "It's one which you'll have to answer sooner or later, and I wish you'd answer it now. For whom did you purchase that malachite jar? You know what I mean."

Pethington showed no surprise. Instead, he merely nodded, as if he had expected to have this question put to him, and he pulled out his watch, noting the time.

"Instead of asking me to answer that question, Mr. Marshford," he said, "I wish you'd just step round to the police-station."

Marshford stared at this unexpected reply.

"Why?" he exclaimed.

"Because I think you'll get an answer to it there," replied Pethington, dropping his watch into his pocket.

The two men exchanged looks. Then Pethington nodded.

"You'll find I'm right," he said.

Marshford went away from the house without a word. He walked rapidly up the deserted High Street towards the town hall, wondering what this sudden development implied. And suddenly, rounding a corner, and in the full light of a street-lamp, he ran into Peasegood.

"I was just coming to you," said the solicitor. "Well, the truth's out at last—just got it. Good heavens, what a world this is!"

"What is it?" demanded Marshford. "You don't mean that somebody's confessed to poisoning Walshawe?"

"That's just what I do mean," replied Peasegood; "the last man in the world I should have suspected, too!"

"Who, then?" exclaimed Marshford.

Peasegood took off his hat and wiped his forehead. Then he spoke one word—a name:

"Thorney!"

"What!" said Marshford. "The doctor?"

"The doctor!" repeated Peasegood. "He's just told the inspector and me all about it. It was by inadvertence. Dr. Thorney, you must know, is an ardent collector of certain things, as Walshawe was. He was bent on having a certain jar of malachite, with a history attached to it, which was to be put up at that sale I told you of. Walshawe was bent on it, too—vowed he'd have it. Thorney—you know that these collectors spare no pains to steal a march on each other—resolved to play a trick on Walshawe. It turned out that Walshawe took opium secretly, in pills—Thorney knew it, and knew where he kept his pills, in a little case on his desk. That night when we all dined there, Thorney got into Walshawe's study by himself, took the opium pills out of the case, and substituted veronal which he'd made up himself. His idea was to make Walshawe sleep far into the next day, until he was too late for the sale. If things had gone as Thorney intended, Walshawe would have slept until the afternoon and been all right after. But Thorney forgot one very important thing."

"What?" asked Marshford, eagerly.

"He didn't know how many opium pills Walshawe did, or could, take," answered the solicitor, "and so you see Walshawe took sufficient veronal to poison him. Misadventure, of course, in Thorney's eyes, but—"

He paused, and looked thoughtfully down the long vista of the High Street as the two men turned away together.

"But—what?" asked Marshford.

"I wonder what the judge will tell the jury to call it?" answered Peasegood.

The Message on the Sun-Dial

J. J. Bell

John Joy Bell (1871–1934) was a Scot who studied chemistry at the University of Glasgow before becoming a journalist with the *Glasgow Evening Times* and a sub-editor for the *Scots Pictorial*. His stories and articles about working-class Scots were often written in the vernacular, and were very popular in their day. *Wee Macgregor* enjoyed particular success, but Bell's sentimentalism is unlikely to appeal to fans of gritty realism.

This story provides a pleasing example of a trope of the genre, the "dying message clue". This is a plot device beloved of detective novelists, and features in many of Ellery Queen's novels and short stories, as well as in Agatha Christie's *Why Didn't They Ask Evans?* Bell makes a good enough fist of the story to make one think it is a pity that his excursions into detective fiction were few and far between.

◇ ◇ ◇

For a good many weeks the morning mail of Mr. Philip Bolsover Wingard had usually contained something unpleasant,
but never anything quite so unpleasant as the letter, with
its enclosure, now in his hand. And the letter was from his
cousin, Philip Merivale Wingard, the man to whom he owed
more benefits, and whom he hated more, than any man in
the world. Certainly the letter was rather a shocking one to
have place in the morning mail of a gentleman; but, oddly
enough, it had never occurred to Bolsover, as he was com-
monly called to distinguish him from the other Philip, that
he had long since forfeited his last rights to the designation.

The letter was dated from the other Philip's riverside
residence, and ran as follows:

Cousin Bolsover,

I send you herewith an appeal just received from
a deeply injured woman, to whom you have apparently given my name, instead of your own. This ends
our acquaintance. If you insist on a further reason, I
would merely mention your forgery of my name to a
bill for £500, which fact has also been brought to my
notice this morning. In the face of these two crimes
it does not seem worth while to remind you that for
seven years I have tried to believe in you and to help
you in a material way.

You will receive this in the morning, and it gives
you forty-eight hours to be out of this country. Within
that time there is a sailing for South Africa. My banker
has received instructions to pay you £500, one half
of which you shall send to the writer of the enclosed.
On that condition, and so long as you remain abroad,
your forgery is my secret. This is your last chance.

Philip Merivale Wingard.

Bolsover, enduring a sickness almost physical, reread the letter. The enclosure did not trouble him, except is so far as it looked like costing him £250. But the discovery of his forgery shook him, for it was a shock against which he had been altogether unprepared. He had not dreamed of the moneylender showing the bill, which was not due for six weeks, to his cousin. What infernal luck!

Bolsover read the letter a third time, seeking some glimmer of hope, some crevice for escape. Hitherto he had regarded his cousin as a bit of a softy, a person to be gulled or persuaded; but every word of the letter seemed to indicate a heart grown hard, a mind become unyielding.

Go abroad? Why, that would simply be asking for it! The clouds of debt were truly threatening, but if he continued to walk warily at home they might gradually disperse, whereas the outcry that would surely follow his apparent flight would, like an explosion, bring down the deluge of ruin.

What a fool was Philip! It did not occur to Bolsover then that, during all those seven years, he had lived by fooling Philip. And the most maddening thought of all was that had Philip not come back from the Great War he, Bolsover, would be in Philip's place to-day! That, indeed, was the root of the hatred, planted in disappointment and nourished from the beginning on envy and greed, and lately also on chagrin and jealousy, since Philip had won the girl, as wealthy as himself, whom Bolsover had coveted for his own.

Bolsover's mouth was dry. He went over to the neglected breakfast-table, poured shakily a cup of the cooled coffee and drank it off. He took out and opened his cigarette-case. His fingers fumbled a cigarette, and he noticed their trembling. This would not do. He must get command of his nerves, of his wits. Raging was of no use. He lighted the cigarette and sat down.

Somehow he must see Philip; somehow he must prevail on Philip to abate his terms—either that, or induce Philip to pay all his debts. But the total of his debts amounted to thousands, and some of them were owing to persons whom he would fain avoid naming to his straitlaced cousin. Still, he must make the appeal, in the one direction or the other. The situation was past being desperate.

〉〉〉

He knew that his cousin was entertaining a house-party. On the mantelshelf was a dance invitation, received three weeks ago, for that very evening. He did not suppose that Philip would now expect to see him, as a guest; yet for a moment or two he dallied with the idea of presenting himself, as though nothing had happened. But there was the possibility, a big one, too, to judge from this damned letter, that Philip would simply have the servants throw him out!

He looked at his watch—10.20—and went over to the telephone. He ought to have phoned at the outset, he told himself. Philip might have gone out, on the river with his friends, for the day. The prospect of seven or eight hours of uncertainty appalled him.

But at the end of a couple of minutes he heard Philip's voice inquiring who was speaking.

'Philip,' said Bolsover quickly, 'bear with me for a few moments. I have your letter. I must obey it. But, as a last favour, let us have one more meeting. There are things—'

'No! I have nothing to say to you; I wish to hear nothing from you.'

'There are things I can explain.'

'No! Excuse me. My friends are waiting for me. Good—'

'Philip, let your invitation for to-night stand. Let me come, if only for an hour.'

'What! Let you come among those girls, after that letter from that unhappy woman? A thousand times, no!'

'Well, let us meet somewhere, during the evening, outside the house. I shan't keep you long. Look here, Philip! I'll be at the sun-dial, at ten, and wait till you come. Don't refuse the last request I'll ever make of you.'

There was a pause till Philip said coldly:

'Very well. But, I warn you, it can make not the slightest difference.'

'Thank you, Philip. Ten, or a little after?' Bolsover retained the receiver awhile.

But there was no further word from his cousin.

He went back to his chair and sat there, glowering at space. Undeniably there had been a new firmness in his cousin's voice. While he did not doubt that Philip would keep the tryst, he could no longer hope that anything would come of the interview. That being so, what was left for him?

To a man like Bolsover the disgrace was secondary; the paramount dread was a life without money for personal indulgence. He had been cornered before, but never so tightly, it seemed, as now. For the first time in his unworthy career he thought of death as the way of escape, knowing all the while that were he in the very toils of despair, he could never bring himself to take the decided step in death's direction. But he toyed gloomily with the thought, till his imagination began to perceive its other side.

What if Philip were out of the world?

At first the idea was vague and misty, but gradually it became clear, and all at once his mind recoiled, as a man recoils from the brink of a precipice—recoiled, yet only to approach again, cautiously, to survey the depths, searching furtively the steep, lest haply it should provide some safe and secret downward path. And peering into his own idea, Bolsover seemed to see at the bottom of it a pleasant place where freedom was, where fear was not. For while Bolsover had no illusions of inheriting a penny in hard cash from his cousin, he knew that a small landed estate, unencumbered, was bound on his cousin's death to come to him: and on that estate he could surely raise the wherewithal to retrieve his wretched fortunes. The greatest optimist in the world is the most abandoned gambler.

A maid came in to remove the breakfast things.

'Ain't you well this morning, Mr. Wingard?' she inquired. Bolsover, resident in the private hotel for a good many months, had been generous enough in his gratuities to the servants.

'Feeling the heat,' he answered, wiping his brow. 'Dreadfully sultry, isn't it?'

'It *is* 'ot for May. Guess we're going to 'ave a thunderstorm soon. Shall I fetch some fresh coffee, or would you like a cup of tea?'

'Thanks, but I have got to go out now.'

Perhaps he was thankful for the interruption.

◇◇◇

The bank with which his cousin dealt was in the Strand. Feeling weak, he took a taxi thither. He was known at the bank, his cousin's instructions had been duly received, and the money was handed over to him, without delay. He rather overdid his amusement, as he realized afterwards, at his shaky signature on the receipt. 'Looks as if I had been having a late night,' he remarked, passing the paper back to the grave cashier.

As the door swung behind him, he called himself a fool and wiped his face.

He lunched leisurely at an unusually early hour. He preceded the meal with a couple of cocktails, accompanied it with a pint of champagne, and followed it with a liqueur. He felt much better, though annoyed by an unwonted tendency to perspire. On his leaving the restaurant, the tendency became more pronounced, so much so that he feared it must be noticeable, and once more he took a taxi, telling the man to go Kensington way. A little later, he was sitting in a shady part of Kensington Gardens. He had wanted to get away from people.

For a while he felt comfortable in body, and almost easy in mind. He was now quite hopeful that Philip would see the unreasonableness of the terms of that letter, which had obviously been written in haste. After all, his debts amounted to no more than £6,000—well, say, £7,000—a sum that would scarcely trouble his cousin to disburse, especially as it would not be required all at once. No doubt, Philip would kick, to begin with, and deliver a pretty stiff lecture, but in the end he would capitulate. Oh, yes, it had been a black morning, but there would be another story to tell by midnight. Bolsover smoked a cigarette or two, surrendered himself to a pleasant drowsiness, and fell into a doze.

He awoke heavy of limb—hot in the head and parched, and with a great spiritual depression upon him. He must have a drink. He looked at his watch. Only 4.30. His hotel, however, was not far distant, and thither he went on foot.

The hall porter presented an expressed letter which had come at midday. The writing was familiar, and Bolsover was not glad to see it. In his room he helped himself to brandy before opening the letter—a curt warning that a fairly large sum must be paid by noon on the morrow. It acted as a powerful irritant and brought on the silent frenzy against things and persons which had shaken him in the morning.

He took another drink, and presently his fiery wrath at fortune gave place to the old smouldering hate against his cousin, who now seemed to block the road to salvation. He unlocked and opened a drawer, and for a long while sat glowering at the things it contained, a revolver, which he had purchased years ago on the eve of a trip abroad, and a package of cartridges, never opened.

He saw himself at the sun-dial in Philip's garden, the loaded weapon in his pocket. He saw Philip coming in the darkness, from the house with its lights and music. And then he began to realize that the house was not so very far away, and imagined how the report of the revolver would shatter the night. He must think of another way, he concluded, shutting the drawer, and turned to the bottle once more.

It was near to seven o'clock when he went out. He ought to have been drunk, but apparently he was quite sober when he entered the cutler's shop in the Paddington district. He was going abroad on a game-hunting expedition, he explained, and wanted something in the way of a sheath-knife. This was supplied, and with the parcel he returned to the hotel.

After dinner he dressed, not carelessly. The brandy bottle tempted, and he put off the craving with a dose much diluted. He took train to a riverside station, then a cab for the last two miles of the journey. At five minutes before ten he was in his cousin's grounds.

The ancient sun-dial stood in the centre of a rose garden, which was separated from the house by a broad walk, a lawn and a path, and walled round by high, thick hedges. Beyond the bottom of the rose garden was a narrow stretch of turf, and then the river.

◇〉◇

The night was very dark; the atmosphere heavy, breathless. It seemed to Bolsover, waiting by the dial, that the storm might burst at any moment, and his anxiety was intense lest the deluge should descend and prevent the coming of

Philip. Though the knife, loosened in the sheath, lay ready in the pocket of his cloak, he kept telling himself that he would never use it, save as a threat; that he had bought it only to strengthen his courage and purpose. The effects of the alcohol apart, the man was not quite sane. A brain storm was as imminent as the storm of nature.

Peering, listening, he stood by the dial, seeing above the hedge the glow from the open windows, hearing dimly the chatter and laughter of the guests. He had arrived in the garden to the sound of music, but soon it had ceased, and now the pause between the dances seemed very long. He argued that Philip, who doubtless desired secrecy as much as himself, would leave the house only when a dance was in progress, and, fingering the knife's haft, he cursed the idle musicians and the guests resting on the verandah, or strolling on the lawn.

◇◇◇

The minutes passed, and at last the music started again. And when Bolsover, savage with exasperation, was telling himself that another dance was nearly over, he became aware of a sound of footfalls on gravel, and a dark figure, with a glimmer of white, appeared in the gap.

Philip Merivale Wingard came quickly down to the dial and halted opposite his cousin.

'So you are here, in spite of my warning,' he said.

'Philip, I came to ask—'

'Ask nothing. Did you get the money from the bank?'

'Thank you, yes.'

'Have you sent half of it to the woman?'

'Yes,' Bolsover lied. 'Let me explain—'

'No!' the other interrupted. 'I am going to tell you why I am here. I have decided to let you have a further five hundred, which will give you a start, wherever you may settle abroad. It shall go to you as soon as I receive your address there. But I must have your signature to a promise, that for five years you will not attempt to return to this country, without my permission. Will you sign?'

No man is so infamous that he cannot feel insulted. Bolsover felt insulted, and once more the silent frenzy shook him.

'Come,' said Philip, laying a single sheet of notepaper on the smooth table of granite. 'Here is a simple promise written out by myself—I need not say that all between us is private—and here is a pen. I'll hold a match while you sign. Come, man, unless you wish us to be discovered!'

Bolsover, his right hand in his pocket, moved round till he was against his cousin's left arm.

'Take the pen,' said Philip.

'One moment,' Bolsover returned in a thick voice.

He took a step backwards, threw up his arm, and drove the knife down between Philip's shoulders. In that moment he experienced a sort of sickness of astonishment at the ease with which the blade penetrated; in the next moment he stepped back, withdrawing the knife and holding it away from him.

Philip squirmed, made a choking noise, and fell across the broad dial, one hand clutching at the far edge. The paper, dislodged, fluttered to the feet of Bolsover, who picked it up, pocketed it, and retreated up the path, backwards, yet with eyes averted from his handiwork. And having reached a distance of seven yards, he turned right round and stood with hunched shoulders, waiting for the ghastly labouring sound to cease. Had he not killed Philip after all? For a little while he knew not what he did—prayed, may be—and then the end came, a gasping, choking noise, a slithering sound, a soft thud. He turned slowly about. There was a heap, slightly moving on the path under the dial, and then—there was a heap that was very still.

Bolsover remembered his own safety. Running softly on the grass verge, he came to the gap in the lower hedge, passed through, crossed the strip of turf, and halted at the river's edge. From the river came no sound at all. The most enthusiastic of boating people had sensed the coming storm. Gingerly Bolsover fitted the knife into its sheath, and slung it far out into the darkness. He tore the paper into tiny bits, and scattered them on the black water. Slowly they drifted away.

By a roundabout route he reached the main walk leading to the house, and deliberately went forward to the door. The servant in attendance, who knew him as his master's cousin, received him as a late arriving guest; if he noticed his pallor, he was not interested.

And the pallor was not so extreme. Bolsover was playing a part now, and so intent thereon that in a measure he forgot why he was playing it.

Before long he was among the guests, greeting those whom he knew, explaining that he had just arrived and was looking for the host, his cousin. A curate, a particular friend of Philip's, whom Bolsover had always rather disliked, remarked that he thought he had seen Philip go out by the French window of the library, about ten minutes earlier.

'You appear to be feeling the heat, Mr. Wingard,' he added. 'You look quite haggard.'

'Yes, I want a drink,' Bolsover answered somewhat roughly, and was going to get it, when a girl, who with her partner had strayed to the rose garden, ran into the hall, screaming that Mr. Wingard was lying by the sun-dial, dead—murdered!

It had come sooner than Bolsover could have wished, and for the moment he was staggered—but appropriately so. He was the first to recover his wits, and, as was his natural duty, proceeded to take charge, ordering a servant to phone for doctor and police, and requesting several of the men guests to accompany him to the scene, with the elements of first aid, lest life should still be there.

'We shall want lights!' cried Mr. Minn, the curate, whose company Bolsover had not requested. 'I'll get my torch from my overcoat.'

◇◇◇

Several torches were procured, and the party hurried down to the rose garden. The young man, whose partner had brought the alarm to the house, met them with a word of warning to prepare for a dreadful sight.

'He was alive, and no more, when we found him, but he's gone now,' the young man added. 'I'm glad you've come. I've used all my matches.'

'Did he speak?' asked the curate, as the others gathered round the dial.

'Oh, no; didn't even attempt it, poor chap. I fancied, though, that he tried to make signs.'

'How so?'

'Towards the dial above him. And then he collapsed—in my arms. Heavens, I'm all bloody—everything is bloody!'

'Go up to the house and take some whisky,' said the curate kindly. 'But stay a moment! Did you look at the dial? Was there anything unusual about it?'

'Blood—and a fountain pen.'

'A pen!'

'Lying against the pointer.'

'Did you remove it?'

'Didn't touch it. It's a gold pen with a green stone in the top.'

'His own,' said Mr. Minn. 'What on earth—? Well, don't wait, Mr. Marshall. I think you will find the library window open, so you can slip in and ring for a servant to fetch your overcoat to cover the—the stains. This is terrible!' The curate gave way to emotion. 'Poor Philip! My good friend and the best of men!'

Presently he joined the group. Bolsover was speaking.

'I wish we could take him to the house, but dare we do so before the doctor—and the police—have seen him?'

'I'm afraid we must wait,' said a guest.

'I felt a spot of rain just now,' said another. 'We can't let him lie here if the storm breaks. What do you say, Mr. Minn?'

The curate did not seem to hear. He was playing the shuddering light of his torch on the dial.

'Gentlemen,' he said unsteadily, 'please give me your attention for a moment.'

There was a catching of breaths at the sight of the dark pool and rivulets on the smooth grey stone, followed by faint exclamations as the beam caught and lingered on the gold pen.

'His own pen, gentlemen—and with it he has written something on the dial, for there is one line of ink not quite dry—and the nib of the pen has given way.'

The beam moved towards the right, and stopped.

Here was no blood; only some writing—of a sort. The guests leaned forward, peering—all save Bolsover, who shrank back, open-mouthed, the sweat of terror on his skin. Had the dying man left a message?

'Figures!' softly exclaimed a guest.

'Yes,' said Mr. Minn, producing a pencil, following with the point of it the wavering, broken lines and curves. 'A one—a three—a nought—a six—an eight—another nought—and something that might have been a four, had the nib not broken, or had the hand not failed. One, three, nought, six, eight, nought—'

A big drop of rain splashed on his hand, and he started as though it had been blood.

'If the storm breaks now, this message, which may be a clue, will be lost!' he cried. 'Will one of you run to the house and fetch something waterproof to cover the dial? Hurry, please!'

A guest ran off. Another drop fell, and another, on the dial. Mr. Minn handed the torch to his neighbour, saying:

'Kindly, all of you, direct your lights on the figures.' He whipped out a little notebook. 'In case of accidents, I shall make a copy as exactly as possible.'

There was a silence while he drew, rather than wrote down, the figures.

Bolsover's panic had passed. There was nothing in those large ill-formed figures that could in any way draw attention to himself. He cleared his throat, and said:

'Mr. Minn, do these figures convey anything at all to you, as a friend of poor Philip's?'

'Nothing, Mr. Wingard.' Mr. Minn shook his head. 'But whatever their meaning, they must surely represent almost the last thought—if not the very last thought—of our cruelly murdered friend—and an urgent message. Whether or not they may provide the police with a clue—'

There was a blinding glare, a stunning crash, a throbbing silence in the blackness, and the clouds turned, as it seemed, to water.

〉〉〉

The inquest was over, the jury returning an open verdict, the only verdict in keeping with the evidence, as every person in court had agreed. The fact that Philip must have had an enemy made a mystery in itself. The figures written on the dial were a mystery also; a search through Philip's papers had revealed nothing with which they could be connected. Mr. Minn was, however, congratulated by the coroner on the presence of mind which he had shown in recording them.

Bolsover won the sympathy of all by his quiet, frank answers to the coroner's questions, by his tribute to the high character and generosity of his late cousin, and by his sad, pale, stricken appearance. Yes, there was a small estate to come to him, but other expectations he had none, the gifts of his cousin in the past having been almost princely.

On the fatal night, he explained, being detained in town, he had arrived at his cousin's house, shortly after ten. His inquiries for his cousin brought from Mr. Minn the reply that his cousin had gone out, and immediately thereafter came the shocking news. It was possible that the crime in the rose garden was committed while he was walking up the avenue; but if so, it must have been done silently. At this point he had asked for a glass of water, and the coroner had expressed himself satisfied.

On the morrow, he attended the funeral, as chief mourner, looking a wreck of a man. But with the turning away from the grave, the worst was over. He was safe! Only one duty remained—his presence at the reading of the will.

It was not a large gathering, and Bolsover was the person least interested. The will had been made five years ago. Bolsover, his heavy lids almost closing his eyes, listened indifferently till—

'And to my cousin and friend, Philip Bolsover Wingard, the sum of fifty thousand pounds, free of legacy duty.'

He nearly fainted. It was Mr. Minn, the curate, who brought him a drink.

⟩⟩⟩

Lunch had been provided for the mourners, but Bolsover begged to be excused. He was feeling far from well, he said, and wished to consult his doctor in town, without delay.

'I think you are wise, Mr. Wingard,' said Mr. Minn, kindly. 'You are looking ill, and no wonder. But before you go, I would beg for just a few minutes' talk. Let us go to the rose garden, where we shall not be disturbed.'

'Very well,' assented Bolsover. He had hoped never again to enter the rose garden, but did not see how he could reasonably refuse to do so now. Anyway, it would be the final torment.

In silence they crossed the lawn, and passed through the gap in the hedge. In silence, also, since Bolsover had not the speech for protest, they came to the sun-dial.

Mr. Minn bared his head, and said:

'As God Almighty's rain has washed away all the signs of this tragedy, so is His infinite mercy able to wash away the sin that caused it. Amen.'

He replaced his hat and looked very gently and gravely at Bolsover.

'Mr. Wingard, I wish to show you something. I wish to show you Philip's last thought before he died.' So saying he took out his notebook and a scarlet chalk pencil.

'The figures!' muttered Bolsover, wondering.

'Yes,' replied Mr. Minn, and proceeded to copy them carefully from the page to the stone, thus:

'It is strange,' said Mr. Minn, adding a touch to the '3', 'that the truth did not strike us at once. It did not come to me till early this morning. And yet, once we make allowance for the penmanship of a man dying quickly and in pain, struggling to write in the dark, the thing becomes as plain as day.'

'Not to me,' said Bolsover thickly; 'but, as you know, I am worn out and—'

'Only a minute more,' said Mr. Minn gently. 'I want just to tell you that those marks were not figures at all.'

'Then I'm blind.'

'We were all blind, but now we see clearly. Observe that "1" and that "3"; note how they are rather close together. But bring them quite together and we have a "B".' Mr. Minn drew a sprawling 'B' on the dial. 'Then the nought becomes an "O", and what we took for a six is really an "L"—see, I put them down after the "B"—and what might well pass for an eight must now be accepted as an "S"—so! Then we have another "O", and, next, the greater part of a "V"—and there the nib broke, or the hand failed. But surely—surely enough is there, Mr. Wingard, to show you your cousin's last thought, or message.'

On the dial, written in scarlet by Mr. Minn, appeared these two lines:

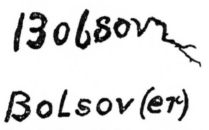

Over the face of Bolsover, gazing dumbly thereon, came a greyish shadow.

Mr. Minn, watching narrowly, raised his left hand as with an effort, while his own countenance paled.

Followed what seemed a long silence. Then, all at once, Bolsover lifted up his face, a dreadful, hunted look in his eyes. His gaze sought the gap in the upper hedge, then fled round to the gap in the lower. In each gap stood a burly man, a stranger.

The curate wiped his eyes.

'My friend,' he said softly, 'I will pray for you.'

The Horror at Staveley Grange

Sapper

"Sapper" was the pen-name used by Herman Cyril McNeile (1888–1937). McNeile was a soldier who was commissioned into the Royal Engineers in 1907, and fought at Ypres and the Somme; he was awarded the Military Cross in 1916. He began to write fiction during the First World War, using a pseudonym because officers on active service were not allowed to publish under their own name. In 1920, he created Hugh "Bulldog" Drummond, who became a popular action hero in a series of thrillers. McNeile had been gassed during the war, and was plagued by ill health; he died of cancer while still quite young.

"The Horror at Staveley Grange" is a rather unexpected piece of work. A personal favourite of the author, this story does not conform to the stereotypical portrayal of Sapper as a crude "blood and thunder" merchant. This is a detective story in the classic mould, offering a well-constructed "impossible crime" puzzle. Drummond is absent, and the mystery is solved by Sapper's second-string hero, Ronald Standish.

◇◇◇

I

'A fact pointing in a certain direction is just a fact: two pointing in the same direction become a coincidence: three—and
you begin to get into the regions of certainty. But you must
be very sure of your facts.'

Thus ran Ronald Standish's favourite dictum: and it was
the astonishing skill with which he seemed to be able to
sort out the facts that mattered from the mass of irrelevant
detail, and having sorted them out, to interpret them cor-
rectly, that had earned him his reputation as a detective of
quite unusual ability.

There is no doubt that had he been under the necessity
of earning his own livelihood, he would have risen to a very
high position at Scotland Yard; or, if he had chosen to set up
on his own, that his career would have been assured. But not
being under any such necessity, his gifts were known only
to a small circle of friends and acquaintances. Moreover, he
was apt to treat the matter as rather a joke—as an interesting
recreation more than a serious business. He regarded it in
much the same light as solving a chess problem or an acrostic.

In appearance he was about as unlike the conventional
detective as it is possible to be. Of medium height, he was
inclined to be thick-set. His face was ruddy, with a short,
closely-clipped moustache—and in his eyes there shone a
perpetual twinkle. In fact most people on first meeting him
took him for an Army officer. He was a first-class man to
hounds, and an excellent shot; a cricketer who might easily
have become first class had he devoted enough time to it,
and a scratch golfer. And last, but not least, he was a man
of very great personal strength without a nerve in his body.

This, then, was the man who sat opposite to me in a first-class carriage of a Great Western express on the way to Devonshire. On the spur of the moment that morning, I had rung him up at his club in London—on the spur of the moment he had thrown over a week's cricket, and arranged to come with me to Exeter. And now that we were actually in the train, I began to wonder if I had brought him on a wild-goose chase. I took the letter out of my pocket—the letter that had been the cause of our journey, and read it through once again.

'Dear Tony,' it ran; 'I am perfectly distracted with worry and anxiety. I don't know whether you saw it in the papers, and it's such ages since we met, but I'm engaged to Billy Mansford. And we're in the most awful trouble. Haven't you got a friend or someone you once told me about who solves mysteries and things? Do, for pity's sake, get hold of him and bring him down here to stay. I'm nearly off my head with it all.—Your distracted Molly.'

I laid the letter on my knee and stared out of the window. Somehow or other I couldn't picture pretty little Molly Tremayne, the gayest and most feckless girl in the world, as being off her head over anything. And having only recently returned from Brazil I had not heard of her engagement— nor did I know anything about the man she was engaged to. But as I say, I rang up Standish on the spur of the moment, and a little to my surprise he had at once accepted.

He leant over at that moment and took the letter off my knee.

'The Old Hall,' he remarked thoughtfully. Then he took a big-scale ordnance map from his pocket and began to study it.

'Three miles approximately from Staveley Grange.'

'Staveley Grange,' I said, staring at him. 'What has Staveley Grange got to do with the matter?'

'I should imagine—everything,' he answered. 'You've been out of the country, Tony, and so you're a bit behindhand. But you may take it from me that it was not the fact that your Molly was distracted that made me give up an excellent I.Z. tour. It was the fact that she is engaged to Mr. William Mansford.'

'Never heard of him,' I said. 'Who and what is he?'

'He is the younger and only surviving son of the late Mr. Robert Mansford,' he answered thoughtfully. 'Six months ago the father was alive—also Tom, the elder son. Five months ago the father died; two months ago Tom died. And the circumstances of their deaths were, to put it mildly, peculiar.'

'Good heavens!' I cried, 'this is all news to me.'

'Probably,' he answered. 'The matter attracted very little attention. But you know my hobby, and it was the coincidence of the two things that attracted my attention. I only know, of course, what appeared in the papers—and that wasn't very much. Mansford senior and both his sons had apparently spent most of their lives in Australia. The two boys came over with the Anzacs, and a couple of years or so after the war they all decided to come back to England. And so he bought Staveley Grange. He had gone a poor man of distinctly humble origin: he returned as a wealthy Australian magnate. Nine months after he stepped into the house he was found dead in his bed in the morning by the butler. He was raised up on his pillows and he was staring fixedly at a top corner of the room by one of the windows. And in his hand he held the speaking tube which communicated with the butler's room. A post-mortem revealed nothing, and the verdict was that he had died of heart failure. In view of the fact that most people do die of heart failure, the verdict was fairly safe.'

Ronald Standish lit a cigarette.

'That was five months ago. Two months ago, one of the footmen coming in in the morning was horrified to find Tom sprawling across the rail at the foot of the bed—stone dead. He had taken over his father's room, and had retired the previous night in the best of health and spirits. Again there was a post-mortem—again nothing was revealed. And again the same verdict was given—heart failure. Of course, the coincidence was commented on in the press, but there the matter rested, at any rate as far as the newspapers were concerned. And therefore that is as much as I know. This letter looks as if further developments were taking place.'

'What an extraordinary affair,' I remarked, as he finished. 'What sort of men physically were the father and Tom?'

'According to the papers,' answered Standish, 'they were two singularly fine specimens. Especially Tom.'

Already we were slowing down for Exeter, and we began gathering our suitcases and coats preparatory to alighting. I leant out of the window as we ran into the station, having wired Molly our time of arrival, and there she was sure enough, with a big, clean-cut man standing beside her, who, I guessed, must be her fiancé. So, in fact, it proved, and a moment or two later we all walked out of the station together towards the waiting motor car. And it was as I passed the ticket collector that I got the first premonition of trouble. Two men standing on the platform, who looked like well-to-do farmers, whispered together a little significantly as Mansford passed them, and stared after him with scarcely veiled hostility in their eyes.

On the way to the Old Hall, I studied him under cover of some desultory conversation with Molly. He was a typical Australian of the best type: one of those open-air, clear-eyed men who came over in their thousands to Gallipoli and France. But it seemed to me that his conversation with Ronald was a little forced; underlying it was a vague uneasiness—a haunted fear of something or other. And I thought he was studying my friend with a kind of desperate hope tinged with disappointment, as if he had been building on Ronald's personality and now was unsatisfied.

That some such idea was in Molly's mind I learned as we got out of the car. For a moment or two we were alone, and she turned to me with a kind of desperate eagerness.

'Is he very clever, Tony—your friend? Somehow I didn't expect him to look quite like that!'

'You may take it from me, Molly,' I said reassuringly, 'that there are very few people in Europe who can see further into a brick wall than Ronald. But he knows nothing of course, as to what the trouble is—any more than I do. And you mustn't expect him to work miracles.'

'Of course not,' she answered. 'But oh! Tony—it's—it's—damnable.'

We went into the house and joined Standish and Mansford, who were in the hall.

'You'd like to go up to your rooms,' began Molly, but Ronald cut her short with a grave smile.

'I think, Miss Tremayne,' he said quietly, 'that it will do you both good to get this little matter off your chests as soon as possible. Bottling things up is no good, and there's some time yet before dinner.'

The girl gave him a quick smile of gratitude and led the way across the hall.

'Let's go into the billiard room,' she said. 'Daddy is pottering round the garden, and you can meet him later. Now, Bill,' she continued, when we were comfortably settled, 'tell Mr. Standish all about it.'

'Right from the very beginning, please,' said Ronald, stuffing an empty pipe in his mouth. 'The reasons that caused your father to take Staveley Grange and everything.'

Bill Mansford gave a slight start.

'You know something about us already then.'

'Something,' answered Ronald briefly. 'I want to know all.'

'Well,' began the Australian, 'I'll tell you all I know. But there are many gaps I can't fill in. When we came back from Australia two years ago, we naturally gravitated to Devonshire. My father came from these parts, and he wanted to come back after his thirty years' absence. Of course he found everything changed, but he insisted on remaining here and we set about looking for a house. My father was a wealthy man—very wealthy, and his mind was set on getting something good. A little pardonable vanity perhaps—but having left England practically penniless to return almost a millionaire—he was determined to get what he wanted regardless of cost. And it was after we had been here about six months that Staveley Grange came quite suddenly on to the market. It happened in rather a peculiar way. Some people of the name of Bretherton had it, and had been living there for about three years. They had bought it, and spent large sums of money on it; introduced a large number of modern improvements, and at the same time preserved all the old appearance. Then, as I say, quite suddenly, they left the house and threw it on the market.

'Well, it was just what we wanted. We all went over it, and found it even more perfect than we had anticipated. The man who had been butler to the Brethertons was in charge, and when we went over, he and his wife were living there alone. We tried to pump them as to why the Brethertons had gone, but they appeared to know no more than we did. The butler—Templeton—was a charming old bird with side-whiskers; his wife, who had been doing cook, was a rather timorous-looking little woman—but a damned good cook.

'Anyway, the long and short of it was, we bought the place. The figure was stiff, but my father could afford it. And it was not until we bought it, that we heard in a roundabout way the reason of the Brethertons' departure. It appeared that old Mrs. Bretherton woke up one night in screaming hysterics, and alleged that a dreadful thing was in the room with her. What it was she wouldn't say, except to babble foolishly about a shining, skinny hand that had touched her. Her husband and various maids came rushing in, and of course the room was empty. There was nothing there at all. The fact of it was that the old lady had had lobster for dinner—and a nightmare afterwards. At least,' added Mansford slowly, 'that's what we thought at the time.'

He paused to light a cigarette.

'Well—we gathered that nothing had been any good. Templeton proved a little more communicative once we were in, and from him we found out, that in spite of every argument and expostulation on the part of old Bretherton, the old lady flatly refused to live in the house for another minute. She packed up her boxes and went off the next day with her maid to some hotel in Exeter, and nothing would induce her to set foot inside the house again. Old Bretherton was livid.'

Mansford smiled grimly.

'But—he went, and we took the house. The room that old Mrs. Bretherton had had was quite the best bedroom in the house, and my father decided to use it as his own. He came to that decision before we knew anything about this strange story, though even if we had, he'd still have used the room. My father was not the man to be influenced by an elderly woman's indigestion and subsequent nightmare.

And when bit by bit we heard the yarn, he merely laughed, as did my brother and myself.

'And then one morning it happened. It was Templeton who broke the news to us with an ashen face, and his voice shaking so that we could hardly make out what he said. I was shaving at the time, I remember, and when I'd taken in what he was trying to say, I rushed along the passage to my father's room with the soap still lathered on my chin. The poor old man was sitting up in bed propped against the pillows. His left arm was flung half across his face as if to ward off something that was coming: his right hand was grasping the speaking-tube beside the bed. And in his wide-open, staring eyes was a look of dreadful terror.'

He paused as if waiting for some comment or question, but Ronald still sat motionless, with his empty pipe in his mouth. And after a while Mansford continued:

'There was a post-mortem, as perhaps you may have seen in the papers, and they found my father had died from heart failure. But my father's heart, Mr. Standish, was as sound as mine, and neither my brother nor I were satisfied. For weeks he and I sat up in that room, taking it in turns to go to sleep, to see if we could see anything—but nothing happened. And at last we began to think that the verdict was right, and that the poor old man had died of natural causes. I went back to my own room, and Tom—my brother—stayed on in my father's room. I tried to dissuade him, but he was an obstinate fellow, and he had an idea that if he slept there alone he might still perhaps get to the bottom of it. He had a revolver by his side, and Tom was a man who could hit the pip out of the ace of diamonds at ten yards. Well, for a week nothing happened. And then one night I stayed chatting with him for a few moments in his room before going to bed. That was the last time I saw him alive. One of the footmen came rushing in to me the next morning, with a face like a sheet—and before he spoke I knew what must have happened. It was perhaps a little foolish of me—but I dashed past him while he was still stammering at the door—and went to my brother's room.'

'Why foolish?' said Standish quietly.

'Some people at the inquest put a false construction on it,' answered Mansford steadily. 'They wanted to know why I made that assumption before the footman told me.'

'I see,' said Standish. 'Go on.'

'I went into the room, and there I found him. In one hand he held the revolver, and he was lying over the rail at the foot of the bed. The blood had gone to his head, and he wasn't a pretty sight. He was dead, of course—and once again the post-mortem revealed nothing. He also was stated to have died of heart failure. But he didn't, Mr. Standish.' Mansford's voice shook a little. 'As there's a God above, I swear Tom never died of heart failure. Something happened in that room—something terrible occurred there which killed my father and brother as surely as a bullet through the brain. And I've *got* to find out what it was: I've *got* to, you understand—because'—and here his voice faltered for a moment, and then grew steady again—'because there are quite a number of people who suspect me of having murdered them both.'

'Naturally,' said Standish, in his most matter of fact tone. 'When a man comes into a lot of money through the sudden death of two people, there are certain to be lots of people who will draw a connection between the two events.'

He stood up and faced Mansford.

'Are the police still engaged on it?'

'Not openly,' answered the other. 'But I know they're working at it still. And I can't and won't marry Molly with this cloud hanging over my head. I've got to disprove it.'

'Yes, but, my dear, it's no good to me if you disprove it by being killed yourself,' cried the girl. Then she turned to Ronald. 'That's where we thought that perhaps you could help us, Mr. Standish. If only you can clear Bill's name, why—'

She clasped her hands together beseechingly, and Standish gave her a reassuring smile.

'I'll try, Miss Tremayne—I can't do more than that. And now I think we'll get to business at once. I want to examine that bedroom.'

II

Ronald Standish remained sunk in thought during the drive to Staveley Grange. Molly had not come with us, and neither Mansford nor I felt much inclined for conversation. He, poor devil, kept searching Ronald's face with a sort of pathetic eagerness, almost as if he expected the mystery to be already solved.

And then, just as we were turning into the drive Ronald spoke for the first time.

'Have you slept in that room since your brother's death, Mansford?'

'No,' answered the other, a little shamefacedly. 'To tell the truth, Molly extracted a promise from me that I wouldn't.'

'Wise of her,' said Standish tersely, and relapsed into silence again.

'But you don't think—' began Mansford.

'I think nothing,' snapped Standish, and at that moment the car drew up at the door.

It was opened by an elderly man with side-whiskers, whom I placed as the butler—Templeton. He was a typical, old-fashioned manservant of the country-house type, and he bowed respectfully when Mansford told him what we had come for.

'I am thankful to think there is any chance, sir, of clearing up this terrible mystery,' he said earnestly. 'But I fear, if I may say so, that the matter is beyond earthly hands.' His voice dropped, to prevent the two footmen overhearing. 'We have prayed, sir, my wife and I, but there are more things in heaven and earth than we can account for. You wish to go to the room, sir? It is unlocked.'

He led the way up the stairs and opened the door.

'Everything, sir, is as it was on the morning when Mr. Tom—er—died. Only the bedclothes have been removed.'

He bowed again and left the room, closing the door.

'Poor old Templeton,' said Mansford. 'He's convinced that we are dealing with a ghost. Well, here's the room, Standish—just as it was. As you see, there's nothing very peculiar about it.'

Ronald made no reply. He was standing in the centre of the room taking in the first general impression of his surroundings. He was completely absorbed, and I made a warning sign to Mansford not to speak. The twinkle had left his eyes: his expression was one of keen concentration. And, after a time, knowing the futility of speech, I began to study the place on my own account.

It was a big, square room, with a large double bed of the old-fashioned type. Over the bed was a canopy, made fast to the two bedposts at the head, and supported at the foot by two wires attached to the two corners of the canopy and two staples let into the wall above the windows. The bed itself faced the windows, of which there were two, placed symmetrically in the wall opposite, with a writing-table in between them. The room was on the first floor in the centre of the house, and there was thus only one outside wall—that facing the bed. A big open fireplace and a lavatory basin with water laid on occupied most of one wall; two long built-in cupboards filled up the other. Beside the bed, on the fireplace side, stood a small table, with a special clip attached to the edge for the speaking-tube. In addition there stood on this table a thing not often met with in a private house in England. It was a small, portable electric fan, such as one finds on board ship or in the tropics.

There were two or three easy chairs standing on the heavy pile carpet, and the room was lit by electric light. In fact the whole tone was solid comfort, not to say luxury; it looked the last place in the world with which one would have associated anything ghostly or mysterious.

Suddenly Ronald Standish spoke.

'Just show me, will you, Mansford, as nearly as you can, exactly the position in which you found your father.'

With a slight look of repugnance, the Australian got on to the bed.

'There were bedclothes, of course, and pillows which are not here now, but allowing for them, the poor old man was hunched up somehow like this. His knees were drawn up: the speaking-tube was in his hand, and he was staring towards that window.'

'I see,' said Standish. 'The window on the right as we look at it. And your brother, now. When he was found he was lying over the rail at the foot of the bed. Was he on the right side or the left?'

'On the right,' said Mansford, 'almost touching the upright.'

Once again Standish relapsed into silence and stared thoughtfully round the room. The setting sun was pouring in through the windows, and suddenly he gave a quick exclamation. We both glanced at him and he was staring up at the ceiling with a keen, intent look on his face. The next moment he had climbed on to the bed, and, standing up, he examined the two wire stays which supported the canopy. He touched each of them in turn, and began to whistle under his breath. It was a sure sign that he had stumbled on something, but I knew him far too well to make any comment at that stage of the proceedings.

'Very strange,' he remarked at length, getting down and lighting a cigarette.

'What is?' asked Mansford eagerly.

'The vagaries of sunlight,' answered Standish, with an enigmatic smile. He was pacing up and down the room smoking furiously, only to stop suddenly and stare again at the ceiling.

'It's the clue,' he said slowly. 'It's the clue to everything. It must be. Though what that everything is I know no more than you. Listen, Mansford, and pay careful attention. This trail is too old to follow: in sporting parlance the scent is too faint. We've got to get it renewed: we've got to get your ghost to walk again. Now I've only the wildest suspicions to go on, but I have a feeling that that ghost will be remarkably shy of walking if there are strangers about. I'm just gambling on one very strange fact—so strange as to make it impossible to be an accident. When you go downstairs I shall adopt the rôle of advising you to have this room shut up. You will laugh at me, and announce your intention of sleeping in this room to-night. You will insist on clearing this matter up. Tony and I will go, and we shall return later to the grounds, where I see there is some very good cover. You will come to bed here—you will get into bed and switch out the light. You will give it a quarter of an hour, and then you will drop out of the window and join us. And we shall see if anything happens.'

'But if we're all outside, how can we?' cried Mansford.

Standish smiled grimly. 'You may take it from me,' he remarked, 'that if my suspicions are correct the ghost will leave a trail. And it's the trail I'm interested in—not the ghost. Let's go and don't forget your part.'

'But, my God! Standish—can't you tell me a little more?'

'I don't know any more to tell you,' answered Standish gravely. 'All I can say is—as you value your life don't fall asleep in this room. And don't breathe a word of this conversation to a soul.'

Ten minutes later he and I were on our way back to the Old Hall. True to his instructions Mansford had carried out his rôle admirably, as we came down the stairs and stood talking in the hall. He gave it to be understood that he was damned if he was going to let things drop: that if Standish had no ideas on the matter—well, he was obliged to him for the trouble he had taken—but from now on he was going to take the matter into his own hands. And he proposed to start that night. He had turned to one of the footmen standing by, and had given instructions for the bed to be made up, while Ronald had shrugged his shoulders and shaken his head.

'Understandable, Mansford,' he remarked, 'but unwise. My advice to you is to have that room shut up.'

And the old butler, shutting the door of the car, had fully agreed.

'Obstinate, sir,' he whispered, 'like his father. Persuade him to have it shut up, sir—if you can. I'm afraid of that room—afraid of it.'

'You think something will happen to-night, Ronald,' I said as we turned into the Old Hall.

'I don't know, Tony,' he said slowly. 'I'm utterly in the dark—utterly. And if the sun hadn't been shining to-day while we were in that room, I shouldn't have even the faint glimmer of light I've got now. But when you've got one bit of a jig-saw, it saves trouble to let the designer supply you with a few more.'

And more than that he refused to say. Throughout dinner he talked cricket with old Tremayne: after dinner he played him at billiards. And it was not until eleven o'clock that he made a slight sign to me, and we both said good-night.

'No good anyone knowing, Tony,' he said as we went upstairs. 'It's an easy drop from my window to the ground. We'll walk to Staveley Grange.'

The church clock in the little village close by was striking midnight as we crept through the undergrowth towards the house. It was a dark night—the moon was not due to rise for another three hours—and we finally came to a halt behind a big bush on the edge of the lawn from which we could see the house clearly. A light was still shining from the windows of the fatal room, and once or twice we saw Mansford's shadow as he undressed. Then the light went out, and the house was in darkness: the vigil had begun.

For twenty minutes or so we waited, and Standish began to fidget uneasily.

'Pray heavens! he hasn't forgotten and gone to sleep,' he whispered to me, and even as he spoke he gave a little sigh of relief. A dark figure was lowering itself out of the window, and a moment or two later we saw Mansford skirting the lawn. A faint hiss from Standish and he'd joined us under cover of the bush.

'Everything seemed perfectly normal,' he whispered. 'I got into bed as you said—and there's another thing I did too. I've tied a thread across the door, so that if the ghost goes in that way we'll know.'

'Good,' said Standish. 'And now we can compose ourselves to wait. Unfortunately we mustn't smoke.'

Slowly the hours dragged on, while we took it in turns to watch the windows through a pair of night glasses. And nothing happened—absolutely nothing. Once it seemed to me as if a very faint light—it was more like a lessening of the darkness than an actual light—came from the room, but I decided it must be my imagination. And not till nearly five o'clock did Standish decide to go into the room and explore. His face was expressionless: I couldn't tell whether he was disappointed or not. But Mansford made no effort to conceal his feelings: frankly he regarded the whole experiment as a waste of time.

And when the three of us had clambered in by the window he said as much.

'Absolutely as I left it,' he said. 'Nothing happened at all.'

'Then, for heaven's sake, say so in a whisper,' snapped Standish irritably, as he clambered on to the bed. Once again his objective was the right hand wire stay of the canopy, and as he touched it he gave a quick exclamation. But Mansford was paying no attention: he was staring with puzzled eyes at the electric fan by the bed.

'Now who the devil turned that on,' he muttered. 'I haven't seen it working since the morning Tom died.' He walked round to the door. 'Say, Standish—that's queer. The thread isn't broken—and that fan wasn't going when I left the room.'

Ronald Standish looked more cheerful.

'Very queer,' he said. 'And now I think, if I was you, I'd get into that bed and go to sleep—first removing the thread from the door. You're quite safe now.'

'Quite safe,' murmured Mansford. 'I don't understand.'

'Nor do I—as yet,' returned Standish. 'But this I will tell you. Neither your father nor your brother died of heart failure, through seeing some dreadful sight. They were foully murdered, as, in all probability you would have been last night had you slept in this room.'

'But who murdered them, and how and why?' said Mansford dazedly.

'That is just what I'm going to find out,' answered Standish grimly.

◇◇◇

As we came out of the breakfast-room at the Old Hall three hours later, Standish turned away from us. 'I'm going into the garden to think,' he said, 'I have a sort of feeling that I'm not being very clever. For the life of me at the moment I cannot see the connection between the canopy wire that failed to shine in the sunlight, and the electric fan that was turned on so mysteriously. I am going to sit under that tree over there. Possibly the link may come.'

He strolled away, and Molly joined me. She was looking worried and *distraite*, as she slipped her hand through my arm.

'Has he found out anything, Tony?' she asked eagerly. 'He seemed so silent and preoccupied at breakfast.'

'He's found out something, Molly,' I answered guardedly, 'but I'm afraid he hasn't found out much. In fact, as far as my brain goes it seems to me to be nothing at all. But he's an extraordinary fellow,' I added, reassuringly.

She gave a little shudder and turned away.

'It's too late, Tony,' she said miserably.

'Oh! if only I'd sent for you earlier. But it never dawned on me that it would come to this. I never dreamed that Bill would be suspected. He's just telephoned through to me: that horrible man McIver—the Inspector from Scotland Yard—is up there now. I feel that it's only a question of time before they arrest him. And though he'll get off—he must get off if there's such a thing as justice—the suspicion will stick to him all his life. There will be brutes who will say that failure to prove that Bill did it, is a very different matter to proving that he didn't. But I'm going to marry him all the same, Tony—whatever he says. Of course, I suppose you know that he didn't get on too well with his father.'

'I didn't,' I answered. 'I know nothing about him except just what I've seen.'

'And the other damnable thing is that he was in some stupid money difficulty. He'd backed a bill or something for a pal and was let down, which made his father furious. Of course there was nothing in it, but the police got hold of it—and twisted it to suit themselves.'

'Well, Molly, you may take it from me', I said reassuringly, 'that Bob Standish is certain he had nothing to do with it.'

'That's not much good, Tony,' she answered with a twisted smile. 'So am I certain, but I can't *prove* it.'

With a little shrug of her shoulders she turned and went indoors, leaving me to my own thoughts. I could see Standish in the distance, with his head enveloped in a cloud of smoke, and after a moment's indecision I started to stroll down the drive towards the lodge. It struck me that I would do some thinking on my own account, and see if by any chance I could hit on some solution which would fit the facts. And the more I thought the more impossible did it appear: the facts at one's disposal were so terribly meagre.

What horror had old Mansford seen coming at him out of the darkness, which he had tried to ward off even as he died? And was it the same thing that had come to his elder son, who had sprung forward revolver in hand, and died as he sprang? And again, who had turned on the electric fan? How did that fit in with the deaths of the other two? No one had come in by the door on the preceding night: no one had got in by the window. And then suddenly I paused, struck by a sudden idea. Staveley Grange was an old house—early sixteenth century; just the type of house to have secret passages and concealed entrances.… There must be one into the fatal room: it was obvious.

Through that door there had crept some dreadful thing—some man, perhaps, and if so the murderer himself—disguised and dressed up to look awe-inspiring. Phosphorus doubtless had been used—and phosphorus skilfully applied to a man's face and clothes will make him sufficiently terrifying at night to strike terror into the stoutest heart. Especially someone just awakened from sleep. That faint luminosity which we thought we had seen the preceding night was accounted for, and I almost laughed at dear old Ronald's stupidity in not having looked for a secret entrance. I was one up on him this time.

Mrs. Bretherton's story came back to me—her so-called nightmare—in which she affirmed she had been touched by a shining skinny hand. Shining—here lay the clue—the missing link. The arm of the murderer only was daubed with phosphorus; the rest of his body was in darkness. And the terrified victim waking suddenly would be confronted with a ghastly shining arm stretched out to clutch his throat.

A maniac probably—the murderer: a maniac who knew the secret entrance to Staveley Grange: a homicidal maniac—who had been frightened in his foul work by Mrs. Bretherton's shrieks, and had fled before she had shared the same fate as the Mansfords. Then and there I determined to put my theory in front of Ronald. I felt that I'd stolen a march on him this time at any rate.

I found him still puffing furiously at his pipe, and he listened in silence while I outlined my solution with a little pardonable elation.

'Dear old Tony,' he said as I finished. 'I congratulate you. The only slight drawback to your idea is that there is no secret door into the room.'

'How do you know that?' I cried. 'You hardly looked.'

'On the contrary, I looked very closely. I may say that for a short while I inclined to some such theory as the one you've just put forward. But as soon as I saw that the room had been papered I dismissed it at once. As far as the built-in cupboard was concerned, it was erected by a local carpenter quite recently, and any secret entrance would have been either blocked over or known to him. Besides McIver has been in charge of this case—Inspector McIver from Scotland Yard. Now he and I have worked together before, and I have the very highest opinion of his ability. His powers of observation are extraordinary, and if his powers of deduction were as high he would be in the very first flight. Unfortunately he lacks imagination. But what I was leading up to was this. If McIver failed to find a secret entrance, it would be so much waste of time looking for one oneself. And if he had found one, he wouldn't have been able to keep it dark. We should have heard about it sharp enough.'

'Well, have you got any better idea?' I said a little peevishly. 'If there isn't any secret door, how the deuce was that fan turned on?'

'There is such a thing as a two-way switch,' murmured Ronald mildly. 'That fan was not turned on from inside the room; it was turned on from somewhere else. And the person who turned it on was the murderer of old Mansford and his son.'

I stared at him in amazement.

'Then all you've got to do', I cried excitedly, 'is to find out where the other terminal of the two-way switch is? If it's in someone's room you've got him.'

'Precisely, old man. But if it's in a passage, we haven't. And here, surely, is McIver himself. I wonder how he knew I was here?'

I turned to see a short thick-set man approaching us over the lawn.

'He was up at Staveley Grange this morning,' I said. 'Mansford telephoned through to Molly.'

'That accounts for it then,' remarked Standish, waving his hand at the detective. 'Good morning, Mac.'

'Morning, Mr. Standish,' cried the other. 'I've just heard that you're on the track, so I came over to see you.'

'Splendid,' said Standish. 'This is Mr. Belton—a great friend of mine—who is responsible for my giving up a good week's cricket and coming down here. He's a friend of Miss Tremayne's.'

McIver looked at me shrewdly.

'And therefore of Mr. Mansford's, I see.'

'On the contrary,' I remarked, 'I never met Mr. Mansford before yesterday.'

'I was up at Staveley Grange this morning,' said McIver, 'and Mr. Mansford told me you'd all spent the night on the lawn.'

I saw Standish give a quick frown, which he instantly suppressed.

'I trust he told you that in private, McIver.'

'He did. But why?'

'Because I want it to be thought that he slept in that room,' answered Standish. 'We're moving in deep waters, and a single slip at the present moment may cause a very unfortunate state of affairs.'

'In what way?' grunted McIver.

'It might frighten the murderer,' replied Standish. 'And if he is frightened, I have my doubts if we shall ever bring the crime home to him. And if we don't bring the crime home to him, there will always be people who will say that Mansford had a lot to gain by the deaths of his father and brother.'

'So you think it was murder?' said McIver slowly, looking at Standish from under his bushy eyebrows.

Ronald grinned. 'Yes, I quite agree with you on that point.'

'I haven't said what I think!' said the detective.

'True, McIver—perfectly true. You have been the soul of discretion. But I can hardly think that Scotland Yard would allow themselves to be deprived of your valuable services for two months while you enjoyed a rest cure in the country. Neither a ghost nor two natural deaths would keep you in Devonshire.'

McIver laughed shortly.

'Quite right, Mr. Standish. I'm convinced it's murder: it must be. But frankly speaking, I've never been so absolutely floored in all my life. Did you find out anything last night?'

Standish lit a cigarette.

'Two very interesting points—two extremely interesting points, I may say, which I present to you free, gratis and for nothing. One of the objects of oil is to reduce friction, and one of the objects of an electric fan is to produce a draught. And both these profound facts have a very direct bearing on...' He paused and stared across the lawn. 'Hullo! here is our friend Mansford in his car. Come to pay an early call, I suppose.'

The Australian was standing by the door talking to his fiancée, and after a glance in their direction, McIver turned back to Ronald.

'Well, Mr. Standish, go on. Both those facts have a direct bearing on—what?'

But Ronald Standish made no reply. He was staring fixedly at Mansford, who was slowly coming towards us talking to Molly Tremayne. And as he came closer, it struck me that there was something peculiar about his face. There was a dark stain all round his mouth, and every now and then he pressed the back of his hand against it as if it hurt.

'Well, Standish,' he said with a laugh, as he came up, 'here's a fresh development for your ingenuity. Of course,' he added, 'it can't really have anything to do with it, but it's damned painful. Look at my mouth.'

'I've been looking at it,' answered Ronald. 'How did it happen?'

'I don't know. All I can tell you is that about an hour ago it began to sting like blazes and turn dark red.'

And now that he had come closer, I could see that there was a regular ring all round his mouth, stretching up almost to his nostrils and down to the cleft in his chin. It was dark and angry-looking, and was evidently paining him considerably.

'I feel as if I'd been stung by a family of hornets,' he remarked. 'You didn't leave any infernal chemical in the telephone, did you, Inspector McIver?'

'I did not,' answered the detective stiffly, to pause in amazement as Standish uttered a shout of triumph.

'I've got it!' he cried. 'The third point—the third elusive point. Did you go to sleep this morning as I suggested, Mansford?'

'No, I didn't,' said the Australian, looking thoroughly mystified. 'I sat up on the bed puzzling over that darned fan for about an hour, and then I decided to shave. Well, the water in the tap wasn't hot, so—'

'You blew down the speaking-tube to tell someone to bring you some,' interrupted Standish quietly.

'I did,' answered Mansford. 'But how the devil did you know?'

'Because one of the objects of a speaking-tube, my dear fellow, is to speak through. Extraordinary how that simple point escaped me. It only shows, McIver, what I have invariably said: the most obvious points are the ones which most easily elude us. Keep your most private papers loose on your writing-table, and your most valuable possessions in an unlocked drawer, and you'll never trouble the burglary branch of your insurance company.'

'Most interesting,' said McIver with ponderous sarcasm. 'Are we to understand, Mr. Standish, that you have solved the problem?'

'Why, certainly,' answered Ronald, and Mansford gave a sharp cry of amazement. 'Oil reduces friction, an electric fan produces a draught, and a speaking-tube is a tube to speak through secondarily; primarily, it is just—a tube. For your further thought, McIver, I would suggest to you that Mrs. Bretherton's digestion was much better than is popularly supposed, and that a brief perusal of some chemical work, bearing in mind Mr. Mansford's remarks that he felt as if he'd been stung by a family of hornets, would clear the air.'

'Suppose you cease jesting, Standish,' said Mansford a little brusquely. 'What exactly do you mean by all this?'

'I mean that we are up against a particularly clever and ingenious murderer,' answered Standish gravely. 'Who he is—I don't know; why he's done it—I don't know; but one thing I do know—he is a very dangerous criminal. And we want to catch him in the act. Therefore, I shall go away to-day; McIver will go away to-day; and you, Mansford, will sleep in that room again to-night. And this time, instead of you joining us on the lawn—we shall all join you in the room. Do you follow me?'

'I follow you,' said Mansford excitedly. 'And we'll catch him in the act.'

'Perhaps,' said Standish quietly. 'And perhaps we may have to wait a week or so. But we'll catch him, provided no one says a word of this conversation.'

'But look here, Mr. Standish,' said McIver peevishly, 'I'm not going away to-day. I don't understand all this rigmarole of yours, and....'

'My very good Mac,' laughed Standish, 'you trot away and buy a ticket to London. Then get out at the first stop and return here after dark. And I'll give you another point to chew the cud over. Mrs. Bretherton was an elderly and timorous lady, and elderly and timorous ladies, I am told, put their heads under the bedclothes if they are frightened.

Mr. Mansford's father and brother were strong virile men, who do not hide their heads under such circumstances. They died, and Mrs. Bretherton lived. Think it over—and bring a gun to-night.'

◇◇◇

For the rest of the day we saw no sign of Ronald Standish. He had driven off in the Tremayne's car to the station, and had taken McIver with him. And there we understood from the chauffeur they had both taken tickets to London and left the place. Following Ronald's instructions, Mansford had gone back to Staveley Grange, and announced the fact of their departure, at the same time stating his unalterable intention to continue occupying the fatal room until he had solved the mystery. Then he returned to the Old Hall, where Molly, he and I spent the day, racking our brains in futile endeavours to get to the bottom of it.

'What beats me', said Mansford, after we had discussed every conceivable and inconceivable possibility, 'is that Standish can't know any more than we do. We've both seen exactly what he's seen; we both know the facts just as well as he does. We're neither of us fools, and yet he can see the solution—and we can't.'

'It's just there that he is so wonderful,' I answered thoughtfully. 'He uses his imagination to connect what are apparently completely disconnected facts. And you may take it from me, Mansford, that he's very rarely wrong.'

The Australian pulled at his pipe in silence.

'I think we'll find out everything to-night,' he said at length. 'Somehow or other I've got great faith in that pal of yours. But what is rousing my curiosity almost more than how my father and poor old Tom were murdered is who did it? Everything points to it being someone in the house—but in heaven's name, who? I'd stake my life on the two footmen—one of them came over with us from Australia. Then there's that poor old boob Templeton, who wouldn't hurt a fly—and his wife, and the other women servants, who, incidentally, are all new since Tom died. It beats me—beats me utterly.'

For hours we continued the unending discussion, while the afternoon dragged slowly on. At six o'clock Mansford rose to go: his orders were to dine at home. He smiled reassuringly at Molly, who clung to him nervously; then with a cheerful wave of his hand he vanished down the drive. My orders were equally concise: to dine at the Old Hall—wait there until it was dark, and then make my way to the place where Standish and I had hidden the previous night.

It was not till ten that I deemed it safe to go; then slipping a small revolver into my pocket, I left the house by a side door and started on my three-mile walk.

As before, there was no moon, and in the shadow of the undergrowth I almost trod on Ronald before I saw him.

'That you, Tony?' came his whisper, and I lay down at his side. I could dimly see McIver a few feet away, and then once again began the vigil. It must have been about half-past eleven that the lights were switched on in the room, and Mansford started to go to bed. Once he came to the window and leaned out, seeming to stare in our direction; then he went back to the room, and we could see his shadow as he moved about. And I wondered if he was feeling nervous.

At last the light went out, and almost at once Standish rose.

'There's no time to lose,' he muttered. 'Follow me—and not a sound.'

Swiftly we crossed the lawn and clambered up the old buttressed wall to the room above. I heard Ronald's whispered greeting to Mansford, who was standing by the window in his pyjamas, and then McIver joined us, blowing slightly.

Climbing walls was not a common form of exercise as far as he was concerned.

'Don't forget,' whispered Standish again, 'not a sound, not a whisper. Sit down and wait.'

He crossed to the table by the bed—the table on which stood the motionless electric fan. Then he switched on a small electric torch, and we watched him eagerly as he took up the speaking-tube. From his pocket he extracted what appeared to be a hollow tube some three inches long, with a piece of material attached to one end. This material he tied carefully round the end of the speaking-tube, thereby forming a connection between the speaking-tube and the short hollow one he had removed from his pocket. And finally he placed a cork very lightly in position at the other end of the metal cylinder. Then he switched off his torch and sat down on the bed. Evidently his preparations were complete; there was nothing to do now but wait.

The ticking of the clock on the mantelpiece sounded incredibly loud in the utter silence of the house. One o'clock struck—then half-past—when suddenly there came a faint pop from near the bed which made me jump violently. I heard Ronald draw in his breath sharply and craned forward to see what was happening. There came a gentle rasping noise, as Standish lit his petrol cigarette lighter. It gave little more light than a flickering glimmer, but it was just enough for me to see what he was doing. He was holding the flame to the end of the hollow tube, in which there was no longer a cork. The little pop had been caused by the cork blowing out. And then to my amazement a blue flame sprang from the end of the tube and burnt steadily. It burnt with a slight hiss, like a bunsen burner in a laboratory—and it gave about the same amount of light. One could just see Ronald's face looking white and ghostly; then he pulled the bed curtain round the table, and the room was in darkness once again.

McIver was sitting next to me and I could hear his hurried breathing over the faint hiss of the hidden flame. And so we sat for perhaps ten minutes, when a board creaked in the room above us.

'It's coming now,' came in a quick whisper from Ronald. 'Whatever I do—don't speak, don't make a sound.'

I make no bones about it, but my heart was going in great sickening thumps. I've been in many tight corners in the course of my life, but this silent room had got my nerves stretched to the limit. And I don't believe McIver was any better. I know I bore the marks of his fingers on my arm for a week after.

'My God! look,' I heard him breathe, and at that moment I saw it. Up above the window on the right a faint luminous light had appeared, in the centre of which was a hand. It wasn't an ordinary hand—it was a skinny, claw-like talon, which glowed and shone in the darkness. And even as we watched it, it began to float downwards towards the bed. Steadily and quietly it seemed to drift through the room— but always towards the bed. At length it stopped, hanging directly over the foot of the bed and about three feet above it.

The sweat was pouring off my face in streams, and I could see young Mansford's face in the faint glow of that ghastly hand, rigid and motionless with horror. Now for the first time he knew how his father and brother had died—or he would know soon. What was this dismembered talon going to do next? Would it float forward to grip him by the throat—or would it disappear as mysteriously as it had come?

I tried to picture the dreadful terror of waking up suddenly and seeing this thing in front of one in the darkened room; and then I saw that Ronald was about to do something. He was kneeling on the bed examining the apparition in the most matter of fact way, and suddenly he put a finger to his lips and looked at us warningly. Then quite deliberately he hit at it with his fist, gave a hoarse cry, and rolled off the bed with a heavy thud.

He was on his feet in an instant, again signing to us imperatively to be silent, and we watched the thing swinging backwards and forwards as if it was on a string. And now it was receding—back towards the window and upwards just as it had come, while the oscillations grew less and less, until, at last it had vanished completely, and the room once more was in darkness save for the faint blue flame which still burnt steadily at the end of the tube.

'My God!' muttered McIver next to me, as he mopped his brow with a handkerchief, only to be again imperatively silenced by a gesture from Standish. The board creaked in the room above us, and I fancied that I heard a door close very gently: then all was still once more.

Suddenly with disconcerting abruptness the blue flame went out, almost as if it had been a gas jet turned off. And simultaneously a faint whirring noise and a slight draught on my face showed that the electric fan had been switched on. Then we heard Ronald's voice giving orders in a low tone. He had switched on his torch, and his eyes were shining with excitement.

'With luck we'll get the last act soon,' he muttered. 'Mansford, lie on the floor, as if you'd fallen off the bed. Sprawl: sham dead, and don't move. We three will be behind the curtain in the window. Have you got handcuffs, Mac?' he whispered as we went to our hiding place. 'Get 'em on as soon as possible, because I'm inclined to think that our bird will be dangerous.'

McIver grunted, and once again we started to wait for the unknown. The electric fan still whirred, and looking through the window I saw the first faint streaks of dawn. And then suddenly Standish gripped my arm; the handle of the door was being turned. Slowly it opened, and someone came in shutting it cautiously behind him. He came round the bed, and paused as he got to the foot. He was crouching—bent almost double—and for a long while he stood there motionless. And then he began to laugh, and the laugh was horrible to hear. It was low and exulting—but it had a note in it which told its own story. The man who crouched at the foot of the bed was a maniac.

'On him,' snapped Ronald, and we sprang forward simultaneously. The man snarled and fought like a tiger—but madman though he was he was no match for the four of us. Mansford had sprung to his feet the instant the fight started, and in a few seconds we heard the click of McIver's handcuffs. It was Standish who went to the door and switched on the light, so that we could see who it was. And the face of the handcuffed man, distorted and maniacal in its fury, was the face of the butler Templeton.

'Pass the handcuffs round the foot of the bed, McIver,' ordered Standish, 'and we'll leave him here. We've got to explore upstairs now.'

McIver slipped off one wristlet, passed it round the upright of the bed and snapped it to again. Then the four of us dashed upstairs.

'We want the room to which the speaking-tube communicates,' cried Standish, and Mansford led the way. He flung open a door, and then with a cry of horror stopped dead in the doorway.

Confronting us was a wild-eyed woman, clad only in her nightdress. She was standing beside a huge glass retort, which bubbled and hissed on a stand in the centre of the room. And even as we stood there she snatched up the retort with a harsh cry, and held it above her head.

'Back,' roared Standish, 'back for your lives.'

But it was not to be. Somehow or other the retort dropped from her hands and smashed to pieces on her own head. And a scream of such mortal agony rang out as I have never heard and hope never to hear again. Nothing could be done for her; she died in five minutes, and of the manner of the poor demented thing's death it were better not to write. For a large amount of the contents of the retort was hot sulphuric acid.

'Well, Mansford,' said Standish a few hours later, 'your ghost is laid, your mystery is solved, and I think I'll be able to play in the last match of that tour after all.'

We were seated in the Old Hall dining-room after an early breakfast and Mansford turned to him eagerly.

'I'm still in the dark,' he said. 'Can't you explain?'

Standish smiled. 'Don't see it yet? Well—it's very simple. As you know, the first thing that struck my eye was that right-hand canopy wire. It didn't shine in the sun like the other one, and when I got up to examine it, I found it was coated with dried oil. Not one little bit of it—but the whole wire. Now that was very strange—very strange indeed. Why should that wire have been coated with oil—and not the other? I may say at once that I had dismissed any idea of psychic phenomena being responsible for your father's and brother's death. That such things exist we know—but they don't *kill* two strong men.

'However, I was still in the dark; in fact, there was only one ray of light. The coating of that wire with oil was *so* strange, that of itself it established with practical certainty the fact that a human agency was at work. And before I left the room that first afternoon I was certain that that wire was used to introduce something into the room from outside. The proof came the next morning. Overnight the wire had been dry; the following morning there was wet oil on it. The door was intact; no one had gone in by the window, and, further, the fan was going. Fact number two. Still, I couldn't get the connection. I admit that the fact that the fan was going suggested some form of gas—introduced by the murderer, and then removed by him automatically. And then you came along with your mouth blistered. You spoke of feeling as if you'd been stung by a hornet, and I'd got my third fact. To get it pre-supposed a certain knowledge of chemistry. Formic acid—which is what a wasp's sting consists of—can be used amongst other things for the manufacture of carbon monoxide. And with that the whole diabolical plot was clear. The speaking-tube was the missing link, through which carbon monoxide was poured into the room, bringing with it traces of the original ingredients which condensed on the mouthpiece. Now, as you may know, carbon monoxide is lighter than air, and is a deadly poison to breathe. Moreover, it leaves no trace—certainly no obvious trace. So before we went into the room last night, I had decided in my own mind how the murders had taken place. First from right under the sleeper's nose a stream of carbon monoxide was discharged, which I rendered harmless by igniting it. The canopy helped to keep it more or less confined, but since it was lighter than air, something was necessary to make the sleeper awake and sit up. That is precisely what your father and brother did when they saw the phosphorescent hand—and they died at once. Mrs. Bretherton hid her face and lived. Then the fan was turned on—the carbon monoxide was gradually expelled from the room, and in the morning no trace remained. If it failed one night it could be tried again the next until it succeeded. Sooner or later that infernal hand travelling on a little pulley wheel on the wire and controlled from above by a long string, would wake the sleeper—and then the end—or the story of a ghost.'

He paused and pressed out his cigarette.

'From the very first also I had suspected Templeton. When you know as much of crime as I do—you're never surprised at anything. I admit he seemed the last man in the world who would do such a thing—but there are more cases of Jekyll and Hyde than we even dream of. And he and his wife were the only connecting links in the household staff between you and the Brethertons. That Mrs. Templeton also was mad had not occurred to me, and how much she was his assistant or his dupe we shall never know. She has paid a dreadful price, poor soul, for her share of it; the mixture that broke over her was hot concentrated sulphuric acid mixed with formic acid. Incidentally from inquiries made yesterday, I discovered that Staveley Grange belonged to a man named Templeton some forty years ago. This man had an illegitimate son, whom he did not provide for—and it may be that Templeton the butler is that son—gone mad. Obsessed with the idea that Staveley Grange should be his perhaps—who knows? No man can read a madman's mind.'

He lit another cigarette and rose.

'So I can't tell you why. How you know and who: why must remain a mystery for ever. And now I think I can just catch my train.'

'Yes, but wait a moment,' cried Mansford. 'There are scores of other points I'm not clear on.'

'Think 'em out for yourself, my dear fellow,' laughed Ronald. 'I want to make a few runs to-morrow.'

The Mystery of Horne's Copse

Anthony Berkeley

Anthony Berkeley Cox (1893–1971), was, like Agatha Christie and Dorothy L. Sayers, one of the new breed of crime writers who, from the 1920s onwards, broke fresh ground in the field. As Anthony Berkeley, he created Roger Sheringham, an amateur sleuth who was far from infallible—as in the superb "multiple solution" mystery *The Poisoned Chocolates Case*. Writing under the name Francis Iles, Cox wrote influential novels such as *Malice Aforethought* which focused on criminal psychology. *Cicely Disappears*, which was published under the name A. Monmouth Platts, is among the rarest and most sought-after detective novels.

"The Mystery of Horne's Copse" was originally published as a serial in *Home and County* in 1931, which accounts for the short, snappy chapters and cliff-hanger endings. The story features both Sheringham and another regular Berkeley character, Chief Inspector Moresby, and its twists and turns illustrate why Agatha Christie, among others, heaped praise on the ingenuity of Berkeley's mysteries.

◇◇◇

Chapter I

The whole thing began on the 29th of May.

It is over two years ago now and I can begin to look at it
in its proper perspective; but even still my mind retains some
echo of the incredulity, the horror, the dreadful doubts as
to my own sanity and the sheer, cold-sweating terror which
followed that ill-omened 29th of May.

Curiously enough the talk had turned for a few minutes
that evening upon Frank himself. We were sitting in the
drawing-room of Bucklands after dinner, Sir Henry and Lady
Rigby, Sylvia and I, and I can remember the intensity with
which I was trying to find a really convincing excuse to get
Sylvia alone with me for half-an-hour before I went home.
We had only been engaged a week then and the longing for
solitary places with population confined to two was tending
to increase rather than diminish.

I think it was Lady Rigby who, taking advantage of a
pause in her husband's emphatic monologue on phosphates
(phosphates were at the time Sir Henry's chief passion),
asked me whether I had heard anything of Frank since he
went abroad.

"Yes," I said. "I had a picture postcard from him this
morning. An incredibly blue Lake Como in the foreground
and an impossibly white mountain at the back, with Cadenabbia sandwiched microscopically in between. Actually,
though, he's in Bellagio for a few days."

"Oh," said Sylvia with interest and then looked extremely
innocent. Bellagio had been mentioned between us as a
possible place for the beginning of our own honeymoon.

The talk passed on to the Italian lakes in general.

"And Frank really does seem quite settled down now, Hugh, does he?" Lady Rigby asked casually, a few minutes later.

"Quite, I think," I replied guardedly; for Frank had seemed quite settled several times, but had somehow become unsettled again very soon afterwards.

Frank Chappell was my first cousin and incidentally, as I had been an only child and Ravendean was entailed, my heir. Unfortunately he had been, till lately, most unsatisfactory in both capacities. Not that there was anything bad in him, I considered he was merely weak; but weakness, in its results, can be as devastating as any deliberate villainy. It was not really his fault. He derived on his mother's side from a stock which was, to put it frankly, rotten and Frank took after his mother's family. He had not been expelled from Eton, but only by inches; he had been sent down from Oxford and his departure from the Guards had been a still more serious affair. The shock of this last killed my uncle and Frank had come into the property. It was nothing magnificent, falling far short of the resources attached to Ravendean, but plenty to allow a man to maintain his wife in very tolerable comfort. Frank had run through it in three years.

He had then, quite unexpectedly, married one of his own second cousins and, exchanging extravagance for downright parsimony, settled down with her to make the best of a bad job and put his heavily mortgaged property on its feet once more. In this, I more than suspected, he was directed by his wife. Though his cousin on the distaff side, Joanna showed none of the degeneracy of the Wickhams. Physically a splendid creature, tall and lithe and with a darkness of colouring that hinted at a Spanish ancestor somewhere in the not too remote past, she was no less vigorous mentally; under the charm of her manner one felt at once a well-balanced intelligence and a will of adamant. She was exactly the right wife for Frank and I had been delighted.

It was a disappointment to me that Sylvia did not altogether share my liking for Joanna. The Rigbys' property adjoined mine and Frank's was less than twenty miles away, so that the three families had always been on terms of intimacy. Sylvia did not actually dislike Joanna but it was clear that, if the thing were left to her, they would never become close friends and as Frank had always had a hearty dislike for me, it seemed that relations between Ravendean and Moorefield would be a little distant. I cannot say that the thought worried me. So long as I had Sylvia, nothing else could matter.

Frank had now been married something over two years and, to set the wreath of domestic virtue finally on his head, his wife six months ago had given birth to a son. The recuperation of Moorefield, moreover, had proceeded so satisfactorily that three weeks ago the pair had been able to set out on a long wandering holiday through Europe, leaving the child with his foster-mother. I have had to give Frank's history in this detail, because of its importance in the strange business which followed that homely scene in the drawing-room of Bucklands that evening.

Sylvia and I did get our half-hour together in the end and no doubt we spent it as such half-hours always have been spent. I know it seemed a very short time before I was sitting at the wheel of my car, one of the new six-cylinder Dovers, and pressing the self-starter. It failed to work. On such trivialities do our destinies hang.

"Nothing doing?" said Sylvia. "The wiring's gone, I expect. And you won't be able to swing her; she'll be much too stiff." Sylvia's grasp of the intricacies of a car's interior had always astonished me. "You'd better take Emma." Emma was her own two-seater.

"I think I'll walk," I told her. "Through Horne's Copse it's not much over a mile. It'll calm me down."

She laughed, but it was quite true. I had proposed to Sylvia as a sort of forlorn hope and I had not nearly become accustomed yet to the idea of being actually engaged to her.

It was a lovely night and my thoughts, as I swung along, turned as always then upon the amazing question: what did Sylvia see in me? We had a few tastes in common, but her real interest was cars and mine the study of early civilizations, with particularly kindly feelings towards the Minoan and Mycenean. The only reason I had ever been able to get out of her for her fondness was: "Oh well, you see, Hugh darling, you're rather a lamb, aren't you? And you *are* such a perfect old idiot." It seemed curious, but I knew our post-war generation has the reputation of being unromantic.

My eyes had become accustomed to the moonlight, but inside Horne's Copse everything was pitch black. It was hardly necessary for me to slacken my pace, however, for I knew every turn and twist of the path. The copse was not more than a couple of hundred yards long and I had reached, as I judged, just about the middle when my foot struck against an obstacle right in the middle of the track which nearly sent me flying to the ground.

I recovered my balance with an effort, wondering what the thing could be. It was not hard, like a log of wood, but inertly soft. I struck a match and looked at it. I do not think I am a particularly nervous man, but I felt a creeping sensation in the back of my scalp as I stood staring down by the steady light of the match. The thing was a body—the body of a man; and it hardly took the ominous black hole in the centre of his forehead, its edges spangled with red dew, to tell me that he was very dead indeed.

But that was not all. My match went out and I nerved myself to light another and hold it close above the dead face to assure myself that I had been mistaken. But I had not been mistaken. Incredibly, impossibly, the body was that of my cousin, Frank.

Chapter II

I took a grip on myself.

This *was* Frank and he was dead—probably murdered. Frank was not in Bellagio. He was here, in Horne's Copse, with a bullet-hole in his forehead. I must not lose my head. I must remember the correct things to do in such a case and then I must do them.

"Satisfy oneself that life is extinct."

From some hidden reserve of consciousness the phrase emerged and, almost mechanically, I proceeded to act on it. But it was really only as a matter of form that I touched the white face, which was quite cold and horribly clammy.

One arm was doubled underneath him, the other lay flung out at his side, the inside of the wrist uppermost. I grasped the latter gingerly, raising the limp hand a little off the ground as I felt the pulse, or rather, where the pulse should have been; for needless to say, nothing stirred under the cold, damp skin. Finally, with some half-buried recollection that as long as a flicker of consciousness remains, the pupils of the eyes will react to light, I moved one of my last matches backwards and forwards and close to and away from the staring eyes. The pupils did not contract the hundredth of a millimetre as the match approached them.

I scrambled to my feet.

Then I remembered that I should make a note of the exact time and this I did too. It was precisely eleven minutes and twenty seconds past twelve.

Obviously the next thing to do was to summon the police.

Not a doctor first, for the poor fellow was only too plainly beyond any doctor's aid.

I am a magistrate and certain details of routine are familiar to me. I knew, for instance, that it was essential that the body should not be touched until the police had seen it; but as I had no-one with me to leave in charge of it, that must be left to chance; in any case it was not probable that anyone else would be using the right-of-way through Horne's Copse so late. I therefore made my way, as fast as I dared in that pitch darkness, out of the copse and then ran at top speed the remaining half-mile to the house. As always I was in sound condition and I dare swear that nobody has ever covered a half-mile, fully clothed, in much quicker time.

I had told Parker, the butler, not to sit up for me and I therefore had to let myself in with my own latch-key. Still panting, I rang up the police station in Salverton, about three miles away and told them briefly what I had discovered. The constable who answered the telephone of course knew me well and Frank too and was naturally shocked by my news. I cut short his ejaculations, however, and asked him to send someone out to Ravendean at once, to take official charge. He undertook to rouse his sergeant immediately and asked me to wait at the house in order to guide him to the spot. I agreed to do so—and it was a long time before I ceased to regret it. It is easy to blame oneself after the event and easy for others to blame one too; but how could I possibly have foreseen an event so extraordinary?

The interval of waiting I filled up by rousing Parker and ringing up my doctor. The latter had not yet gone to bed and promised to come round at once. He was just the kind of man I wanted, for myself rather than Frank; my nervous system has never been a strong one and it had just received a considerable shock. Gotley was his name and he was a great hulking young man who had been tried for England at rugger while he was still at Guy's and, though just failing to get his cap, had been accounted as a good a forward as any outside the team. For a man of that type he had imagination, too, intelligence and great charm of manner; he was moreover a very capable doctor. He had been living in the village for about four years now and I had struck up quite a friendship with him, contrary to my usual practice, for I do not make friends easily.

His arrival was a relief—and so was the whisky and soda with which Parker immediately followed his entrance into the library where I was waiting.

"This sounds a bad business, Chappell," he greeted me. "Hullo, man, you look as white as a sheet. You'd better have a drink and a stiff one at that." He manipulated the decanter.

"I'm afraid it has rather upset me," I admitted. Now that there was nothing to do but wait I did feel decidedly shaky.

With the plain object of taking my mind off the gruesome subject Gotley embarked on a cheerful discussion of England's chances in the forthcoming series of test matches that summer, which he kept going determinedly until the arrival of the police some ten minutes later.

These were Sergeant Afford whom, of course, I knew well and a young constable. The sergeant was by no means of the doltish, obstinate type which the writers of detective fiction invariably portray, as if our country police forces consisted of nothing else; he was a shrewd enough man and at this moment he was a tremendously excited man, too. This fact he was striving nobly to conceal in deference to my feelings for, of course, he knew Frank as well as myself and by repute as well as in person; but it was obvious that the practical certainty of murder, and in such a circle, had roused every instinct of the bloodhound in him: he was literally quivering to get on the trail. No case of murder had ever come his way before and in such a one as this there was, besides the excitement of the hunt, the certainty that publicity galore, with every chance of promotion, would fall to the lot of Sergeant Afford—if only he could trace the murderer before his Superintendent had time to take the case out of his hands.

As we hurried along the sergeant put such questions as he wished, so that by the time we entered the copse he knew almost as much of the circumstances as I did myself. There was now no need to slacken our pace, for I had a powerful electric torch to guide our steps. As we half ran, half walked along I flashed it continuously from side to side, searching the path ahead for poor Frank's body. Somewhat surprised, I decided that it must lie further than I had thought; though, knowing the copse intimately as I did, I could have sworn that it had been lying on a stretch of straight path, the only one, right in the very middle; but we passed over the length of it and it was not there.

A few moments later we had reached the copse's further limit and came to an irresolute halt.

"Well, sir?" asked the sergeant, in a tone studiously expressionless.

But I had no time for nuances. I was too utterly bewildered. "Sergeant," I gasped, "it—it's *gone*."

Chapter III

There was no doubt that Frank's body had gone, because it was no longer there; but that did not explain its remarkable removal.

"I can't understand it, Sergeant. I know within a few yards where he was: on that straight bit in the middle. I wonder if he wasn't quite dead after all and managed to crawl off the path somewhere."

"But I thought you were quite sure he was dead, sir?"

"I was. Utterly sure," I said in perplexity, remembering how icy cold that clammy, clay-like face had been.

The constable, who had not yet uttered a word, continued to preserve his silence. So also did Gotley. After a somewhat awkward pause the sergeant suggested that we should have a look round.

"Well, I can show you where he was, at any rate," I said. "We can recognise the place from the dead matches I left there."

We turned back again and the sergeant, taking my torch, examined the ground. The straight stretch was not more than a dozen yards long and he went slowly up it one side and back the other. "Well, sir, that's funny; there isn't a match anywhere along here."

"Are you sure?" I asked incredulously. "Let me look."

I took the torch, but it was a waste of time: not a match-stalk could I find.

"Rum go," muttered Gotley.

I will pass briefly over the next hour, which was not one of triumph for myself. Let it be enough to say that search as we might on the path, in the undergrowth and even beyond the confines of the copse, not a trace could we discover of a body, a match-stalk, or anything to indicate that these things had ever been there.

As the power of my electric torch waned so did the sergeant's suspicions of my good faith obviously increase. More than once he dropped a hint that I must have been pulling his leg and wasn't it about time I brought a good joke to an end.

"But I did see it, Sergeant," I said desperately, when at last we were compelled to give the job up as a bad one and turn homewards. "The only way I can account for it is that some man came along after I'd gone, thought life might not be extinct and carried my cousin bodily off with him."

"And your burnt matches as well, sir, I suppose," observed the sergeant woodenly.

Gotley and I parted with him and his constable outside the house; he would not come in, even for a drink. It was clear that he was now convinced that I had been playing a joke on him and was not by any means pleased about it. I had to let him carry the delusion away with him.

When they had gone I looked enquiringly at Gotley, but he shook his head. "My goodness, no, I'm not going. I want to go into this a little deeper. I'm coming in with you, whether you like it or not."

As a matter of fact I did. It was nearly half-past one, but sleep was out of the question. I wanted to talk the thing out with Gotley and decide what ought to be done.

We went into the library and Gotley mixed us each another drink. I certainly needed the one he handed to me.

"Nerves still a bit rocky?" Gotley remarked, looking at me with a professional eye.

"A bit," I admitted. I may add in extenuation that I was supposed to have been badly shell-shocked during the war. Certainly my nervous system had never been the same since. "I'm glad you don't want to go. I want your opinion on this extraordinary business. I noticed you didn't say much up there."

"No, I thought better not."

"Well, it'll be light in just over an hour. I want to get back and examine that copse by daylight, before anyone else gets there. I simply can't believe that there aren't some indications that I was telling the truth."

"My dear chap, I never doubted for one moment that you were telling what you sincerely thought was the truth."

"No?" This sounded to me rather oddly put, but I didn't question it for the moment. "Well, the sergeant did. Look here, are you game to stay here and come up with me?"

"Like a shot. If any message comes for me, they know at home where I am. In the meantime, let's try to get some sort of a line on the thing. I thought your cousin was abroad?"

"So did I," I replied helplessly. "In fact I had a card from him only this morning, from Bellagio."

"Did he give the name of his hotel?"

"Yes, I think so. Yes, I'm sure he mentioned it."

"Then I should wire there directly the post office opens and ask if he's still there."

"But he isn't," I argued stupidly. "How can he be?"

Gotley contemplated his tumbler. "Still, you know," he said airily—rather too airily, "still, I should wire."

The hour passed more quickly than I could have expected. I knew now that Gotley did not consider that I had been deliberately romancing, he suspected me merely of seeing visions; but he did not give himself away again and discussed the thing with me as gravely as if he had been as sure as I was that what I had seen was fact and not figment. As soon as the dawn began to show we made our way to the copse; for no message had arrived from the police station to throw any light on the affair.

Our journey, let me say briefly, was a complete failure. Not a single thing did we find to bear out my story—not a burnt match, a drop of blood, nor even a suspicious footprint on the hard ground.

I could not with decency retain Gotley any longer, especially as he was having more and more difficulty in concealing from me his real opinion. I made no comment or protestation. His own suggestion of the telegram to Bellagio could be left to do that; for I had now determined to adopt it in sheer self-defense, to prove that there was at least the fact of Frank's absence to support me. If he had been in Horne's Copse he could not be in Bellagio and, conversely, if he had suddenly left Bellagio, he could have appeared in Horne's Copse.

I did not go to bed till past eight o'clock, at which hour I telephoned my telegram.

The rest of the day dragged. Sylvia telephoned after lunch to say that the chauffeur had now put my car right, but I put her off with a non-committal answer. The truth was that nothing would induce me to leave the house until the answer to my telegram had arrived.

Just after six o'clock it came.

I tore open the flimsy envelope with eager fingers. "Why the excitement?" it ran. "Here till tomorrow, then Grand Hotel, Milan. Frank."

So Gotley had been right. I *had* been seeing visions.

Chapter IV

I sank into a chair, the telegram between my fingers.

But I had *not* been imagining the whole thing. It was out of the question. The details had been too vivid, too palpable. No, Gotley was wrong. I had seen someone—it might not have been Frank.

I hurried to the telephone and rang up Sergeant Afford. Had he heard anything more about last night's affair? I might possibly have been mistaken in thinking the dead man my cousin. Had any other disappearance been reported? The sergeant was short with me. Nothing further had developed. He had been himself to the scene of the alleged death that morning and found nothing. He advised me, not too kindly, to think no more about the affair.

I began to feel annoyed. Now that it was proved that the body could not possibly have been Frank's, my feeling towards it was almost resentment. Only by the chance of a defective wire on my car had I stumbled across it and the contact had resulted in suspicion on the part of the police of an uncommonly callous practical joke and the conviction on the part of my doctor that I was mentally unbalanced. The more I thought about it, the more determined I was that the mystery must be unveiled. I resolved to tell Sylvia the whole story that very evening.

Unlike Gotley, Sylvia asked plenty of questions; still more unlike him she accepted what I said as a statement of fact. "Rot, Hugh," she said bluntly, when I told her of that young man's suspicions. "If you say you saw it, you did see it. And anyhow, how could you possibly imagine such a thing? Hugh, this is terribly exciting. What are we going to do about it?" She took her own part in any subsequent action for granted.

I looked at her pretty gray eyes sparkling with excitement and, in spite of the gravity of the affair, I could not help smiling. "What do you suggest, dear?" I asked.

"Oh, we must get to the bottom of it, of course. We'll make enquiries in the neighbourhood and go round all the hospitals, oh and everything." As I had often noticed before, Sylvia had been able to translate into realities ideas which to me had remained a trifle nebulous.

So for the next few days we played at being detectives enquiring into a mysterious murder and traveled all over the country in pursuit of our ridiculous but delightful theories. We enjoyed ourselves tremendously; but if real detectives got no further in their cases than we did, the number of undetected murders would see a remarkable increase; for we discovered exactly nothing at all. No man resembling Frank had been seen in the vicinity; there was not the vaguest report of a man with a bullet wound in his forehead.

All we really did determine was that the man must have been dead (for that he had been dead I was absolutely convinced) for about four to six hours because, though the body was cold, the wrist I had held was still limp, which meant that *rigor mortis* had not set in. This information came from Gotley who gave it with a perfectly grave face and then quite spoilt the effect by advising us to waste no more time on the business. Sylvia was most indignant with him.

Perhaps it is not true to say that we discovered nothing at all, for one rather curious fact did come to light. Although we knew now that the man must have been dead at least four hours, must have died, that is, not later than eight o'clock, we found no less than three persons who had passed over the path between that hour and midnight; and at none of those times had he been there.

"There's a gang in it," Sylvia pronounced with enjoyment. "He was shot miles away, brought to the copse and then carried off again, all by the gang."

"But why?" I asked, wondering at these peripatetic activities.

"Heaven only knows," Sylvia returned helplessly.

And there, in the end, we had to leave it.

At least a month passed and my mysterious adventure gradually became just a curious memory. Gotley ceased to look at me thoughtfully and when I met him at the local flower show even Sergeant Afford showed by his magnanimous bearing that he had forgiven me.

At first, I must confess, I had tended to avoid Horne's Copse at night, although it was much the shortest route between Bucklands and Ravendean. Then, as the memory faded, reason reasserted itself. By the third of July I had shed the last of my qualms.

That third of July!

There is a saying that history repeats itself. It did that night with a vengeance. Once again I had been dining at Bucklands. Before leaving home my chauffeur had found a puncture in one of the back tyres of the Dover and had put the spare wheel on. I risked the short journey without a spare, only to find, when it was time to go home, that another puncture had developed. Once again Sylvia offered me her own car: once again I refused, saying that I should enjoy the walk. Once again I set out with my mind busy with the dear girl I had just left and the happiness in store for me. That very evening we had fixed our wedding provisionally for the middle of September.

Indeed, so intent was I upon these delightful reflections, that I had got a third of the way through Horne's Copse before I even called to mind the sinister connection which the place now held for me. It was not quite such a dark night as that other one, but inside the copse the blackness was as dense as before as I turned the last twist before the stretch of straight path in the centre.

"It was just about six yards from here," I reflected idly as I walked along, "that my foot struck, with that unpleasant thud, against–"I stopped dead, retaining my balance this time with ease, as if I had subconsciously been actually anticipating the encounter. For my foot had struck, with just such another unpleasant thud, against an inert mass in the middle of the path.

With a horrible creeping sensation at the back of my scalp, I struck a match and forced myself to look at the thing in my way, though I knew well enough before I did so what I should see. And I was right. Lying across the path, with unnaturally disposed limbs and, this time, a small dagger protruding from his chest, was my cousin Frank.

Chapter V

The match flickered and went out and still I stood, rigid and gasping, striving desperately to conquer the panic which was threatening to swamp my reason.

Gradually, in the darkness, I forced my will to control my trembling limbs. Gradually I succeeded in restoring my brain to its natural functions. Here, I told myself deliberately, was the real thing. As for the other—vision, pre-knowledge, clairvoyance, or whatever it might have been, I had at the moment no time to find explanations; here I was in the presence of the real thing and I must act accordingly.

I suppose it can really have been scarcely more than a couple minutes before, restored to the normal, I felt myself not merely calm but positively eager to investigate. With fingers that no longer quivered I struck another match and bent over my unfortunate cousin. It did not even repel me this time to touch the cold, clammy face, glistening in the match-light with unnatural moisture, as I made sure that he really was dead.

It was with an odd sense of familiarity that I made my swift examination. Except for the dagger in his chest and the bloodstained clothes around it instead of the bullet wound in his forehead, everything was exactly the same as before and my own actions followed more or less their previous course. There was the same outflung arm, cold wrist uppermost, whose motionless pulse I could conveniently feel for; there were the staring eyes, unresponsive to the movements of my match; there was the damp, chilled skin of his face. It was only too plain that he was dead, without it being necessary for me to disarrange his clothing to feel his heart and I was again unwilling to do this, knowing how much the police dislike a body to be tampered with before they have examined it themselves.

But one thing further I did this time. I made sure that the body was, beyond all possibility of dispute, that of Frank himself. Frank had a scar on his left temple, just at the edge of the hair. I looked for the scar and I found it. Then I hurried home at the best speed I could, to ring up Sergeant

Afford and Gotley. I was conscious as I did so of a rather ignoble feeling of triumph. But after all, self-vindication *is* a pleasant feeling.

Sergeant Afford himself was not at the police station, but to Gotley I spoke directly. "Right-ho," he said with enthusiasm. "Really has happened this time, has it?"

"Yes," I replied. "There's no doubt this time. I shall want to go into that other affair with you some time. It must have been a vision of some kind, I suppose."

"Yes, extraordinary business. And apparently not quite an accurate one. What about getting the Psychical Research Society on to it?"

"We might. In the meantime, I'm going back to the copse now. Meet me there. I'm taking no risks this time."

Gotley promised to do so and we rang off.

As I passed out of the front door I looked at my watch. The time was three minutes to twelve. It had been twenty-one minutes to the hour within a few seconds, when I left the body. I walked back at a good pace and the journey took me about twelve minutes. In all, then, I was absent from the centre of Horne's Copse for about half-an-hour. The importance of these figures will be apparent later.

I am not sure what motive prompted my return alone to the spot where I had left the body. I think I wanted, in some vague way, to keep guard over it, almost as if it might run away if left to itself. Anyhow I certainly had the feeling, as I had mentioned to Gotley, that this time I would take no chances.

I had my torch with me now and I turned it on as I reached the copse. It threw a powerful beam and as I turned the corner on to the straight I directed the light along to the further end. The whole dozen yards of straight path was thus illuminated, the undergrowth at the sides and the dense green foliage beyond the twist at the end. But that was all. Of Frank's body there was no sign.

Incredulously I hurried forward, thinking that I must have been mistaken in my bearings; the body must have lain round the further corner. But neither round the corner was there any sign of it, nor anywhere along the path right to the further edge of the copse. Filled with horror, I retraced my steps, sweeping the surface of the ground with my beam. It was as I feared. Again there was not even a litter of spent matches to show where I had knelt by Frank's remains.

In the middle of the path I halted, dazed with nameless alarm. Was my reason going? The thing was fantastic, inexplicable. If I had had my suspicions about the reality of my former experience, I had none concerning this one. I *knew* there had been a body; I *knew* I had handled it, physically and materially; I *knew* it was Frank's—Frank who was supposed to be that moment in Rome. I knew all these things as well as I knew my own name, but…But the alternative simply did not bear thinking about.

But for all that, hallucinations…

And yet I felt as sane as ever I had been in my life. There *must* be some ordinary, simple, logical explanation…

I was still trying to find it when the police and Gotley arrived together.

I turned to meet them. "It's gone!" I shouted. "Would you believe it, but the damned thing's gone again. I saw him as plainly as I see you, with the dagger in his chest and the blood all round the wound—I touched him! And now there isn't a sign that he was ever there at all. Damn it, the very matches have disappeared too." I laughed, for really if you looked at it one way, the thing was just absurd.

Sergeant Afford eyed me austerely. "Is that so, sir?" he said, in his most wooden voice.

He was going to say more, but Gotley brushed him aside and took me by the arm.

"That's all right, Chappell, old man," he said, very sooth-ingly. "Don't you worry about it any more tonight. I'm going to take you home and fill you up with bromide and tomorrow we'll go into it properly."

Gotley thought I was mad, of course. After all it was only to be expected.

Chapter VI

"Ought I to marry, then?" I asked drearily. I had been trying for some minutes to summon up the courage to put this question.

It was the next evening and Gotley and I had been talking for over an hour. He had succeeded in convincing me. I had seen nothing, felt nothing, imagined everything. To pacify me he had telegraphed that morning to Frank in Rome; the answer, facetiously couched, had left no room for doubt.

Gotley had been perfectly open with me during the last hour. It was better, he said, to face this sort of thing frankly. The thing was not serious; I must have been overworking, or suffering from nervous strain of some kind. If I took things easily for a bit these hallucinations would disappear and probably never return. Above all, I must not brood over them.

"Ought I to marry, then, Gotley?" I repeated.

"Oh dear, yes. In time. No need to hurry about it."

"You mean, not in September?"

"Well, perhaps not quite so soon. But later, oh, yes."

"Is it fair? I mean, if there are children."

"My dear chap," Gotley said with great cheerfulness, "it's nothing as bad as that. Nothing but a temporary phase."

"I shall tell Sylvia."

"Ye-es," he agreed, though a little doubtfully. "Yes, you could tell Miss Rigby; but let me have a word with her too.

And look here, why not go away somewhere with her and her mother for a bit of a holiday? That's what you want. Drugs can't do anything for you, but a holiday, with the right companionship, might do everything."

And so, the next day, it was arranged.

I told Sylvia everything. She, of course, was her own loyal self and at first refused to believe a word of Gotley's diagnosis. If I thought I had seen a body, then a body I had seen, and felt, and examined. Even Frank's facetious telegram did not shake her. But her private talk with Gotley did, a little. She was not convinced, but she went so far as to say that there might be something in it, conceivably. In any case there was no reason why I should not have a holiday with herself and her mother, if that was what everyone seemed to want; but neither Sir Henry nor Lady Rigby were to be told a word about anything else. To this, though somewhat reluctantly, I agreed.

Nevertheless, rumours of course arose. Not that Gotley said a word, but I cannot think that Sergeant Afford was so discreet. When we got back, in August, from Norway, I was not long in gathering, from the curious looks which everywhere greeted me, that some at any rate of the cat had escaped from its bag.

I saw Gotley at once and he expressed his satisfaction with my condition. "You'll be all right now," he predicted confidently. "I shouldn't go to that place at night for a bit yet, but you'd be all right now really, in any case."

A couple of days later I had a letter from Frank. It was in answer to one I had written him from Norway, asking him, just as a matter of curiosity, exactly what he had been doing just before midnight on the 3rd of July, as I had had rather a strange dream about him just at that time. He apologised for not having answered earlier, but the hotel in Rome had been slow in forwarding my letter, which had only just now caught him up in Vienna, from which town his own letter was written. So far as he could remember, he was just coming out of a theatre in Rome at the time I mentioned: was that what I wanted? My recovery had been so far complete that I could smile at a couple of very typical spelling mistakes and then dismiss the matter from my mind.

That was on the 9th August. The next morning was a blazing day, the sort of shimmering, cloudless day that one always associates with the month of August and, about once in three years, really gets. I made a leisurely breakfast, read the newspaper for a little and then set off to keep an appointment with a farmer, a tenant of mine, concerning the re-roofing of his barn. The farm adjoined the Bucklands estate and lay about three miles away by road, but little over a mile if one cut through Horne's Copse. It was a little hot for walking and I had intended to take the Dover, but a message reached me from the garage that something had gone mysteriously wrong with the carburetor and a new float would have to be obtained before I could take her out. Rather welcoming the necessity for exercise, I set off on foot.

As I approached Horne's Copse I reflected how complete my recovery must be, for instead of feeling the slightest reluctance to pass through it I positively welcomed its prospect of cool green shade. Strolling along, my thoughts on the coming interview and as far as they well could be from the unhappy memories that the place held for me, I turned the last corner which hid from me the little length of straight path which had played so sinister a part in those memories—even, I think, whistling a little tune.

Then the tune froze abruptly on my lips and the warmth of the day was lost in the icy sweat of sheer terror which broke out all over me. For there at my feet, incredibly, impossibly, lay the body of Frank, the blood slowly oozing round the dagger that projected from his heart.

This time I stayed to make no examination. In utter panic I took to my heels and ran. Whither, or with what idea, I had no notion. My one feeling was to get away from the place and as soon and as quickly as possible.

Actually I came to my senses in a train, bound for London, with a first-class ticket clutched in my hand. How I had got there I had no conception but the vaguest. It had been a blind flight.

Fortunately the compartment was an empty one and I was able to take measures to control the trembling of my limbs before trying to take stock of the situation. I was not cured, then. Far from it. What was I to do?

One thing I determined. I would stay a few days in London now that I was already on the way there and, when I felt sufficiently recovered to tell my story coherently, consult some experienced alienist. Obviously I was no longer a case for Gotley.

It was no doubt (as I reflected in a strangely detached way), a part of my mania that I did not go to my usual hotel, where I was known, but sought out the most obscure one I could find. In an effort to shake off my obsession and complete the process of calming myself I turned after the meal into a dingy little cinema and tried to concentrate for three hours on the inanities displayed on the screen.

"Shocking murder in a wood!" screamed a newsboy almost in my ear, as I stood blinking in the sunlight outside again. Mechanically I felt for a copper and gave it to him. It was in a wood that I had seen...

And it was an account of the finding of Frank's body that I read there and then, on the steps of that dingy cinema— Frank who had been found that morning in Horne's Copse with a dagger in his heart.

"The police," concluded the brief account, "state that they would be grateful if the dead man's cousin, Mr. Hugh

Chappell, who was last seen boarding the 11.19 train to London, would put himself in touch with them as soon as possible."

Chapter VII

I turned and began to walk quickly, but quite aimlessly, along the pavement. The one idea in my mind at the moment was that nobody should guess, from any anxiety I might display, that *I* was the notorious Hugh Chappell with whom the police wished to get in touch as soon as possible. It never occurred to me to doubt that I was notorious, that my name was already on everyone's lips and that not merely every policeman but even every private citizen was eagerly looking for me. Such is the effect of seeing one's name, for the first time, in a public news sheet.

By and by my mind recovered from this temporary obsession and I began to think once more. So this time my hallucination had not been a hallucination at all. Frank *had* been killed—murdered, almost certainly: it *was* his body I had seen that morning. But what, then, of the two previous times I had seen that same body and even handled it? Or so I had fancied at the time. Obviously they were not the meaningless delusions that Gotley and, finally, I myself, had believed them to be; they really were definite pre-visions of the real event. It was most extraordinary.

In any case, be that as it might, my own immediate action was clear. I must return at once to Ravendean and offer Sergeant Afford any help in my power.

It did not take me much over half-an-hour to ring up my hotel, cancel my room and make my way to Paddington. There I found that a train was luckily due to start in ten minutes and, having taken my ticket, I strolled to the bookstall to see if any later edition with fuller details was yet on sale.

As I approached the stall I noticed a figure standing in front of it which looked familiar to me. The man turned his head and I recognised him at once as a fellow who had been on my staircase at Oxford, though I had never known him well: his name was Sheringham and I had heard of him during the last few years as a successful novelist with an increasing reputation, Roger Sheringham.

I had not the least wish, at the present juncture, to waste time renewing old acquaintances, but as the man was now staring straight at me I could hardly do less than nod, with what pleasantness I could muster and greet him by name.

His response surprised me enormously. "Hullo, Hugo!" he said warmly, indeed with a familiarity I resented considering that we had never been on terms of anything but surnames before. "Come and have a drink." And he actually took me by the arm.

"I'm sorry," I said, a little stiffly, "I have a train to catch." And I endeavoured to release myself.

"Nonsense!" he said loudly. "Plenty of time for a quick one." I was going to reply somewhat peremptorily when, to my astonishment, he added in a hissing sort of whisper without moving his lips: "Come *on*, you damned fool."

I allowed him to lead me away from the bookstall, completely bewildered.

"Phew!" he muttered, when we had gone about thirty yards. "That was a close shave. Don't look round. That man in the grey suit who was just coming up on the left is a Scotland Yard man."

"Indeed?" I said, interested but perplexed. "Looking for someone, you mean?"

"Yes," Sheringham said shortly. "You. One of a dozen in this very station at this very minute. Let's get out—if we can!"

I was surprised to hear that so many detectives were actually looking for me. Evidently the police considered my evidence of the first importance. I wondered how Sheringham knew and asked him.

"Oh, I'm in touch with those people," he said carelessly. "Lord," he added, more to himself than to me, "I wish I knew what to do with you now I've got you."

"Well," I smiled, "I'm afraid you can't do anything at the moment. If you're in touch with Scotland Yard, you'll have heard about my poor cousin?" He nodded and I explained my intentions.

"I thought so," he nodded, "seeing you here. Well, that confirms my own opinion."

"What opinion?"

"Oh, nothing. Now look here, Chappell, I don't want you to take this train. There's another a couple of hours later which will do you just as well; there's no particular urgency so far as you're concerned. In the interval, I want you to come back with me to my rooms at the Albany."

"But why?"

"Because I want to talk to you—or rather, hear you talk. And I may say I was about to travel down to your place by that same train for just that purpose."

This was the most surprising news I had yet received. I demurred, however, at missing the train, but Sheringham was so insistent that at last I agreed to accompany him.

"We'd better get a taxi, then," I remarked with, I fear, no very good grace.

"No," Sheringham retorted. "We'll go by tube."

And by tube we went.

Sheringham took me into a very comfortable paneled sitting-room and we sat down in two huge leather armchairs.

"Now," he said, "don't think me impertinent, Chappell, or mysterious, and remember that I'm not only in touch with Scotland Yard but I have on occasions even worked with them. I want you to tell me, from beginning to end, in as much detail as you can, your story of this extraordinary business of your cousin's death. And believe me, it's entirely in your own interests that I ask you to do so, though for the present you must take that on trust."

The request seemed to me highly irregular, but Sheringham appeared to attach such importance to it that I did, in fact, comply. I told him the whole thing.

"I see," he said. "Thank you. And you proposed to go down and give the police what help you could. Very proper. Now I'll tell you something, Chappell. What do you think they want you for? Your help? Not a bit of it. They want you in order to arrest you, for killing your cousin."

"What!" I could only gasp.

"I have it from their own lips. Shall I tell you what the police theory is? That your two false alarms were the results of hallucinations, which left you with the delusion that you had a divine mission to kill your cousin and that, meeting him accidentally in the flesh in that same place you, under the influence of this mania, actually did kill him."

Chapter VIII

For a minute or two Sheringham's revelation of this hideous suggestion left me quite speechless with horror. I was beginning to stammer out a repudiation when he waved me into silence.

"My dear chap, it's all right: *I* don't believe anything of the sort. I never did and now I've seen and talked to you I do still less. You're not mad. No, I'm convinced the business isn't so simple as all that. In fact, I think there's something pretty devilish behind it. That's why I was on my way down to try to find you before the police did and ask you if I could look into things for you."

"Good heavens," I could only mutter, "I'd be only too grateful if you would. I've no wish to end my days in a madhouse. This is really terrible. Have you any ideas at all?"

"Only that those first two occasions were no more delusions than the last. You did see something that you were meant to see—either your cousin or somebody made up to resemble his. And the plot which I'm quite certain exists is evidently aimed against you as well as against your cousin. For some reason a certain person or persons do want you locked up in an asylum. At least, that seems the only possible explanation, with the result that the police are thinking exactly what they have been meant to think. Now, can you tell me of anyone who would benefit if you were locked up in a madhouse?"

"No one," I said in bewilderment. "But Sheringham, how can it possibly be a deliberate plot? It was only by the merest chance on all those three occasions that I went through Horne's Copse at all. Nobody could possibly have foreseen it."

"Are you sure? On each occasion, you remember, you had to pass from one point to another, with Horne's Copse as the nearest route, provided you were on foot. And on each occasion, you also remember, your car just happened to be out of action. You think that's coincidence? I don't."

"You mean—you think my car had been tampered with?"

"I intend to have a word or two with your chauffeur; but I'm ready to bet a thousand pounds here and now what the implications of his answers will be—though doubtless he won't realise it himself. What sort of a man is he, by the way? Sound?"

"Very. A first-rate mechanic and an excellent fellow. In fact, he has rather a sad story. Not that he's ever told me a word himself; actually I had it from Frank who sent him along to me, not being able to find a job for him himself. He's a public school and University man whose people lost all their money while he was up at Cambridge, where Frank knew him slightly. So, having a bent for engineering, he buckled down to it, worked his way through the shops and turned himself into a most efficient chauffeur."

"Stout fellow," Sheringham commented. "We may find him very useful. Now look here, Chappell, you're absolutely convinced that the man you saw each time in Horne's Copse was your cousin? You're sure it wasn't somebody disguised as him?"

"I'm practically certain," I replied.

"Yes; well, we must check up on that; which means that someone must go abroad and cover the ground."

"But you forget the telegrams I had from Frank."

"Indeed I don't," Sheringham retorted. "A telegram's no evidence at all."

"But who is to go?"

"There you have me," he admitted. "I simply can't spare the time myself if I'm to go into things properly at this end, and we've got none of it to lose. I want to get the case cleared up before the police find you and we don't know when that may be."

"Oh! I'm to go into hiding, then?"

"Well, of course. Once arrested it's the dickens of a job to get free again. We must put it off as long as we possibly can."

"But where am I to hide?"

"Why, I thought here. Meadows, my man, is perfectly safe. Any objection?"

"None, indeed. This is extraordinarily good of you, Sheringham. I needn't say how very grateful I am."

"That's all right, that's all right. Now then, if I'm to do any good down in your neighbourhood I must put a few questions before I leave you. I'm going to catch that train."

Sheringham hurriedly put his queries, some concerning my own affairs and Frank's and some upon local conditions and personages and rushed off to catch his train. Before he went I obtained his promise to see Sylvia and secretly inform her of my plans and whereabouts, together with his own hopes of getting me out of this trouble, which I urged him to put as high as possible to save the poor girl anxiety. This he undertook to do and I was left alone.

It need not be said that my reflections were not pleasant ones; but rack my brains as I might, I could see no possible solution of the mystery of my cousin's death, nor even discover the least bit of evidence to support Sheringham's theory that some person or persons unknown, having murdered Frank, were now trying to get me confined as a homicidal lunatic. Who was there who could possibly benefit by this double crime?

To all practical purposes I was a prisoner in the Albany for an indefinite period. Outside the shelter of Sheringham's rooms I did not dare to put my nose. And for all the company that the silent-footed, respectfully taciturn Meadows proved himself, I might just as well have been completely alone. The time hung heavily on my hands, in spite of the numbers of newspapers I examined, Meadows silently bringing me each fresh edition as it appeared. There was, however, little fresh to be found in the reports so far as real information went, though columns of balderdash were printed concerning myself, Frank and everything relevant and irrelevant to the case. The only piece of complete news was that the dagger with which Frank had been stabbed had been identified as my own dagger, from the wall in my library, a fact which lent superficial support to the police theory but, to me, more to Sheringham's.

The latter had not been able to say how long he would be absent. Actually it was nearly forty-eight hours before he returned, looking considerably graver than when he departed.

I had jumped up eagerly to question him as to his success and his reply was anything but reassuring.

"I've found out a little, but not much. And the police have found out a good deal more. They've got evidence now which has made them change their theory completely. You'd better prepare for a shock, Chappell. They think now that you feigned the first two hallucinations in order to create the impression that you were mad and then, having established that, killed your cousin in extremely sane cold blood in accordance with a careful plan of murder, knowing that as a homicidal maniac you couldn't be executed but would get off with a year or so in Broadmoor before proving that you'd recovered your sanity. That's what we're up against now."

Chapter IX

I had still found no words to answer Sheringham's appalling news when the door behind him opened and Sylvia herself appeared.

"Oh, Hugh!" she said, with a little cry and ran to me.

"She would come," Sheringham said gloomily. "I couldn't stop her. Well, I'll go and unpack." He left us alone together.

"Hugh dear," Sylvia said, when our first disjointed greetings were over, "what does this terrible business all mean? Frank dead and you suspected of killing him! I knew all the time there was something dreadful behind those 'hallucinations' of yours, as that idiot of a Dr. Gotley would call them."

"I can tell you one thing it must mean, darling," I said sadly, "and that is that our engagement must be broken off. It wouldn't be fair to you. Though when I'm cleared I shall—"

"Hugh!" she interrupted me indignantly. "How dare you say such a thing to me! What kind of a girl do you imagine I am? Engagement broken off indeed. Do you know *why* I've come up with Mr. Sheringham?"

"Well, no," I had to admit.

But I was not destined to learn just then exactly why Sylvia had come up to London, for Sheringham himself followed his own discreet tap on the door into the room.

We settled down into a council of war.

"There's no disguising the fact," Sheringham said gravely, "that the position's uncommonly serious, Chappell. The hunt for you is up, with a vengeance."

"Look here," I returned, "in that case I must leave your rooms. You could get into serious trouble for harbouring a wanted man, you know."

"Oh, that," Sheringham said scornfully. "Yes, you can go all right, but you'll have to knock me out first. I'll hold you here if necessary by main force."

Sylvia's face, which had become highly apprehensive at my remark, lightened again and she shot a grateful smile at our host.

"Then you really don't think I should surrender to the police and let them hold me while you're working?" I asked anxiously, for, magistrate as I was, the way in which I was evading arrest seemed to me just then almost more reprehensible than the ridiculous charge which was out against me.

"I do not," Sheringham replied bluntly. "That is, not unless you want to turn a short story into a long one. Give me just a few days and I'll clear the mystery up—granted one thing only."

"And what's that?"

"Why, that the agent we send abroad is able to establish the fact that your cousin was *not* at his hotel abroad on those first two occasions; because unless you're completely mistaken in your identification, there can't be any doubt about that, as a fact."

"But wait a minute!" Sylvia cried. "Mr. Sheringham, that would mean that—that his wife is in it too."

"Oh, yes," Sheringham agreed carelessly. "Naturally."

"Joanna!" I exclaimed. "Oh, that's impossible."

"I wouldn't put it past her," said Sylvia. "But why 'naturally,' Mr. Sheringham? Have you got a theory that brings her in?"

"Yes. My idea is that so far as your cousin and his wife were concerned, Chappell, the thing was a joke, just to give you a fright. Rather a gruesome joke, perhaps, but nothing more. He was home on business for a day or two and, with the help of somebody else, rigged himself up as a sham corpse. *Then* that unknown third person turned the joke against him most effectively by really killing him the third time. All we've got to do, therefore, is to find this mysterious person (which, with your cousin's wife's help, shouldn't be difficult), and we've got the murderer."

"Joanna's on her way home now, of course," Sylvia told me. "They expect her to arrive tonight or tomorrow. Mr. Sheringham's going down again to see her."

"I understand," I said slowly, though I was not altogether sure that I did. "And supposing that she says that Frank was with her all the time and our agent confirms that?"

"Well, in that case there's only one possible explanation: your identification was mistaken."

"I'm sure it wasn't," I said. "And what's more I'm equally sure that Frank was dead the first time of all—quite dead. I tell you, his face was icy cold and his heart wasn't beating; I felt his pulse most carefully. It's impossible that I could have been mistaken."

"That does make things a little more difficult," Sheringham murmured.

There was a gloomy little pause, which I broke to ask Sheringham what this fresh evidence was which the police imagined they had discovered against me. Apparently it amounted to the facts that, according to Jefferson, my chauffeur, the car had on each occasion shown every sign of having been deliberately tampered with (which Sheringham had expected), and by myself (which he had not); that the police had obtained my finger-prints from articles in the house and the finger-prints on the dagger corresponded with them; and that I had been heard to use threatening language as regards Frank—which so far as his escapades before marriage were concerned, was possibly in some degree true, though I could not in any way account for the finger-prints.

"Whom are you going to send abroad for us, Mr. Sheringham?" Sylvia asked suddenly, when our discussion on these points was over.

"Well, I've been thinking about that. It must be someone who knew the dead man and all the circumstances. In my opinion the very best thing would be for Hugh to go and act as his own detective. We can easily lay a trail to make the police think he's still in London, so the foreign forces won't be warned."

"Hugh!" Sylvia echoed in surprise. "Well, really, that mightn't be at all a bad idea. Though as to detecting…Still, I can do that part of it."

"You?" we exclaimed in unison.

"Oh, yes," said Sylvia serenely. "I shall go with him, of course."

"But, darling," I was beginning to expostulate.

"Which brings me back to my real reason for coming up to London, Hugh," Sylvia went on with the utmost calmness. "It was so that we can get married at once, of course. Or at any rate, within the usual three days. It will have to be in false names, I'm afraid, owing to this fuss, but it's just as legal and we can go through a ceremony again in our own names if you like after it's all over. I've applied for the special license already, in the name of—" She began to giggle and dived into her handbag, from which she extracted a crumpled piece of paper. "Yes, Miss Arabella Whiffen. And you, darling, are Mr. Penstowe Stibb."

Chapter X

And so, in spite of my misgivings, Sylvia and I actually were married three days later. In my own defence I may say that when Sylvia has really made her mind up to a thing…

How we got safely out of the country, while the police were feverishly chasing clues ingeniously laid by Sheringham to show that I was still in London, I do not propose to say. In the public interest such things are better kept quiet.

It was a strange honeymoon upon which we embarked, with its object of finding out whether or not Frank really had been abroad at the time when I had seen him (as I was now more convinced than ever that I had), lying dead in Horne's Copse. Nor was there any time to lose. With only one night to break the journey in Bâle on the way, we went straight through to the Italian lakes. We did not, however, stay in Bellagio, where Frank had been (or said he had been), but at Cadenabbia opposite. For all we knew, we might encounter an English detective in Bellagio and we did not intend to remain in the danger zone longer than necessary.

We arrived at Cadenabbia late at night. The next morning, before crossing the lake to Bellagio, I received a letter from Sheringham, addressed to me in the assumed name in which we were traveling. Its contents were most disturbing:

DEAR STIBB,

I am keeping in close touch with S.Y. and they still have no doubt that London is the place. Meanwhile here is news.

Both the police and I have seen J. and she tells the same story to both of us: that her husband never came back to England at all, until the day before his death, when he had to return for a few hours to see in person to some business connected with the estate and left saying that he was going straight to you to ask you to put him up. That is bad enough, but this is worse. The police now think they have found a definite motive for you. They say you were in love with J. (Your late marriage, of course, would be put down to an act of panic.)

Now this information can have come from one person only, J. herself, so I tackled her about it. She was very reluctant to tell me anything but finally, while admitting the possibility that she might have been totally mistaken, did hint that in her opinion your attentions to her since her marriage have been a good deal more marked than one might have expected in the case of a man engaged to another girl. I need not tell you my own opinion that J. is a vain hussy and all this is pure moonshine due to her inordinate conceit; but I must admit that it would not sound at all a pretty story in court.

I am more than ever certain that everything now hinges on your being able to establish that F. was not where he pretended to be. So do your level best.

Yours, R.S.

P.S. J. is very bitter against you. She seems to have no doubt in her empty head that you did the deed.

"Well, I am blessed!" I exclaimed and showed the letter to Sylvia. "Really, I can't imagine how Joanna can have got such an extraordinary idea into her head. I'm quite certain I never gave her the least grounds for it."

Sylvia read the letter through carefully. "I never did like Joanna," was all she said.

It can be imagined that, after this news, we were more anxious than ever to succeed in the object of our journey. It was, therefore, with a full realisation of the fateful issues involved that we approached the Grand Hotel in Bellagio, which Frank had given as his address there.

While Sylvia engaged the reception clerk in a discussion regarding terms for a mythical stay next year I, as if idly, examined the register. My heart sank. There was the entry for the date in question. "Mr. and Mrs. Francis Chappell," unmistakably in Joanna's handwriting. Apparently they had only stayed for two nights.

Concealing my disappointment, I turned to the clerk. "I believe some friends of ours were staying here last May. English, of course. I don't suppose you remember them. The lady was very dark, with quite black hair and her husband was just about my build and not at all unlike me in face, except that he had a scar just here." I touched my right temple.

"Was he a gentleman of fast temper—no, quick temper, your friend?" asked the clerk, who spoke excellent English, with a slight smile.

"Yes," I agreed. "Occasionally perhaps he is. Why?"

"Oh, nothing. It was nothing at all," said the clerk hastily. Too hastily, for it was evidently something. "Just something that displeased the gentleman. Quite natural. Yes, signor, I remember your friends very well. Their name is Chappell, is it not? And they went on from here to Milan. I remember he told me he got the scar playing cricket when a boy. Is it not so?"

"It is," I said gloomily.

"You have a very good memory," remarked Sylvia.

"It is my business," beamed the clerk, evidently pleased with the compliment.

Disconsolately we made our way back across the lake to our hotel, where Sylvia vanished indoors to write a letter.

Rather to my surprise, considering how urgent our business was, Sylvia refused to go on to Rome the next day, nor even the day after that. She had always wanted to see the Italian lakes, she said and now she was here she was going to see them all. And see them all we did, Lugano, Maggiore and the rest at the cost of a day apiece. It was almost a week later before at last we found ourselves in Rome.

And there it seemed that our enquiries were to meet with just the same fate. The conversation with the hotel clerk was repeated almost word for word. Did he remember my friend? Certainly he did and again by name as well as behaviour (Frank seemed from the hints we had had to have traveled across Europe blazing a trail of fiery temper). There was no doubt at all about his having been there. Even the scar was once more in evidence.

Sylvia drew something out of her bag and pushed it across the counter. I saw what it was as she did so. It was a small but excellent photograph of Frank himself.

"Is that anything like Mr. Chappell?" she asked, almost carelessly.

The clerk took the photograph up and looked at it carefully. "It is like him, just a little. But it is not Mr. Chappell himself, as the Signora well knows. Oh, no."

Sylvia glanced at me. "I knew you'd need someone with you to do the real detecting," she said calmly, though her eyes were dancing.

Chapter XI

But that was not the end of my surprises.

Sylvia was contemplating the clerk thoughtfully. "Are you ever able to get away from here for the weekend?" she asked. "A long weekend?"

The man shook his head regretfully. "No, never. We do not have the English weekend in Italy."

"Oh!" said Sylvia.

"Only a week's holiday in a year we have. My holiday begins in three days time. I shall not be sorry."

Sylvia brightened. "Look here, how would you like to go to England for your week's holiday, all expenses paid?"

The man's voluble answer left no doubt of his liking for the idea. Sylvia arranged the details with him there and then.

"My darling," I said, when at last we were seated in a café a few streets away and could talk properly, "what on earth is it you're doing and how did you know the man with Joanna wasn't Frank at all?"

She gave me a superior smile. "It didn't strike you as curious, Hugh, that both those men remembered Frank so well, what with his temper and his scar, about which he was so confidential, and the rest? It didn't occur to you to wonder whether they remembered all the visitors at their hotels quite so thoroughly? It didn't strike you as though Frank had almost gone out of his way to be remembered at those two places so clearly?"

"Go on. Rub it in. No, it didn't."

"Poor lamb! Well, why should it have? You haven't got such a suspicious mind as I have. But all those things struck me. Also the fact that it was Joanna who signed the register. Very fishy, I thought. So I wrote off to Mr. Sheringham to get hold somehow of a photograph of Frank and send it to me *poste restante* at Rome. That's why I insisted on staying so long on the lakes, to give it time to arrive."

"Well, well," I said. "I'm quite glad I married you. So what is our programme now?"

"I must write to Mr. Sheringham at once and tell him what we've discovered and that we're bringing the witness back with us in two or three days' time."

"But why are we doing that?"

"I'm not going to let him go off on his holiday where we can't get hold of him," Sylvia retorted. "Besides, aren't there things called affidavits that he'll have to swear? Something like that. Anyhow, Mr. Sheringham will know, so to Mr. Sheringham he's going."

And to Mr. Sheringham, three days later, the man went. I think I have already hinted in this chronicle that when Sylvia makes up her mind to a thing...

Sheringham seemed scarcely less pleased to see him than us. He handed him over to Meadows with as much care as if he had been made of glass and might fall into pieces at any moment.

As soon as he had gone and Sylvia had received Sheringham's congratulations on her perspicacity, I asked eagerly whether anything further had come to light at this end of the affair.

Sheringham smiled, as if not ill-pleased with himself. "I think I've made some progress, but I'd rather not say anything just at the moment. I've arrived at one decision, though, Chappell, and that is that you must now come out in the open."

"Stop skulking?" I said. "I shall be only too pleased. I've nothing to hide and I dislike this hole and corner atmosphere I've been living in."

"But is it safe?" Sylvia asked anxiously.

"On that we've got to take a chance," Sheringham told her. "Personally, I think it will be. In any case, since getting your letter I've arranged a conference here this evening. I'm going to do my best to bring everyone into the open and with any luck developments may result."

"Who's coming?" I asked, a little uneasily. I was not sure that I cared for the sound of the word "conference."

"Well, Mrs. Chappell, for one."

"Joanna? Really, Sheringham, do you think it advisable—"

"And her brother, for another," he interrupted me. "You know him, I expect?"

"Well, very slightly. I met him at the wedding. That's all. I've heard of him, of course. Rather a—a—"

"Bad egg?"

"Exactly."

"Well, bad egg or not he's coming to support his sister in my omelet."

"Yes, but what have you found out, Mr. Sheringham?" Sylvia insisted. "What have you been doing these last ten days?"

"What have I found out?" Sheringham repeated whimsically. "Well, where to buy ice in your neighbourhood, for one thing. Very useful, in this hot weather."

Sylvia's eyes dilated. "Mr. Sheringham, you don't mean that Frank was killed right back in May and—and—"

"And kept on ice till August?" Sheringham laughed. "No, I certainly don't. The doctor was quite definite that he hadn't been dead for more than a couple of hours at the outside when he was found. And now don't ask me any more questions, because I'm determined not to spoil my conference for you."

It was by then nearly dinner time and Sheringham, refusing to satisfy our curiosity any further, insisted on our going off to dress. We had to take what heart we could from the fact that he certainly seemed remarkably confident.

Joanna and her brother, Cedric Wickham, were to arrive at nine o'clock. Actually they were a minute or two early.

The meeting, I need hardly say, was constrained in the extreme. From the expression of acute surprise on their faces it was clear that the other two had had no idea that we were to be present, a fact which Sheringham must have purposely concealed from us. Recovering themselves, Joanna greeted

us with the faintest nod, her brother, a tall, good-looking
fellow, with a scowl. As if noticing nothing in the least amiss,
Sheringham produced drinks.

Not more than three minutes later there was a ring at the
front door bell. The next moment the door of the room was
opened, a large, burly man was framed in the doorway and
Meadows announced: "Detective Chief Inspector Moresby."

Expecting as I did to be arrested on the spot, I put as
good a face on the encounter as I could, though I had a
task to appear altogether normal as the C.I.D. man, after a
positively benevolent nod to the others, advanced straight
towards me. But all he did was to put out a huge hand and
say: "Good evening, Mr. Chappell. And how are you, sir?
I've been wanting to meet you for some time." His blue eyes
twinkled genially.

I returned his smile as we shook hands—a proceeding
which Joanna and her brother watched decidedly askance.
They too, I think, had been expecting to see me led off, so
to speak, in chains.

"Now," said Sheringham briskly, "I'm glad to say I've
got news for you. A new witness. No credit to me, I'm
afraid. Mrs. Hugh Chappell is responsible. We'll have him
in straightaway, shall we, and hear what he's got to say." He
pressed the bell.

The Chief Inspector, as it were casually, strolled over to
a position nearer the door.

I think our little Italian thoroughly enjoyed his great
moment, though his English suffered a little under the strain.
He stood for a moment in the doorway, beaming at us and
then marched straight up to Cedric Wickham.

"Ah, it is a pleasure to meet antique faces again, *non è
vero?* Good evening, Mr. Frank Chappell!"

Chapter XII

Joanna, her brother and Chief Inspector Moresby had gone.

Almost immediately, as it seemed, after the little Italian clerk's identification of Cedric Wickham as the impersonator of Frank at Bellagio and Rome the room had appeared to fill with burly men, before whom the Chief Inspector had arrested Joanna and Cedric, the latter as the actual perpetrator of the murder and the former as accessory to it both before and after the fact. My own chauffeur, whose real name I now learned was Harvey, not that under which I had engaged him on poor Frank's recommendation, was already under arrest as a further accessory.

It was a terrible story that Sheringham told Sylvia and myself later that evening.

"There were two plots in existence," he said when we were settled in our chairs and the excitement of the treble arrest had begun to calm down. "The first was invented by your cousin himself, who called in his wife, his brother-in-law and Harvey to help him carry it out. The second was an adaptation by these three aimed against the originator of the first. Both, of course, were aimed against you, too.

"This was the first plot. I'm not quite clear myself yet on some of its details, but—"

At this point the telephone bell in the hall rang and Sheringham went out to answer it.

He was away a considerable time and when he returned it was with a graver face even than before.

"Mrs. Chappell has confessed," he said briefly. "She puts all the blame on the other two. I have every doubt of that and so have the police, but I can give you her whole story now. It fills up the gaps in my knowledge of the case." He sat down again in his chair.

"The first plot, then," he resumed, "was aimed against you, Chappell, by your cousin. It did not involve murder, although it was designed to put your possessions in his hands. To put it shortly, Frank had worked hard for two years and he didn't like it; what is more, he did not intend to work any longer. He determined to anticipate his inheritance from you. But, rotter though he was, he drew the line at murder. To get you shut up in a lunatic asylum for the rest of your life, with the result that he as your heir and next-of-kin would have the administering of your estate, was quite enough for his purpose.

"To achieve this result he hit on the idea of causing you several times to come across his apparently dead body, knowing that you would give the alarm and then, when the searchers and the police came, have no body to show for it. When this had happened three or four times, the suspicion that you were mad would become a certainty and the rest would follow. I think it only too likely that if the plan had been left at that it would almost certainly have succeeded."

"The devil!" Sylvia burst out indignantly.

"I'm quite sure it would," I agreed soberly. "The police were taken in and Gotley too and, upon my word, I was ready to wonder myself whether I wasn't mad. But what I can't understand is how he copied death so well. I hadn't the slightest suspicion that he wasn't dead. He not only looked dead, he *felt* dead."

"Yes—in the parts you did feel, which were the ones you were meant to feel. If you'd slipped your hand inside his shirt and felt his actual heart, instead of only the pulse in his wrist, you'd have felt it beating at once.

"Anyhow, the way he and Harvey went about it was this. About an hour before you were expected, Frank gave himself a stiff injection of morphia. They couldn't use chloroform, because of the smell. Harvey meantime was watching for you to start, having, of course, already put the car out of action so as to ensure your walking and through Horne's Copse at that. As soon as you set out or looked like doing so, Harvey ran on ahead at top speed for the copse, which he would reach about ten minutes before you.

"Ready waiting for him there was a tourniquet, a bottle of atropine drops and a block of ice fashioned roughly to the shape of a mask and wrapped in a blanket. He clapped the ice over your cousin's face and another bit over his right hand and wrist and fastened it there, put the tourniquet on his right arm above the elbow and slipped off the ice mask for a moment, when his hand was steadier, to put a few of the atropine drops into Frank's eyes to render the pupils insensible to light. Then he arranged the limbs with the dead pulse invitingly upwards and so on, waited till he could actually hear you coming, and then whipped off the ice blocks and retreated down the path. After you'd gone to give the alarm, of course, he cleared the ground of your traces, match sticks and so on and carried Frank out of the way, coming back to smooth out any footprints he might have made in so doing.

"In the meantime, Joanna's brother was impersonating Frank abroad, just in the unlikely event of your making any enquiries over there, though, as your wife very shrewdly spotted, he overdid his attempts to impress the memory of himself on the hotel staff. And, of course, she answered your telegrams. By the way, as an example of their thoroughness I've just heard that your cousin engaged two single rooms instead of one double one through the whole tour, so that the fact of it being done at Bellagio and Rome, where it was necessary, wouldn't appear odd afterwards. Well, that's the first plot and, as I say, it very nearly came off.

"The second was, in my own opinion, most probably instigated by Joanna herself, or Joanna and Harvey. Frank didn't know, when he brought into his own scheme a man who would help because he was in love with Frank's wife, that Frank's wife was in love with him. You told me yourself that the Wickhams are rotten stock, though you didn't think that Joanna was tainted. She was, worse than any of them (except perhaps her own brother), but morally, not physically. To take advantage of Frank's plot by having him actually killed in the hope that you (if the evidence was rigged a little on the spot, which Harvey was in a position to do) would be hanged for his murder, was nothing to her."

"Is that what was really intended?" Sylvia asked, rather white.

Sheringham nodded. "That was the hope, in which event of course her infant son would inherit and she would more or less administer things for him till he came of age, marrying Harvey at her leisure and with a nice fat slice of the proceeds earmarked for brother Cedric. If things didn't go so well as that, there was always Frank's original scheme to fall back on, which would give almost as good a result, though with that there was always the danger of your being declared sane again."

"And the police," I exclaimed, "were for a time actually bamboozled!"

"No," Sheringham laughed. "We must give Scotland Yard its due. I learned today that, though puzzled, they never seriously suspected you, and what's more, they knew where you were the whole time and actually helped you to get abroad, hoping you'd help them to clear up their case for them, and in fact you did."

"How silly of them," Sylvia pronounced. "When we were out of the country they lost track of us."

"Yes?" said Sheringham. "By the way, did you make any friends on the trip?"

"No. At least, only one. There was quite a nice man stay-ing at Cadenabbia who was actually going on to Rome the same day as we did. He was very helpful about trains and so on. We took quite a fancy to him, didn't we, Hugh?"

"He is a nice fellow, isn't he?" Sheringham smiled.

"Oh, do you know him? No, of course you can't; you don't even know who I mean."

"Indeed I do," Sheringham retorted. "You mean Detec-tive Inspector Peters of the C.I.D., though I don't think you knew that yourself, Mrs. Chappell."

The Perfect Plan

James Hilton

Born in Lancashire and educated at Cambridge, James Hilton (1900–1954) published his first novel at the age of twenty, and was an established author by the time his solitary detective novel, *Murder at School* (also known as *Was it Murder?*), appeared in 1931, under the pen-name Glen Trevor. Two years later came *Lost Horizon*, filmed famously by Frank Capra and decades later as a Seventies musical. *Goodbye, Mr Chips*, *Random Harvest*, and *We are Not Alone* soon followed, and the film versions also became box office hits. Hilton moved to California, and won an Academy Award for his contribution to the screenplay for *Mrs Miniver*.

Hollywood's gain was detective fiction's loss. Hilton's rare ventures into the crime genre show a distinctive talent in the making. *Murder at School* was a soundly crafted story, and "The Perfect Plan" is an accomplished take on the familiar concept of the perfect criminal scheme that might just turn out to have a fatal flaw.

◇◇◇

Every public man has his enemies, but few of these enemies would wish to murder him, or are in a position to do so in any case. Sir George Winthrop-Dunster, however, was unfortunate in these respects. He had his enemies, and one of them, his secretary, both wished to murder him, and did so.

Sir George, as chairman of the Anglo-Oceanic group of companies, was what is called "a well-known figure in the City." He belonged to the modern school of financiers who instead of being fat, heavy-jowled, gold-ringed, and white-spatted, look more like overgrown public-school prefects. He was fifty-five, played energetic squash-rackets, wore neat lounge suits, and as often as not lunched in a pub off a glass of sherry and a ham sandwich.

Scarsdale, his private secretary, was not unlike him in physique, but nearly a quarter of a century younger. With a First in Greats at Oxford and a B.Sc. Econ. of London, he was well equipped to deal with the numerous complications of Sir George's affairs, and for five years he had given every satisfaction. Well, almost. Just one little rift had once appeared—in 1928, when Scarsdale had rashly bought Amal. Zincs in greater quantities than he had cash to pay for. He had not exactly pledged Sir George's credit in the transaction, but he had made use of Sir George's stockbroker, and when the account finished with Amal. Zincs well down, it was to Sir George that he had perforce to confess the little mishap. A hundred pounds more than covered everything, and Sir George wrote a check instantly. He did not lecture, or even rebuke; he merely specified arrangements by which the sum could be repaid out of Scarsdale's monthly salary.

This amounted to three hundred a year, and within two years the debt had been fully repaid, plus interest at 5 per cent. No other unfortunate incident had occurred, and the relations between the two men seemed as good as ever. Then, in 1930, Scarsdale received a tentative offer of a better post. It was an important one, and his prospective employer, purely as a matter of routine, wished to effect a fidelity insurance for which a testimonial from Sir George would be necessary.

When Scarsdale approached Sir George about this, the financier talked to him with all the suavity he usually reserved for shareholders' meetings. "My dear Scarsdale," he replied, in his curiously high-pitched voice, "I have no objection whatever to your leaving me, but I have, I admit, a certain reluctance to putting my name to any statement that is not absolutely correct. Take this question, for instance: 'Have you always found him to be strictly honest and reliable while in your service?' Now, my truthful reply to that would be: 'With one exception, yes.' Do you think that would help you?"

Obviously it would have been worse than no reply at all, and in default of the required testimonial the offer of the job fell through, and Scarsdale remained Sir George's secretary. Sir George, no doubt, congratulated himself on having secured a permanently good bargain. He was that kind of a man.

But had he known it, he was really much less to be congratulated. For just as Sir George was *that* kind of a man, so Scarsdale was another kind, equally rare perhaps.

It was not until a year had passed that Scarsdale decided that the time had come to murder Sir George. During the interval he had come to regard the matter with something of the detachment of the chess player; indeed, the problem had rather comforted than worried him amid the botherations of a secretary's life. He had always, since his school days, been interested in the science of crime, and never for a moment did he doubt his own capacity to do the job; it was merely a question of waiting until the perfect moment offered itself. That moment seemed to him to be arriving in February 1931—his choice being determined by two fortuitous circumstances—(1) that at 8 p.m. on Saturday the 22nd, Sir George was to deliver a broadcast talk on "Post-War Monetary Policy," and (2) that immediately after the talk, which was to be given from the London studio, he intended to travel to Banbury to spend the weekend with his brother Richard.

On the morning of the 22nd Scarsdale awoke at his usual time at Bramstock Towers, Berkshire. It was a pleasant establishment, surrounded by a large and well-wooded estate, and Scarsdale, glancing through the window as he dressed, was glad to see that there had been no rain during the night and that the weather was fine and cold.

Sir George always breakfasted in his bedroom, and did not meet his secretary until ten o'clock, in the library. By this time Scarsdale had, as usual, been at work for an hour or so opening letters and typing replies for Sir George's signature. After an exchange of good mornings, Sir George made a very customary announcement. "I'll just look through these letters, Scarsdale; then we'll take a turn round the garden while I tell you about my wireless talk tonight. I want you to prepare a few notes for me...."

"Certainly, Sir George," replied Scarsdale. A great piece of luck, for the after-breakfast tour of the estate, though almost an institution in fine weather, might just, for one reason or another, have been foregone.

The men were soon dressed for outdoors and strolling briskly across the terrace towards the woods—the usual gambit, Scarsdale observed, with continuing satisfaction. Sir George meanwhile divided his attention between the garden and his impending radio talk. "You see, Scarsdale, I want those figures about the American Federal Reserve note issue.... Ah, that *cupressus macrocarpa* seems to be doing nicely.... And a month-to-month table of Wall Street brokers' loans...." And so on, till they were deep in the woods, over half a mile from the house. The thickets, even in mid-winter, were very dark. "I want your notes by three at the latest, so that I can catch the 3:50 from Lincott and work up my talk in the train.... Ah, just look at that—Fanning really ought to notice these things. Confound the fellow!"

Fanning was the head gardener, and "that" was nothing more dreadful than an old kettle under a bush. But to Sir George it was serious enough, for if there were one thing that annoyed him more than another it was the suggestion of trespassers on his land. "Why the devil don't Fanning and his men keep their eyes open?" he exclaimed crossly; but in that he did Fanning an injustice, since the kettle had not been there more than a few hours; Scarsdale, in fact, had placed it there himself the evening before.

Suddenly Scarsdale cried: "Why, look there, sir—the door of the hut's open! A tramp, I suppose. Wonder if he's still inside, by any chance."

At this point Sir George began to behave precisely as Scarsdale had guessed and hoped he would. He left the path and strode vehemently amid the trees and undergrowth towards the small square erection just visible in the near distance. "By Jove, Scarsdale," he shouted, "if I do catch the fellow, I'll teach him a lesson."

"Yes, rather," agreed Scarsdale.

Striding together through the less and less penetrable thickets, they reached the hut at last. It was built of grey stone, with a stout wooden door—the whole edifice intended originally as a sort of summerhouse, but long disused. For years it had functioned at rare intervals as a store place for sawn-up logs; but now, as Scarsdale entered it, it proved empty even of them. Nor was there a tramp in it, either. "He must have gone, sir," said Scarsdale, pulling wide open the half-gaping door. "Though it does look as if he's left a few relics.... I say, sir, what do you make of this?" He waited for Sir George to enter. "Damnation, that's my last match gone! Have you a match, Sir George?"

As Sir George began to fumble in his pocket in the almost complete darkness Scarsdale added: "I say, sir, you've dropped something—your handkerchief, I think."

Sir George stooped, and at the same instant Scarsdale shot him neatly through the head with a small automatic pistol which he had that very morning abstracted from the drawer of the Boule cabinet in Sir George's private study.

Afterwards, still wearing gloves, of course, he placed the weapon by the side of the dead man, closed the door carefully from the outside, and walked away.

All murders—all enterprises of any kind, in fact—carry with their accomplishment a certain minimum of risk; and at this point, as Scarsdale had all along recognized, the risks began. Fortunately, they were very small ones. The hut was isolated and only rarely visited; Fanning and his men were not interested in it at all and the whole incident of the visiting tramp had been a mere invention to lure Sir George to the spot. Scarsdale felt reasonably sure that the body would remain undiscovered until a deliberate search were made.

Leaving the woods, he returned to the house by way of the garages. There he took out his two-seater car, drove it round to the front of the house, and had a friendly chat with Wilkes, the butler. "Oh, Wilkes, would you mind bringing down Sir George's suitcase? He's decided to go right on to town immediately, so he won't be in to lunch. He's walking over to Lincott through the fields…. Oh, and you might label the bag for Banbury—I've got to get it sent off at the station."

"Will you be returning to lunch yourself, sir?"

"Oh, yes."

"Very good, sir."

Lincott, which Scarsdale reached through winding lanes within a quarter of an hour, was a middle-sized village with a large and important railway junction. There were three facts about Lincott that were, from Scarsdale's point of view, fortunate—(1) its railway station was large, frequented, and badly lit; (2) there were convenient expresses to London, as well as a late "down" train at night; and (3) Sir George's estate offered a pleasant short cut to the village, a short cut which Sir George was fond of traversing on foot and alone, even after dark.

Scarsdale drove direct to the junction and left the suitcase for despatch to Banbury, whence it would be forwarded immediately to the house of Sir George's brother. Then he proceeded to a neighboring garage, arranged to leave his car until called for, and asked to use the telephone. Ringing up the Towers, he had a second amiable talk with Wilkes. "Oh, hullo, Wilkes—this is Scarsdale speaking—from Lincott. Sir George has slightly changed his plans again—or rather my plans. He wants me to go along to town with him right away. Yes…. Yes…. I'm leaving my car here….Yes, that's what I want to tell you—I've decided that as I'm going to town I may as well spend the weekend there at my club…. I'll be back on Tuesday, you know…. Yes…. Good-bye…."

Scarsdale then walked to the junction, booked a third-class single ticket to Paddington, and caught the 1 p.m. train. At Paddington he did several things. First he went to the local booking-office and purchased a third-class single ticket to Ealing. Then he took a snack at a nearby A.B.C. shop, and about 3 p.m. travelled by omnibus to the bank, whence he walked to the Anglo-Oceanic offices in Bishopsgate. There he met several people whom he knew very well, chatted with them affably, and busied himself for some time in Sir George's private office. "Yes, Sir George is in town, but he's very busy—I don't suppose you'll see him here today."

Williamson, one of the head-office people, grinned. "Yes, he's busy," Scarsdale repeated, faintly returning the grin. They both knew that there were aspects of Sir George's life that had nothing to do with the Anglo-Oceanic companies. "Taking her to the theatre, eh?" queried Williamson.

"More likely to the cinema," returned Scarsdale. "He's not free tonight, anyhow—he's got a date at the B.B.C.—and left me the devil's own pile of work to finish, too."

It was quite natural, therefore, that Scarsdale should still be at work in Sir George's private office when Williamson and the rest of the staff left. At 6 p.m., by which time the huge office building was tenantless, Scarsdale, having previously made fast the door on the inside, turned to a little job that he had not cared to tackle before. Opening the safe by means of the combination, he carefully abstracted certain documents—to be precise, South American bearer bonds to the value of between thirty and forty thousand pounds. How odd, he reflected, that Sir George, who would not give him a simple testimonial of honesty, had never scrupled to leave the keys and combination of his private safe in an unlocked bureau drawer at the Towers!

Leaving the Anglo-Oceanic offices about 6:30 p.m., Scarsdale took an omnibus to Piccadilly Circus and entered a cinema that was showing a film so remarkably bad that in the five-and-ninepenny seats he had almost an entire row to himself at that early hour of the evening. There and then, in the surrounding gloom, he managed to transform himself into a fairly credible impersonation of Sir George Winthrop-Dunster. In build and dress they were rather similar: nothing else was required but a few touches of grease-paint, a false moustache, and the adjustment of Sir George's characteristic type of horn-rimmed spectacles. The disguise would have deceived anyone who did not know Sir George intimately.

Scarsdale left the cinema about 7:30, choosing the middle of a film. A few moments in a telephone booth enabled him, with the help of a pocket-mirror, to make good any small deficiencies in his quick change. It had all, so far, been delightfully easy. At 7:55 he took a taxi to the old B.B.C. headquarters in Savoy Hill.

Neither he nor Sir George had ever broadcast before, and Scarsdale was quite genuinely interested in the experience. In the reception room he had an amiable chat with one of the studio officials, and found no difficulty at all in keeping up the character and impersonation of Sir George. Indeed he not only talked and behaved like Sir George, but he found himself even thinking as Sir George would have thought—which was rather horrible.

At eight o'clock he took his place in the thick-carpeted studio and began to read from his typed manuscript. It was a cosy and completely restful business. With the little green-shaded lamp illuminating the script and the perfectly silent surroundings, it was a comfort to realize that, by such simple means, he was fabricating an alibi that could be vouched for afterwards by hundreds of thousands of worthy folk all over the country. He read Sir George's views on monetary policy with a perfection of utterance that surprised even himself, especially the way he had got the high-pitched voice.

Leaving the studios half an hour later he asked the commissionaire in the hall to get him a taxi, and in the man's hearing told the driver "Paddington." There he commenced another series of operations. First he put through a long distance call to Richard Winthrop-Dunster, of Banbury. "That you, Richard?" sang out the high-pitched voice, still functioning. "I'm extremely sorry, but I'm afraid I won't be able to spend the weekend at your place after all. Fact is, I've got a rather worrying piece of business on hand at the moment, and I can't spare the time.... Yes, things *are* infernally worrying just now…. Next week I might come—I'll try to, anyhow, so you might keep my bag, if it's arrived—oh, it *has*, has it? Yes, I told young Scarsdale to send it….Yes, that's right—keep it till next week….I'm at Paddington, just about to catch the 9:15 home—yes, I've just come from the studio—were you listening?…Yes…. Yes….Goodbye, then—next week, I hope…."

Then Scarsdale went to the booking office and purchased a first-class single ticket to Lincott. Passing the barrier, he even risked a word or two with the man who snipped his ticket, and who knew Sir George very slightly. "Cold evening, Sir George," the man said.

Scarsdale found an empty first-class compartment and as soon as the train moved out from the platform, opened the small nondescript attaché-case which he had carried with him all day. With the help of its contents, he began to make sundry changes in his personal appearance; then taking from his pocket the single ticket to Ealing purchased earlier in the day, he cut out of it a triangular section similar to that snipped from his Lincott ticket. Finally, at Ealing, a slim, clean-shaven fellow in a cloth cap might have been seen to leave the train and climb the steps to the street. He carried a brown-paper parcel which, if examined, would have been found to contain (rather oddly) an attaché-case.

Scarsdale boarded a bus going east, and at Ealing Common changed to an Underground train. At 10 p.m.— long before the train from Paddington would have reached Lincott—Scarsdale, himself again, was entering a West End restaurant and exchanging a cordial good evening with a head waiter who knew him well by sight.

Throughout the weekend Scarsdale stayed in London, visiting numerous friends—indeed, there was scarcely an hour from morning to midnight which he did not spend in company. His nights at the club were conveniently preluded by friendly chats with the hall porter, and in the mornings, at breakfast, he was equally affable to the waiter.

On Tuesday afternoon he returned to the Towers, collecting his car at Lincott on the way, and got to work immediately on Sir George's accumulated correspondence. "I know Sir George will expect to find everything finished," he explained to Wilkes.

But dinner time came and Sir George did not arrive. It was peculiar, because he was usually back by the six o'clock train when he visited his brother.

At nine Scarsdale decided to have dinner without further waiting; but when ten o'clock came and it was clear that Sir George had not caught the last train from Banbury, Scarsdale agreed with Wilkes that Richard Winthrop-Dunster had better be informed of the situation. "Maybe Sir George is staying there an extra night," said Scarsdale, as the butler hurried to the telephone.

Five minutes later Wilkes returned with a pale and troubled face. "Mr. Richard says that Sir George never visited him at all, sir," he began falteringly. "He says Sir George rang him up late on Saturday night from Paddington cancelling the visit and saying he was on his way back here."

"Extraordinary!" exclaimed Scarsdale. "Why isn't he here then? Where the devil can he be?"

They discussed the problem with an increasing degree of consternation until midnight, and went to bed with mutually expressed hopes that some message might arrive by the morning's post. But none came. At noon, after consultation with Scarsdale and further telephoning to Banbury, Wilkes notified the police. Inspector Deane, of the local force, arrived during the afternoon, and after acquainting himself with the known details of the situation, motored over to Banbury to see Mr. Richard Winthrop-Dunster. All that was on Wednesday.

On Thursday morning enquiries began at Paddington station, with immediate and gratifying result. As Inspector Deane put it: "Well, Mr. Scarsdale, we've traced Sir George as far as the Lincott train on Saturday night—there's a ticket inspector at Paddington who remembers him. We're not quite sure of him at Lincott, but no doubt he must have been seen there too."

Everything, Scarsdale was glad to perceive, was still working out perfectly according to plan. From Paddington the trail had already led to Lincott; soon it would lead from Lincott to the Towers—and on the way, to be discovered inevitably when the constabulary intelligence had progressed so far, was that little hut in the woods. But it was not part of Scarsdale's plan to anticipate this inevitability by any hint or suggestion. He merely said; "Perhaps you could advertise for information. The taximen in the station yard may have noticed him, or one of them may have driven him somewhere. Of course, if it was a fine night he may have walked. He often walks. It was a fine night in London, I remember."

"Quite so, sir," agreed Inspector Deane. "I'm sure I'm greatly obliged to you for the idea."

It was queer how the two men "took to" each other; Scarsdale had a delightful knack of putting people at their ease. But for the mischance of working for Sir George, he would probably never have murdered anybody.

The plan remained perfect—indeed, he thought, as he settled for sleep that night, he could afford almost to be indifferent now; the dangerous interval was past, and it no longer greatly mattered when or how the body was discovered. Perhaps it would be tomorrow, or the next day, or the next week even, if the police were exceptionally stupid. He had in mind exactly what would happen subsequently. The medical evidence would, of course, be vague after such a lapse of time, but fully consistent with Sir George's death having taken place late on Saturday night, at an hour (if the matter were ever called into question) when he, Scarsdale, had several complete alibis sixty miles away. Then would come the question: How had it happened? At such a juncture the dead man's brother would probably recall that Sir George had stated over the telephone on the fatal night, that he was "worried" about some business affair. Scarsdale would then, with a little reluctance to discuss the private affairs of his late employer, admit that Sir George had had certain financial troubles of late. The next stage of revelation would doubtless be enacted at the Anglo-Oceanic office, when and where the disappearance of the bonds would be discovered. That would certainly cause a sensation, both in the City and beyond. Clearly it would suggest that Sir George, having monkeyed with the assets of his companies, had taken his life rather than face the music.

All this, of course, was according to Scarsdale's plan, and when, on Thursday morning, the police found the body of Sir George in the little hut in the woods, Scarsdale might have been excused for reckoning his plan ninety-nine per cent infallible. Unfortunately for him, the remaining one per cent took a hand, with the rather odd result that a man named Hansell was arrested a few hours later and charged with the murder of Sir George.

Hansell was an unemployed workman turned tramp, and had been arrested in a Lincott public-house after trying to pawn a watch which an alert shopman recognized as Sir George's. At first Hansell gave the usual yarn about having found the watch, but after a severe questioning at the police station he told a much more extraordinary story. On the previous Saturday, he said, about a quarter past eight in the evening, he had been trespassing in the woods belonging to the Towers estate. Finding the little hut he had pushed open the door and had there, to his great alarm and astonishment, come across the dead body of a man. At first he thought of going for help immediately, but as he felt that his own position might be thought rather questionable, he had contented himself in the end with rifling the pockets and decamping. He admitted having taken some papers and a wallet, which he had since destroyed, except for a few treasury notes it had contained. He had also taken the watch.

But at 8:15 p.m., as the police detectives did not fail to point out, Sir George had been broadcasting a talk from the B.B.C. studio in London. How, then, could he have been found sixty miles away, dead, at the same hour? Obviously Hansell must be a great liar.

He was brought before the local magistrates and speedily committed for trial at the assizes. Meanwhile Scarsdale, in the midst of well-simulated grief at the loss of a respected employer, was thinking hard. The arrest of Hansell had given him a shock at first, but he was not long in finding a way of fitting it into his plan. Indeed, now that the suicide theory was all out of focus, Scarsdale himself thought fit to make the discovery about the missing bonds, and was inclined to agree with the police when they suggested that the bonds might have been among the papers that Hansell had stolen from Sir George's pockets and afterwards destroyed.

The trial of Hansell came on in due course. He pleaded "Not Guilty," but his story sounded pretty thin, and was not improved by the fact that he still insisted that he had found the body at 8:15 p.m. He had heard the Lincott church clock chime the quarter, he said, and no amount of cross-examination could shake him. Moreover, the prosecution were able to prove that his fingerprints were on the automatic pistol. Hansell explained this by saying that he had found the weapon lying beside the body and had picked it up; but the story was unconvincing. Was it not more likely that Sir George had been taking the short cut home from

Lincott station (as he often did), that he had been attacked by Hansell and had drawn his automatic (which he often carried) to defend himself, that Hansell had wrested it from him, and had shot him with it, and had afterwards dragged the body into the shed and, in sheer panic, left the telltale weapon behind?

Defending counsel could only offer the alternative theory of suicide, which, in the case of so well-respected a personage as Sir George, seemed a breach of taste as well as a straining of probability. As for Hansell, he must, whatever he said, have mistaken the time of his visit to the hut. Neither of these suggestions appealed to judge and jury, and it was not surprising that Hansell was found guilty and sentenced to death. This was afterwards commuted to penal servitude for life.

Scarsdale, with the trial over and everything settling down, had now only the tail end of his plan to put into cautious execution. He would wait, he had decided, for twelve months (to avoid any semblance of flight), and then go abroad, probably to the Argentine, taking with him the bonds. After a year or two in Buenos Aires he would doubtless have formed a sufficiently intimate connection with some banker or stockbroker to enable him to begin disposing of the booty.

It has already been noted that the verdict of "murder" instead of "suicide" did not at first disturb the vast and almost terrifying equanimity of Scarsdale. What did trouble him, however, as time passed and the death of Sir George became history, was the gradually invading consciousness that the only thing that had saved him from the dock, and possibly from the gallows, was not his precious plan at all, but sheer luck! For if Hansell had reported the finding of the body without delay, the faked alibi of the broadcast would have been discovered. Scarsdale had been saved, then, not by the flawlessness of his own brainwork but by a casual circumstance entirely outside of his control!

It was an unwelcome conclusion to reach, partly because it robbed him of pride in achievement, but chiefly because it laid him open to disquieting thoughts of the future.

During the year of waiting in England he lived at Kew, renting a house near the river and living on his savings while he devoted himself to writing a book on his favourite subject—criminology. It passed the time; besides which, he had hopes that it would eventually establish his reputation.

He received several minor shocks during this period. One happened when an acquaintance named Lindsey accosted him suddenly at his club (and apropos of nothing at all): "You know, Scarsdale, you're awfully like old Dunster in appearance. Did you ever realize that? I'm sure you could easily have passed for him during his lifetime with the help of a false moustache and those goggles of his! Especially, too, if you could have managed that rather shrill way of talking he had. And you *are* a bit of an actor-chap, aren't you? Didn't you once play in something at Oxford?"

Scarsdale wondered whether his face were turning fiery red or ashen pale. He managed to laugh, and an hour or so later reached the satisfying conclusion that it had all been pure chance—nothing but that. But it was upsetting, all the same, and it was about this time that he began the habit of carrying a small automatic pistol about with him wherever he went. He would not be taken alive.

Just about a month before the year was up, Lindsey telephoned him with immense cheerfulness one morning. "Oh, hullo, Scarsdale. I'm in a job now, and you'll never guess where. It's in the B.B.C...." Several minutes of excited chatter, and then: "By the way, how would you like to do a short talk on Crimes and Criminals, or something of the sort? We're getting up a series here and your name occurred to me—you've always been keen on the subject, haven't you? What about June 11th, say?"

Scarsdale had hoped to be in Buenos Aires by that date, but he could not very well say so, and some kind of caution urged him not to make excuses. Besides, he could not help being slightly thrilled at the prospect of making a whole country listen to his views on crime and criminals. He told Lindsey that the date would suit him quite well.

During the eight weeks' interval, however, there came to him once or twice the faintest possible misgiving—soon banished, but leaving nevertheless a flavour of anxiety behind.

On the evening of June 11th he did not feel at his best as he set out for Savoy Hill. He was due to speak from 8 p.m. until 8:20, and he could not escape the recollection of the last time he had entered the building. It was odd, perhaps, that the very same announcer should be welcoming him again now, though it was quite natural, no doubt, that the announcer, knowing that Scarsdale had been Sir George's secretary should begin to chat about the deceased gentleman. "Awfully sad business that was," commented the familiar dulcet tones. "I talked to him that very evening just as I'm talking to you now. Amazing that he should have been so near his tragic end—indeed, I often wonder if he had any premonition of it himself, because he seemed just slightly uneasy in manner."

"Did he?" said Scarsdale.

"Of course it may have been my imagination. I was only comparing him with other times I'd heard him speak—at company meetings. Fortunately, I'd already sold all my Anglo-Oceanics. Queer he should have been carrying all those bonds about with him—forty thousand pounds' worth of them, wasn't it?"

"It was never absolutely proved."

"But bearer bonds, weren't they? Doesn't that mean that anybody who got hold of them could raise money on them?"

"More or less," answered Scarsdale absently. He had suddenly begun to feel troubled. He wished he had not arrived early enough for this chat.

By 7:55 the announcer had reached the stage of offering a few general tips about broadcasting. "This is your first experience of the microphone, I understand, Mr. Scarsdale?"

Scarsdale nodded.

"Curious—I thought I recognized your face. Or perhaps you're very like someone else…. However, you'll soon get over mike-fright, even if you do have a touch of it at first. The chief point to remember is, never to speak too fast or in a very high-pitched voice. But then, you don't, as a matter of fact, do you?"

Scarsdale was a trifle pale. "I don't think so," he murmured.

Five minutes later he sat at the little desk before the microphone, with the green-shaded lamp before him. He was certainly nervous, and beyond his nervousness, strangely uneasy in a deeper sense. It was peculiar; he hadn't been like it before. As he sat down, his foot caught in the flex that connected the lamp with the wallplug; the lamp went out, but it did not matter; the globes overhead were sufficient to see by. He waited for the red light to deliver its signal, indicating that he had been properly introduced to his unseen audience; then he began to read his manuscript.

But all the time he was reading, he was thinking and pondering subconsciously…he had been there before…the announcer had thought so, too…the announcer had seen and heard Sir George in the flesh at company meetings… the announcer had told him he must avoid a high-pitched voice…bearer bonds…this was the very same studio—and the same time also—eight o'clock…and it was Lindsey who had fixed up his talk, and Lindsey who had once commented on his likeness to Sir George....

Suddenly the idea burst over him in full force, monstrous, all-conquering: this was all a plant—engineered jointly by Lindsey and the B.B.C.—with perhaps Scotland Yard in the discreet background—they were testing him, and by the very latest psychological methods, as expounded by the great French criminologists.... They guessed the truth and were probing subtly—it was *their* perfect plan seeking to undermine *his*...

At that moment, while Scarsdale's eyes and voice were reading automatically, the announcer stole into the room and silently replaced the lamp-plug in the wall-socket. The green light blazed suddenly into Scarsdale's face as the intruder, in a whisper too soft to be audible to the microphone, murmured: "Pulled it off, didn't you? I thought that's what must have happened...."

Scarsdale's broadcast talk on Crimes and Criminals will never, it is safe to say, be forgotten in the history of the radio. Most listeners, as the talk progressed, must have been aware of a growing tension in the speaker's delivery—a tension ill-suited both to matter and theme. But it is certain that no listener remained unthrilled when, about sixteen minutes past eight, Scarsdale exclaimed, in a voice vibrating with excitement: "And here, if I may be permitted, I will interpose an example of what I consider to be the really perfect, undetectable crime...*I myself murdered Sir George Winthrop-Dunster*...."

At this point the loud-speakers in some hundreds of thousands of homes delivered themselves of a mysterious crashing sound, followed by a long silence until 8:35, when a familiar Oxford accent expressed regret for the delay and gave out, without further comment, the continuation of the evening's programme.

In the morning, however, the newspapers were less reticent. Scarsdale, it appeared, had made history by being the first person actually to commit suicide before the microphone. He had shot himself.

The inquest was held the following day and attracted great attention. The announcer was very gentle and soothing in giving evidence—almost as if he were reading an S.O.S. "It seemed to me," he said, "that Mr. Scarsdale was rather upset about something when he arrived at the studio. He was a few minutes early and we chatted together. We talked a little about Sir George Winthrop-Dunster. I concluded that Mr. Scarsdale was probably nervous, as it was his first broadcast. About halfway through the talk I noticed that the lamp over his desk had gone out—he must have caught his foot in the flex and pulled the plug away. I went in to put it right for him and noticed then that he wasn't looking at all well. He was very pale, and he stared at me in a rather queer way when I mentioned something about the light. A few minutes later I had to put up the signal warning him not to talk in such a high-pitched voice because the sound wasn't coming through properly. The next I heard was his extraordinary statement about—er—Sir George Winthrop-Dunster. Of course I rushed to cut off the microphone immediately, but before I could do so I heard the shot...."

The verdict was naturally one of "Suicide during temporary insanity."

Even the last of Scarsdale's plans went astray. Instead of being fearfully acknowledged as the perpetrator of the world's perfect murder, he was dismissed as that familiar and rather troublesome type—the neurotic person who confesses to a crime of which he is quite obviously innocent. "Poor Scarsdale," said Inspector Deane, in a special interview for one of the Sunday papers, "had been deeply distressed by the tragic death of his employer, and that, coupled with his interest in criminology (I understand he was writing a book on the subject), had combined to unhinge his mind....We often get similar confessions during well-known murder trials, and as a rule, as on this occasion, we can spot them at a glance." Answering a further question, Inspector Deane remarked: "As a matter of fact, Scarsdale wasn't within fifty miles of Lincott during the whole of the time that the crime could possibly have been committed. We know that, because in the ordinary course of police routine we had to check up his movements....Poor fellow, we all liked him. He helped us a good deal in our work though it was clear all the time that he was feeling things badly."

Just one point remains—about those bonds. If ever it should be discovered that Scarsdale had had in his possession a small fortune in South American bearer certificates, a certain measure of suspicion would inevitably be cast upon him—albeit posthumously. But will such a discovery be made? Scarsdale had put them in a tin box and had buried the box three feet deep in the back garden of the house he rented at Kew; and who, pray, is ever likely to dig them up?

The Same to Us

Margery Allingham

Margery Allingham (1904–1966) came from literary stock and published her first novel whilst still a teenager. Her most famous character, Albert Campion, had a low-key role in *The Crime at Black Dudley* (1929), but soon moved to centre stage. Originally a rather mysterious scoundrel, he (like Raffles long before) developed into a more appealing character; he remained enigmatic, however, and Allingham amused herself by dropping hints that he was connected to the royal family.

Allingham was a talented writer who became increasingly keen to shake off the constraints of the conventional whodunit. Some of her experiments were more successful than others, but the quality of her best work is such that her reputation endures to this day, and the Margery Allingham Society is thriving. This story, first published as long ago as 1934, makes a telling point.

◇◇◇

It was particularly unfortunate for Mrs Christopher Molesworth that she should have had burglars on the Sunday night of what was, perhaps, the crowningly triumphant week-end of her career as a hostess.

As a hostess Mrs Molesworth was a connoisseur. She chose her guests with a nice discrimination, disdaining everything but the most rare. Mere notoriety was no passport to Molesworth Court.

Nor did mere friendship obtain many crumbs from the Molesworth table, though the ability to please and do one's piece might possibly earn one a bed when the lion of the hour promised to be dull, uncomfortable and liable to be bored.

That was how young Petterboy came to be there at the great week-end. He was diplomatic, presentable, near enough a teetotaller to be absolutely trustworthy, even at the end of the evening, and he spoke a little Chinese.

This last accomplishment had done him but little good before, save with very young girls at parties, who relieved their discomfort at having no conversation by persuading him to tell them how to ask for their baggage to be taken ashore at Hong Kong, or to ascertain the way to the bathroom at a Peking hotel.

However, now the accomplishment was really useful, for it obtained for him an invitation to Mrs Molesworth's greatest week-end party.

This party was so select that it numbered but six all told. There were the Molesworths themselves–Christopher Molesworth was an M.P., rode to hounds, and backed up his wife in much the same way as a decent black frame backs up a coloured print.

Then there was Petterboy himself, the Feison brothers, who looked so restful and talked only if necessary, and finally the guest of all time, the gem of a magnificent collection, the catch of a lifetime, Dr Koo Fin, the Chinese scientist himself–Dr Koo Fin, the Einstein of the East, the man with the Theory. After quitting his native Peking he had only left his house in New England on one memorable occasion when he delivered a lecture in Washington to an audience which was unable to comprehend a word. His works were translated but since they were largely concerned with higher mathematics the task was comparatively simple.

Mrs Molesworth had every reason to congratulate herself on her capture. 'The Chinese Einstein', as the newspapers had nicknamed him, was hardly a social bird. His shyness was proverbial, as was also his dislike and mistrust of women. It was this last foible which accounted for the absence of femininity at Mrs Molesworth's party. Her own presence was unavoidable, of course, but she wore her severest gowns, and took a mental vow to speak as little as necessary. It is quite conceivable that had Mrs Molesworth been able to change her sex she would have done so nobly for that week-end alone.

She had met the sage at a very select supper party after his only lecture in London. It was the same lecture which had thrown Washington into a state of bewilderment. Since Dr Koo Fin arrived he had been photographed more often than any film star. His name and his round Chinese face were better known than those of the principals in the latest *cause célèbre*, and already television comedians referred to his great objectivity theory in their patter.

Apart from that one lecture, however, and the supper party after it, he had been seen nowhere else save in his own closely guarded suite in his hotel.

How Mrs Molesworth got herself invited to the supper party, and how, once there, she persuaded the sage to consent to visit Molesworth Court, is one of those minor miracles which do sometimes occur. Her enemies made many unworthy conjectures, but, since the university professors in charge of the proceedings on that occasion were not likely to have been corrupted by money or love, it is probable that Mrs Molesworth moved the mountain by faith in herself alone.

The guest chamber prepared for Dr Koo Fin was the third room in the west wing. This architectural monstrosity contained four bedrooms, each furnished with french windows leading on to the same balcony.

Young Petterboy occupied the room at the end of the row. It was one of the best in the house, as a matter of fact, but had no bathroom attached, since this had been converted by Mrs Molesworth, who had the second chamber, into a gigantic clothes press. After all, as she said, it was her own house.

Dr Koo Fin arrived on the Saturday by train, like a lesser person. He shook hands with Mrs Molesworth and Christopher and young Petterboy and the Feisons as if he actually shared their own intelligence, and smiled at them all in his bland, utterly-too Chinese way.

From the first he was a tremendous success. He ate little, drank less, spoke not at all, but he nodded appreciatively at young Petterboy's halting Chinese, and grunted once or twice most charmingly when someone inadvertently addressed him in English. Altogether he was Mrs Molesworth's conception of a perfect guest.

On the Sunday morning Mrs Molesworth actually received a compliment from him, and saw herself in a giddy flash the most talked-of woman in the cocktail parties of the coming week.

The charming incident occurred just before lunch. The sage rose abruptly from his chair on the lawn, and as the whole house party watched him with awe, anxious not to miss a single recountable incident, he stalked boldly across the nearest flower bed, trampling violas and London Pride with the true dreamer's magnificent disregard for physical obstacles, and, plucking the head off a huge rose from Christopher's favourite standard, trampled back with it in triumph and laid it in Mrs Molesworth's lap.

Then, as she sat in ecstasy, he returned quietly to his seat and considered her affably. For the first time in her life Mrs Molesworth was really thrilled. She told a number of people so afterwards.

However, on the Sunday night there were burglars. It was sickeningly awkward. Mrs Molesworth had a diamond star, two sets of ear-rings, a bracelet and five rings, all set in platinum, and she kept them in a wall safe under a picture in her bedroom. On the Sunday night, after the rose incident, she gave up the self-effacement programme and came down to dinner in full war paint. The Molesworths always dressed on Sunday and she certainly looked devastatingly feminine, all blue mist and diamonds.

It was the more successful evening of the two. The sage revealed an engaging talent for making card houses, and he also played five-finger exercises on the piano. The great simplicity of the man was never better displayed. Finally, dazed, honoured and happy, the house party went to bed.

Mrs Molesworth removed her jewellery and placed it in the safe, but unfortunately did not lock it at once. Instead, she discovered that she had dropped an ear-ring, and went down to look for it in the drawing-room. When at last she returned without it the safe was empty. It really was devastatingly awkward, and the resourceful Christopher, hastily summoned from his room in the main wing, confessed himself in a quandary.

The servants, discreetly roused, whispered that they had heard nothing and gave unimpeachable alibis. There remained the guests. Mrs Molesworth wept. For such a thing to happen at any time was terrible enough, but for it to occur on such an occasion was more than she could bear. One thing she and Christopher agreed: the sage must never guess…must never dream…

There remained the Feisons and the unfortunate young Petterboy. The Feisons were ruled out almost at once. From the fact that the window catch in Mrs Molesworth's room was burst, it was fairly obvious that the thief had entered from the balcony; therefore, had either of the Feisons passed that way from their rooms they would have had to pass the sage, who slept with his window wide. So there was only young Petterboy. It seemed fairly obvious.

Finally, after a great deal of consultation, Christopher went to speak to him as man to man, and came back fifteen minutes later hot and uncommunicative.

Mrs Molesworth dried her eyes, put on her newest negligée, and, sweeping aside her fears and her husband's objections, went in to speak to young Petterboy like a mother. Poor young Petterboy gave up laughing at her after ten minutes, suddenly got angry, and demanded that the sage too should be asked if he had 'heard anything'. Then he forgot himself completely, and vulgarly suggested sending for the police.

Mrs Molesworth nearly lost her head, recovered herself in time, apologised by innuendo, and crept back disconsolately to Christopher and bed.

The night passed most wretchedly.

In the morning poor young Petterboy cornered his hostess and repeated his requests of the night before. But the sage was departing by the 11.12 and Mrs Molesworth was driving with him to the station. In that moment of her triumph the diamonds seemed relatively unimportant to Elvira Molesworth, who had inherited the Cribbage fortune a year before. Indeed, she kissed poor young Petterboy and said it really didn't matter, and hadn't they had a wonderful, wonderful week-end? And that he must come down again some time soon.

The Feisons said good-bye to the sage, and as Mrs Molesworth was going with him, made their adieux to her as well. As the formalities had been accomplished there seemed no point in staying, and Christopher saw them off in their car, with poor young Petterboy leading the way in his.

As he was standing on the lawn waving somewhat perfunctorily to the departing cars, the post arrived. One letter for his wife bore the crest of the Doctor's hotel, and Christopher, with one of those intuitions which made him such a successful husband, tore it open.

It was quite short, but in the circumstances, wonderfully enlightening:

'Dear Madam,

In going through Dr Koo Fin's memoranda, I find to my horror that he promised to visit you this week-end. I know you will forgive Dr Koo Fin when you hear that he never takes part in social occasions. As you know, his arduous work occupies his entire time. I know it is inexcusable of me not to have let you know before now, but it is only a moment since I discovered that the Doctor had made the engagement.

I do hope his absence has not put you to any inconvenience, and that you will pardon this atrocious slip.

I have the honour to remain, Madam,

Yours most apologetically
Lo Pei Fu
Secretary.

P.S. The Doctor should have written himself, but, as you know, his English is not good. He begs to be reminded to you and hopes for your forgiveness.

As Christopher raised his eyes from the note his wife returned. She stopped the car in the drive and came running across the lawn towards him.

'Darling, wasn't it wonderful?' she said, throwing herself into his arms with an abandonment she did not often display to him.

'What's in the post?' she went on, disengaging herself.

Christopher slipped the letter he had been reading into his pocket with unobtrusive skill.

'Nothing, my dear,' he said gallantly. 'Nothing at all.' He was amazingly fond of his wife.

Mrs Molesworth wrinkled her white forehead.

'Darling,' she said, 'now about my jewellery. Wasn't it too odious for such a thing to happen when that dear, sweet old man was here: what shall we do?'

Christopher drew her arm through his own. 'I think, my dear,' he said firmly, 'you'd better leave all that to me. We mustn't have a scandal.'

'Oh, no,' said Mrs Molesworth, her eyes growing round with alarm. 'Oh, no; that would spoil everything.'

In a first class compartment on the London train the elderly Chinese turned over the miscellaneous collection of jewellery which lay in a large silk handkerchief on his knee. His smile was child-like, bland and faintly wondering. After a while he folded the handkerchief over its treasure and placed the package in his breast pocket.

Then he leaned back against the upholstery and looked out of the window. The green undulating landscape was pleasant. The fields were neat and well tilled. The sky was blue, the sunlight beautiful. It was a lovely land.

He sighed and marvelled in his heart that it could be the home of a race of cultivated barbarians to whom, providing that height, weight and age were relatively the same, all Chinese actually did look alike.

The Murder at the Towers

E. V. Knox

Edmund George Valpy Knox (1881–1971), also known as "Evoe", or E. V. Knox, came from a gifted family. His brother, Monsignor Ronald Knox, was a leading light of detective fiction in the Golden Age; as well as writing novels and short stories, Ronald was an accomplished exponent of the Sherlockian pastiche, and famously devised "the Detective's Decalogue", ten mostly tongue-in-cheek "commandments" for writers of detective stories. Their sister Winifred Peck also wrote a couple of crime novels. Evoe was best known as a poet and humorist and was editor of *Punch* from 1932 to 1949.

Neither Evoe nor Ronald took crime fiction too seriously; for them, detective stories were a form of game-playing. This story wittily employs the country house setting for a display of detective work by one of those "gifted amateurs" who so often appear in Golden Age fiction. In classic whodunits, victims were often unpleasant characters who supplied plentiful motives for murder, and it is clear from the outset that the victim here is no exception.

◇◇◇

I

Mr. ponderby-wilkins was a man so rich, so ugly, so cross, and so old, that even the stupidest reader could not expect him to survive any longer than Chapter I. Vulpine in his secretiveness, he was porcine in his habits, saturnine in his appearance, and ovine in his unconsciousness of doom. He was the kind of man who might easily perish as early as paragraph two.

Little surprise, therefore, was shown by Police-Inspector Blowhard of Nettleby Parva when a message reached him on the telephone:

"You are wanted immediately at the Towers. Mr. Ponderby-Wilkins has been found dead."

The inspector was met at the gate by the deceased's secretary, whom he knew and suspected on the spot.

"Where did it happen, Mr. Porlock?" he asked. "The lake, the pigeon-loft, or the shrubbery?"

"The shrubbery," answered Porlock quietly, and led the way to the scene.

Mr. Ponderby-Wilkins was suspended by means of an enormous woollen muffler to the bough of a tree, which the police-officer's swift eye noticed at once to be a sycamore.

"How long has that sycamore tree been in the shrubbery?" he inquired suspiciously.

"I don't know," answered Porlock, "and I don't care."

"Tell me precisely what happened," went on the inspector.

"Four of us were playing tennis, when a ball was hit out into the bushes. On going to look for it at the end of the set, I found Mr. Wilkins as you see him, and called the attention of the other players to the circumstances at once. Here they all are."

And pushing aside the boughs of a laurel, he showed the police-officer two young women and a young man. They were standing quietly in the middle of the tennis-court, holding their tennis-racquets soberly in their hands.

"Do you corroborate Mr. Porlock's account of the affair?" inquired Blowhard.

"We do," they answered quietly in one breath.

"Hum!" mused the inspector, stroking his chin. "By the way," he continued, "I wonder whether life is extinct?"

He went and looked at the body. It was.

"A glance showed us that life was extinct when we found it," said the four, speaking together, "and we thought it better to go on playing tennis as reverently as possible until you arrived."

"Quite right," said Blowhard. "I shall now examine the whole household *viva voce*. Kindly summon them to the drawing-room."

They went together into the large, white-fronted mansion, and soon the notes of a gong, reverberating through the house and all over the grounds, had summoned the whole house-party, including the servants, to the Louis-Seize *salon* overlooking the tennis lawn. The gathering consisted, as the inspector had foreseen, of the usual types involved in a country house murder, namely, a frightened stepsister of the deceased, a young and beautiful niece, a major, a doctor, a chaperon, a friend, Mr. Porlock himself, an old butler with a beard, a middle-aged gardener with whiskers, an Irish cook, and two servants who had only come to the place the week before. Every one of them had a bitter grudge against the deceased. He had been about to dismiss his secretary, had threatened to disinherit his niece, sworn repeatedly at his stepsister, thrown a port decanter at the butler's head, insulted the guests by leaving *Bradshaws* in their bedrooms, pulled up the gardener's antirrhinums, called the cook a good-for-nothing, and terrified the housemaids by making noises at them on the stairs. In addition, he had twice informed the major that his regiment had run away at Balaclava, and had put a toad in the doctor's bed.

Blowhard felt instinctively that this was a case for Bletherby Marge, the famous amateur, and sent him a telegram at once. Then he ordered the body to be removed, walked round the grounds, ate a few strawberries, and went home.

II

Bletherby Marge was a man of wide culture and sympathy. In appearance he was fat, red-faced, smiling, and had untidy hair. He looked stupid, and wore spats. In fact, whatever the inexperienced reader supposes to be the ordinary appearance of a detective, to look like that was the very reverse of Bletherby Marge. He was sometimes mistaken for a business man, more often for a billiard-marker or a baboon. But whenever Scotland Yard was unable to deal with a murder case—that is to say, whenever a murder case happened at a country house—Bletherby Marge was called in. The death of an old, rich, and disagreeable man was like a clarion call to him. He packed his pyjamas, his tooth-brush, and a volume of *Who's Who*, and took the earliest train.

As soon as he had seen the familiar newsbill:

HOST OF COUNTRY HOUSE-PARTY INEXPLICABLY SLAIN

he had expected his summons to The Towers. Telegraphing to the coroner's jury to return an open verdict at Nettleby Parva, he finished off the case of the Duke of St. Neots, fragments of whom had mysteriously been discovered in a chaff-cutting machine, and made all haste to the scene of the new affair. It was his forty-ninth mystery, and in every previous affair he had triumphantly slain his man. A small silver gallows had been presented to him by Scotland Yard as a token of esteem.

"We are in deep waters, Blowhard—very deep," he said, as he closely scrutinized the comforter which had been wrapped round Mr. Ponderby-Wilkins's throat. "Just tell me once more about these alibis."

"Every one of them is perfect," answered the police inspector, "so far as I can see. The butler, the cook, and the two housemaids were all together playing poker in the pantry. Miss Brown, the deceased's stepsister, was giving instructions to the gardener, and the doctor was with her, carrying her trowel and her pruning scissors. The chaperon and the friend were playing tennis with Mr. Porlock and the major, and the niece was rowing herself about on the lake, picking waterlilies."

A gleam came into Bletherby Marge's eyes.

"Alone?" he queried.

"Alone. But you forget that the lake is in full view of the tenniscourt. It almost seems as if it must have been constructed that way on purpose," added the inspector rather crossly. "This girl was seen the whole time during which the murder must have occurred, either by one pair of players or the other."

"Tut, tut," said Bletherby Marge. "Now take me to the scene of the crime."

Arrived at the sycamore tree, he studied the bark with a microscope, and the ground underneath. This was covered with dead leaves. There was no sign of a struggle.

"Show me exactly how the body was hanging," he said to Blowhard.

Police-Inspector Blowhard tied the two ends of the comforter to the bough and wrapped the loop several times round Bletherby Marge's neck, supporting him, as he did so, by the feet.

"Don't let go," said Bletherby Marge.

"I won't," said Blowhard, who was used to the great detective's methods in reconstructing a crime.

"Have you photographed the tree from every angle?" went on Bletherby.

"Yes."

"Were there any finger-prints on it?"

"No," replied Blowhard. "Nothing but leaves."

Then together they wandered round the grounds, eating fruit and discussing possible motives for the murder. No will had been discovered.

From time to time one or other of the house-party would flit by them, humming a song, intent on a game of tennis, or a bathe in the lake. Now and then a face would look haggard or strained, at other times the same face would be merry and wreathed with smiles.

"Do you feel baffled?" asked Blowhard.

Bletherby Marge made no reply.

III

The house-party were having a motor picnic at Dead Man's Wood, ten miles from the The Towers. The festivity had been proposed by Bletherby Marge, who was more and more endearing himself, by his jokes and wide knowledge of the world, to his fellow-guests. Many of them had already begun to feel that a house-party without a detective in it must be regarded as a literary failure.

"Bless my soul!" said Marge suddenly, when the revelry was at its height, turning to Blowhard, who was out of breath, for he had been carrying the champagne across a ploughed field. "I ask you all to excuse me for a moment. I have forgotten my pipe."

They saw him disappear in a two-seater towards The Towers. In little more than an hour he reappeared again and delighted the company by singing one or two popular revue songs in a fruity baritone. But, as the line of cars went homeward in the dusk, Bletherby Marge said to Blowhard, seated beside him, "I want to see you again in the shrubbery to-morrow at ten-thirty prompt. Don't begin playing clock-golf."

Inspector Blowhard made a note of the time in his pocketbook.

IV

"Perhaps you wonder why I went away in the middle of our little outing?" questioned Marge, as they stood together under the fatal sycamore tree.

"I suspected," answered Blowhard, without moving a muscle of his face, except the ones he used for speaking, "that it was a ruse."

"It was," replied Marge.

Without another word he took a small folding broom from his pocket and brushed aside the dead leaves which strewed the ground of the shrubbery.

The dark mould was covered with foot-prints, large and small.

"What do you deduce from this?" cried Blowhard, his eyes bulging from his head.

"When I returned from the picnic," explained the great detective, "I first swept the ground clear as you see it now. I then hastily collected all the outdoor shoes in the house."

"All?"

"Every one. I brought them to the shrubbery on a wheel-barrow. I locked the servants, as though by accident, in the kitchen and the gardener in the tool-shed. I then compared the shoes with these imprints, and found that every one of them was a fit."

"Which means?"

"That every one of them was here when the murder took place. I have reconstructed the scene exactly. The marks of the shoes stretch in a long line, as you will observe, from a point close to the tree almost to the edge of the tennis-lawn. The heels are very deeply imprinted; the mark of the toes is very light indeed."

He paused and looked at Blowhard.

"I suppose you see now how the murder was done?" he barked loudly.

"No," mewed the inspector quietly.

"Ponderby-Wilkins," said Marge, "had the comforter twisted once round his neck, and one end was tied to the tree. Then—at a signal, I imagine—the whole house-party, including the servants, pulled together on the other end of the comforter until he expired. You see here the imprints of the butler's feet. As the heaviest man, he was at the end of the rope. Porlock was in front, with the second housemaid immediately behind him. Porlock, I fancy, gave the word to pull. Afterwards they tied him up to the tree as you found him when you arrived."

"But the alibis?"

"All false. They were all sworn to by members of the household, by servants or by guests. That was what put me on the scent."

"But how is it there were no finger-prints?"

"The whole party," answered Bletherby, "wore gloves. I collected all the gloves in the house and examined them carefully. Many of them had hairs from the comforter still adhering to them. Having concluded my investigations, I rapidly replaced the boots and gloves, put the leaves back in their original position, unlocked the kitchen and the tool-house, and came back to the picnic again."

"And sang comic songs!" said Blowhard.

"Yes," replied Marge. "A great load had been taken off my mind by the discovery of the truth. And I felt it necessary to put the murderers off their guard."

"Wonderful!" exclaimed Blowhard, examining the foot-prints minutely. "There is now only one difficulty, Mr. Marge, so far as I can see."

"And that is?"

"How am I going to convey all these people to the police-station?"

"How many pairs of manacles have you about you?"

"Only two," confessed Blowhard, feeling in his pocket.

"You had better telephone," said Bletherby, "for a motor-omnibus."

V

The simultaneous trial of twelve prisoners on a capital charge, followed by their joint condemnation and execution, thrilled England as no sensation had thrilled it since the death of William II. The Sunday papers were never tired of discussing the psychology of the murderers and publishing details of their early life and school careers. Never before, it seemed, had a secretary, a stepsister, a niece, an eminent K.C., a major, a chaperon, a friend, a cook, a butler, two housemaids, and a gardener gone to the gallows on the same day for the murder of a disagreeable old man.

On a morning not long after the excitement had died away, Bletherby Marge and a house-agent went together to The Towers, which for some reason or other was still "To Let." As they looked at the library, Bletherby Marge tapped a panel in the mantelpiece.

"It sounds hollow," he said.

Finding the spring, he pressed it. The wood shot back and revealed a small cavity. From this he drew a dusty bundle of papers, tied together with a small dog-collar.

It was Ponderby-Wilkins's will. On the first page was written:

> *I am the most unpopular man in England, and I am about to commit suicide by hanging myself in the shrubbery. If Bletherby Marge can make it a murder I bequeath him all my possessions in honour of his fiftieth success.*

"Extraordinary!" ejaculated the house-agent.

Mr. Bletherby Marge smiled.

An Unlocked Window

Ethel Lina White

Ethel Lina White (1876–1944) had, like Ernest Bramah and Anthony Berkeley Cox, a horror of personal publicity, and relatively little is known about her, although she did have a lifelong love of writing. Born in Abergavenny, she worked in the Ministry of Pensions before the success of her fiction enabled her to write full-time. Her most famous novel is *The Wheel Spins*, which was filmed by Alfred Hitchcock as *The Lady Vanishes*, and has also been adapted for television and the stage.

White specialised in domestic suspense; typically, her novels and short stories feature "women in jeopardy". Stories of this kind are often suited to screen adaptation, and "An Unlocked Window" featured in the long-running TV series *The Alfred Hitchcock Hour* in 1965, starring Dana Wynter, and directed by the Master of Suspense himself. The teleplay won an Edgar, and to this day, it receives plaudits as one of "TV's scariest episodes".

◇◇◇

"Have you locked up, Nurse Cherry?"

"Yes, Nurse Silver."

"Every door? Every window?"

"Yes, yes."

Yet even as she shot home the last bolt of the front door, at the back of Nurse Cherry's mind was a vague misgiving.

She had forgotten—*something*.

She was young and pretty, but her expression was anxious. While she had most of the qualities to ensure professional success, she was always on guard against a serious handicap.

She had a bad memory.

Hitherto, it had betrayed her only in burnt Benger and an occasional overflow in the bathroom. But yesterday's lapse was little short of a calamity.

Late that afternoon she had discovered the oxygen-cylinder, which she had been last to use, empty—its cap carelessly unscrewed.

The disaster called for immediate remedy, for the patient, Professor Glendower Baker, was suffering from the effects of gas-poisoning. Although dark was falling, the man, Iles, had to harness the pony for the long drive over the mountains, in order to get a fresh supply.

Nurse Cherry had sped his parting with a feeling of loss. Iles was a cheery soul and a tower of strength.

It was dirty weather with a spitting rain blanketing the elephant-grey mounds of the surrounding hills. The valley road wound like a muddy coil between soaked bracken and dwarf oaks.

Iles shook his head as he regarded the savage isolation of the landscape.

"I don't half like leaving you—a pack of women—with *him* about. Put up the shutters on every door and window, Nurse, and don't let *no one* come in till I get back."

He drove off—his lamps glow-worms in the gloom.

Darkness and rain. And the sodden undergrowth seemed to quiver and blur, so that stunted trees took on the shapes of crouching men advancing towards the house.

Nurse Cherry hurried through her round of fastening the windows. As she carried her candle from room to room of the upper floors, she had the uneasy feeling that she was visible to any watcher.

Her mind kept wandering back to the bad business of the forgotten cylinder. It had plunged her in depths of self-distrust and shame. She was overtired, having nursed the patient single-handed, until the arrival, three days ago, of the second nurse. But that fact did not absolve her from blame.

"I'm not fit to be a nurse," she told herself in bitter self-reproach.

She was still in a dream when she locked the front door. Nurse Silver's questions brought her back to earth with a furtive sense of guilt.

Nurse Silver's appearance inspired confidence, for she was of solid build, with strong features and a black shingle. Yet, for all her stout looks, her nature seemed that of Job.

"Has he gone?" she asked in her harsh voice.

"Iles? Yes."

Nurse Cherry repeated his caution.

"He'll get back as soon as he can," she added, "but it probably won't be until dawn."

"Then," said Nurse Silver gloomily, "we are *alone*."

Nurse Cherry laughed.

"Alone? Three hefty women, all of us able to give a good account of ourselves."

"*I'm* not afraid." Nurse Silver gave her rather a peculiar look. "*I'm* safe enough."

"Why?"

"Because of *you*. He won't touch me with you here."

Nurse Cherry tried to belittle her own attractive appearance with a laugh.

"For that matter," she said, "we are all safe."

"Do you think so? A lonely house. No man. And two of *us*."

Nurse Cherry glanced at her starched nurse's apron. Nurse Silver's words made her feel like special bait—a goat tethered in a jungle, to attract a tiger.

"Don't talk nonsense," she said sharply.

The countryside, of late, had been chilled by a series of murders. In each case, the victim had been a trained nurse. The police were searching for a medical student—Sylvester Leek. It was supposed that his mind had become unhinged, consequent on being jilted by a pretty probationer. He had disappeared from the hospital after a violent breakdown during an operation.

Next morning, a night-nurse had been discovered in the laundry—strangled. Four days later, a second nurse had been horribly done to death in the garden of a villa on the outskirts of the small agricultural town. After the lapse of a fortnight, one of the nurses in attendance on Sir Thomas Jones had been discovered in her bedroom—throttled.

The last murder had taken place in a large mansion in the very heart of the country. Every isolated cottage and farm became infected with panic. Women barred their doors and no girl lingered late in the lane, without her lover.

Nurse Cherry wished she could forget the details she had read in the newspapers. The ingenuity with which the poor victims had been lured to their doom and the ferocity of the attacks all proved a diseased brain driven by malignant motive.

It was a disquieting thought that she and Nurse Silver were localized. Professor Baker had succumbed to gas-poisoning while engaged in work of national importance and his illness had been reported in the Press.

"In any case," she argued, "how could—*he*—know that we're left tonight?"

Nurse Silver shook her head.

"*They* always know."

"Rubbish! And he's probably committed suicide by now. There hasn't been a murder for over a month."

"Exactly. There's bound to be another, *soon*."

Nurse Cherry thought of the undergrowth creeping nearer to the house. Her nerve snapped.

"Are you trying to make me afraid?"

"Yes," said Nurse Silver, "I am. I don't trust you. You forget."

Nurse Cherry coloured angrily.

"You might let me forget that wretched cylinder."

"But you might forget again."

"Not likely."

As she uttered the words—like oil spreading over water—her mind was smeared with doubt.

Something forgotten.

She shivered as she looked up the well of the circular staircase, which was dimly lit by an oil-lamp suspended to a cross-bar. Shadows rode the walls and wiped out the ceiling like a flock of sooty bats.

An eerie place. Hiding-holes on every landing.

The house was tall and narrow, with two or three rooms on every floor. It was rather like a tower or a pepper-pot. The semi-basement was occupied by the kitchen and domestic offices. On the ground-floor were a sitting-room, the dining-room and the Professor's study. The first floor was devoted to the patient. On the second floor were the bedrooms of the nurses and of the Iles couple. The upper floors were given up to the Professor's laboratorial work.

Nurse Cherry remembered the stout shutters and the secure hasps. There had been satisfaction in turning the house into a fortress. But now, instead of a sense of security, she had a feeling of being caged.

She moved to the staircase.

"While we're bickering," she said, "we're neglecting the patient."

Nurse Silver called her back.

"I'm on duty now."

Professional etiquette forbade any protest. But Nurse Cherry looked after her colleague with sharp envy.

She thought of the Professor's fine brow, his wasted clear-cut features and visionary slate-grey eyes, with yearning. For after three years of nursing children, with an occasional mother or aunt, romance had entered her life.

From the first, she had been interested in her patient. She had scarcely eaten or slept until the crisis had passed. She noticed too, how his eyes followed her around the room and how he could hardly bear her out of his sight.

Yesterday he had held her hand in his thin fingers.

"Marry me, Stella," he whispered.

"Not unless you get well," she answered foolishly.

Since then, he had called her "Stella." Her name was music in her ears until her rapture was dashed by the fatal episode of the cylinder. She had to face the knowledge that, in case of another relapse, Glendower's life hung upon a thread.

She was too wise to think further, so she began to speculate on Nurse Silver's character. Hitherto, they had met only at meals, when she had been taciturn and moody.

To-night she had revealed a personal animus against herself, and Nurse Cherry believed she guessed its cause.

The situation was a hot-bed for jealousy. Two women were thrown into close contact with a patient and a doctor, both of whom were bachelors. Although Nurse Silver was the ill-favoured one, it was plain that she possessed her share of personal vanity. Nurse Cherry noticed, from her painful walk, that she wore shoes which were too small. More than that, she had caught her in the act of scrutinizing her face in the mirror.

These rather pitiful glimpses into the dark heart of the warped woman made Nurse Cherry uneasy.

The house was very still; she missed Nature's sounds of rain or wind against the window-pane and the cheerful voices of the Iles couple. The silence might be a background for sounds she did not wish to hear.

She spoke aloud, for the sake of hearing her own voice.

"Cheery if Silver plays up to-night. Well, well! I'll hurry up Mrs. Iles with the supper."

Her spirits rose as she opened the door leading to the basement. The warm spicy odour of the kitchen floated up the short staircase and she could see a bar of yellow light from the half-opened door.

When she entered, she saw no sign of supper. Mrs. Iles—a strapping blonde with strawberry cheeks—sat at the kitchen-table, her head buried in her huge arms.

As Nurse Cherry shook her gently, she raised her head.

"Eh?" she said stupidly.

"Gracious, Mrs. Iles. Are you ill?"

"Eh? Feel as if I'd one over the eight."

"What on earth d'you mean?"

"What *you* call 'tight.' Love-a-duck, my head's that swimmy—"

Nurse Cherry looked suspiciously at an empty glass upon the dresser, as Mrs. Iles's head dropped like a bleached sunflower.

Nurse Silver heard her hurrying footsteps on the stairs. She met her upon the landing.

"Anything wrong?"

"Mrs. Iles. I think she's drunk. Do come and see."

When Nurse Silver reached the kitchen, she hoisted Mrs. Iles under the armpits and set her on unsteady feet.

"Obvious," she said. "Help get her upstairs."

It was no easy task to drag twelve stone of protesting Mrs. Iles up three flights of stairs.

"She feels like a centipede, with every pair of feet going in a different direction," Nurse Cherry panted, as they reached the door of the Ileses' bedroom. "I can manage her now, thank you."

She wished Nurse Silver would go back to the patient, instead of looking at her with that fixed expression.

"What are you staring at?" she asked sharply.

"Has nothing struck you as *strange?*"

"What?"

In the dim light, Nurse Silver's eyes looked like empty black pits.

"To-day," she said, "there were four of us. First, Iles goes. Now, Mrs. Iles. That leaves only two. If anything happens to you or me, there'll only be *one.*"

As Nurse Cherry put Mrs. Iles to bed, she reflected that Nurse Silver was decidedly not a cheerful companion. She made a natural sequence of events appear in the light of a sinister conspiracy.

Nurse Cherry reminded herself sharply that Iles's absence was due to her own carelessness, while his wife was addicted to her glass.

Still, some unpleasant suggestion remained, like the sediment from a splash of muddy water. She found herself thinking with horror of some calamity befalling Nurse Silver. If she were left by herself she felt she would lose her senses with fright.

It was an unpleasant picture. The empty house—a dark shell for lurking shadows. No one on whom to depend. Her patient—a beloved burden and responsibility.

It was better not to think of that. But she kept on thinking. The outside darkness seemed to be pressing against the walls, bending them in. As her fears multiplied, the medical student changed from a human being with a distraught brain, to a Force, cunning and insatiable—a ravening blood-monster.

Nurse Silver's words recurred to her.

"*They* always know." Even so. Doors might be locked, but *they* would find a way inside.

Her nerves tingled at the sound of the telephone-bell, ringing far below in the hall.

She kept looking over her shoulder as she ran downstairs. She took off the receiver in positive panic, lest she should be greeted with a maniac scream of laughter.

It was a great relief to hear the homely Welsh accent of Dr. Jones.

He had serious news for her. As she listened, her heart began to thump violently.

"Thank you, doctor, for letting me know," she said. "Please ring up directly you hear more."

"Hear more of what?"

Nurse Cherry started at Nurse Silver's harsh voice. She had come downstairs noiselessly in her soft nursing-slippers.

"It's only the doctor," she said, trying to speak lightly. "He's thinking of changing the medicine."

"Then why are you so white? You are shaking."

Nurse Cherry decided that the truth would serve her best.

"To be honest," she said, "I've just had bad news. Something ghastly. I didn't want you to know, for there's no sense in two of us being frightened. But now I come to think of it, you ought to feel reassured."

She forced a smile.

"You said there'd have to be another murder soon. Well—there *has* been one."

"Where? Who? Quick."

Nurse Cherry understood what is meant by the infection of fear as Nurse Silver gripped her arm.

In spite of her effort at self-mastery, there was a quiver in her own voice.

"It's a—a hospital nurse. Strangled. They've just found the body in a quarry and they sent for Dr. Jones to make the examination. The police are trying to establish her identity."

Nurse Silver's eyes were wide and staring.

"Another hospital nurse? That makes *four*."

She turned on the younger woman in sudden suspicion.

"Why did he ring you up?"

Nurse Cherry did not want that question.

"To tell us to be specially on guard," she replied.

"You mean—he's near?"

"Of course not. The doctor said the woman had been dead three or four days. By now, he'll be far away."

"Or he may be even nearer than you think."

Nurse Cherry glanced involuntarily at the barred front door. Her head felt as if it were bursting. It was impossible to think connectedly. But—somewhere—beating its wings like a caged bird, was the incessant reminder.

Something forgotten.

The sight of the elder woman's twitching lips reminded her that she had to be calm for two.

"Go back to the patient," she said, "while I get the supper. We'll both feel better after something to eat."

In spite of her new-born courage, it needed an effort of will to descend into the basement. So many doors, leading to scullery, larder and coal-cellar, all smelling of mice. So many hiding-places.

The kitchen proved a cheerful antidote to depression. The caked fire in the open range threw a red glow upon the Welsh dresser and the canisters labelled 'Sugar' and 'Tea.' A sandy cat slept upon the rag mat. Everything looked safe and homely.

Quickly collecting bread, cheese, a round of beef, a cold white shape, and stewed prunes, she piled them on a tray. She added stout for Nurse Silver and made cocoa for herself. As she watched the milk froth up through the dark mixture and inhaled the steaming odour, she felt that her fears were baseless and absurd.

She sang as she carried her tray upstairs. She was going to marry Glendower.

The nurses used the bedroom which connected with the sick chamber for their meals, in order to be near the patient. As the night-nurse entered, Nurse Cherry strained her ears for the sound of Glendower's voice. She longed for one glimpse of him. Even a smile would help.

"How's the patient?" she asked.

"All right."

"Could I have a peep?"

"No. You're off duty."

As the women sat down, Nurse Cherry was amused to notice that Nurse Silver kicked off her tight shoes.

"You seem very interested in the patient, Nurse Cherry," she remarked sourly.

"I have a right to feel rather interested." Nurse Cherry smiled as she cut bread. "The doctor gives me the credit for his being alive."

"Ah! But the doctor thinks the world of you."

Nurse Cherry was not conceited, but she was human enough to know that she had made a conquest of the big Welshman.

The green glow of jealousy in Nurse Silver's eyes made her reply guardedly.

"Dr. Jones is decent to every one."

But she was of too friendly and impulsive a nature to keep her secret bottled up. She reminded herself that they were two women sharing an ordeal and she tried to establish some link of friendship.

"I feel you despise me," she said. "You think me lacking in self-control. And you can't forget that cylinder. But really, I've gone through such an awful strain. For four nights, I never took off my clothes."

"Why didn't you have a second nurse?"

"There was the expense. The Professor gives his whole life to enrich the nation and he's poor. Then, later, I felt I *must* do everything for him myself. I didn't want you, only Dr. Jones said I was heading for a break-down."

She looked at her left hand, seeing there the shadowy outline of a wedding-ring.

"Don't think me sloppy, but I must tell some one. The Professor and I are going to get married."

"*If* he lives."

"But he's turned the corner now."

"Don't count your chickens."

Nurse Cherry felt a stab of fear.

"Are you hiding something from me? Is he—worse?"

"No. He's the same. I was thinking that Dr. Jones might interfere. You've led him on, haven't you? I've seen you smile at him. It's light women like you that make the trouble in the world."

Nurse Cherry was staggered by the injustice of the attack. But as she looked at the elder woman's working face, she saw that she was consumed by jealousy. One life lay in the shadow, the other in the sun. The contrast was too sharp.

"We won't quarrel to-night," she said gently. "We're going through rather a bad time together and we have only each other to depend on. I'm just clinging to *you*. If anything were to happen to you, like Mrs. Iles, I should jump out of my skin with fright."

Nurse Silver was silent for a minute.

"I never thought of that," she said presently. "Only us two. And all these empty rooms, above and below. What's that?"

From the hall, came the sound of muffled knocking.

Nurse Cherry sprang to her feet.

"Some one's at the front door."

Nurse Silver's fingers closed round her arm, like iron hoops.

"Sit down. It's *him*."

The two women stared at each other as the knocking continued. It was loud and insistent. To Nurse Cherry's ears, it carried a message of urgency.

"I'm going down," she said. "It may be Dr. Jones."

"How could you tell?"

"By his voice."

"You fool. Any one could imitate *his* accent."

Nurse Cherry saw the beads break out round Nurse Silver's mouth. Her fear had the effect of steadying her own nerves.

"I'm going down, to find out who it is," she said. "It may be important news about the murder."

Nurse Silver dragged her away from the door.

"What did I say? *You* are the danger. You've forgotten already."

"Forgotten—what?"

"Didn't Iles tell you to open to no one? *No one?*"

Nurse Cherry hung her head. She sat down in shamed silence.

The knocking ceased. Presently they heard it again at the back door.

Nurse Silver wiped her face.

"He *means* to get in." She laid her hand on Nurse Cherry's arm. "You're not even trembling. Are you never afraid?"

"Only of ghosts."

In spite of her brave front, Nurse Cherry was inwardly quaking at her own desperate resolution. Nurse Silver had justly accused her of endangering the household. Therefore it was her plain duty to make once more the round of the house, either to see what she had forgotten, or to lay the doubt.

"I'm going upstairs," she said. "I want to look out."

"Unbar a window?" Nurse Silver's agitation rose in a gale. "You shall *not*. It's murdering folly. Think! That last nurse was found dead *inside* her bedroom."

"All right. I won't."

"You'd best be careful. You've been trying to spare me, but perhaps I've been trying to spare you. I'll only say this. *There is something strange happening in this house.*"

Nurse Cherry felt a chill at her heart. Only, since she was a nurse, she knew that it was really the pit of her stomach. Something wrong? If through her wretched memory, she again were the culprit, she must expiate her crime by shielding the others, at any risk to herself.

She had to force herself to mount the stairs. Her candle, flickering in the draught, peopled the walls with distorted shapes. When she reached the top landing, without stopping to think, she walked resolutely into the laboratory and the adjoining room.

Both were securely barred and empty. Gaining courage, she entered the attic. Under its window was a precipitous slope of roof without gutter or water-pipe, to give finger-hold. Knowing that it would be impossible for any one to gain an entry, she opened the shutter and unfastened the window.

The cold air on her face refreshed her and restored her to calm. She realized that she had been suffering to a certain extent from claustrophobia.

The rain had ceased and a wind arisen. She could see a young harried moon flying through the clouds. The dark humps of the hills were visible against the darkness, but nothing more.

She remained at the window for some time, thinking of Glendower. It was a solace to remember the happiness which awaited her once this night of terror was over.

Presently the urge to see him grew too strong to be resisted. Nurse Silver's words had made her uneasy on his behalf. Even though she offended the laws of professional etiquette, she determined to see for herself that all was well.

Leaving the window open so that some air might percolate into the house, she slipped stealthily downstairs. She stopped on the second floor to visit her own room and that of Nurse Silver. All was quiet and secure. In her own quarters, Mrs. Iles still snored in the sleep of the unjust.

There were two doors to the patient's room. The one led to the nurses' room where Nurse Silver was still at her meal. The other led to the landing.

Directly Nurse Cherry entered, she knew that her fear had been the premonition of love. Something was seriously amiss. Glendower's head tossed uneasily on the pillow. His face was deeply flushed. When she called him by name, he stared at her, his luminous grey eyes ablaze.

He did not recognize her, for instead of "Stella," he called her "Nurse."

"Nurse, Nurse." He mumbled something that sounded like "man" and then slipped back in her arms, unconscious.

Nurse Silver entered the room at her cry. As she felt his pulse, she spoke with dry significance.

"We could do with oxygen now."

Nurse Cherry could only look at her with piteous eyes.

"Shall I telephone for Dr. Jones?" she asked humbly.

"Yes."

It seemed like the continuation of an evil dream when she could get no answer to her ring. Again and again she tried desperately to galvanize the dead instrument.

Presently Nurse Silver appeared on the landing.

"Is the doctor coming?"

"I—I can't get any answer." Nurse Cherry forced back her tears. "Oh, whatever can be wrong?"

"Probably a wet creeper twisted round the wire. But it doesn't matter now. The patient is sleeping."

Nurse Cherry's face registered no comfort. As though the shocks of the last few minutes had set in motion the arrested machinery of her brain, she remembered suddenly what she had forgotten.

The larder window.

She recollected now what had happened. When she entered the larder on her round of locking up, a mouse had run over her feet. She ran to fetch the cat which chased it into a hole in the kitchen. In the excitement of the incident, she had forgotten to return to close the window.

Her heart leapt violently at the realization that, all these hours, the house had been open to any marauder. Even while she and Nurse Silver had listened, shivering, to the knocking at the door, she had already betrayed the fortress.

"What's the matter?" asked Nurse Silver.

"Nothing. Nothing."

She dared not tell the older woman. Even now it was not too late to remedy her omission.

In her haste she no longer feared the descent into the basement. She could hardly get down the stairs with sufficient speed. As she entered the larder the wire-covered window flapped in the breeze. She secured it and was just entering the kitchen, when her eye fell on a dark patch on the passage.

It was the footprint of a man.

Nurse Cherry remembered that Iles had been in the act of getting fresh coal into the cellar when he had been called away to make his journey. He had no time to clean up and the floor was still sooty with rain-soaked dust.

As she raised her candle, the footprint gleamed faintly. Stooping hastily, she touched it.

It was still damp.

At first she stood as if petrified, staring at it stupidly. Then as she realized that in front of her lay a freshly-made imprint, her nerve snapped completely. With a scream, she dropped her candle and tore up the stairs, calling on Nurse Silver.

She was answered by a strange voice. It was thick, heavy, indistinct. A voice she had never heard before.

Knowing not what awaited her on the other side of the door, yet driven on by the courage of ultimate fear, she rushed into the nurses' sitting-room.

No one was there save Nurse Silver. She sagged back in her chair, her eyes half-closed, her mouth open.

From her lips issued a second uncouth cry.

Nurse Cherry put her arm around her.

"What is it? Try to tell me."

It was plain that Nurse Silver was trying to warn her of some peril. She pointed to her glass and fought for articulation.

"Drugs. Listen. When you lock out, you lock *in*." Even as she spoke her eyes turned up horribly, exposing the balls in a blind white stare.

Almost mad with terror, Nurse Cherry tried to revive her. Mysteriously, through some unknown agency, what she had dreaded had come to pass.

She was alone.

And somewhere—within the walls of the house—lurked a being, cruel and cunning, who—one after another—had removed each obstacle between himself and his objective.

He had marked down his victim. *Herself.*

In that moment she went clean over the edge of fear. She felt that it was not herself—Stella Cherry—but a stranger in the blue print uniform of a hospital nurse, who calmly speculated on her course of action.

It was impossible to lock herself in the patient's room, for the key was stiff from disuse. And she had not the strength to move furniture which was sufficiently heavy to barricade the door.

The idea of flight was immediately dismissed. In order to get help, she would have to run miles. She could not leave Glendower and two helpless women at the mercy of the baffled maniac.

There was nothing to be done. Her place was by Glendower. She sat down by his bed and took his hand in hers.

The time seemed endless. Her watch seemed sometimes to leap whole hours and then to crawl, as she waited—listening to the myriad sounds in a house at nightfall. There were faint rustlings, the cracking of wood-work, the scamper of mice.

And a hundred times, some one seemed to steal up the stairs and linger just outside her door.

It was nearly three o'clock when suddenly a gong began to beat inside her temples. In the adjoining room was the unmistakable tramp of a man's footsteps.

It was no imagination on her part. They circled the room and then advanced deliberately towards the connecting door.

She saw the handle begin to turn slowly.

In one bound, she reached the door and rushed on to the landing and up the stairs. For a second, she paused before her own room. But its windows were barred and its door had no key. She could not be done to death there in the dark.

As she paused, she heard the footsteps on the stairs. They advanced slowly, driving her on before them. Demented with terror, she fled up to the top storey, instinctively seeking the open window.

She could go no higher. At the attic door, she waited.

Something black appeared on the staircase wall. It was the shadow of her pursuer—a grotesque and distorted herald of crime.

Nurse Cherry gripped the balustrade to keep herself from falling. Everything was growing dark. She knew that she was on the point of fainting, when she was revived by sheer astonishment and joy.

Above the balustrade appeared the head of Nurse Silver.

Nurse Cherry called out to her in warning.

"Come quickly. There's a man in the house."

She saw Nurse Silver start and fling back her head, as though in alarm. Then occurred the culminating horror of a night of dread.

A mouse ran across the passage. Raising her heavy shoe, Nurse Silver stamped upon it, grinding her heel upon the tiny creature's head.

In that moment, Nurse Cherry knew the truth. Nurse Silver was a man.

Her brain raced with lightning velocity. It was like a searchlight, piercing the shadows and making the mystery clear.

She knew that the real Nurse Silver had been murdered by Sylvester Leek, on her way to the case. It was her strangled body which had just been found in the quarry. And the murderer had taken her place. The police description was that of a slightly-built youth, with refined features. It would be easy for him to assume the disguise of a woman. He had the necessary medical knowledge to pose as nurse. Moreover, as he had the night-shift, no one in the house had come into close contact with him, save the patient.

But the patient had guessed the truth.

To silence his tongue, the killer had drugged him, even as he had disposed of the obstructing presence of Mrs. Iles. It was he, too, who had emptied the oxygen-cylinder, to get Iles out of the way.

Yet, although he had been alone with his prey for hours, he had held his hand.

Nurse Cherry, with her new mental lucidity, knew the reason. There is a fable that the serpent slavers its victim before swallowing it. In like manner, the maniac—before her final destruction—had wished to coat her with the foul saliva of fear.

All the evening he had been trying to terrorize her— plucking at each jangled nerve up to the climax of his feigned unconsciousness.

Yet she knew that he in turn was fearful lest he should be frustrated in the commission of his crime. Since his victim's body had been discovered in the quarry, the establishment of her identity would mark his hiding-place. While Nurse Cherry was at the attic window, he had cut the telephone-wire and donned his own shoes for purposes of flight.

She remembered his emotion during the knocking at the door. It was probable that it was Dr. Jones who stood without, come to assure himself that she was not alarmed. Had it been the police, they would have effected an entry. The incident proved that nothing had been discovered and that it was useless to count on outside help.

She had to face it—alone.

In the dim light from the young moon, she saw the murderer enter the attic. The grotesque travesty of his nursing disguise added to the terror of the moment.

His eyes were fixed on the open window. It was plain that he was pretending to connect it with the supposed intruder. She in her turn had unconsciously deceived him. He probably knew nothing of the revealing footprint he had left in the basement passage.

"Shut the window, you damned fool," he shouted.

As he leaned over the low ledge to reach the swinging casement window, Nurse Cherry rushed at him in the instinctive madness of self-defence—thrusting him forward, over the sill.

She had one glimpse of dark distorted features blotting out the moon and of arms sawing the air, like a star-fish, in a desperate attempt to balance.

The next moment, nothing was there.

She sank to the ground, covering her ears with her hands to deaden the sound of the sickening slide over the tiled roof.

It was a long time before she was able to creep down to her patient's room. Directly she entered, its peace healed her like balm. Glendower slept quietly—a half-smile playing round his lips as though he dreamed of her.

Thankfully she went from room to room, unbarring each window and unlocking each door—letting in the dawn.

The Long Shot

Nicholas Blake

Nicholas Blake was the pen-name which Cecil Day-Lewis (1904–1972) adopted for writing detective fiction. The first Blake novel, *A Question of Proof*, introduced Nigel Strangeways, who became a popular series character. He appears in Blake's most renowned mystery, *The Beast Must Die*, although that story—which has been filmed twice, once by Claude Chabrol—is structured very differently from the stereotypical whodunit.

In the Thirties, Blake became a Communist, and was one of a number of writers with passionately held left-wing opinions who wrote interesting Golden Age detective fiction, although his views modified with the passage of time. "The Long Shot", written and set in the post-war era, is a late example of a short story whodunit in the classic tradition. Strangeways, as usual, does the detective work.

⟡⟡⟡

"His Lordship," announced Amphlett as he received me in the hall, "his lordship is in the rookery, sir."

He crooked a little finger at the maid. "Alice, Mr.

Strangeways' baggage. We have put you in your old room, sir. I trust you will enjoy your visit."

Did I detect a faint, quite unprofessional lack of conviction in the butler's tone? Why shouldn't I enjoy my visit? Any civilised person is bound to enjoy staying at a beautiful, perfectly run country house, where money is no object. Besides, Gervase was an old friend of mine, and I hadn't seen him for nearly two years.

"I think I'll go straight out," I said.

"Very good, sir. His lordship has been anticipating your arrival with the keenest pleasure."

I noticed that Gervase had still not succeeded in training dear old Amphlett to disregard his title. Twenty years ago, as a young man, Gervase had had a sort of Tolstoyan conversion. The eldest son of the Earl of Wessex, he had decided to give up his title and be called by the family name, plain Mr. Musbury. Friends, neighbours, relations, servants—all had to toe the line. That was the time he started to run his estate on a co-operative basis.

His struggles to become poor had been singularly unsuccessful, however. His co-operative farming prospered; the fortune left him in securities by his American mother throve on his neglect of it. And if he lost any friends through discarding his title, it may be assumed that they were not worth keeping anyway.

As we walked over the lawn, Amphlett delicately mopped his brow. It was certainly a very hot day for April. The cawing of rooks in the elm trees we were approaching sounded cool as a waterfall. I quite envied Gervase up there; but I didn't much fancy climbing the rope ladder to reach him.

Looking up, I descried a small object, which presently resolved itself into a ginger-beer bottle on a string descending erratically from the top of the nearest elm.

A young footman silently received it, took a fresh bottle from a silver tray, tied the string round its neck, and gave a signal to haul away. The bottle was drawn up again into the heights, toward a narrow, well-camouflaged platform laid across two of the topmost branches.

"You've got a new footman, I see. A nice-looking young chap."

"Henry gives satisfaction, sir," said Amphlett gloomily, and not—I thought—with entire conviction.

"Been with you long?" I asked.

"Some eight months, sir."

Henry had held his job, under the exacting Amphlett, for eight months. Well, perhaps I was wrong. Perhaps he did give satisfaction.

"His lordship finds it very hot up there," remarked Amphlett.

I perceive that the reader may be feeling a certain resistance to my narrative. Either this friend of yours was a lunatic, he is saying, or else you're making the whole thing up. That is because he did not know Gervase Musbury.

Gervase was an eccentric who could afford to give his eccentricities a blank cheque and knew how to run them at a profit. Eccentricity, as I see it, is nothing more than the visible track of the libido taking a short cut to the desired object. When Amphlett told me his master was in the rookery, knowing Gervase I never doubted but that he was there for some rational purpose.

Equally when I saw the bottle travelling up to that eyrie in the elm top, I accepted it as something quite natural; it was much simpler for Gervase to haul up his ginger-beer than for the footman to scale the rope ladder every time his master wanted a drink.

The ladder began to wriggle. Gervase had seen me and was climbing down—with great agility for a man approaching fifty. He jumped the last six feet, put his hands eagerly on my shoulders, and said, "You've not changed, Nigel."

Nor had he. The piercing blue eyes, the moustache cut like a thicker version of Adolphe Menjou's and appearing to bristle with electricity, the infectious manner of the enthusiast—Gervase was just the same.

"You'd better stay here, Henry," he said to the footman. "I'll be back presently." Then to me, "Henry gives me my bottles at regular intervals. Like a baby."

His blue eyes grew abstracted. "Let me see, Amphlett: who have we staying in the house? I am rather out of touch."

"Your brother and his wife, sir. Mr. Prew. And Miss Camelot."

"Ah, just so." He took my arm. "Better come and meet them. Get it over. Then we can spend the rest of the afternoon watching the rooks. Absorbing, I assure you. I built a nice little hide up there before the nesting season. Fit you in easily."

"No, Gervase," I said firmly. "There is not room for two on that appalling little platform. And I am not madly interested in the habits of rooks. Since when have you taken up bird-watching?"

"Just a relaxation, dear boy, that's all. I got a bit stale this winter, working on a new explosive. MacMaster called me in. Working against time—that's the trouble. We shall have war in two years. Or sooner."

We emerged from the shadow of the elm trees, to be greeted by a small, stoutish man, whose photograph I had seen often enough in the papers. It was Thomas Prew, M.P., a notable defender of lost causes. If Gervase was right, the hardest-fought cause of Prew's life was now as good as lost too, for he was an out-and-out pacifist, who had gone to prison for his convictions in the last war and cried them up and down the country ever since.

I was surprised to find the pacifist Member of Parliament here, and when we left Prew I asked Gervase about it.

"Oh, Tom Prew's an honest man," he said. "Besides, he's an education for my brother. You know what an old war-monger Hector is. He and Tom had quite an argument at dinner the other night. Tom won on a technical knockout. Hector and Diana have barely been on speaking terms with him since. Let's go and find them."

We found them at last in the garage yard, up to the elbows in the engine of their Bentley. I had almost forgotten what a magnificent couple they made. Tall, handsome, golden-haired—there was something leonine about them, both in their restlessness and repose. Hector had all his elder brother's super-abundance of energy, but lacked Gervase's many outlets for it: war might well prove his release and *métier*.

Diana I admired without liking; she was too ambitious, too overpowering for my taste. Besides, she was wrapped up in her husband. They gave one, more than any other couple I ever met, the impression of being a team, of physical and mental co-ordination. I felt it again now, watching them as they worked in a sort of telepathic unison over the engine of the car in which they tore restlessly over the face of Europe.

My sensation was obviously shared by the beautiful Miss Anthea Camelot, who had been standing by with an odd-man-out expression on her face. She turned to Gervase with relief—and something more than relief, I fancied. Poor girl, I thought: if you were Circe and Sheba rolled into one, your enchantments would break against Gervase; the name written on his heart is burned too deep for any other woman to erase it.

Though ten years younger than Gervase, I had been for a long time his confidant. I was one of the very few people outside his own family who knew about the tragedy of Rose Borthwick. She had been the daughter of one of his father's tenant farmers. Gervase, in his youth, had fallen passionately in love with her. His father, knowing that Gervase was determined to marry the girl, had managed to have her sent away out of his reach.

There were terrible scenes and a final estrangement between Gervase and his father. Gervase had nearly gone off his head, trying to find Rose again. But all his searches were in vain.

I was still thinking of this sad business a quarter of an hour later, as we were all at sea on the lawn. Presently the conversation turned to Hitler.

"We should have called his bluff long ago," said Hector Musbury. "If our politicians hadn't all got cold feet—"

"Your politicians have a responsibility, too," said Thomas Prew, in the beautiful deep voice that contrasted so strangely with his dumpy, rather insignificant figure. "Look at that young man"—he pointed toward Henry, who was standing a little distance away, in the shadow of the elm trees. "Multiply him by several millions. Imagine those millions torn, maimed, rotting in the earth…Can you wonder if the politicians have cold feet?"

A shade of anger came over Hector's face. "That's just sentimental special-pleading. The alternatives are possible death or certain slavery for us. Evidently some of you people prefer the idea of being slaves."

Diana flicked a warning glance at him, I noticed. Anthea Camelot broke in, "But Mr. Prew wasn't talking about the politicians. He was talking about the people who'd have to be killed. About Henry. Let's see what *he* thinks. Henry!" she called.

The young footman came a few paces forward. There was a piquant blend of respectfulness and irony on his face.

"Henry, would you rather be killed by the Germans or enslaved by them?"

Henry took his time, gazing levelly at us all. "If it comes to that, Miss Camelot," he said at last, "many might think I'm a slave already."

I saw Amphlett flinch. Even for Gervase's equalitarian *ménage*, this was a bit too much. No wonder the old butler had been unconvincing about Henry's giving satisfaction. Diana evidently felt the same.

"Your servants, Gervase," she exclaimed, "seem to enjoy a perpetual Saturnalia."

"You mustn't be hard on Henry," said Anthea Camelot. "After all, he's spent most of the day standing at attention over a tray of ginger-beer bottles. If that isn't slavery, my name is Pharaoh."

I was sitting very near Gervase, and got the feeling that the words he now murmured were for my ears alone. "Youth must have its tests, its ordeals," I heard.

Diana broke in, "Oh, dear, I've left my handkerchief indoors. Henry"—she was the kind of woman who gives orders to servants without bothering to look at them—"fetch the handkerchief from my dressing table."

"My orders are to stay here, madam."

I was afraid there would be an explosion. Gervase evidently intended to give no help: he was glancing quizzically from Diana to the young footman. But Hector was already on his feet, moving toward the house, as though his wife's wish had been communicated to him before she uttered it.

"I'll fetch it," he said.

After tea, Gervase retired up his elm tree again. Hector and Diana set up a target on the lawn and tried to lure the rest of us into archery. But Anthea, well aware no doubt that this particular sport would set off her charms to less advantage than Diana's, indicated that she would not object to my walking her round the rose garden.

As we strolled off, in the wake of Amphlett and Henry who were bearing the tea-things back to the house, we noticed Hector and Diana fastening upon a not-too-obviously-enthusiastic Mr. Prew and beginning to instruct him in the art of drawing a six-foot bow.

"The thin end of the wedge," remarked Anthea. "Start off the wee pacifist on a bow and arrow, and he'll soon be romping round with a loaded Tommy gun."

Gervase's rose garden is a charming enough place even when there are no roses out, with its neat grass walks, its fountains and statues, and the box-hedges yielding their fragrance to the sun. Anthea and I sat down on deck chairs, prepared to enjoy each other's company. At least, I was. But it soon became clear that she had brought me here for a purpose.

"You *are* a detective of sorts, aren't you?" she said.

"Of sorts. Why?"

Her eyes followed an early butterfly for a moment. "Oh, everything seems so queer here this time."

"Such as?"

"Well, little Prew wandering about like a lost soul, and Hector quarrelling with him, and Diana nagging at Gervase about that new footman, and Gervase sitting up a tree ignoring us all."

And ignoring you in particular, I thought. I said, "It's odd, no doubt. But this always was an odd household."

"Gervase does treat young Henry in an extraordinary way, though, don't you think? Spoiling him half the time, and tyrannising over him the rest. He's hardly let him out of his sight this afternoon, for instance."

"Perhaps it's Henry who's guarding Gervase," I said idly.

"Guarding him!" Anthea gave me a look from her warm, dark eyes. "You'd not say that if— Listen. The other night I came down late to get a book out of the library, and I heard Gervase telling somebody off in the study next door. He was shouting, 'You'll not get any more of my money! I've a better use for it now.'"

"That is interesting. You don't know who he was talking to?"

"No. But any fool could make a good guess. There's only one person in this household who fits the role of blackmailer."

"You're judging Henry on rather flimsy evidence. Why, it might have been Hector. Hasn't Hector been sponging on Gervase most of his life?"

Anthea rose impatiently. I had not taken her seriously enough. Or so she thought. We strolled back to the lawn, where the archers were still at it. Diana made a fine goddess, standing bright-haired with the bow at full stretch. Hector was near her, his hands in the pockets of his tweed jacket. Thomas Prew looked an uninspiring figure beside them.

Diana's arrow flew into the gold. Then she turned to us, her face flushed and excited.

"Now I'll shoot the golden arrow. We used to do it when we were children. Watch, everyone! Henry, you must watch too!"

She made the footman come a little way out from the elm tree and join us on the lawn. Everyone must see her triumph.

She took an ordinary arrow from her quiver and fitted it to the bowstring. "It'll turn to gold in the sky," she said.

Her body bent gracefully back, and she shot straight upward. The dark arrow soared, almost invisible in its speed. The sun had gone down behind the low hill to our west; but, higher up, its rays were still streaming laterally from over the hilltop, so that the arrow was suddenly caught in them, flashed golden, and pursued its course for a little, shining like a gold thread against the sky's deepening blue.

For us, it was a strangely fascinating sight, a moment of pure innocence. Like children, we all wanted to do it. But the lower the sun sank behind the hill, the higher we had to shoot.

After a quarter of an hour only Hector and Diana could get an arrow up into the golden stream. Then Diana failed. Then Hector made a last effort. His arrow just turned gold before it began to wobble, slowly reversed, and streaked down toward the elms just behind us.

We heard it strike a branch, and fall clattering from branch to branch. The sound of its falling grew and grew, was hideously amplified, as if in a nightmare the arrow had turned into a human body hurtling down.

A few seconds later, the body of Gervase Musbury crashed to the ground, only half a dozen yards from where we stood.

It seemed, for a moment, to put into words what we were all thinking, when Anthea Camelot cried out bitterly to Hector, who was standing there, the bow still in his hand, looking stupid and frightened like a child who has broken some treasured ornament. "You've shot him!"

Diana said, in a brisk, motherly sort of voice, "Don't let's get hysterical. Of course Hector couldn't have shot him."

Thomas Prew was staring at the body, an expression of white horror on his face, his mouth moving soundlessly. It must have been some shock in childhood, some spectacle like this of blood and shattered bone, which created the pacifist in him.

Henry was kneeling beside the body, making as if to lift Gervase's head on to his lap. Then he said, dully, "I think his neck's broken."

"I kept telling him that platform wasn't safe," said Anthea, staring up into the treetops. The rooks, which had risen out of them in hundreds, cawing and crawking when the body fell, were beginning to return.

I stepped forward and put my hand on Henry's shoulder. I could feel it trembling. We gazed down at the wreck of Gervase. His face was a queer bluish-pink colour. My heart missed a beat. This was too much; it was grotesque and impossible.

I bent and sniffed at his lips. Then I found, a few yards away on the grass, an object whose fall had been disregarded in the tragic moment—the shattered fragments of a ginger-beer bottle. I picked one of them up. The same scent of peach blossom clung to it as I had smelled on Gervase's lips.

I turned angrily to the cluster of people. "The arrow may have struck him," I said, "and his neck is certainly broken. But what killed him was poison—prussic acid—conveyed to him through that ginger-beer bottle."

An hour later we were all together again, sitting round the table in the dining room. The village constable had taken statements, and was now on guard over the body. A super-intendent, police surgeon, and the rest of it were on their way from the county town. In the meanwhile, I had made use of Gervase's keys and had the run of his study, where I had found out one or two interesting things.

I looked round the group at the table. Anthea was crying quietly. Thomas Prew's face remained white, dazed, incredulous. Hector, for some reason, was still holding an arrow and the bow, as though it had frozen to his fingers. Only Diana appeared relatively normal.

"I thought we might clear up a few things before the Westchester police come," I said. "Suicide seems to be out of the question. Gervase had no motive for it, he wasn't that kind of person, and there's no farewell message. So I'm afraid he was murdered."

The four of them stirred, almost as if in relief at knowing the worst. "Somehow the poison was introduced into that bottle," I continued flatly. "Gervase hauled it up, drank it in the ginger-beer—prussic acid works very quickly—and was overcome just at the moment when Hector happened to send up his last arrow, and toppled off the platform."

"But how could the poison—?" began Anthea.

"I've been talking to Amphlett. The ginger-beer is kept in the cellar. Only he and Gervase had keys to the cellar. Gervase's key was on the ring in his pocket. So it's unlikely that anyone but he or Amphlett could have tampered with one of the bottles while they were still in the cellar. Amphlett opened the cellar after lunch, gave half a dozen bottles to Henry, who carried them out on a tray, and locked the cellar door again immediately."

"But Henry was out there beside the tray the whole afternoon," said Mr. Prew.

"Yes. The odd thing is that he admits it. Almost like a sentry on guard, swearing he never left his post. He swears no one could have got at the bottles, except during the couple of minutes after tea when he and Amphlett were carrying the tea-things back to the house."

"Well," said Anthea, "you and I were walking over to the rose garden just then, so we can give each other alibis."

"I suppose Mr. Prew, Hector, and I can do the same," said Diana, in a tone of some distaste, as though giving people an alibi was a vulgar and disgusting thing, like giving them ringworm.

"In that case, no one but Henry or Amphlett could have put the poison into the bottle," said Mr. Prew.

"So it would seem. Logically."

"But Amphlett was devoted to Gervase," said Hector after a pause. "And Henry wouldn't do it. I mean, he wouldn't murder his own father, would he?"

Anthea gave a gasp of astonishment. It was no surprise to me. I had found a will in Gervase's desk, leaving the bulk of his fortune to Henry Borthwick. There could be little doubt that Henry was Gervase's long-lost child by the love of his youth, Rose Borthwick.

The relationship explained his peculiar treatment of the young man. I remembered him murmuring to me, "Youth must have its tests, its ordeals." There was always method in Gervase's eccentricity. It was quite in character for him to have tested the young man, like the hero in a fairy tale, given him a period of probation, imposing on him the menial duties of a servant.

"So it *was* Henry who was trying to blackmail Gervase," exclaimed Anthea. She told the others what she had heard that night in the library.

"But why," I asked, "should he blackmail Gervase, when Gervase had left him most of his fortune in a will?"

"Is this true?" demanded Diana.

I nodded.

Hector said, "The question about blackmail doesn't seem important now. The point is, Henry *had* a motive for *killing* Gervase. If he knew that Gervase had made a will in his favour, that is."

"We'd better ask him." Before anyone had time to object, I sent Amphlett to fetch Henry. When the young man came in, I asked him, "Did you know Gervase was your father, and was leaving you his fortune?"

"Oh, yes," said Henry, gazing defiantly at us all. "But if you think I murdered him, you're—"

"What else can you expect us to think?"

"I expect you to credit me with some brains. If I'd wanted to kill my father, d'you suppose I'd be fool enough to do it by putting poison in a bottle which points to me as the most likely suspect?"

"There's something in what he says," remarked Mr. Prew. "But who else could have had a motive for—"

"There's yourself for one," I interrupted. "You're a militant pacifist. You heard that Gervase was on the way to perfecting a new explosive. Maybe you wanted to spare humanity the horror of it."

"Oh, but that's fantastic!"

"Then there's Diana and Hector. Diana is an ambitious woman, with a not very rich husband and a very rich brother-in-law. Dispose of the latter, and she'd have the means to gratify all her ambitions—at least, she would as soon as Hector's father dies, and he's a very old man now."

"I think perhaps you had better leave these matters to the police," began Diana icily.

I paid no attention to her. "What Anthea heard in the library that night is significant. It fits the theory that it was Hector, not Henry, who was demanding money from Gervase. Gervase said, 'You'll not get any more of my money! I've a better use for it now.' A better use for it *now*, because he had found his son, Henry. No doubt Hector then asked him what he meant by the last phrase, and was told that Gervase proposed to leave his money to his son."

"In that case, Nigel, you silly ass, what would be the point of my killing Gervase?" Hector was blushing, yet triumphant, like a boy making a decisive point in a school debate.

"None. Unless you did it in such a way as to incriminate Henry. He would be hanged for your crime, and Gervase's fortune in due course would pass to you. And, I must say, if Henry didn't commit the murder, someone took great pains to make it look as if he did. Why—"

We all started, as Anthea burst out hysterically, "Oh, for God's sake stop this! I loved Gervase. Why not say I did it, because—because he wouldn't look at me? Hell hath no fury—"

"Be quiet, Anthea!" I commanded. "I'm not finished with Hector and Diana yet. You see, two rather peculiar things happened which the police may well ask them to explain."

"Well?" asked Diana indifferently; but I could see her curiosity was aroused.

"It was peculiar that you two, who—Gervase told me—were hardly on speaking terms with Mr. Prew, should suddenly become so chummy with him after tea and insist on showing him how to shoot with the bow. But not peculiar if you wanted him to give you an alibi for just then—the only few minutes in the afternoon when Henry wasn't standing by the ginger-beer bottles. Not peculiar if it was absolutely vital for both of you to be able to prove you didn't go near them."

"But, my dear good Nigel, you've admitted, only a few minutes ago, that no one but Henry or Amphlett could have tampered with that bottle. Why pick on us?" said Hector.

"I said that logically it seemed so. But Diana did another funny thing. She became matey also with Henry—Henry, whom she'd been treating like dirt up to that point."

Mr. Prew and Anthea had grown tense. They were staring at me as if I was the Apocalypse.

"Yes," I went on, "when she was getting ready to shoot the golden arrow, for the first time, Diana called out to Henry to come and watch. Terribly out of character that was, Diana. But suppose you had to get him away from under the elm trees, get him looking up in the sky like the rest of us, following the course of your arrow, for the seven or eight seconds Hector would need to move the few yards to that silver tray under the elms and substitute a poisoned bottle of ginger-beer for the one that stood there? Hector," I went on quickly, "where's that handkerchief you fetched for Diana during tea? You never gave it to her, did you?"

Hector was angry now, but he gave me a queer smile of triumph, reached in the poacher's pocket of his tweed coat, and took a handkerchief out of it.

"I see what you're driving at, old boy. The idea is that I really went indoors to fetch a bottle of poisoned ginger-beer?

Well, I didn't. I just brought the handkerchief. So now," he advanced on me menacingly, "you'll kindly apologise to my wife for—"

I snatched the handkerchief from him and put it cautiously to my nose.

"As I thought. Since when did you start using a perfume of peach blossom, Diana?" I was round the other side of the table from them now. "You fetched both the handkerchief *and* the poisoned bottle, Hector. In that nice big poacher's pocket. The handkerchief was needed to keep your fingerprints off the bottle, no doubt. It was unlucky for you that some of the poisoned ginger-beer leaked out onto it."

Hector and Diana were certainly a good team. I had hardly finished speaking when they were at the door, Hector threatening us with the arrow he had notched on his bowstring.

"If any of you calls out, he gets this arrow in him. Diana, fetch the car."

Diana was out of the door like a flash. Prew, Anthea, and old Amphlett were staring at Hector, dazed out of all movement. I felt like one of the suitors in the banqueting hall when Odysseus turned his great bow on them. Then I heard a scurry of movement behind me.

Henry had snatched up one of the huge, heavy silver dish-covers from the sideboard and, shielding his face and breast with it, was running headlong at Hector. The bow twanged deeply. The arrow clanged against the edge of the dish-cover, ricocheted off, and stuck quivering in the far wall.

Henry's charge brought Hector down. He half killed Hector before we could pull him off. He would have been a good son to Gervase, if Gervase had lived.

I had loved Gervase too. If I hadn't, I don't think I should have played that trick on Hector.

The perfume on the handkerchief I snatched from him was not peach blossom, not the lethal fragrance of prussic acid at all. The handkerchief smelled of nothing more dangerous than fresh linen, though he *had* used it to hold the poisoned bottle.

Yes, it was a very long shot on my part—as long a shot in its way, as that last one of Hector's which had just caught the golden gleam, and then fallen into the treetops where Gervase died.

Weekend at Wapentake

Michael Gilbert

Michael Gilbert (1912–2006) achieved eminence in two very different fields. For many years a partner in a leading London firm of solicitors, he enjoyed an even longer career as one of the most distinguished male British crime writers of the second half of the twentieth century, and received the UK's most prestigious crime writing award, the CWA Diamond Dagger. His novels are diverse in their subject matter and setting, but the most celebrated of them, *Smallbone Deceased*, benefits from a wittily evoked background in a law firm.

Gilbert was a prolific writer of short stories, a number of which featured solicitors; two series characters were Henry Bohun (who also appeared in *Smallbone Deceased*) and Jonas Pickett. The title of *Stay of Execution and Other Stories of Legal Practice* is self-explanatory, and "Weekend at Wapentake" comes from that surprisingly little-known collection. The tale is told in Gilbert's characteristically smooth and readable style.

◇◇◇

When Kilroy Martensen and his wife died in the Skyliner

crash at Prestwick, it brought the family settlement to an end and gave Bohun a lot of work to do.

The memorandum came to light when he was searching through the old files. It was in a handwriting that he did not recognise, thin, rounded, not educated, not attractive, but extremely easy to read. "The Surviving Martensen of the last generation," it started baldly, "is Christabel; Of this generation, Kilroy and Harriett, who are the only children of Christabel's late cousin Alastair. Under the settlement created by the will of Christabel's grandfather—"

And so on. It was a clear exposition of a complex set of facts. The man who had penned it had obviously been a sound lawyer with a certain talent for exposition.

"—Christabel enjoys the family property at Wapentake during her life. The house and estate is in first and second mortgage (see separate files) and would hardly clear these debts on realisation. The property is in a poor state of repair. The contents of the house, apart from the pictures and plate which are entailed, stand at Christabel's disposition. She lives alone, using part only of the house, with two servants, a married couple called Sherman. Mrs. Sherman appears to exercise a greater influence on Christabel than is really desirable. I am visiting Wapentake at the end of next week to talk to her on trust matters. I shall explain to her the disadvantages of dying intestate—" There the memorandum stopped. It was dated "12.x.48", and was the last paper on that file.

Bohun stared at the date for a moment, then went to the shelf and opened another fat wallet of papers. From it he extracted a Death Certificate. It stated that Christabel Drusilla Martensen had died, of cardiac distension, on the seventeenth day of October, 1948. Bohun clipped the memorandum and the Death Certificate together and carried them into the next room where his senior partner, Mr. Craine, lived.

"That's Sam Tucker's fist," said Tubby Craine, as soon as he spotted the paper. "I expect he wrote that just before he retired. He left us notes on all his clients. Not a qualified solicitor at all, you know. Started as an office boy with old Horniman, and worked his way up. Took night classes. People like that are the backbone of any law firm. You don't find them growing on every tree."

"This Christabel Martensen—"

"Of course, in theory he was only a managing clerk, but actually, in my time, he interviewed clients himself. And they were well advised to see him. Knew more Law than any of us. I remember Martello—the old Duke, I mean, who was a bigger bastard than the present one, and that's saying something—wanted to raise money on his mother's reversion. Sam told him he couldn't do it. The old boy blew his top properly. When he'd finished shouting, Sam said, 'I've told you what the Law is. You can hear it again from a High Court Judge if you prefer. It'll cost you a couple of thousand guineas, but I guarantee it'll be just the same law.' Marvellous, marvellous. No real offence, either. We still act for the Martellos."

"You notice that coincidence of dates," said Bohun, persevering. "He was going down at the end of next week. Christabel died suddenly on the seventeenth."

"How do you know it was sudden?"

"If she'd been ill when Tucker wrote that memorandum, surely he'd have mentioned it."

"I suppose so. I really don't remember. Look here, if anything turns on it, why don't you go and see Sam?"

"See him?" Bohun sounded slightly startled. "I imagined—"

"Good Lord, no. Right as rain. Nearly ninety, but going very strong. Lives at Streatham. I'll give him a ring and warn him to expect you."

◇◇◇

Mr. Tucker lived in a neat, bright house on the exclusive side of Streatham Common. The middle-aged lady who opened the door said that she thought he was in the garden. He usually played clock-golf when the morning was fine. She desposited Bohun in the sitting room.

It was a cheerful room. The only outstanding piece of furniture was a towering, polished mahogany bookcase which must have been divided several times, laterally and transversely, to get it through the low door. Bohun strolled across to look at it and found that it was entirely filled with Law Reports—the old sets of Chancery and King's Bench which terminated in the year of Mr. Tucker's retirement— and a bound set of Law Reports which had been kept up to date, and clearly represented Mr. Tucker's current reading. There were no other books in the room.

When Mr. Tucker came hopping in, agile, spry, indestructible, Bohun realised at once that he was in the presence of a natural centenarian. He turned his mind to the Martensen family. The old fellow had no difficulty in recollecting them. His memory was as sharp as when he had quitted the office.

"Yes," he said. "I went down to Wapentake, just as I had planned to do. It was not quite the social visit I had anticipated, you understand. Christabel's sudden death put a stop to that. But there was a lot that could only be decided on the spot. Mr. Horniman was in Geneva. I was the only person available."

"You said 'sudden death'?"

"Oh, very," said Mr. Tucker. He looked at Bohun steadily for a moment, then added, "Most unexpected. She was seventy at the time, but in fair health as far as anyone knew."

"Cardiac distension," said Bohun. "I asked a doctor about it. It only really means that the heart stopped beating."

"Yes," said Mr. Tucker again. His head was tilted. He looked like a crafty old robin, uncertain whether to pick up an attractive crumb.

"Have you ever considered," he said unexpectedly, "how far old people put themselves into the power of their servants? Christabel was living quite alone. A mile in any direction from the nearest mortal. No telephone, even. She was substantially bedridden. Every moment of her day was governed by her servants, Mr. and Mrs. Sherman." He gave a disconcerting little laugh. "Well, if they were good, kind-hearted people, that was all right. If they were the contrary, consider their power. They prepared all her food. They helped her up and down stairs. They drove her in the pony-cart. They tucked her up at night. They could have killed her at their own convenience."

"If they had any reason to do so," said Bohun softly. "And were cleverer than the police. Who are quite clever men."

"Police?" said Mr. Tucker. "I don't underestimate the police. They are extremely effective in what I might perhaps call an arm's length murder. But what chance would they have in a cosy, domestic little tragedy of this sort? There were so many things the Shermans could do, or abstain from doing, that would kill an old woman of seventy. One pillow too many or too few. A wedged-open window on a foggy night. The wrong sort of food even, if they kept it up long enough. When things get serious, Miss Christabel wants the doctor. 'Yes, madam,' they say. 'He's coming as soon as he can. Tom's gone off in the trap to get him.' But of course they don't. Or not until it's just too late."

Bohun was listening with only half of his attention. With the other half he was trying to track down an echo. In the end he realised what it was. Mr. Tucker had spent so much of his life among legal documents that he had come to speak like them. 'Substantially bedridden', he said, and 'Do or abstain from doing'.

"Did you enjoy your visit?"

"It was the most remarkable weekend I have ever spent," said Mr. Tucker simply. "Do you know Wapentake?"

"I've seen pictures of it. It was a show place at one time, wasn't it?"

"I'm not a great hand at architecture," said Mr. Tucker. "It was too draughty for my taste." He looked affectionately round his own snug room. "All pillars and porticoes and arches of which someone had tired and had them bricked up."

"Blind arches," said Bohun. "I don't think they were ever meant to be used. Just ornaments."

"It may have been beautiful once. I should not like to state positively. It was after dark when I arrived. And then, so little of it was really being used. The two great wings had been shut for thirty years, and of the main part of the house only one corner was really lived in. It was like—" Mr. Tucker sought about him for the precise description. "It was like living in a box, inside another box, inside another box."

"Oil lamps and log fires, I suppose," said Bohun. He had a very clear picture of the little lawyer hopping down from the trap in the misty autumn dusk and advancing upon the huge, silent house.

"It wasn't uncomfortable," said Mr. Tucker. "As far as it went. I had a very nice dinner in the small dining room, sitting all alone at a table laid for eighteen. The Shermans waited. He was an odd character. White-haired with a sort of absent-minded distinction. You might have taken him for an Oxford don. It was only when you looked at his hair and finger-nails in a better light that you changed your mind. She was a terrible woman. Perhaps I'm being wise after the event, but I don't think so. Real, hard selfishness writes with an unmistakable pen on the human face. It can be oddly charming in the young. Not so as we come to middle age. She was a big woman, with a white face, and dressed in black. I can really tell you little more about her."

Bohun said that he now had a most accurate picture of Mrs. Sherman.

Mr. Tucker bowed fractionally as counsel do when the judge commends their efforts.

"After dinner," he said, "Mr. Sherman went for the coffee and I apprehended that his wife wanted to talk business. I had no objection. For my taste the less time I had to spend there the better. She said, 'I understand that the heirs are cousins.'

"'Second cousins,' I said. 'Alastair Martensen's children.'

"'But it's only the settled property that goes to them.'

"'That is so. The house and land pass to them under the Settlement.'

"'Little profit they'll get out of that,' she said.

"I must have looked my surprise, for she added rather defiantly, 'Miss Christabel had no secrets from us. We knew that the land and house and pictures and plate were tied up. But the rest of what's in the house, she could do what she liked with that.' She looked at me out of the corners of her eyes.

"'Yes,' I said. 'She could dispose of her free estate as she wished. But perhaps you'll excuse me saying,' I went on, for I was a little nettled, 'that it's no concern of yours.'

"'Indeed it concerns me—or us, rather,' said Mrs. Sherman, for her husband had come in with the coffee at that moment. 'All that she *could* leave she left to us.'

"I must have sat staring at her.

"She swept to the sideboard, picked up a paper she had put ready to hand and laid it before me. Then she went on with the clearing of the table, but with a sort of subdued and ferocious triumph.

"It was not a long paper, but I read it slowly, because I wanted time to think.

"The body of the document was in a strange handwriting, but well written and well phrased. As I looked at it my eye fell again on Mr. Sherman and I thought that perhaps my first guess had not been so far from the truth. Here was an educated man who had fallen on evil days. A schoolmaster, or possibly even that professor that my imagination had painted. I felt no doubt that his was the hand that had penned the document. I cannot now recall the precise terms, but its effect was clear and unambiguous. Christabel Martensen left everything that she could leave, including the entire contents of the house (these were specifically mentioned) to the pair of them in grateful recognition of their faithful services. And it was signed by Christabel. I had seen her vast disjointed signature too often to doubt it. Under what compulsion or misapprehension I could not guess, but she had signed it all right.

"I said, 'But you know, this isn't worth the paper it's written on.'

"Mrs. Sherman stopped clearing the table. She had the bread-board in one hand and the knife in the other and as she turned the light ran up the blade.

"'It's signed and witnessed,' she said, quite quiet.

"'You and your husband witnessed it,' I agreed. 'Unfortunately that means that neither of you can take any benefit under it.'

"'Is that the rule?' she said, and she took a slanting look at her husband, who stood there dumb.

"'I'm afraid so,' I said.

"I knew, then, as plainly as if they had told me, that they had done murder, and all for nothing. To break the long silence I said, 'I've changed my mind. I'll have coffee in the library.'

"Sherman picked up the tray and followed me in. Apart from the dining room the library was the only inhabited room on the ground floor. I fancy Christabel had used it as a sitting room. There was a fire of logs alight in the grate, but by that time I wanted somewhere where I could get my back up against a solid wall.

"'I'll sit there,' I said, pointing to a table in an alcove completely lined by books.

"'Oh, I wouldn't do that, sir,' said Sherman. 'It's rather damp, and there's a draught from the ventilator. You'll find it very chilling. I should sit by the fire.'

"He couldn't disguise the fact that he was an educated man.

"'All right,' I said. After all, I could move as soon as he had gone. I pulled the armchair up to the fire, and added, 'I hope there's plenty of oil in the lamps. I may be sitting up late.' In fact I had made up my mind not to go to bed at all. As soon as I was alone, and the door had shut (sound died very quickly in that old house. I never heard Sherman move away down the passage), I started to do some thinking. And there was a lot to think about.

"They had killed the old lady, that I knew. But why in the name of Providence had they done it? She was overpaying them—and those sort of jobs were few and far between. They were not a stupid pair. Far from it. Yet they had done a foolish thing. They must have known the value of everything in the house. The heavy, unfashionable furniture, riddled with woodworm. The carpets which looked regal in the dim light, but fell to pieces the moment you tried to prise them off the floor. A few clothes and a very few jewels. The whole lot would go to Probate for less than a thousand pounds. And on the debit side of the account a sheaf of bad debts and an overdraft at the bank. Net result, nothing. Murder for nothing? Impossible. Then murder for what?

"My eye fell on the books and this started a new train of thought. The Wapentake library had been a good one—"

"I thought I remembered the name," said Bohun. "'Mercy' Martensen was a well-known eighteenth-century collector, wasn't he? A friend of Horace Walpole. He was a nob on Elizabethan poetry and Court Chronicles. I'm sorry. Please go on."

"Not at all," said Mr. Tucker. "That's very interesting. I knew the library was valuable, but I hadn't realised it was historic. Everything in it of value had been disposed of in the salerooms over the last, lean, twenty years. But the thought which had occurred to me was this. Suppose that there were books—one really valuable book would do—which we had overlooked. The library had never been offered as a whole, and the books which had been sold had not been selected on any very logical principle. Outstanding ones, like the *Book of Masques*, had gone early on—Christabel had lived on that book for nearly three years. But I felt a doubt whether any instructed person had gone right through the collection."

"But how—?" said Bohun, and stopped. "Oh, I see. You thought that Mr. Sherman might have been knowledgeable enough to spot a winner if he saw one?"

"Yes. And it made sense of their insistence that 'all the contents' should pass to them. Really, it would have been such a—such a safe crime."

"Foolproof," said Bohun. "Can't you see the story in the newspapers? Devoted old couple get left a houseful of worthless junk. The exciting discovery that among the rubbish has come to light some priceless book. The sale at Sotheby's and the final close-up of the old pair fading away into well-earned retirement clasping a large cheque."

"I am not sure," said Mr. Tucker, "that I thought it all out there and then, but I remember getting up, picking up one of the lamps and starting a sort of search. It was hopeless, of course. You could have put the most valuable book in the world right down in front of me and I would have lacked the skill to identify it. But I did think of one thing. I walked over to the recess where I had first intended to sit, held the lamp up and looked about me. No sign of damp. No draught. Not even a ventilator.

"Then why, I asked myself, had Mr. Sherman troubled to lie about it? There was no question of a misunderstanding. He had said, quite clearly, 'Don't sit there. It's damp. There's a draught through the ventilator.' Following my previous train of thought, I argued that if there was a valuable book they would not dare remove it from the library, since that would arouse just those suspicions they were anxious to avoid. But they might move it into some out-of-the-way corner, and this was the dimmest corner in the library. So I got the ladder and climbed up to the top shelf, and there, in the darkest angle, between two large volumes, I certainly found a curious book. Whether it was valuable or not, I couldn't say, even now. Would you care for something? I myself have a glass of warm milk at this hour."

The maid had come into the room, but Bohun had been so engrossed that he had not heard her.

"What—oh, milk will suit me. What sort of book was it?"

"I took it back to the light," said Mr. Tucker, "and examined it. The outer cover was a sort of yellowish wallet—it had once been white, I suppose—of vellum. The inside came right out, and was a series of pages, some old, of parchment, others rather newer, of paper. When I looked more closely I saw that at some time—the work was by no means recent—the original parchment pages had been taken apart and interleaved. I looked first at the writing on the parchment, but I couldn't make a lot of it, except that it was in English. The letters were difficult. There was nothing to choose between 'n' and 'u' and 'v', and the 'e' looked like an 's' and the 's' like a straggly 'f'."

"Extremely interesting," said Bohun. "Was there writing on the interleaving?"

"Yes. A transcription of what was on the parchment, or so I judged. It was old-fashioned writing, such as I've seen in legal deeds, but perfectly legible. It was a play. I've never been a reader, apart from the law"—Mr. Tucker glanced with apologetic pride at his bookcases—"but once I had got into it, do you know, I found it interesting. It was about a family—I can't remember many of the names—but this girl was very beautiful and was being wooed by a boy who lived near her home. The boy had a so-called friend, but he was a bad lot really. He told a nobleman, who was his patron—the friend's patron—about this girl, and the nobleman lured her away. He was actually helped by the girl's mother, Megira. *She* wasn't a very nice character, either. The boy went after the girl to try and rescue her. The queen of the country, who was on a progress, was staying near the nobleman's house. The boy appealed to her, but the nobleman and Megira told the queen a lot of lies, and she refused even to give him audience. The boy had a friend, a sort of clown, called Euthio, who was always trying to comfort him. Rather a superior sort of man for a clown. I suppose this is all terribly difficult for you to follow."

"Far from it," said Bohun. "Tell me, are you familiar with the works of Scott?"

Mr. Tucker's face lighted up. "Of course, of course," he said. "I think I have them all. His book on Contingent Remainders is the one I have found most useful."

"Not that Scott," said Bohun. "Another one."

"Oh," said Mr. Tucker. "Yes. You mean the novelist. I'm afraid that I've never found much time for that sort of reading."

"Then that," said Bohun, "makes it even more interesting. Can you recall anything that was said in the play? What form was it in? Some sort of verse?"

"Well, it didn't rhyme. Most of it was in—what would you call it?—blank verse. That's right. One line sticks in my memory. When Euthio was talking to the boy, trying to comfort him, you see. He said: 'What Time has swallowed comes not forth again.' I thought that rather neat. In fact, it was all a good readable yarn and a lot of it was very nicely expressed. I got quite engrossed.

"I never heard the door open. And when I suddenly saw that woman's face behind me, I thought for a second it was Megira! She had some heavy thing in her hand and she slashed at my head with it. It was the woodworm that saved me. I had noticed that the chair was rickety, and as I twisted round sharply one of the chair-legs snapped right off, so I was already falling sideways when the thing hit my head, and instead of breaking my skull, it only dazed me. I had the sense to lie still. I could see Mrs. Sherman's face from where I lay. There was no room for doubt. She was quite mad. She must have been going that way for some time and the shock of what I had told her at dinner had toppled her over.

"I don't think she had much idea of what she was doing. She stood for a few minutes peering round the bookshelves, then she picked up the lighted lamp and tossed it on to the floor. It went plop and there was a woof of flame and the paraffin ran all over the carpet with the fire chasing after it. I scrambled up on to my knees. If she saw me, she took no notice. She picked up the other two lamps, and tossed them down too. Then she went out and I heard her shut and lock the door. It was awkward for a moment because the windows up my end of the room were all the thin sort which you open at the top with a rope. Then I remembered there was another door in the corner beside the fireplace. I ran through and found myself in an annexe. It had larger windows, of plain glass, and I stood on the sill, kicked a hole and climbed out. I rolled down the grass bank into a flower-bed, and then fainted off properly."

"Good gracious me, yes," said Bohun. "Of course, I remember now. The house was burned to a shell. And the Shermans with it."

"He was in bed. They doubt if he ever woke up. She was in the dining room, what was left of her, when they got the fire out. At some stage in the proceedings I must have been found by the firemen, or the police, and packed off to hospital. Anyway, I had plenty of time to think things out, and I said that I had been in my bedroom, but not undressed, when the fire caught me. It was too late for the stairs, so I dropped from my bedroom window. Which happened to be just above where they found me. Nobody questioned my story. The fire had obviously started in the library and, as Mrs. Sherman was the only one downstairs, it was assumed that she had started it, by accident, when putting the lamps out. The insurance company paid up, and the cousins got what was left after the mortgages had been paid off."

"But," said Bohun, in a rather desperate voice, "didn't you—did you—did anyone—I mean, was there nothing left of the library?"

"Not a scrap," said Mr. Tucker cheerfully. "The brigade said it was one of the fiercest fires they had seen. An absolute furnace. The old woodwork burned like tinder."

"'Not a wrack'," said Bohun. "'Leave not a wrack behind.' 'Such stuff as dreams are made of.'"

He said all this to himself, as he walked slowly along the north side of the Common. He was trying to believe something.

To believe that it was possible that the one, complete, lost play of William Shakespeare, the one that all scholars know about but none had been able to find, the one that fear of the Queen had confined to a single version in the poet's own hand, that even after the Queen's death could not be put on any stage while the Leicester faction had power to stop it, the original of *Kenilworth* and a dozen stories and legends beside, the tragedy of Amy Robsart; lost to sight after Shakespeare's death, lighted on and transcribed by that eccentric but knowledgeable bibliophile, 'Mercy' Martensen, standing unremarked on the Wapentake library shelves through five generations of port-drinking, pheasant-shooting Martensens; that this unimaginable treasure, as rich as *Antony*, more lurid than *Hamlet*, part of the birthright of the civilised world, had been revealed at the last to Mr. Tucker, who had read it carefully, through one long autumn evening, and had found it a good yarn, and nicely expressed.

Bohun looked back at the front of Mr. Tucker's house, winking in the sun; at the neat lawn and at the plaster dwarf beside the plaster mushroom.

"What Time has swallowed comes not forth again."

He shook his head angrily and jumped on the bus that would take him back to Lincoln's Inn.

To receive a free catalog of Poisoned Pen Press titles, please provide your name, address, and e-mail address in one of the following ways:

Phone: 1-800-421-3976
Facsimile: 1-480-949-1707
Email: info@poisonedpenpress.com
Website: www.poisonedpenpress.com

Poisoned Pen Press
6962 E. First Ave. Ste 103
Scottsdale, AZ 85251

CPSIA information can be obtained at www.ICGtesting.com
Printed in the USA
LVOW07s1322270916

506397LV00003B/146/P